W9-CFL-194

HOW LIKE A God

HOW LIKE A God

BRENDA W. CLOUGH

TOR®

A TOM DOHERTY ASSOCIATES BOOK
NEW YORK

This is a work of fiction. All the characters and events portrayed in this novel are either fictitious or are used fictitiously.

HOW LIKE A GOD

This book is printed on acid-free paper.

A Tor Book
Published by Tom Doherty Associates, Inc.
175 Fifth Avenue
New York, NY 10010

Tor Books on the World Wide Web:
http://www.tor.com

Tor® is a registered trademark of Tom Doherty Associates, Inc.

Edited by Delia Sherman

Library of Congress Cataloging-in-Publication Data

Clough, B.W.
    How like a god / Brenda W. Clough.
        p.   cm.
    ISBN 0-312-86263-6
    I. Title.
    PS3553.L628H68   1997   96-33981
    813'.54—dc20   CIP

First Edition: March 1997

Printed in the United States of America

0 9 8 7 6 5 4 3 2 1

To Simon, who slept, and Larry, who put him to bed

Midway in our life's journey, I went astray
  from the straight road and woke to find myself
  alone in a dark wood. How shall I say
what wood that was! I never saw so drear,
  so rank, so arduous a wilderness!
  Its very memory gives a shape to fear.

  —*Dante's Inferno*, Canto 1 (translated by John Ciardi),
  Dante Alighieri

One

It was Rob's turn to drive the kids to day care. As usual the noise and chaos of the morning departure were stupendous, enough to make a strong man quake. Davey, eighteen months old, was perfecting a full-throated imitation of Tarzan of the Apes. Julianne carried him yodeling out to the minivan on one hip, her briefcase slung over her shoulder and a bulging diaper bag hooked over the other arm. In the living room Rob wedged the filled baby bottles into Angela's diaper bag and scooped his daughter up. "No!" she shrieked. She raised her arms into noodle position and almost slipped right out of his grasp. He foiled her by grabbing one chubby leg.

"Come along, sugar pie." With his free elbow he pushed the new storm door open. He had installed it himself only last weekend, and made a good job of it—a white steel frame and door with a safety grate over the glass and a self-storing screen.

"No no no no!" Angela howled. Rob stuffed her expertly into the carseat in the center seat of the van. Before she could wiggle away he clicked the latch home. In the other carseat, Davey had already accepted the inevitable and was philosophically eating Cheerios by the fistful.

Rob slid the door shut on the pair of them and waved at Julianne's retreating back. "Bye, darling!"

"Have a good day, hon!" she called over her impeccably tailored pink shoulder. "Don't forget to tell Miss Linda about the shots!" Then the Washington, D.C., commuter bus roared into view at the far end of the suburban street. Julianne sprinted to catch it, her satin blonde hair bobbing.

Julianne was always in a rush. Years of hurrying in high-heeled designer pumps had taught her to run as fast in them as in sneakers. But she had cut it too fine this time, Rob decided. The bus showed no signs of slowing down. The gray diesel plume of its exhaust streamed out straight behind like a fox's tail. Probably the driver hadn't even seen her. Shaking his head, Rob went around the maroon van to the driver's side. If only Julianne would allow herself five more minutes! Now she would need a lift to the Vienna Metro station, and that would make them both late. The family schedule had no slack in it at all.

The revelation came to him suddenly, just as his fingers touched the van's fake wood door panel. The bus driver had indeed seen Julianne. Rob was absolutely certain of it. The blue of the May morning sky over his head was not more obvious. The rotten bastard! Taking out his petty frustrations on an innocent commuter . . . Rob jerked open the door, seething.

A warm solid wall of sound and odor hit him in the face. The twins yelled in stereo and he realized that at least one diaper was very thoroughly soiled indeed. Bitter experience had taught Rob there was never any percentage in postponing the inevitable. Holding his breath, he climbed up between the front seats and clawed a diaper bag out of the back with one hand, unlocking Angela with the other. It was fifty-fifty the diaper was hers, and she was sobbing with rage, in desperate need of soothing. Cheerios crunched underfoot as he backed out. Davey had broadcast his snack with happy liberality onto the dashboard, over all the seats, and into his sister's clothing and hair. Out of the car again, Rob stared, the screaming child muffled against the knot of his necktie. The bus had stopped after all. But not at the bus stop, not for Julianne. It had halted right in the middle of the street. A few passengers were climbing out, and others were crowded at the front. Julianne came trudging back. "Thank god you haven't left yet," she said. She tossed her briefcase into the front seat. "You'll have to drop me at the station."

With his free hand Rob shook the orange plastic changing pad open and laid it on the driver's seat. "Sure—can you hold her for me?"

Out here in the open air it was evident that Angela wasn't the culprit. Julianne took the hiccuping toddler and said, "Now what?" But when Rob hauled Davey out in a hail of falling Cheerios no further explanations were necessary. The stay-dry gathers had utterly and visibly failed in their duty. Rob held his reeking son and heir at arm's length to save his tan sports jacket. Sighing, Julianne pulled the wipes and a complete change of clothing out of Davey's bag.

"What happened to the bus?" Rob asked as he wiped.

"I didn't see. The other passengers said the driver went into convulsions or something. A woman with a cellular phone called 911."

"Lucky there wasn't an accident." An ambulance sped past the bus and halted, lights flashing. Rob didn't look up. The appalling condition of Davey's clothing and car seat commanded his full attention.

There was heavy traffic on the way to the train station, and then Miss Linda had to be brought up to date on the twins' vaccinations. Rob didn't have a chance to catch his breath until he got to Chasbro Corporation, in a Fairfax City brick-and-glass office complex. Luckily nobody noticed he was late. He dropped his briefcase on his desk, hung up his jacket, and hurried to the kitchen alcove for that first reviving cup of coffee. "Yo, Bobster," Danny Ramone said. He was bearded and generously built, like a rollicking black Santa Claus. "How they hangin'?"

If there was a name worse than Bob, Rob thought, it was Bobster. But he didn't want to say this to the head of the software project. Instead he said, "Low, Dan, very low—in need of coffee. Traffic on 66 was all shot to hell this morning."

"You should leave earlier. Hey, I got in at 5:30 this morning! The commute was a breeze!"

Once more Rob held back his first words. Daycare didn't start until 8 A.M., and it was impossible to ask for more. Miss Linda already kept the twins until 6 P.M. And Julianne's job at the Garment Design Association demanded so much from her—

Again there came that opening sensation, as if a skylight gaped wide in his forehead. In the driveway at home it had been a mere flicker of enlightenment, a camera shutter opening and then shutting again. Now Rob stared at his boss, amazed at the flood of sightless unheard perception. Danny was pouring coffee and saying something about the joys of unlocking the office and having the mainframe all to himself. He hadn't intended to annoy or criticize. He was too busy contemplating his own vigor, efficiency and intelligence. There was no more malice in him than there was in the elevator doors that shut before the passengers crowd on board. Rob could almost taste Danny's magnificent, glistening self-absorption, like a Thanksgiving turkey huge enough to shrink everyone in Chasbro Corporation into small potatoes and side dishes. "Wow, that's weird," Rob said.

"Coffee too strong for you, huh, Bobster?" Danny clapped him on the back with a meaty hand and turned away. Rob stood staring at nothing for a few moments. Had he always been able to do this? It felt so natural, to inspect personalities in fine detail through this new mental microscope. Then why had he never done it before?

But self-examination had never been Rob's habit, and anyway the oddity of the whole business made him uncomfortable. He dismissed all these peculiar thoughts and went back to his cubicle to immerse himself in the day's work. Since the days of the abacus, no software has ever been developed smoothly, cheaply, or on time. Nor was Chasbro going to be the first to do it. Rob, like everyone else on the team, in the division, and in the entire company, was racing the clock to produce, lurching from one looming deadline to another without letup. It was a crazy way to make a living.

As the program booted up, he briefly considered getting away from it all—doing something entirely different with his life. But the thought was a fleeting one. The mortgage, the twins, the car payments: All these turned his paycheck into golden handcuffs. Although Rob was only in his early thirties, his life was already laid out from here to retirement.

Absorbed in writing C++ computer code, Rob jumped when one of the junior programmers stuck her head in the door. "Lunch in five, Rob," Tawana called. "Can we count on your van for the ride?"

"Sure," he said. "Uh, we're going out?"

"C'mon, you remember—Jean's getting married next month, and we're going to give her the present. Lori chose this absolutely buff Fiestaware salad set."

Rob had completely forgotten, and scrambled to put on his jacket. At Chasbro it was important to fit into the corporate culture, to make all the right noises and touch all the bases. He liked people, but since social skills didn't come naturally to him, Rob had learned to compensate by deliberately joining things and saying yes to all invitations. He followed Tawana over to Lori's desk and duly admired the salad set before the gift box was taped shut.

For the luncheon the bride had chosen the Blackeyed Pea, a restaurant just up the road that advertised its comforting American-style food. Rob ordered the meat loaf special and ate without tasting it, hardly listening to the technical chat around the table. He was too busy observing people.

What a fascinating variety of personalities there were! It

was like looking out over a delightful intricate garden in which every flower was totally different, not only a different color from its neighbor but a different species entirely—a cactus next to a rose, a sequoia shading a pansy. Here, a staid computer nerd with a lurid second career writing leather porn; across the room a waitress working on a Ph.D. in heuristics. He worked among Trekkies and canoeing fanatics, an ex-CIA agent and a world-class glazer of chocolate truffles.

Rob had never wanted or been able to delve into his associates' private lives. Now this painless panorama delighted him. The charm of living in the greater Washington area was its diversity. There were so many different kinds of people here, and now he could really appreciate and enjoy it. The kaleidoscopic view reminded him of his first experience of computer bulletin boards—a hundred thousand topics to surf through, each holding a hundred thousand messages.

"Yoo-hoo, Earth to Rob! Would you pass the ketchup?"

With a start Rob looked up. Lori, one of the secretaries, smiled impatiently at him and pointed at the ketchup bottle. Everyone was looking at him. This was obviously not her first request. He lunged awkwardly for the bottle in front of him, his hand feeling as large as hams. Rob had never been graceful—even as a boy he had dreaded Little League and square dancing. Now his reaching hand closed an instant too soon. He could feel the glass bottle sliding across his fingertips. It went spinning onto its side across the table and a gush of ketchup hit Danny Ramone dead center.

"Damn it!" Danny exclaimed, leaping up. When he dabbed with a napkin, the stain merely spread down the broad white expanse of his shirt.

Two of the younger programmers applauded. "Definitely hit points!"

"Holy mackerel, Danny, I apologize!" Horrified, Rob held his own napkin to Danny's belt buckle, to save his pants. The secretaries giggled. Their waiter bustled over with a towel. People at other tables craned their necks to see. Rob yearned for the earth to open and swallow the entire restaurant. He wouldn't live this one down for weeks—celebration lunches always made the company newsletter, and any incident was fodder for it.

Danny burst into one of his braying laughs. "I look like a drive-by shooting victim! You're lucky I don't hold grudges, Rob!"

"What with salary review coming up next quarter," Lori said.

Other people at the table chimed in with wisecracks too. Rob ignored them and said, "I'll swing by the mall on the way back and pick up another shirt for you, okay?"

"I sure can't go to the design meeting this afternoon like this!" Danny laughed. He mimed being hit by a bullet, clutching his stained chest and slumping back in his chair. "Bitch set me up," he moaned, sounding enough like D.C.'s ex-con mayor to get another big laugh.

Rob could only be glad that Danny was being such a good sport. Still, he wished with all his heart that everyone would forget his role in the entire stupid incident. And the all-important software design meeting with the customer had completely slipped his mind! He was too flustered to hang on for dessert. He left a twenty with Lori to cover his share of the meal and hurried off to the mall. A men's shirt sale was on at Hecht's. Rob bought three plain white shirts in the three most likely sizes, since he had forgotten to ask what Danny wore. For good measure he bought a tie too, in a vivid Wile E. Coyote pattern that Danny would be sure to appreciate.

His stomach was in a knot by the time he got back, and Rob swung by his own desk to pop a few Tums before rushing to Danny's office. "Thank goodness you're still here," he exclaimed. "When's that design meeting?"

"Doesn't start until three," Danny said absently, staring at his computer screen. When he looked up and noticed the bag in Rob's hand astonishment spread over his plump brown face. "Good god, Bobster!"

Rob took the shirts out of the shopping bag. "Didn't know your size," he said. "I'll return the ones that don't fit."

"This is above and beyond the call of duty, my man! And a necktie, my god! You're really determined I'll represent the division with pride!" With genuine surprise and pleasure Danny held the coyote necktie up, unbuttoning the stained shirt with his other hand.

"Well, this is the least I could do, considering my part in the whole debacle," Rob said uneasily.

"What part?" Danny demanded. He flung off the ruined shirt and tore open the largest new one. "All my own clumsiness! I better not tell the wife either. She'd never let me forget it." He buttoned the fresh shirt up over his pot-belly and tucked in the shirttail. "Damn, I need a mirror to do the tie."

"But—don't you remember? When I pushed the ketchup bottle over?"

Danny rapidly transferred three pens, a pink highlighter, and a 0.5 millimeter mechanical pencil from the old shirt pocket into the new one, and sat down. "That was *me*, Bobster. I pushed it over. Stupidest thing I've done this week—except for this damned code here." He frowned at the glowing screen and tapped a few keys, the unknotted necktie draped around his neck already forgotten. Stunned, Rob began to retreat. "Leave the receipt and I'll reimburse you later, Bobster," Danny surfaced briefly to say. "Appreciate your thoughtfulness, pal. I won't forget it."

"It was nothing, really," Rob muttered, and left him to it.

Obviously the thing to do was to interview the witnesses, talk to the other people who went to lunch. Rob made a quiet circuit through the division, eavesdropping. As long as he frowned down at the printout in his hands he blended in completely. No one mentioned the luncheon at all, so he was forced to bring it up himself. He caught up with Jean, the upcoming bride, at the water cooler. "Pretty messy scene at lunch there, huh?" he greeted her.

"Oh, I've seen worse," Jean said. "My future father-in-law is like Danny—so involved in his thoughts that there's, like, no one at the helm."

"It was Danny who spilled the ketchup," Rob said.
"You're sure."

She stared at him. "Well, yeah. We all saw it."

"I, uh, must have been lost in my thoughts myself."

Jean shook her head, smiling. "That's like, an occupational
hazard around here."

As obliquely as he could, Rob quizzed a few more friends.
Testimony was unanimous. "A typical Dano trick," Lori pronounced it. Unable to let it rest, Rob slipped out of the building and drove back to the restaurant. It was midafternoon, and
the dining room was nearly empty. The hostess chirped,
"Would you like the lunch menu, sir? We don't start the dinner menu until four-thirty."

"I don't want a menu," Rob said. "I was here at lunchtime,
with a group from Chasbro. Could I speak to our waiter? We
were sitting right over there."

"That would be Julio's table, but he's gone now. But I was
here. Maybe I can help?"

"There was a little accident—someone spilled ketchup on
one of the guys."

"It wasn't our server's fault," she said quickly.

"I know that—but who did it? Who actually knocked the
bottle over?"

The hostess wrinkled her brow in puzzlement. "If your as-
sociate would bring us the dry-cleaning bill for his suit, we'd
be happy to—"

"No, no! Besides, I already bought him a new shirt. Did
you actually see the incident? Who knocked the bottle over?"
He wanted to shake the answer out of her.

She began to look nervous. "From where I was standing it
looked like he picked the bottle up himself, and it slipped out
of his hand and down his front. Look, let me see the receipt
for the shirt. If the manager gives an okay—"

Rob turned on his heel and almost ran out of the restaurant. He stood on the sidewalk, swaying on his feet, sweating
in spite of the mild spring weather. His brain seemed to have

overloaded. He couldn't think properly. It would be crazy to try and drive in this state. He'd have to get a grip on himself first. Across the street he saw the post office and, just beyond, the Fairfax City branch of the library. He took a deep breath and crossed with the light.

Libraries were one of Rob's favorite places. In college he had even written a paper about how the entire goal of civilization was to build libraries and produce books to fill them. Now he stepped through the double glass doors and collapsed gratefully into an ugly institutional armchair. The library's familiar atmosphere of friendly neglect enveloped him. As long as he didn't become noisy or destructive he could do anything here—sleep, use the restroom, read lowbrow military adventure novels. Nobody would bother him with questions, or descend on him demanding why he was wasting time when there was software to be debugged and diapers to be changed. He relaxed and took the nearest paperback from the rack for camouflage.

Now he felt able to analyze his problem rationally. What the hell has happened to me? he wondered. Can I really be looking into people's heads? Altering their memories? I know what happened at lunch today! How did everyone at Chasbro forget? He took out the pocket notebook he always carried, and made a list:

1. Ketchup
2. Danny at the coffee machine

Slowly, he added:

3. Julianne's bus driver

But before this morning, there had been no weirdnesses. Vague memories of the comic books of his boyhood came to him, of unlikely accidents involving meteors or lightning bolts. "Was it my Wheaties this morning?" he asked out loud. But he couldn't remember anything special. His routine yesterday and last night—in fact, for the entire past year—was set in concrete. Having twins did that for you. He and Julianne hadn't even gone out to a movie since Before Children.

But a search for a cause was time-wasting. Instead, what

should he do about this? Rob got up and took the elevator upstairs to the reference room. The librarian showed him the directories for doctors and medical specialties. The thickness of the books was disheartening, and he moved over to the more popularized medical books on the nonfiction shelves. A fast skim through indexes and tables of contents showed him this was hopeless too. Nobody seemed to have his disease, if it was a disease. If he wanted a medical opinion he'd have to consult a doctor in person, and would Chasbro's health insurance cover such a speculative visit? "Holy mackerel, Chasbro!" Rob exclaimed. He should be at the office!

Dashing out of the library and up the street to his car, Rob realized he had made a default decision. This wasn't an important or interesting ailment. It was just a weirdness. He was going to ignore it and carry on with regular life. Eventually, like a cold sore, it would go away by itself.

There was no time to ponder matters further. Rob stepped into the office and was instantly collared by Lori. "Danny needs you!" she exclaimed. "The customer doesn't like the way the GUI is laid out—can you fold in these changes right away?"

"I'm on it," Rob said, and dove for his cubicle. Graphical Unit Interface was always a royal pain in the neck. He spent the next two hours moving multicolored widgets around on the screen. Danny phoned in twice with yet more alterations. His opinion of the customer was sulphurous.

"Everybody's a critic," he groused. "Everybody! Now they want the menu at the top of the screen, not the bottom. They don't know squat about what's under the hood, noooo! But everybody's got an opinion about the user interface!"

Rob was stuck at the computer until past six. He did phone Julianne, but she didn't have the car and therefore couldn't pick up the twins. Rob picked them up himself very late, which made Miss Linda positively icy. When he pulled up in their driveway Julianne stood in the doorway, frantic. "I told you I was running late," he protested.

She ignored him, seizing a twin instead. "How's Mommy's

big boy, then?" she cooed to Davey. "And Mommy's darling Angel?" With a tot in each arm she marched up the walk and into the house, leaving Rob to bring in the diaper bags.

She was deliberately making her peeve quite clear. Rob was resigned. Juggling twins plus a two-career lifestyle took incredible drive and organization, and it was mostly Julianne who kept those particular balls in the air. Rob's sphere was more traditionally male: car maintenance, home repair and improvement, the lawn—all the Harry Homeowner stuff. There was no point in complaining about occasionally getting caught in the machinery. Julianne never stayed in a snit for long. Over the years Rob had learned that reconciliation was lots of fun. Besides, getting steamed about things might lead to weirdness. Much better to pick up the ball and run.

He grabbed the phone off its hook and punched one of the preprogrammed buttons. While it rang he began emptying the diaper bags, sorting out the empty bottles and dirty clothes. "Hello, China Garden? I'd like a delivery: two egg rolls, one shrimp lo-mein, no MSG . . ."

A tumultuous meal and the kids' bedtime routine gave them no time to work it out. The twins insisted, as they always did, on hearing their favorite story, "The Three Billy Goats Gruff." After a hundred readings Rob had honed his dramatic technique finely. He made his voice go deep and gluey for the troll's words, "Who's that tripping over my bridge?" And when he bleated the reply, "It's only meeee, the tiiiniest Billy Goat Gruff," Davey giggled and Angela crowed in delight.

After the story and the final kisses, Rob came into the undersized master bedroom and pushed the lock button on the doorknob. Julianne lay on her side under the king-sized duvet, pretending to be asleep. But he saw the smile dimpling the corner of her mouth.

Kneeling by the bed he bent and kissed that dimple, tracing the line of her upper lip with the tip of his tongue. Her mouth quivered under his as she giggled. She raised the covers and slid an arm out to circle his neck. Under the edge of the duvet she was naked. Her creamy-pale breasts in their post-pregnancy state sagged charmingly slightly sideways across her chest. "Rise and shine, sleepy," he said a little breathlessly. If his family was the center of Rob's life, then the white-hot molten core of it was here, in bed with Julianne. Plunging into that sweetness refreshed and renewed him like nothing else. The tensions of the day burned off in her embrace, and he touched an exquisite reality that didn't exist in other areas of his life. After five years of marriage he knew her body well, all the hot buttons and favorite places. And her orgasm always drove him wild, right over the edge.

Afterwards she rested on his chest to catch her breath. He lay beneath her with his eyes closed, savoring the lassitude and occasionally running a hand down her sweaty back and firm buttocks. This was the best time to talk, about the past, the future, or just nothing in particular at all.

". . . if you get a raise," she was saying drowsily into his neck. "And I talk Debra into bumping me up one grade. It'll be three hundred dollars extra every month once we pay off the van. If we save that, put it into a money market or something, in a couple years we'd have some real money. That's my idea—buy a bigger house. With more bedrooms, and a bigger yard for the kids."

"Sure, Jul," Rob yawned. "A raise. Your wish is my command."

She laughed, knowing as well as he did that she was daydreaming. He could feel her rib cage expand under his palms as she sighed contentedly. "I love you, hon. You put up with a real pushy dame."

"There are compensations." He squeezed her butt gently as she rolled off him. It was only at times like this that Rob could say, "There's nothing I wouldn't do for you and the kids."

"Me too," she murmured, already more than half asleep. An unwelcome little flashbulb pop of weirdness showed him that she hadn't really heard his avowal. But words weren't important. Enacting this love, in bed and out, was enough: bringing home the bacon, as well as sex.

They both liked to keep in contact during sleep—nothing grabby, but maybe her hand on his flank, or his foot against her leg. As she settled against him, Rob thought sleepily about doing something with the weirdness for Jul. For instance, could he use it to convince the head of the department to give him that raise? Probably it wouldn't fly—salary review took place only in September, and Chasbro had no procedure for midcourse corrections. Was there any way he could use it to pick a winning Lotto number? Or influence Ed McMahon? Jul was right—it would be so nice to have some money for a change! Take a vacation, buy a bigger house . . . Holding her, he slipped into sleep, skipping like a stone over the sunny wavetops of materialistic dreams.

*J*ulianne got the car the next day. On the way to dropping him at the office she said, "Is that a new tie?"

Rob looked down at the beige silk necktie against his white
shirt front. "I think your brother Ike gave it to me a few
Christmases ago."

"Maybe it's the way you parted your hair. Something different, anyway."

Rob glanced at her, but Julianne was giving most of her attention to the road. In the back Angela murmured, "Troll,
troll, troll," as she pretended to read her favorite book, and
Davey sucked on a bottle. "I haven't changed anything," Rob
said as casually as he could. He had looked at his reflection in
the bathroom mirror this morning to shave. As he recalled, he
looked just like usual: tall but not really good-looking, his
thick light brown hair not yet due for a trim, his gray-blue eyes
surrounded by fair-skinned and slightly doughy flesh. As bland
as supermarket white bread.

But he never did pay much attention to how he looked. It was Julianne who had a sharp eye for appearances—as part of her job. She had revamped his entire wardrobe after they married, for instance, ruthlessly tossing out the polyester neckties and shirts with overly-long collar points.

"What sort of different?" he asked, and was immediately sorry he had. What if some sign of the weirdness was becoming visible?

But Julianne was no longer listening. A green sports-utility van cut in too close in front, and Julianne as usual got ticked. "Bastard," she muttered between clenched teeth, and gunned the engine to bring the van right up behind the other vehicle.

"You're going to clip him!" Rob exclaimed, instinctively flinging one hand back to shield the twins.

"Gimme a break. When have I ever made contact?"

"If you wouldn't take your driving so personally—" They had this same pointless fight about every other month, every time Rob let Julianne's pushy driving style get his goat. Now he made a deliberate effort to simmer down. Suppose—suppose he could *fix* Julianne's little foible here? Transform her into a sensible, conservative driver? As the idea seized him his confidence rose, warm and heady. It could be done. He was sure he could do it. How funny! Yesterday it never would have occurred to him to do stuff to her—to fool her into believing he hadn't been late, for instance. And fixing her style behind the wheel would be a good thing to do, he argued to himself. Julianne was a lousy driver. One of these days she'd piss off a crack dealer or a psycho, and get shot or something. Or she'd rear-end somebody, endangering the kids and incurring outrageously costly body-work on the van. He would be saving her from herself, really.

He turned in his seat to try it. With a hand-over-hand motion Julianne cut the van hard right and jerked to a halt in front of the Chasbro building. "Here you are," she said. "Have a nice day, hon." She leaned over to give him a peck on the cheek.

Flustered, Rob grabbed his briefcase. "Bye, Jul. Bye-bye,

kids!" He flapped a hand vigorously at them through the window. Both twins stared at him but only Davey flapped a fist back. With a squeal of tires Julianne pulled away.

Just as well, Rob reflected. To mess with her driving style while she was driving—wouldn't that be as stupid as changing the oil in a moving car? Absorbed in his thoughts, Rob headed for the building entrance.

"Spare change, mister?"

Rob blinked. By the double doors slouched a homeless person, a heap of gray tatters with eyes. He or she—hard to say which—occasionally hung out here, until the building security people noticed. A plastic 7-Eleven cup sat on the pavement with a dime inside. Automatically Rob felt in his pants pocket for change.

"Wait a minute, wait a minute here." Rob took his hand out. Now here was the perfect subject for a little experiment. Hardly anything that happened to this street person could make his situation much worse—when Rob concentrated he could tell that the beggar was male. He put his briefcase down and brought the weirdness to bear on him. It felt like reading a newspaper obituary, all the biographical data in chronological order. "You are Joe McNeal Moore," Rob said. "You are fifty-seven years old, a veteran of the Korean War, former bartender, truck driver, janitor . . ."

"What you say, man?" The homeless man scuttled back against the granite facade of the building. His watery brown eyes, bloodshot and rimmed with yellow matter, glanced frantically to either side. "Look, I ain't got no money, okay?"

"Alcohol," Rob announced. "And borderline schizophrenia. Let me see . . ." It was like fixing one of Angela's toys, a SpeakNSpell or the pull-toy shaped like a turtle. Unwind a tangle here, straighten out a bit there—his power encompassed Joe Moore completely. This was easy. "Okay. If you go to the homeless shelter, that Open Door Center over at Fairfax Circle, I bet you can get a shower and shave and some clothes. Here's a couple bucks for the bus fare." Rob held out the money with one hand, and pointed down the road with the other. The homeless man stared up at him for a minute, and then slowly took the dollars and tottered to his feet. Without a word or a look back he shuffled off towards the bus stop.

Lori came up from the parking lot and said, "Morning, Rob. You give them money, they just drink it up."

"Oh, I don't know." Rob picked up his briefcase and politely held the big glass door for her. "You can always hope they'll turn a corner and get better."

"Optimist," Lori snorted.

Now Rob knew what the Amazing Spider-Man felt like, in the comic books he had once loved. With great power comes great responsibility, he quoted to himself—wasn't that Spider-Man's motto? He could straighten out every steam-grate crazy in the greater Washington area if he wanted to. The power sang through his nerves, beat in his veins. And what other evils could he not battle? Was he going to have to wear a cape and spandex?

With a laugh he tried to come down to earth. A brief fiddle with a schizo's head, and he was ready to save the world. Surely it would be only sensible to see how Joe Moore turned out first. After lunch he borrowed a phone book from Lori and phoned the shelter. "I gave your center's name to a homeless person this morning," he said. "I was wondering if he got there okay. His name was Moore, Joe Moore. Kind of an older white guy."

"Oh him," the person on duty said. "He's doing great—in with the jobs counsellor right now. Could I have him call you back?"

"No, no, that's okay. I'll check back later." Rob set the receiver back into place. If he really had done it, actually turned a street bum into a productive normal member of society, there was nothing he couldn't accomplish. Suddenly he was sweating, sick with dread. He would have to do it, then: take apart and reassemble the head of every wino in D.C., on the East Coast, in the world.

"No, I don't," he muttered, clutching his forehead. "Why do I have to? Just because I *can?* Who says?" How did really rich or really powerful people manage? Surely Malcolm Forbes had never felt impelled to feed every hungry person in America.

Danny pounded a brisk tattoo on the cubicle wall as he approached the door opening. "You look like hell," he remarked cheerfully. "If it's the flu don't share it, okay? There's too much work to be done." Leaning over Rob's shoulder he clicked the mouse and called a new section of the computer program onto the screen.

Rob watched it scroll by eagerly. "This is the medicine I need, pal."

"Attaboy, Bobster." Danny double-clicked the mouse to highlight a section of code on the screen. "Lookit, I figure the error's got to be about *here.* The subroutine works fine up to about *there . . .*"

Good god, a burglar!" Julianne exclaimed as they turned onto their own street that evening. She stamped so hard on the brakes the van skidded a bit.

Rob stared at the dark-clad figure fiddling with their living room window. "No it's not," he said with resignation. "It's Angie." His sister, for whom baby Angela had been named, ran a restaurant supply firm in Chicago, but came often to the D.C. area on business.

"About time you came home," she called, climbing out from behind the holly bush. "Look at what your jungle has done to my pantyhose!" Her dark hair straggled out of its French twist, and pine-bark mulch stuck to her skirt.

"You can't break in, Angie. I installed bolts on the windows last month. If you'd phoned, I could have left you a key." Rob gave her a peck on the cheek and picked her garment bag up off the hose rack.

"And how are my darling twinlets?" Angie demanded. "Look at what Aunty Angie's brought you, Davey—a toy machine gun! And what's in here for Angela, a bongo drum!"

Behind her Julianne made a horrified face. Rob shrugged—aunthood has its privileges. Angie had a gift for choosing noisy, inappropriate toys that the kids loved. "Come on in and have a beer," he suggested. "When did you get in?"

"Flew in on the red-eye this morning, did meeting all day, and now I'm a wreck." Angie paused on the doormat, stuck a cigarette between her high-gloss lips, and flicked the lighter.

"Oh no, Angie dear, not in the house," Julianne wailed.

Rob laid the bag on a chair and looked his sister in the eye. "You must quit, Angie," he said firmly. "For your own health, not the kids or anybody else." Come on, weirdness, kick in, he said to himself. To his relief Angie clicked the lighter shut and took the cigarette out of her mouth. She looked at it with a sort of surprise, as if she had forgotten how it got there.

There couldn't be anything at all wrong with getting Angie to lay off smoking for good. The entire family nagged her about it, and she had failed SmokEnders twice now. But Rob felt a twinge of guilt all the same. It came to him that he hadn't truly grasped the magnitude of his fidget with Joe Moore's head this morning. That had been a straightforward cure of a mental illness, inarguably a good deed. But smoking? That was a lot less clear-cut. This was his sister he was adjusting, a real person, not some anonymous recipient of casual charity. To hide his discomfort he said, "I'm starving. Let's order pizza!"

It was Friday, and Angie was in town only over Saturday. On Saturday morning there was no hope of extra sleep, since the twins knew nothing of weekends. But an extra adult on hand was always helpful. Angie played joyfully with the twins, bouncing balls, reading Barney books, pounding the bongo drum. This freed Rob up to run two loads of laundry, mend a window screen and mow the lawn, and Julianne to cook lasagne and vacuum. "I can't stand you two," Angela announced. "You've got to take a break! I know, let's go out for lunch."

"There speaks the single woman," Rob said.

"With these wild things," Julianne explained, "we

wouldn't get to eat, just chase them around a restaurant."
They compromised on a gourmet carry-out picnic in the
park. The blue May sky was clear as a jewel, and it was too
early in the season for the notorious Washington humidity. Julianne and Angie, on their perpetual diets, ate salad stuffed into
pita bread, while Rob loaded his pita with chicken dijonnaise.
He noticed that Angie didn't reach for a cigarette, not even at
the crucial after-meal moment, and secretly congratulated himself.

Angela and Davey burrowed into the sand area, nominally
finished with their food. Every now and then Julianne would
go over and pop a grape or a bit of pita into their mouths. "It's
so neat that they're getting independent," Angie marveled.
"Only a year ago they were totally helpless, remember? Now
they're eighteen months old, playing by themselves, eating
real food—next thing you know they'll be getting their ears
pierced and borrowing the car."

"God forbid!" Julianne said.

"It's only temporary, playing by themselves," Rob said
lazily. He lay on his back on the picnic quilt. "In a minute
they'll yell for Mommy or Daddo to help with the shovels."

At that moment Davey did yell. "Siren!" he shouted.
"Momma, siren!"

"It sure is, poopsie!" Julianne picked Davey up to look for
the vehicle, and Rob sat up too.

A Jeep careened around the corner on two wheels. Behind
it came a police car, sirens howling and lights flashing.
"They're chasing a bad car, just like on TV," Angie told Angela.

"That guy's a menace," Rob exclaimed. Automatically he
reached out and scanned the driver. The roiling chaos in his
head was dizzying—the kid must be hyped up on drugs. All
three adults winced as the Jeep screeched around the minivan
parked at the curb.

Rob's first thought was to wait for the chase to vanish. The
police were paid to do this kind of thing. But a deep atavistic
instinct rose up in his chest: defend the women and children!

And Batman would never have let it go by. Quietly Rob said, "Stop." For good measure he added, "Foot on the brake, not the accelerator." The Jeep slowed immediately, and almost got rear-ended by the police car.

Davey squealed with pleasure at the sight so Julianne didn't notice, but Angie stared at Rob narrowly. "Rob, did you just tell that car to stop?"

Rob was pleased that he didn't tense up. With his enhanced perception he could strike exactly the right note for his sister. "You think I did it?" he asked smiling. "Superman and Green Lantern ain't got nothin' on me."

"Oh, very funny." Angie rolled her eyes. "I told you when you were nine that all those comic books would warp your brain. That's right, baby dumpling, wave at the nice policeman!"

Of course Angie was right—she frequently was. Rob knew that the comic books were a bad precedent to follow. Besides, he was just a little too plump around the middle these days to wear tights with dignity. Any public display would be repugnant, not his style at all. If he was going to dabble in crimefighting and world-saving he was going to be private about it. The idea of being a secret benefactor was powerfully attractive—all the pleasures of do-gooding without having to cope with the people involved.

He went to work on Monday and got the day off by announcing to several people, "I'm really here." Anyone looking for him would now be told something like, "Well, I just saw Rob a second ago. Isn't he in the Xerox room?"

He still only had today to act in. The software would continue to accumulate on the company computer net, and eventually he'd have to debug it. What was the most efficient use of this short time? He got into the minivan and thought about it. What he needed was a large concentration of criminals in one place that he could easily visit. "Of course," he murmured. "Lorton Reformatory." He opened the glove compartment and rooted around for a map.

It was in Fairfax County, but due to archaic regional regulations Lorton Reformatory housed convicts from nearby Washington, D.C., not suburban baddies. The two-lane highway ran incongruously right through the prison complex. One moment Rob was cruising past subdivisions full of six-figure mansions, and then the road was flanked with tall razor-wire fences and guard towers. He turned off onto a side street and unfolded the map, pretending to be lost—no point in exciting the perimeter guards.

He closed his eyes and reached out. How many prisoners were detained here, maybe nine thousand? For a second he wondered if he'd bit off more than he could chew. But when he called on the power it was there, inexhaustible. There were limits to everything, but not, apparently, to this. Or hadn't he found the limits yet? This would be an interesting test.

He phrased it carefully. "Decency," he said aloud. "Honesty. Politeness." Should he mention honor? Maybe not—too complicated a concept. "Law-abiding"—there was a useful one. He scribbled the words on the edge of the map, so as not to omit one, and concentrated on broadcasting them, impressing each on the soft clay of the brains around him. Vaguely he realized how vastly his abilities had multiplied in less than a week. First he had just observed, then he could interfere, and now he knew he could impose a mindset on nine thousand people. Amazing. Where would it end?

"Excuse me, sir—do you need help?"

A frowning uniformed cop tapped on Rob's window. Hastily he powered it down. "I was looking for Occoquan," Rob said, rustling his map. "But I seem to have turned myself around."

The policeman relaxed. A Plymouth Voyager with fake wood paneling on the sides and two child seats in the back was a preposterous vehicle for a prison break. And Rob knew that he looked supremely uncriminal: an out-of-shape white guy in a brown sports jacket and khakis. "You didn't go far enough south down Route 123," the cop said, pointing. "Another three-four miles'll get you there."

"I get it," Rob said, nodding at his map. "Thanks a lot!" He started the engine again and, turning in a driveway, returned to 123 and joined the traffic rolling south. Might as well grab a sandwich in Occoquan before heading back to work. Five minutes' worth of weirdness should be enough. Cruising past the prison again Rob began to laugh. "I can't believe I'm doing this," he said out loud. "It's like something on TV!" He could imagine himself, in an Armani suit, simpering beside Phil Donahue. "Yes, Phil, I am indeed personally responsible for the 27 percent drop in the D.C. crime rate . . ."

*R*ob took his time driving back after lunch, stopping to raid the ATM machine and fill up on gas. It was a sunny warm day, the kind of afternoon that insidiously encourages idleness. How long has it been, Rob wondered, since I went to Great Falls and sat on the rocks by the river? But he didn't feel comfortable playing hooky any longer. He was too conscientious to enjoy the thought of all those software bugs piling up in cyberspace. Sighing, he turned onto the side street that led to Chasbro's building.

Lost in thought, he almost side-swiped the fire engine. "Holy mackerel," he muttered, swerving around it. There was another pumper truck pulled up in the circular driveway at the main door. The air was hazy and foul with smoke. An oily black plume of it streamed from the roof of the building. On the grassy strip beside the parking garage huddled his coworkers, clutching handbags and briefcases.

Rob pulled into a parking space and reached out. A fire?

What about the software? But to his horror, when he peeked into the others' minds, he found them full of images of himself. When he powered down the window the smoke made him cough. He could hear Danny yelling, "We know he's in there, man! You gotta find him!"

"Damn. Oh, damn." Rob slouched in his seat so that no one would see him. He had "told" people he was really in the office, and they truly and totally believed it. Everyone could see he was missing, and therefore he must still be inside. No hope now of slipping out and just joining the group, letting them assume he'd followed everyone out. He'd have to go into the building and allow himself to be rescued—be seen, carried out by a fireman.

Lori was weeping loudly, saying, "And poor Julianne, with the twins! They have to get him out, they just have to!" Rob opened the van door and stepped out, concentrating hard. Invisible, he thought. I'm not here. I'm wearing a tarnhelm, an invisibility hat, just like in the Norse myth. You don't see me. He walked past a group of firemen in yellow and brown slickers and stepped over a tangle of canvas hoses to the side door. Nobody saw him. It was a fire door, usually shut but now propped open. Inside, the acrid smoke burned his throat and made his eyes water. I am not Superman, he told himself. The power, whatever it is, will in no way save me from burning to death. I have got to keep my ass safe! Nevertheless it seemed impossibly incorrect to be found standing just inside the door. Coughing, he moved a little farther in.

Everything was chaos, noisy and strange. Under his feet the carpet squelched with water from the hoses. From above came shouts and the crashing of fire axes against doors, and the thump of booted running feet. Rob thought he couldn't see anything, but then an orange glow lit the smoky air. The building's on fire, he noticed idiotically. He found he really hadn't quite believed it until now. Somehow he was slumping to his knees as the menacing light and glare slowly increased. Cause of death, smoke inhalation. Damn it. What a stupid, stupid way to die.

A dark tornado seemed to whirl down the hallway. It caught Rob up and sent him jostling back out the door into the blessed clean air. He fell onto the grass and stared up at the tornado, which revealed itself to be a fireman in full protective gear and gas mask. Other hands seized him, starting an IV, thrusting a cold stethoscope disc inside his shirt, slipping a mask over his nose and mouth. He pushed it away to cough, and coughed until he gagged. The shriek of the siren as the ambulance pulled up beside him almost split his head in two.

Then he was in the ambulance, strapped to a wheeled stretcher and covered with a cheap scratchy blanket. Oh boy, now I'm in big trouble, he worried. They'll do a CAT scan or something, and discover I'm weird. Scientists from the National Institutes of Health will come and dissect me. And Julianne will be stranded without the car. She'll hit the ceiling. The constant siren noise filled his skull, making connected thought impossible. He wanted to beg the paramedics to turn the horrible thing off, but couldn't get the words past the oxygen mask.

Finally it was quiet. Bliss! He opened his eyes. His stretcher stood in a nook curtained all around with green cloth. He was completely alone. Suppose I was really ill, Rob thought crossly as he sat up. A guy could die in here and nobody would notice.

His shoes had been removed, but nothing else. When he stood up his chest ached from all that coughing, but otherwise he felt okay. He reached out. The emergency room people were all busy somewhere nearby, on something more important than Rob Lewis. He pulled the curtain aside and shuffled off in his stocking feet to find out what.

All the action seemed to be happening across the room, in another bay of the ER. Nurses scudded towards it pushing laden instrument carts. Mysterious machines with lots of dials and LED displays beeped and booped. In the center, tense doctors in green scrub suits clustered two deep around a gurney. Rob went to a sink and helped himself to a paper cup of water. A very young nurse said, "Excuse me, sir," and reached past him to open a drawer.

"What's happening there?" Rob asked.

"Oh, there was a fire in an office building."

Rob could feel the blood draining away from his face. "Somebody was hurt?"

"A fireman—he was searching the building, and had some kind of attack. Heart, I guess."

The nurse hurried off. Rob leaned against the sink, sweating. My god, the poor devil was searching for *me!* And I told them I was there, but I wasn't. If this guy dies, I will have killed him. Rob's stomach twisted even worse than before. He retched into the sink, clinging to the chilly stainless-steel rim.

"What are you doing up? You should be lying down!" A passing nurse grabbed him and hustled him back to his own bed.

"Is he going to die?" Rob croaked.

"Who?"

"The fireman . . ."

"Now you have enough to worry about, with your own self," she said, firmly tucking the sheet around him. But Rob read the truth easily enough. He lay shivering behind the shelter of his green curtains, his mind racing madly. I could make them forget, he thought. Everybody, just like at the restaurant. Chasbro, the fire department, the ambulance people, the doctors: everyone would forget this ever happened. But what about the burned building? And, more to the point, what about this fireman? Maybe he has a wife, parents, some kids. Do they forget him too? I could wipe him out utterly from all living memory. It would be like he was never born. But what a shitty thing to do to someone who was only trying to save your life! And—and *I* would remember, Rob realized. I can't wipe myself.

If only the weirdness could make the fireman get better! Heal the sick, raise the dead . . . he tried it. "Get better," he whispered sternly, glaring at the curtain in the direction of the sick man. But the muted bustle of medical wizardry out there didn't change in tempo or tone. If it had only been a matter of the guy's head Rob felt he might have pulled it off. But a physical problem, a heart or pancreas or whatever, didn't seem to come under his jurisdiction. And suppose the guy died? The thought of being anywhere near made Rob cringe.

From outside came a purposeful tip-tap of high heels. The curtain was jerked aside, and Julianne stared down at him. "Oh my god, Rob!" she exclaimed. "Are you very badly hurt?"

"I'm not hurt at all," Rob said hoarsely. "Get them to let me out of here, Jul—please!"

"You poor thing, you're upset!" Julianne hugged him, feeling his forehead and straightening his shirt collar. She wasn't taking him seriously, Rob saw, and no wonder. Reflected in her mind better than any mirror he saw how he looked—smoke-begrimed, red-eyed, distraught. I could make her do it, he thought desperately. Really inspire her with a sense that she has to get me away from here. But he winced away from the idea. Lighthearted and casual mental dabbling had generated enough misery for today.

"Jul, the fireman is dying, and it's all my fault," he blurted. "I did it."

"What, get trapped in a burning building? You big silly, what you need is something to calm you down." With a swish of the curtains she was gone, and then back again with a doctor in tow.

"Not quite ourself, are we?" the doctor said cheerfully. He pressed a stethoscope to Rob's chest. "Now, breathe! In, out, good!"

"He's been talking a little disjointedly," Julianne told the doctor.

"No, I haven't!" Rob said indignantly. "I'm trying to tell you something important!"

"Breathe again," the doctor commanded. "Perhaps a mild sedative to take home with him, Mrs. Lewis. It's probably not necessary to hospitalize him overnight, but he should certainly take it easy the next few days."

Rob kept his mouth shut. If they were inclined to let him go there was no reason to argue. Let the doctor talk over him as much as he liked. Paperwork still had to get filled out and signed. Julianne and a nurse conferred on it. Rob wanted to hold the pillow over his ears. What did they do in hospitals when somebody died—ring a bell, take off their hats? If they did, he didn't want to know about it. He couldn't help straining his ears for bad news about the fireman, but he was damned if he'd trawl in minds. If he could just go home! But the nurse had to take his temperature and blood pressure one more time, and then he had to sign to get his wallet, digital watch, and shoes back. All this time he hadn't even noticed the wallet was gone. He pocketed it again with embarrassment.

He put his shoes on. Then, shod, he felt foolish sitting on the edge of the bed. He stood up. "Just stretching my legs," he said to no one in particular. But there wasn't enough space in his curtained alcove, and he didn't want to jog Julianne's elbow while she filled out forms. So he found himself unwillingly walking through the ER, drawn back towards the other nook.

He was more collected about it this time, able to tarnhelm himself so that none of the nurses and doctors noticed him. A peek at a clipboard, clutched in a passing hand, showed him the fireman's name: Vernon Shultz. For the first time it occurred to him to wonder how Vernon Shultz felt about this whole thing. From wondering to finding out was for Rob a step so small now that he hardly noticed it. This close, scarcely three yards away, he could dive right into the sick man's head.

The first thing he noticed was an ill-fitting, gritty quality, like putting on sneakers after a day at the beach. Rob realized this must be from the heart attack, and all the medicines they were pumping into Vernon Shultz's system. The real Vernon was safe in a deep inner fortress, beyond the discomforts besieging the outer defenses. Rob walked up to this central keep and knocked politely on the door, which, in contrast to the rest of the castle, looked like an ordinary modern wooden door.

Vernon opened it cautiously to the limit of the door chain. "Not buying any today, man."

"I'm not selling anything," Rob assured him. "I'm the guy you were searching for today, in that burning office building off Waples Mill Road. My name's Rob. And you're Vernon, right?"

"Holy shit. It's Vern, actually. Nice to meetcha." Unsurprised, Vern undid the chain and held the door open. "Get a move on, there's bad shit happenin' out there."

Rob stepped inside. The space within was totally uncastlelike. In fact it was a college boy's room, furnished by a fairly hip early-seventies undergrad. A blacklight Grateful Dead poster was stuck to the wall with poster putty, and brown shag carpet covered the floor. Vern refastened the chain and gestured towards the waterbed. "Have a sit, man. 'Less you want a floor cushion."

"No, this is fine." Rob perched on the edge of the bed. How funny—the man in the ER looked twenty years older than this kid, who had shaggy ringlets and a Ho Chi Minh beard. But, of course! This was Vern's mental image of himself, perpetually young and hip—probably hipper than Vern had really been at that age. "What do you think is happening out there?"

"Oh, smoke inhalation, probably—carbon monoxide poisoning, that kind of stuff. But I'll be okay. Take more than this to kill me."

"That's good to hear," Rob said with relief. "I really appreciate your searching for me. I would've felt terrible if you died doing it."

"All part of the job, man." Vern shrugged. He took his heroism utterly for granted, which disconcerted Rob a little.

"I hope you won't be sick long."

"Maybe I'll retire on medical disability," Vern said. "Move down to Florida and go fishing every day."

"That would be fun." This was not how Rob wanted the conversation to go. Platitudes and small talk he could do in a bar. He didn't have to storm Vern's central soul to sit on a waterbed. But there didn't seem to be any way to move out of the mundane, to explain and apologize.

Looking around the room, Rob rather thought Vern was a fairly mundane man. This was Vern's space. He was calling the shots. Maybe any other way of interacting would make him uncomfortable. Possible comments flitted through Rob's head: "So, you a Deadhead?", "How long you been into fishing?", "I went to Florida once." Guy talk, all of it. He had not realized how paltry most male conversation was, how trivial and shallow. With the weirdness he could peer deeper now. But even then the insights were incommunicable because Rob himself was a man, trapped in that same tight-lipped Clint Eastwood mold. Women were luckier—at least in the volleys of their female chatter some feelings came through.

A deep noise, not very loud but almost subsonic, made the entire room quiver. "Damn, it's getting bad," Vern said. Then Rob noticed that the dorm wall was dissolving behind Vern. He pointed, and Vern whirled. Suddenly Vern wore his full fireman gear, the helmet, the rubber coat, the boots, everything. He brandished a fireman's axe at the onrushing darkness. "No way!" he yelled, flailing.

Rob knew there was nothing for him to do. This was the absolute last place he wanted to be, stuck in a dying man's head. He stood up on the jelly-like surface of the water-bed as the dark washed up around it. The walls were gone. Even the bed was melting away like an ice cube in hot chocolate. Vern stood alone in the nothingness. His axe drooped. "Oh, well," he said reluctantly. "Maybe I'll go. I guess. I dunno."

He didn't look back at Rob. Rob called, "Hey, thanks again for your help!" But Vern still didn't look back.

Haul ass before it's too late, Rob told himself. He launched himself up and out through the icy dark, refusing to think about getting lost in here. But it wasn't far. He blinked and found himself staring at an annoyed nurse. His tarnhelm trick must have slipped while he was 'away.' "This is a restricted area, sir," she said. She thought he was ghoulish.

"I'm sorry," he said meekly. Something was urgently beeping behind Vern's curtain, and a doctor was talking rapidly at somebody. The intercom was paging a Doctor Mallory, and a nurse ran by with a rattling trayful of instruments. Rob shuffled back to his side of the ER. The misery that had made him frantic five minutes ago still oppressed him. At least he had done something. Finding Vern and saying thanks was a minor achievement, better than nothing. But none of these cheer-up reflections had much impact. He went back into the cubicle and sat on his bed again. Unhappiness seemed to press down on the back of his neck, so that the pillow looked very attractive. He lay down.

"You can't nap here any more," Julianne said indignantly. "They've just discharged you!"

The nurse put down her pen and grabbed Rob's arm to hitch a blood-pressure cuff around it. "Do you feel bad anywhere, Mr. Lewis? Dizzy, nauseous?"

"No no, I'm fine!" Rob sat up.

Julianne felt his forehead. "You don't feel feverish."

"I'm fine! Let's go!"

The nurse stared narrowly at the gauge on the blood-pressure cuff. "Well, I guess you'll do," she said reluctantly. She ripped the Velcro cuff free. "Your wife has the list of the doctor's recommendations there. Stick to them like glue!"

"I'll see to that," Julianne promised. "And if he gets sick, he's coming straight back here."

"I won't get sick," Rob muttered. There was nothing wrong with him that unloading to Julianne wouldn't cure. All this secret identity stuff seemed utterly juvenile, the power fantasies of little boys. Strength is in partnership, he thought as they left. I can tell my wife anything. And she'll help me. Julianne's such a sharp one, she'll have ideas, give me guidance. The very presence of their minivan in the parking lot was testimony to Julianne's resourcefulness. She had taken emergency medical leave from the association, phoned Miss Linda to set up the twins' care, taken a taxi to Chasbro to get the van, and then driven to the hospital, all without knowing whether Rob was alive or dead.

It was almost midnight now, and Rob shivered in the cool sweet air. Somewhere this afternoon he had lost his sports coat. The sleeve of his shirt scraped annoyingly at the edge of the Band-Aid in the crook of his elbow, where the IV had been stuck. Suddenly exhausted, he collapsed into the passenger seat of the van. He buckled the seat belt and fell into sleep the way he would flick off a light.

✳ CHAPTER
4

In the morning Rob woke luxuriously, stretching all the way down to his toes like a cat. A year and a half of fatherhood had taught him to sleep alertly, with one ear open for the sounds of a baby vomiting or choking or climbing out of the crib. But the twins had spent last night with Miss Linda, and somehow the knowledge had permeated his rest. Rob slept deeper and better last night than he had in months. He felt great.

Adhering to the doctor's order sheet, Julianne had let him sleep. A Post-It note stuck to the lampshade said, "Gone to get the kids, back by 11, XX OO." It was only ten-thirty, plenty of time for a shower and a cup of coffee. Rob's nose told him that Julianne—wonderful woman!—had already brewed a pot. Yawning, he padded downstairs to the kitchen to get some.

The sight of his own image in the hall mirror brought it all back. He looked like a junkyard dog. Black oily soot had been wiped, not very thoroughly, off his face. His light-brown hair was thick with it. The bedsheets must be a total loss. Rob looked down at his hands and saw how the grime stopped at the shirt-cuff line. "Priority shift," he announced. Turning, he went straight back up to the bathroom.

Thoroughly clean, he sat down at the sunny dining table with coffee and the paper. The headline was about Congressional legislation, but just below was a smaller column headed: FIRE IN FAIRFAX OFFICE PARK KILLS ONE. His pleasure in the morning evaporated. Quickly he turned to the comics, hoping to recapture his mood, but there was Spider-Man, pouring out some inane work problem to his wife. Rob wondered if it was an omen.

The Spider-Man family, being child-free, could indulge in confidences any time. When the Lewis household reunited there was no chance to talk for hours. Angela trotted in and pointed at him, screaming "Daddo!" in an imperious tone. "Where were you?" You disrupted my routine! she would have accused him if she could.

Rob picked her up and said, "How's my girl, huh? Is she a baby bat?" Holding her upside down made her squeal with glee.

Davey came in at a run, tripped over his own sneaker toes, and fell. Unhurt, he howled anyway. Still clutching Angela by the ankles, Rob could only say, "Hey, sport! C'mon, you're not hurt! Where's the owie, huh?" Davey thought it over and pointed at his head. "Well, c'mere then, let me kiss it." Rob dropped a peck on the damp buttercup hair. "Holy mackerel, kid, is that food there? Jul, he's got half a graham cracker welded to his scalp, did you see?"

"Damn, I thought I got it all." Julianne came in and dumped the diaper bags down in a corner. "How do you feel, hon?"

"Never better. Here, sweetie, down you go. Time to be a wiggly snake."

He laid Angela down on the rug and she shouted, "Hiss!"

Rob seized Davey before he could join her, and began wiping cracker out of his hair.

"We have to feed them lunch," Julianne said feverishly, and surveying the situation, Rob agreed. It was past eleven. This was the last flush of sweet temper before empty tummies and low blood sugar forced the twins into whininess. Julianne hurried into the kitchen and opened a can of Spaghetti-Os. The microwave beeped just as Angela began to scowl.

"Lunchies," Rob announced. "Up into your chair, that's a big girl! What about you, sport, you need a boost?" But Davey felt himself quite old enough today to climb into a high chair. Rob hovered in back in case he slipped.

"Chow time," Julianne said. "Oooh, our fave!"

"You think they'll ever learn to use a spoon?" Rob drew back from the splash as Angela dove into her bowl with both fists.

"Oh yeah, maybe by high school. Keep an eye on them, and I'll rustle up something for us."

Armed with a roll of paper towels, Rob kept the major spurts cleaned up. The highchairs stood on an inadequately-sized old shower curtain that could be hosed off outside. From the kitchen came more microwave sounds—leftover pizza, Rob could foresee. The weekend-type meal was going to taste strange on a Tuesday. Ordinarily the family never ate lunch together during the week. Julianne set a small paper plate with a large limp wedge of pizza draped over it in front of him. Rob asked her, "Would you change anything in our life if you had the chance, Jul?"

Julianne sat down across from him and raked her blonde bangs with her fingers. "Potty training," she said. "God, if they would just be dry during the day, that's all I ask! We'd save a fortune on the Pampers alone, you know that?"

"Yeah, but that's not what I meant." Rob bit off the dangling point of his pizza.

As he set the paper plate down Davey lunged for it. Pepperoni and sausage pellets went flying, but Davey had the pizza tight in both hands. "Haw, haw!" he bellowed proudly. "Oh, look at this!" Rob dove to his knees to gather up pepperoni.

"No no, dearest!" Julianne tried to take the plate and its pizza away, but Davey had his fingers sunk in to the knuckles and the struggle was undignified. "It's hopeless, Rob, the carpet's shot."

"We'll have to shampoo it again."

"That's something I'd like," Julianne said, setting the mangled pizza slice well out of reach. "In our next house, the dining area will have a washable floor—linoleum, or concrete, or something."

"Something we can sandblast," Rob agreed. Talking to Julianne was impossible with the kids on deck, he decided. Even connected conversation was impractical. But they took a nap right after lunch—that would be his time.

The drill for naptime when both of them were on hand was for Rob to take Angela up to her crib first. Angela didn't approve of rest in any form. While she kicked up her heels in bed, singing "Twinkle twinkle!" at the top of her voice, Rob sat out in the hall, officially not present but within reach in case Angela decided to climb out. Usually he used the time to catch up on magazines, but today he took the cordless phone and the Chasbro office directory up with him. It would be really useful to know if he still had a job or not.

Rob dialed the main Chasbro number just to see what would happen. "—not in service," the mechanical voice said. Then he phoned Danny at his home number. The answering machine, great. He left a message: "Just checking in, Danny. Hey, are we still pulling paycheck, or what?" Then he tried Lori.

"Ohmigosh, Rob, how are you?" she demanded. "You looked like hell, we were so worried—"

"I'm perfectly okay," Rob interrupted her. "They couldn't even fudge up an excuse to keep me in the hospital overnight."

"Wasn't it scary! I was terrified! I was with Maura in the

copier room when the alarm rang, and we didn't really take it seriously for a while, but then, when this smoke started filling up the hall—"

Rob let her babble on for as long as he dared. Since he'd been playing hooky yesterday morning it might be very wise to catch up on what had been going on in the office. Also with his free ear he could hear Angela winding down a little with a rendition of a Barney song. Inevitably Lori came around to asking, "But where *were* you? Nobody noticed you weren't following along down the fire stairs, until Danny counted noses out on the front lawn and you were missing!"

Rob had given this some thought and was able to say, "Well, you know I never heard the alarm ringing at all? I needed the number off my health insurance card, and when I reached for my wallet I remembered I'd left it in the van. So I went out to get it, and that's when the alarm must have gone off. I went back up to the office, and by the time I noticed what was going on—"

"How awful, you could have been killed!"

"But what I really want to know now is, what's the damage? What's the status of the project?"

"The mainframes are insured, that I know," Lori said uncertainly. "But the disks are trashed, I bet anything you like."

"Something can be salvaged."

"Only if the head office decides it's worth while."

"There is that," Rob admitted. "Listen, Lori, I have to run. You'll keep me up to date, huh?"

So that was taken care of—although it was a startling thought, that Chasbro's parent corporation might cut their losses and fold. Granted, Chasbro hadn't run in the black last year, but surely the powers that be wouldn't throw them all to the wolves?

Julianne came softly up the narrow stair, Davey nodding on her shoulder. With a visible effort Davey raised his flaxen head and grinned sleepily at Rob, who couldn't help smiling back. Julianne sidled into the now silent bedroom and, after a long suspenseful pause, came out on tiptoe. "Let's beat it!" she whispered, and they sneaked downstairs again like burglars.

"Another triumph of nap management," she congratulated him in the kitchen.

"It's all in my dull personality," Rob boasted. "Bore any kid to sleep, guaranteed." He cracked open a large bottle of cola and took two glasses out.

"Aren't you a sweetie," Julianne said, sipping. She took her glass into the toy-strewn living room and lay down on the sagging sofa. "It's so great to have a surprise day off. I wouldn't mind a nap myself." She winked at him, wickedly.

"Could we talk first?" Rob sat down in a shabby green armchair, a relic of grad school days.

"Sure—what is it, Chasbro? Are they going to reopen the office, or what?"

"Who knows? When they decide they'll tell me about it. But that's not what I wanted to say."

"Okay, what?"

Now that the time had come, Rob couldn't find a good way to begin. To mention Spider-Man would surely be madness, but he couldn't think of any other comparable person. He stared at Julianne, whose eyes were closed. She held the cold glass to her forehead and said, "I warn you, Rob, if you're thinking divorce, you get the kids. I am not taking them."

That made him laugh a little. Julianne knew him so well . . . "You remember what you were saying last week in the car, Jul? About how I had changed?"

She opened her eyes. "You've discovered you're gay."

"Cut it out, Jul, I'm serious! Something's happened to me. Not from the fire, but from before. I can do stuff now. Things that nobody can do."

Julianne's raised eyebrows made him stop. "I'm waiting for the punch line," she said. "God's gift to comedy you're not, hon. Okay, I'll bite—what kind of things?"

She was humoring him. Rob felt his face getting red with annoyance. "Well, mind reading, for instance."

"Read my mind, then."

"You don't believe me."

"Of course not. C'mon, Rob, let me in on the gag. April Fool's Day was last month. Or—good god! Your head doesn't ache, does it? Do you see spots, or feel numb or anything?" She sat up, staring at him with narrowed hazel eyes and setting down her drink.

"No, no!" Rob exclaimed in dismay. "I feel fine, never better!"

"But it's not like you to talk like this." Julianne advanced purposefully on him. Brushing his protesting hand aside she clapped a chilly hand to his forehead. "I don't know. Let me get the thermometer."

"Look, you want to know what else I can do?" Rob demanded, a little desperately.

"That does it. I'm calling the doctor."

"Julianne, listen to me. I can change your mind. Make you believe me. Okay?"

"Anything you say, hon. I have the name of that emergency room doctor written down right here."

She had seized the cordless phone and was already punching out the number. "This is ridiculous," Rob said. "All right. It *shall* be as I say. Julianne, you do believe me. Everything I said to you is a plain fact."

He watched with relief and a little guilt, as she clicked the cordless phone off and pushed the little antenna back in again. "How—how did it happen, Rob? Did you, like, do radiation treatments as a kid? Get exposed to kryptonite or something?"

"I haven't the faintest idea," Rob admitted. "And I can't think of any way to find out."

"What have you done with it?"

"Nothing much. It's been, gosh, only about a week—I can hardly believe it. I think I might've made your bus driver sick that day. I guess I should find out about him." Rob winced at the thought of another Vernon Shultz.

"Can you, like, do anything useful?"

"I might've turned some of the Lorton convicts around. I

sneaked out yesterday to experiment with it. And I told the office I was there. So when the fire broke out they all swore to the fire department that I was still in the building. I'm afraid I'm responsible for that fireman's death yesterday."

There, it was out. Rob sagged in his chair with relief. Disappointingly, the horror of it didn't seem to strike Julianne very greatly. "That's a fireman's job, hon. They know what they're getting into. And what are you wasting your energy at Lorton for? There's lots of better things to do with this!"

"I knew you'd have some ideas," Rob said with pride.

Julianne began to pace slowly back and forth from the sofa to the TV cart, frowning with thought. "You can tell people what to think. Let me see. Lobbyist, of course. We get the National Rifle Association or somebody to hire you as a lobbyist, and bingo, all the senators help you ram through gun legislation."

"Holy mackerel!" Rob exclaimed in horror. "You know, Jul, I'm not a mover-and-shaker kind of guy! Besides, I think there are too many guns already!"

"That's just an example, hon. What about PR? Convince everybody to drink Florida orange juice, or buy panty hose. Or, I know! You could run for public office! If you tell people to vote for you, they would, right?"

"Well, sure, but—"

"How lucky that this is the off year! I don't think it's too late yet to file to be on the ballot this November. You could start in one of the local races, say for the state legislature. Then in two years pick up a House seat, run for governor in '98—" Julianne counted quickly on her perfectly-manicured fingers. "You'd be in a good position to make a Presidential run in 2004!"

"But I don't want to be President!"

"But you literally can't lose! So why not?"

Rob almost stuttered, trying to get the words out. "For one thing, if I was President, I'd actually have to do stuff—meet with foreign leaders, declare war, run the government—things like that. And I don't know anything about it."

"So what? Does anybody? What difference will that make?"

"Jul! We live in this country! Do you want it run into the ground by an ignoramus? Suppose I declare war against Canada or something?" Rob tried to stick to the point. "And another thing—would it be right, to make people vote for me? Or to buy orange juice, even?"

"I don't see how that's different from running ads in the paper."

"But you can choose to read the ad. You can choose what kind of juice to buy. If I tell you which kind, you have no choice, Jul—none at all. You'd have more options if I held a gun to your head."

Julianne's eyes flashed. "Well, by that argument, you're just going to sit on this thing, and not accomplish anything with it!"

On Thursday he had sworn there was nothing he wouldn't do for her. Rob felt trapped. He stood up and grabbed her hand. "Look, we don't have to jump into anything right away. What I really want us to think about is, what kind of life do we want? Where do we want to go with this? For instance, have you really envisioned living with the twins in the White House?"

The image made Julianne shudder. "And I never could stand Colonial furniture," she admitted.

"We have all the time in the world," Rob said. "There's no need to rush."

"How do you know that this ability won't just go away, as fast as it came?"

"It's possible, but I don't think so." Rob turned away towards the window and looked out into the back yard. A chain-link fence enclosed the worn grass, and the cement patio was furnished with two aluminum lawn chairs, a rust-streaked barbecue grill, and a turtle-shaped sand box. "I've only gotten stronger, Jul. The number of people I can reach seems to be growing exponentially. Sometimes I wonder, is there any upper limit for me? How much more can it increase?"

Julianne joined him, tucking her arm through his. From up-stairs came a small tentative whoop. The twins were awake. "You know, what we do need is a picnic table," she said. "We need money." The ceiling bumped alarmingly above their heads as Angela rocked her crib on its casters. No more dis-cussion was possible.

The rest of the afternoon had to be frittered away on a se-ries of minor errands. Rob bought a kitchen sink aerator and a concrete splash block from Hechinger's, and the kids needed shoes. Angela and Davey were used to visiting the hardware store, but the relative novelty of Kmart intoxicated them. They ran screaming up and down the aisles of the shoe department while Julianne wavered between Barney sneakers and orange canvas high-tops.

"I can't concentrate," she said peevishly. "It's all your fault, you know."

"Me? What about them?" Rob protested, but then he un-derstood. "Right—why can't I have normal ailments, like everybody else?"

She held up a midget pair of sneakers. "Rob, what would happen if you told the clerk we'd already paid for these?"

Rob's mouth opened in dismay. "But—I guess she'd believe me, but—it wouldn't be true, Jul! It'd be shoplifting!"

"I just *wondered*," Julianne said in a nettled tone.

Rob took a deep breath, but the words froze solid in his mouth. At the far end of the aisle, in naughty silence, the twins were scaling a floor-to-ceiling rack of men's work boots. The entire unit was pulling away from the wall, toppling forwards under their combined toddler weight. Already the upper boots were falling.

Julianne screamed. Rob reacted instinctively. There were trying-on benches and clusters of startled customers blocking the aisle, and he had never possessed bodily deftness. Instead he now thrust like a javelin into the head of the closest per-son, a black shoe clerk in a red Kmart shirt. As if by remote control, Rob twirled the slim young man around and jammed

him like a two-by-four under the teetering boot rack. The
shoe clerk whinnied with shock.

Faster on her feet, Julianne plunged past the other shop-
pers and snatched a twin away with either hand. "You mon-
keys!" she cried.

Rob followed and shoved the rack rattling back into a
more stable configuration again. Around him a hail of tan
work boots tumbled to the floor. "You saved them!" he said
loudly to the stunned shoe clerk. He caught Julianne's eye
pleadingly.

Julianne covered for him magnificently. "That was so brave
and clever of you!" she caroled. She seized the clerk's slim
black hand in both her own and wrung it. "You saved my children from certain death! You're a hero!"

Everyone in earshot began to talk loudly and rapidly, exclaiming in wonder or explaining the situation to each other.
Outraged at the abrupt interruption of their mountaineering
expedition, the twins began to yowl. The store manager and
several assistants hurried up, peppering everyone with questions and nervously examining the boot rack, visions of lia-
bility lawsuits dancing in their heads. The noise was immense.

Trembling with reaction, Rob sat down on a try-on bench
and hugged a wailing child in each arm. He had never done
that before, forced a crude action on somebody like that.
Thoughts, motives, memories even, but not action. Somehow
the physical reality of this thing was a shock worse than a blow
in the face. "I could do anything now," he muttered into Angela's damp blond curls. "Anything at all." Shoplifting, dere-
licts, all that was small change. He could rule this country not
like a President, but like a god. The thought made the sweat
run cold down his armpits.

Under the pure horsepower of Julianne's praise, the store
manager relaxed. "I'll see to it that Mr. Akkam is our next Em-
ployee of the Month," he said. "Good work, Akkam!" He patted the shoe clerk on the back.

In a thick foreign accent Akkam said, "I did nothing. I did

not know to move. I just do it." His dark face was completely confused.

"You were wonderful," Julianne assured him. "What a superb sales staff you have here!"

Keeping up a steady fulsome barrage, she swept the family up and through the cashier checkout to the door. At the last moment Rob pulled himself together enough to mutter to an assistant manager, "I'd use six-inch T-toggles to refasten that rack to the wall."

When the kids were safely buckled into their car seats, Julianne turned towards Rob. "Are you all right, hon?" He nodded, and in an undertone she said, "That was you, wasn't it? You made that poor little man a hero."

"I wasn't close enough to help with my own hands."

"So you borrowed his instead? Good job! I didn't know you could jerk people around like that! Did it take a lot out of you, though? You look kind of shook up."

Rob sat down in the van's open doorway. "It took nothing out of me, Jul. It was easy as snapping my fingers." Very softly he added, "Jul, I'm scared."

"Pooh, you did exactly right." She patted his cheek and slung the bagful of sneakers past him into the rear seat. "Come on, I'll drive if you like. If we don't feed them soon they'll start whining."

✳ CHAPTER 5

*T*hings *began to roll at Chasbro the following day. Rob* drove to a temporary setup at the building next to the old one. When everyone was assembled in the large echoing unfurnished space Danny announced, "Okay. The powers that be have given a tentative green light. The general game plan is this. A subcontracted salvage team flies in from L.A. tomorrow. The more daring of us will join them in digging through the rubble for disks and documentation and the backup tapes. Jeans and work boots, boys and girls. Lori, remember to swing by Hechinger's for two dozen pairs of work gloves. The rest of us will start setting up diagnostic programs here. The mainframes will be delivered and set up by next week. And may God have mercy on us all, they still expect us to meet the October delivery deadline."

Groans burst out on all sides, but they were cheerful ones. Obviously everyone would continue to have a job for now. Workmen began to arrive to install partitions and telephones.

A truckload of rented office furniture pulled up at the delivery dock. Someone set up the all-important coffee machine on the first unloaded desk. A pleasant uproar filled the sprawling space as it came to life.

When one of the phone lines came on, Rob plugged a phone in and sat on the rug to phone Julianne. "Good news," he said. "I'm still employed."

"Oh, super!" Her sigh of relief rattled in his ear. "Because I may be losing mine."

"You're kidding!"

"That rat's ass Debra is going to squeeze me out, I just know it," she murmured. Debra was Julianne's boss, the bane of her professional life.

"Jul, don't they say that you should never attribute to malice what you can blame on ignorance?"

"This woman is both, Rob, I swear it. Dumb and mean together."

"You two get into this every few months," Rob said reasonably. "A flurry of memos, and it's all over until the next time. Don't take it so personally, Jul. Look at Debra—she isn't giving herself an ulcer about it."

"How do you know?" Julianne asked, her voice sharp with suspicion.

"No, Jul, I can't read her mind over the phone," Rob said impatiently. "I'm using my common sense. If she was as hassled by you as you are by her, you would've been out on your ear months ago."

"Look, Rob, how busy are you? You have the van. Can you join me for lunch?"

"Julianne, what do you have in mind?" Rob wished he really could probe her thinking over the phone.

"The pizza place at 12:30, okay? Look, I've got to scoot. See you then."

Click! She hung up. Rob put his receiver back more slowly. What on earth did she have in mind? Suddenly it really worried him. How far could he reach these days? Julianne's office was in Crystal City, a good 15 miles away.

There were desks now, but still no chairs. Rob moved over to a far window where nobody was hammering partitions or tucking cables into baseboards. Across the sunny parking lot was their old office building. From here the only signs of the fire were the smears of black soot above the windows at the far end. A workman in an orange hard hat was sealing a broken window with black plastic and duct tape. Rob leaned against the window frame and closed his eyes.

It was as if he stood on a high place, a rooftop or a mountain peak, with a view all around. As far as he could see down below were flowers, cup-shaped blossoms like buttercups or crocuses. There were hundreds of them, in every color imaginable, the fantasy of a gardener with megalomania. And when Rob leaned over to look more closely, he saw the flowers were heads, the heads of people. The tops of their skulls were transparent. He could make out the busy secret life inside each one, humming and spinning away, hidden from everyone but him.

A little dizzy, he straightened up again and gulped. Either the mountain peak was growing, or he was going up, straight up towards the zenith. The horizon widened and widened, spreading out to show more flowers and yet more, millions of them. How many people could he encompass now—everyone in the greater Washington area? The state? The entire eastern seaboard? And he had more than a view. He had supreme power over these little flowers. He could tell them how to think, what to want, how to feel. He could force moralities and actions on them. He was omnipotent. Suddenly he couldn't bear to contemplate it any more. With a shudder he wrenched himself away, back to the window overlooking the parking lot. He opened his eyes and wiped his wet forehead.

"You don't look so good, Bobster," Danny said behind him. "Just this second, you've gone gray."

"The doctors said I'd be okay," Rob said. "But maybe you're right. I should take it easier. Go home and take a nap."

"Good idea," Danny said. "Nothing's going to get going here until all this housekeeping crap is set up. Next week we hit the ground running. You want to take a shot at sifting through rubble? You recognize the disks."

"Sure, Dan. Have Lori set aside a pair of work gloves for me." Rob had to force a smile as he said that. Next week— what will I be, next week? At this rate I'm not even going to be human. He gathered up his jacket and briefcase with trembling hands, and almost ran out.

Behind the wheel of the van he tried to relax. At least there'd be no problem now meeting Julianne for lunch. He arrived in good time at the Pizza Palace. It had been their favorite restaurant when they lived in Alexandria after the wedding. There was something enormously comforting in sitting up to a red-checked tablecloth in the familiar poky dining room. "Pepperoni, extra cheese, red peppers, and half anchovy," he told the waitress. "And a small carafe of red." It was the standard Lewis order. When Julianne came striding in she laughed at him.

"How long has it been since we did this?" she asked, sliding into the booth across from him. "Do you remember when we ate here practically once a week?"

"Those were the days," Rob said. "B.C.—before children! Remember?" He leaned forward on his elbows, taking her hand.

She sighed, smiling. She wasn't thinking about pizza. Rob didn't need telepathy to see that. He grinned back. There's another idea, he thought. Use this thing in bed—it might be a lot of fun. What did sex do for women? How good was it for Jul, when she moaned and juddered in his arms? Inquiring minds want to know! Their love life was terrific, but you never knew. There might be room for improvement. Julianne's face grew pinker, as if his ideas were contagious.

Suddenly it occurred to him that they really were. He was so powerful now. And sitting so close to Julianne, thinking intently about something that she naturally shared with him— he was transmitting like a powerful radio tower, overriding her own weaker signal. It wasn't her own desire glowing so deliciously in her hazel eyes, but just an echo of his own. The thought instantly pulled the plug on his lust. He let go of her hand.

Luckily the wine and food arrived just then and he could fill up her glass. Julianne shook her head, blinking. Damn, he was going to have to be more careful. "Tell me, uh, about Debra," he said quickly. "What's the big deal this time?"

"Debra? Oh god, Rob, I wish I could strangle her. You know the report she had me draft for the Atlanta division? Four of the graphs—four of them!—turn up in her presentation this morning! On viewgraph slides, no less . . ."

Rob chewed pizza and kept the glasses filled. Nodding and making an intelligent noise every now and then was enough to keep Julianne going until she had vented all her frustrations. Which was really the point of this entire exercise—there was nothing anybody could do about Debra's alleged cussedness. It was as much a feature of Julianne's job as wearing designer suits and pearls. Besides, Rob didn't entirely believe in Debra's demonic aspect. It might be like the ineffectiveness of the postal system, or the collapse of the American family—a nugget of truth bloated way out of proportion by overzealous newspapers and TV talk shows.

At this moment overzealous was a good word for Julianne. She waved her pizza slice in the air. "—and when I checked with Mr. Thomas he said the fax had never been sent! Now wouldn't you think that if she was going to be so devious she'd at least send a cover sheet, and then blame it on line noise?"

"Oh sure, Jul, that would be obvious," Rob agreed absently.

"So my idea was to get you in on it," Julianne continued.

Rob choked on a sip of wine. "Me?"

"Yeah—you could drive me back to the office after lunch, and come up for a few minutes. It shouldn't take you but a jiffy to tell Debra that I'm right. You can tell when she's lying, right?"

"Well, yeah, but—"

"And then I'll write a memo, an accurate memo, to send upstairs. And she'll sign it."

"Jul, think a minute! How can I *make* the poor woman do something? It wouldn't be fair."

"But you're making her do something *right*. How is that different from making a bunch of dipsticks in Lorton do something right? Or pushing that shoe clerk around? You're being really inconsistent!"

For a second Rob's mouth hung open, as his thought processes spun their wheels to catch up. "So I'm inconsistent—I've been dealing with this for less than a week! At the shoe department it was an emergency, okay? Just in and out of the guy's head, nothing permanent. And I like to think I was performing a service to society at the prison, Jul. How does my leaning on your boss advance the common good?"

"It'll advance *my* good, and I'm your wife," Julianne said firmly. "I told you how important it'll be this month, to put up a good show for the Atlanta division. If I'm smart enough— if Debra doesn't undo all my good work the second I turn my back—the whole department gets a gold star."

"That is not what you could call a broad-impact goal, Jul," Rob protested. "Look, isn't it time to start on back? We can discuss this on the way."

"Oh my god, yes—look at the time! You better let me drive, otherwise I'll be late."

Rob willingly let her take the driver's seat. When she was in a rush Julianne put even more energy than usual into her driving. She would have little attention to give to persuading him, which meant he could think. Now that she wasn't prodding at him, it didn't seem so unreasonable to lend her a hand. She needed help with Debra and had asked him for it. The cons in Lorton hadn't even asked—he had just dumped a new mindset on them. And he wouldn't do anything nearly so drastic to Debra. Just a very slight adjustment, so that she wouldn't undercut Julianne so often. What could be the harm in that?

So when they arrived at Julianne's building he let her park the van in the basement parking lot and hustle him up to her office. The Association of Garment Design had the eighteenth and nineteenth floors in the building. Their suites were ostentatiously modern in decor and gave a fine view of the airplanes landing and taking off at National Airport. In his rumpled computer jockey clothing, Rob always felt underdressed at the Association. Operating anywhere in the garment industry seemed to demand very high fashion standards.

Rob had met Debra several times before, at Christmas parties mostly, but he always had trouble recognizing her. Partly it was the disguising effect of changes in hair color, hairstyle, and makeup. The one year she had become a redhead had really shaken his confidence. And today his difficulties would be compounded by the certainty that Debra would be in ordinary business attire rather than a killer party dress. Fortunately he now had a powerful booster to his feeble social skills. He scanned the minds around him, hoping to pick her out. Immediately he tapped into excitement and anticipation. "Something's going on today, huh?" he asked Julianne.

"Oh, it's Joubert. He's in town getting the red-carpet tour of the Association."

"Who is Joubert?"

"Oh, Rob! If you have to be a barbarian don't announce it, okay? Joubert is the famous French couturier. But don't worry. Mr. Rowe will keep him upstairs."

"Don't you believe it, Jul. He's just around the corner, over by the file cabinets."

Julianne shot him a quick surprised glance, but there was no time to talk about it. They came round the corner and the illustrious visitor was indeed there, dressed in green suede from head to toe and flirting with a delighted secretary. Mr. Rowe stood uncomfortably by, and hailed Julianne with relief. "Let me introduce one of our most energetic account execs, Phillipe. This is Julianne Lewis. And, er . . ." He looked at Rob in confusion.

"Rob Lewis, her husband," Rob said helpfully.

"Enchanté, madame," Joubert said without taking his eyes off the secretary. "Enchanté, m'sieur." He was absurdly young, in his mid-twenties perhaps, with a carefully wild shock of dark hair. Mr. Rowe looked like his disapproving grandfather.

From pure mischief Rob said, "I've always admired your work, Mr. Joubert. Is that suit your own design?"

"Rob!" Julianne mouthed almost silently at him.

"Surely," Joubert said. He brushed his palms over the studs and fringes. "I hope to reform, revamp, American male fashions, as I have revolutionized the ladies'." He raised one fastidious eyebrow at Rob's beige sports jacket.

"But suede will be so hot in the summertime," Rob said.

"So it is." Surprised, Joubert glanced down at his own fringed sleeve. "Too oppressive! I shall remake this in silk!"

"Green is all right, I guess," Rob said with a straight face. "But I always liked yellow myself."

"Yellow!" Joubert seemed to be seeing heavenly visions. "Yellow, a Naples yellow with a lot of orange in it! I think of sunflowers, of sunsets, of marigolds—"

"Rob, cut it out!" Julianne hissed.

"Plaid," Rob suggested wickedly.

"A piece of paper," Joubert demanded feverishly. "I must draw!"

The secretary handed the great man a pad. Mr. Rowe contributed his own fountain pen. Julianne seized Rob by the elbow and hauled him away. "How could you?" she whispered. "What have you done to him? What will his Paris collection look like next autumn?"

"Heaven knows," he laughed. "But anything'll be an improvement over green suede."

"How you can shuffle Monsieur Joubert's design inspirations around like that, and be so mealy-mouthed about Debra, I will never understand."

"Oh, but Julianne, couturier fashion design has absolutely no relationship to reality anyway!"

"But—but the industry, the balance of trade, the—" She sputtered to a stop and then announced in despair, "Oh, you're hopeless!"

Rob knew he shouldn't be surprised at how easy that had been. He no longer had to pronounce a command, even in silent words, or to harness a strong emotion to get the weirdness moving. A mere suggestion was enough, when he put the muscle of his will behind it. That was what to call it, muscle. And maybe poor Joubert was the malleable type anyway? But when he confronted Debra, Rob felt a small nagging doubt. Yes, interference was easy to do and subtle to execute. The woman would never know, just as Joubert hadn't noticed his interference. But Julianne would know. Rob couldn't help wondering if that knowledge would be good for her.

Julianne was saying, "You remember my husband Rob, don't you? We sat together at the company picnic last fall."

"Of course I remember you," Debra said cordially. "The father of those beautiful twins! Did you drop by to get a glimpse of Monsieur Joubert?"

Rob stared in fascination at her new hair color, a sort of strawberry blonde. Even her eyebrows matched. "He's just bringing me back from lunch," Julianne interposed, "and wanted to say hi." She frowned and nodded at Rob to get on with it.

Again Rob felt an impulse to delay. "I've run into Monsieur Joubert already. Doesn't he have a keen suit on, though!"

Debra beamed at Julianne. "And you were telling us about his conservative taste in clothes!"

"Look at what he's wearing now, Deb," Julianne said.

"Office uniform," Rob said airily.

"A good-looking guy like you would really set off designer menswear," Debra said.

"I know what I'm getting you for Christmas," Julianne threatened. "Green suede!"

Rob stared soberly into Debra's eyes—at least those were unchanged—and said, "Julianne's always right about this sort of thing." He gave the words the push, the muscle.

Debra blinked. "Of course she is," she assured him. "Why, without her nothing would get done around here!"

"I'm so glad you think so," Rob said uncomfortably.

Julianne instantly seized the offensive. "Don't you think we should send that fax off to Atlanta this afternoon?"

"Oh, for sure—do you have the revised draft?"

Rob didn't feel like contributing to the conversation any more. He wondered, is this how a rapist feels? Someone who slinks around forcing weaker people to do things they have no intention of doing? Fiddling with Joubert's clothing ideas had been a laugh riot, but would Joubert himself agree? By no stretch of the imagination could you argue that anyone would benefit from today's meddling. At the first moment he could, Rob made a show of consulting his watch and said, "My gosh, I better get going. I'll pick you up at the Metro station, okay, Jul?"

"You got it, hon." She blew him a kiss, her eyes sparkling with pleasure. Rob trundled gloomily off down the shiny modern hall to find the elevator. Had he ever seen that glitter in Julianne's eye before?

CHAPTER 6

*A*fter all the crises of this past week the Lewises were deeply in hock to Miss Linda. Rob was well aware it wasn't only a question of money. Miss Linda was irreplaceable and she knew it. No money in the world could have purchased a reliable and, above all, familiar sitter for the twins the other night, at such short notice. Rob knew that it would be only decent of him to apply the rest of this afternoon off to quality time with the twins. Miss Linda would get an unexpected holiday, thus giving the Lewis family a psychological leg up again.

When Rob halted the van at the curb the twins shrieked with joy. Their sandbox was set up in the fenced side yard of a modest brick rambler. What with the kids and the scattered sand, almost all the grass was dead. Miss Linda rose from her seat on the porch swing and waved. Rob unlatched the chain-link gate and, slipping in quickly, shut it smartly behind himself to prevent escapes. Living with two active kids forced everyone involved into a kind of paranoia.

Davey flung himself onto a leg and locked on, yelling, "Da!"

Angela dashed up with a double handful of sand. "Here, Daddo! Annie give!"

"No way, sugar pie, I'm on to that one. Hi, Miss Linda— I got the afternoon off, so I thought I'd give you a break."

"You feeling better, Mr. Rob? I saw that fire on TV."

"Sure, I'm fine. But it was scary, huh?" At this moment Angela dumped the handfuls of sand onto Rob's feet. Since he was wearing loafers his shoes filled immediately. "Oh, no no, Angela!"

"No no," she replied, inspecting her work calmly.

"You better let me fetch their diaper bags out to you," Miss Linda said kindly. "Maybe you should just empty your shoes back into the sandbox again."

Rob did so. By the time he got his shoes and socks back on, and loaded both kids into the van, Miss Linda was back with the bags. "Use your afternoon wisely," he urged her. "Watch Oprah. Go to the hairdressers. Have a good time."

"You can count on me, Mr. Rob. Good-bye, loveys, I'll see you tomorrow!" She blew kisses to the kids through the window, and they enthusiastically blew kisses back.

It would be shameful to waste such adorable toddler moods, and besides it was a glorious afternoon, full of birdsong and the green juicy smells of spring. Rob said, "Shall we go to the playground again, huh, kids?"

The twins had nothing to say against it, so Rob drove to the park. Having had enough sand for the day, Angela tugged imperiously at a toddler swing. Rob lifted her up and fastened the lap belt, all the while keeping a sharp eye on Davey climbing the tot slide. "Now push," Angela commanded.

The park wore an entirely different aspect midweek. Last Saturday with Aunt Angela, there had been adults as well as kids. Today some local preschool had taken over. Two harried-looking women chased after maybe forty kids. And some of those boys should have been in kindergarten, Rob judged.

They were huge. Luckily most of them were waving sticks and horsing around near the monkey bars. "Higher!" Angela squealed. "Go under!" Rob knew what that meant, and obediently ran with the swing until he dashed right under Angela's high-kicking feet. She screamed with delight.

He had only turned his back for a second, no more. But there was Davey, flat on his back at the foot of the slide, howling. A trio of bigger boys galloped past, heading for the teeter-totters. Rob ran over and picked Davey up. "Hey, poor little guy! Don't cry, let me look you over!"

Rob found nothing obviously wrong, no broken limbs or flowing blood, as he dusted his son off. Had those budding thugs knocked him off the slide? "What happened, sport?" Davey hiccuped and stuck a dirty thumb in his mouth. Rob gently pulled the hand down. "Davey, can you tell me how you fell?"

Davey had inherited Julianne's preposterously long eye-lashes, but his eyes were blue-gray like Rob's. When Rob looked into them he saw only a little-boy mind, not much more than a baby's. He didn't really expect Davey to answer. But suddenly Davey said, quite clearly, "The big boys ran by. They waved a stick at me. I got scared and my shoes slipped."

Rob's jaw dropped. Three whole sentences: his son had never yet been so articulate. Angela was the chatterbox of the two. "Oh my god," he whispered. "Davey, little guy, did I just make you say that?"

He knelt in the dirt hugging the little torso to his chest, and felt cold all over. What was he doing, just with his powerful presence, to these tiny impressionable brains? Was he warping them, the way plutonium might mutate their DNA?

There was no time to consider this now. Davey, already completely recovered, wiggled to be set free. The outraged Angela, trapped in her motionless swing, wailed, "Push, Daddo! Push!" at the top of her lungs. Rob staggered to his feet and pushed. He felt winded, as if he had taken a thunderous blow over the heart.

. . .

Another thing Rob felt obliged to do with an afternoon off was to cook some real food. The family was forced to do far too much carryout and TV dinner. Rob had only two menus in his repertoire, chicken à la king and spaghetti. Since chicken was on sale when he got to the store, the choice was easy. He knew the recipe by heart, which was good. Speed was essential when shopping with the twins. He had to seat them side by side in the body of the shopping cart, and then dash through the store tossing cream of mushroom soup and frozen peas into the small front area. By the time the kids were bored enough to try climbing out, Rob was breezing through the checkout line.

At home there was time to get the chicken going, change diapers, and feed the kids a snack. The child-care books didn't approve of TV as a babysitter, but Sesame Street kept them quiet and happy while he cooked. Then he piled them back into the van to go to the station to fetch Julianne. "Have you had a lovely restful afternoon?" she greeted him.

"No, I haven't," Rob groaned. "I've been running around doing things till my tongue's hanging out."

"Well, I had a great day! Come on, let's get it in gear—I'm dying for a drink, and I bet you are too."

She almost sparkled in the front seat beside him, her bell of blonde hair throwing back the last of the day's sunshine. In her sharp hound's-tooth jacket and green skirt she looked like a model, not at all like the mother of two. How on earth did such a beautiful girl marry me? Rob wondered idly, as he sometimes did. But quickly he caught himself up. He was too strong now. If he pursued that line of thought he'd find the answer.

When Rob unlocked the front door the smell of cooking chicken was marvelous, filling the house. Suddenly he knew he'd feel better after dinner. On his arm Davey remarked, "Hungry."

"Your wish is my command, sport! Into the highchair with you!"

"This is so nice!" Julianne exclaimed as she came in with Angela. "The table set, dinner cooking—I love it!"

"Makes a nice change from pizza, doesn't it? By the time you get your shoes off, the food'll be on the table."

A scattering of Cheerios on their trays as an appetizer kept the twins busy as Rob dished up and poured some beer. Julianne came clattering downstairs again in jeans, and took her seat. She raised her glass to him. "To the chef, long may he wave!"

"Thank you, thank you." Rob bowed to an imaginary audience on either side. "And what's your discerning assessment, madame?" he asked Angela, as he spooned chicken onto her dinosaur plate.

"Yum!" She squelched the food through her fingers.

"Thank god for bibs," Julianne said shuddering. "All right, baby boy, here's your peas, Davey's favorite!"

The twins gobbled their usual fast and messy meal, while their parents cut up chicken as quickly as possible and kept the plates filled. Once fully fed, they could be cleaned off, lifted down, and allowed to roister with toys underfoot. Then an adult meal became possible at last. Rob heaped his plate with chicken for himself this time, and asked, "So what's the story with Debra now?"

"Oh, you won't believe what a difference!" Julianne piled her fork with noodles and chicken. "You remember those graph slides? Well, she told me all about it. It was Gordon Rowe's fault after all! He took the graphs and had the graphics people transfer them without telling a soul, just boom! Like that . . ."

Rob's attention drifted a little. He had heard this sort of thing before. Directly between his ankles Angela was playing with her new bongo drum. At least it felt like the drum, whacking irregularly against his instep. He put his foot on it, casually pinning it against the rug, but she jerked it away, exclaiming, "Naughty Daddo!" Now, was it normal for an eighteen-month-old to be so assertive?

Suddenly he focused on Julianne again. The flavor and tone of her complaint was powerfully familiar, and it only took him a second to recognize it from lunchtime. She was working up to a demand. Resigned, he waited for it.

"—the simplest thing, all things considered, would be for me to take over Rowe's position, when he retires next year."

"What, become director of the Association? I thought the garment designer members got to vote on the director."

"Why shouldn't they choose me? You could tell them to do it."

Rob concentrated on scraping food up with his fork. "And Rowe has been promising to retire next year since the Reagan Administration. What makes you think he's serious this time?"

"He's going to have to bite the bullet some time." Julianne said it as if this were the most obvious fact in the world. "He's never there anyway, except when someone important comes by. All he does is work on his golf handicap."

"Nothing has to be done about it right away, right?" Rob said. "Let's wait on it awhile. See how things develop." He stared unhappily at the congealing mess on his plate. It looked like library paste studded with carrots and peas. Maybe he should learn another recipe.

"And there was another idea I had." Julianne speared another chicken wing and transferred it deftly to her plate. "You know how Ike is getting his degree next month?"

"Is he really?" Rob turned his attention to Ike's problems with relief. Julianne's younger brother, a perpetual student, had stretched his four-year undergraduate degree program well into his twenties. "What's his major now?"

"Oh god, some time-waster, I think it's sociology. The point is, he'll need a job in the real world."

"Not easy in this economic climate, Jul. He doesn't exactly have a stellar resume."

"Well, I told him to leave the bar gigs off," Julianne said. "And all those part-time busboy jobs at Shoney's. But what I figure is, once he decides what field to go into, you could give him a boost."

"Me?" Rob wanted to clutch his forehead with both hands. "And suppose he wants to be a rock drummer, like he did in the eighties? Jul, I don't know that I can create talent where there isn't any!"

"Did I say he was going to be a drummer?" Julianne demanded. "We wouldn't let him do that. I think he'd make a great CPA. Or maybe a lawyer."

"He'd make a lousy CPA," Rob said flatly. "Ike can't balance his own checkbook! How on earth will you talk him into graduate school, and on such a tough track?"

"You can do it."

"No way!"

"Oh, come on, Rob," Julianne coaxed. "We want him to support himself, right? God knows my parents won't last forever, and once they're gone he'll sponge off of us, unless he develops some openings."

"No. Zero. Nada. Not one cent, not one finger lifted in his direction. Ike's only hope is to make it off his own bat."

"And what about Angie?" Julianne demanded.

"What about her?" Rob asked, caught off balance by the sudden change of subject.

"Her real problem is that lukewarm boyfriend of hers, what's-his-name, Jerry. If there's one thing that gets on my nerves it's a commitment-phobic man."

"Good gosh, you don't want me to stampede Jerry Catharing, do you? Maybe Angie hasn't made up her own mind about him—have you thought of that?"

"True, but—" At that moment a squall of rage came from the living room. Rob got up to investigate and found the twins wrestling over a toy. "Now, sugar pie, you know that the walrus is Davey's special friend," Rob said reasonably.

"No!"

"Where's Angela's special pal, huh? Where's Tigger?" He snagged the toy out of the playpen and thrust it into Angela's arms. "Okay, now everybody's ready to go upstairs, right?"

"No upstairs!" Angela said. She hated bedtime.

"We'll take a bath first," Rob reminded her.

"Bath," Davey said happily.

"You're up for it, huh sport? Jul, I'm taking Davey upstairs for his bath. And then we'll read 'The Three Billy Goats Gruff.' "

Angela wavered. They might squabble, but the twins hated to be separated. And the story was an irresistible lure. "Okay, bath," she conceded.

Rob hoisted them both up. "We're all going up for a bath," he told Julianne as they passed the kitchen.

Julianne was speeding through the dinner cleanup, rattling the silverware into the dishwasher and rinsing plates. "What you really ought to find her, Rob," she said, "is a better boyfriend. Angie, I mean. A nice rich one, not too old or too flaky."

Rob didn't bother to answer that one. On either side of his head the twins were hooting, achieving their famous stereo effect that cancelled all rational thought. He galloped up the stairs with them, shouting, "Gangway!" They screamed with delight. How wonderfully simple it was, to please them!

✳ CHAPTER 7

*T*he next day was Thursday. The West Coast salvage team wouldn't arrive till this afternoon, so there was nothing for Rob to go in to work for. Julianne took the bus to the station, leaving him to drop off the twins at his leisure. Rob watched her trot off, glancing at her watch, her high heels clicking. It was a week ago today, exactly, that the bus driver had tried to ignore her. It might have been a decade. Certainly Rob felt as if he'd had ten years' worth of experiences.

He herded the kids into the van and drove them to Miss Linda's. "Going in a little late today, huh, Mr. Rob?" she greeted him.

"I'm sure sleeping in did us all good," he answered. She was assuming he was going in to the office, and he didn't correct her.

Instead he drove to Great Falls. It was a less than ideal day to go—he remembered with regret the piercingly mild days earlier in the week. Today was cooler, tending to rain. He wore new jeans and a nylon Redskins warm-up jacket, and hoped the drizzle wouldn't become a downpour.

The unpaved trail wound through a strip of woodland. Beyond was an infinity of cloudy gray sky between the tall trunks. He came out onto a shoulder of rock the size of an office building. The water-seamed granite sloped slightly downhill, and he picked his way carefully to the verge.

Twenty yards straight down the Potomac River thundered past, sleek and green as glass. Elsewhere on the river you could pretend the water was safe, tame. Its power was hidden. Here, squeezed between the shelves of rock, the current's strength was like a naked sword. People drowned here every year. One false step and Rob knew that nothing could save him, not the weirdness, not even the U.S. Park Police. Their helicopter would fish his battered body out of the current ten miles downstream.

The cliff made a perfect right angle. Sitting on it was like sitting on a curbstone. He could look right across the river to the Maryland side, where a lookout platform had been build among the boulders on Olmstead Island. A few Marylanders hung over the rail, snapping pictures and taking in the view. One of them waved. Rob pretended he didn't notice. He didn't want to communicate with anyone, even with a gesture.

He had to force himself to face the truth. It had been a terrible mistake to tell Julianne. She was just not the type of person who could handle power over others, even at one remove. It would have been just as bad, Rob sadly supposed, if they had won the Reader's Digest Sweepstakes, or if she had been nominated to be Treasury secretary or something. Julianne had never known when to quit. She had never been able to put herself in someone else's shoes. He could easily imagine her riding roughshod over all the Treasury undersecretaries, sparking off Congressional investigations and acerbic articles in the *Washington Post*.

Reluctantly he reviewed his options. How pleasant it would be to have a supportive wife who wouldn't insist on appalling interference with other people's lives! The only way to transform Julianne into such a person would be with massive adjustments of her personality. Fiddling with the homeless guy's head would be a fleabite compared to it. Even the Lorton convicts—he hadn't known them, been married to them. It felt outrageous, wrong—like meddling with nature, or stealing her soul.

And suppose he did. Suppose he successfully warped Julianne's character until she was like—well, like Lois Lane. Then she wouldn't be Julianne any more. He'd have remodeled her into a stranger, one that he might not even like, might never learn to love. "And the devil of it is, I do love her," he said out loud. The roar of the tumbling waters drowned his words.

Another, easier, possibility might be to just excise the knowledge from her mind. That would be far less drastic. He could make her forget completely about the weirdness and everything associated with it. If he was going to take this route he had to act soon. He had told her on Tuesday, and today was Thursday. Already she had had two days of thought, of action, of *memory*. The longer he waited, the more pruning he'd have to do.

He considered it carefully. The episode about Debra— well, Jul was constantly complaining of Debra's inconsistency. Maybe her latest about-face could be blamed on that. He had been able to drag his heels on all of Jul's more grandiose proposals. The whole thing was so wacky she probably hadn't confided it to any of her friends. Although he realized, now he looked back on it, that he had never told her to keep it secret. She had made no promises, and Rob, his head full of Spider-Man's home life, had not thought to demand one.

"Damn, I better move on it," he muttered. Carefully he stood up. A fine mist had been falling all this time, and he was chilled to the core. His jeans were clammy with the wet, and when he ran his hand over his hair droplets fell onto his jacket collar. A baseball cap would've been smart. Maybe the hike back to the car would get his blood moving.

The parking lot was nearly empty as he made his way to

the van. A trio of class-cutting teenage girls sat in the only other car, passing a joint around. As Rob went by a spiky-haired head popped out the driver's window. "Hey mister, do you have any cigarettes?"

"Sorry, I don't smoke."

"Then maybe you could give us some money to buy some, instead."

Her tone was threatening. Rob looked. Surely that was the gleam of a gun barrel in the rear window. But no rush of law-enforcement zeal overtook him. "Oh, for god's sake." Tiredly he marched up to the car. "Give me that."

The window descended. The girl in back meekly put something in his hand—a large silvery tube from a roll-on foundation container. The Revlon insignia was visible on the top. He gave it back. "Don't ever try that again," he said, turning away. "Oh, and all of you, quit smoking," he added over his shoulder. Probably he ought to do more. But he couldn't deal with it today. Wearily he climbed into the van and drove off.

Halfway to Crystal City it occurred to Rob that he could do the job long-distance. He didn't have to see Julianne or touch her to edit her memories. He pulled off the parkway onto a side road. There was a coffee shop in a strip mall just up the way.

With a hot mug cupped in his hands Rob felt better. Julianne would never know about the adjustments in her head. Everything would be okay. They could go on being married and life would carry on as it always did. He would never tell anybody else about the weirdness, and maybe someday it would dry up and go away.

He sat in a booth towards the rear, well back from the bustling pastry counter. For further camouflage he spread out the sports page on the table. A man meditating on the box scores wouldn't be interrupted.

He let the real world drop like a curtain to reveal the other place behind. Yesterday Rob remembered it had been a vast field of minds, all growing and blowing. Today it was like a crystal or a lattice, still a growing and organic thing but with more dimension, more depth.

Rob walked down glassy corridors lined with clear crystals. Or maybe it was a passageway right through a crystal, a gigantic diamond, perhaps. And each of these hand-sized crystals that made up the walls and floor and ceiling was one molecule of that diamond, a single twist of tightly-knotted carbon atoms.

He stopped and touched one crystal at random. "Why can't I get my ear pierced, Mom? All the guys at school are doing it." Unsurprised, he tried another. "Oh, no no, not like that. First you loosen the nuts, like this. Here, hold the wrench. Take the weight on your shoulder evenly, before you spin the nuts right off . . ." People, Rob thought. These were all people. He was walking through Mansoul, the entire agglomeration of minds on, say, this half of the continent. How many? Well, how many carbon atoms make up the Hope Diamond?

It didn't matter. He knew where he was and who he was looking for. After an uncounted time of walking through the cool labyrinth of passageways he found her. The crystal was low down on one wall. He knelt and touched it gently. Julianne.

Here, safely wrapped in crystal, he could be dispassionate. All that there was of Julianne he could hold in one hand. As on his computer at the office, he could call up the directory and see the files without opening each one. When he got to the right file, he knew it immediately. It was the only one with his own mark, his own fingerprint at the beginning, when he had forced Julianne to believe him. He picked it up. It was like a glass bead in his hand, a tiny translucent pearl. Would simply removing the file be enough? If Julianne were a computer he would be sure of it. But she wasn't. He would have to go through the file's contents.

There was no point in refinements. This glass pearl was doomed anyway. So he squeezed it hard between the heels of his hands. It shattered in a smear of moisture, and suddenly he fell.

For a moment Rob thought he was back at Great Falls

again, and had slipped on the rocks. A foaming torrent washed over him, tumbling him head over heels in the current. But this couldn't be the Potomac. The water was warm. In fact it was downright uncomfortable, warmer than the water in a hot tub.

He tried not to panic. This dark and rather dirty stuff wasn't real water. He wasn't drowning, could breathe perfectly well even though his head was under. All this turmoil was in that pearl, and now he was in the pearl with it. A battering waterfall was just as much of a construct as—well, as crystal corridors lined with computer-gems. He realized the enormous Mansoul diamond had been his own creation, the kind of image he was comfortable with, cool and hard-edged and organized. Julianne's imagery was obviously very different. He was in her playground, and she had set the rules.

Was this really a river? Or was it a closed sphere of turbulence, a salad dressing shaken in its bottle? Up, he thought. If I can get up and out, it's a river. For some moments he struggled against the currents, which seemed to batter at him from all directions. Then he was through, up above the turmoil like a seagull in a storm.

"It's a river," he said with satisfaction. The obvious next step was to find the source. The air was thick and supportive, and he had no trouble dog-paddling along in it. The torrent below soared down from a high cliff. At the top he saw floodgates, like the gates on the spillways of big dams. The gates were wide open, so that the muddy water gushed out unimpeded. He swooped lower. There was just room to stand on that rock by the open gate.

From this vantage point Rob could relax a little and survey the situation. A shock of recognition hit him. This flood was familiar, though he had never seen it as water before. It was another image: the torrent of Julianne's ambition. His tumbling struggle in the undertow just now was the exact analogy of his struggle with her in real life. And there was another proof of the parallel, right here. He surveyed the floodgates beside him. They seemed to be made of poured concrete, gleaming wet and festooned with slimy green weeds. About halfway up the farther gate was a whiter splotch—a hand-print, sunk deep into the concrete. Rob didn't bother to go up and fit his hand against it. He knew it was his own mark. He had thrust open these gates himself.

And now he had to close them again. But first, where else had the water run? Now he realized the usefulness of the river metaphor. The computer-crystal picture would have been much less convenient. From here he could track exactly where the water was going.

He kicked off again into the thick soupy air. The stream was fast and strong but surely couldn't be very long yet. He glided above as it fountained over rocks and rushed through a gorge. "Oh boy," he exclaimed. The river split into several smaller streams—Julianne had indeed told people!

Suddenly the humid thick air was intolerably oppressive. How much more pleasant crystal corridors were! Enough— he wanted out of this tiny worldlet. Rob made a gesture of reaching, pushing, and broke right through. Panting a little, he found himself sitting in the back booth again, clutching a cold mug of coffee.

As soon as he caught his breath Rob got up and made for the pay phone. It was in the back corner by the men's room. Let's keep this simple, he thought. His fingers were cramped and clumsy as he punched out the number. "This is Rob," he told the secretary. "Is Julianne there?"

She picked up. "Hi hon, are you at work?"

"No, I didn't go in. Julianne, who have you talked to about this weird thing of mine?"

It was only yesterday, wasn't it? When he had told her he couldn't exert the weirdness over the phone? Well, a day was a long time in Rob's life these days. He could tell now that she was lying. "Only Angie, this morning. But how on earth did you know?"

He didn't answer that. "And who else?"

"Well . . . I did ask Ike about his career plans."

"And?"

For a moment she hesitated. "You know my secretary, Pat?

She has a daughter Nadine in junior high. Well, Nadine is going out for the cheerleading squad, and—"

"No," Rob interrupted. "Is that everyone, Jul?" She didn't say anything, but he knew that it was all. "This is the end, Julianne. Forget it all: everything I told you about these powers, everything that you've thought and done on the subject. I'm wiping the slate clean." Still she didn't speak. Of course—she couldn't, not on this subject, not now. He hung up the receiver quietly.

Rob's knees felt a little shaky. He was glad to slide back into his booth. The waitress brought the pot over. "Hot that up for you, dear?" She topped off his mug.

He had drunk so little of the first cup that the mixture was scarcely lukewarm. He sipped it anyway. His hand trembled so that the cup clicked against his teeth, and he set it down again with a grunt of annoyance. There was no need to get upset about this. Julianne would be exactly as she was before. Nothing would be different, except—

Except that there was nobody now to turn to. He'd have to carry this thing alone, however huge it got, however long it took. Rob stared down into his cup, his shoulders bowed with the weight of it. Maybe it would be easier to drive to someplace like NIH and hand himself over to the research doctors. At least then he could talk to people about it—probably more than he would want to, after a while.

No, he wouldn't make the same mistake again. No hasty, emotion-driven decisions. Anything he did with the power from now on, Rob resolved to consider carefully. There was no reason why he shouldn't survey those scientists at NIH, for instance—try to predict what they might want to do, maybe select a sympatico one. Nobody who was into dissection, for instance . . .

With a start he remembered there were still loose ends to tie up: Angie, Ike, Pat the secretary and maybe her cheerleader daughter. Calling his sister and Ike would be long distance. He could do that cheaper from home. He put a big tip under his cup and hurried out.

That afternoon driving over to pick up the kids, Rob had another idea. He had done his telephoning and found that it was easy to make people forget stuff. It was a piece of cake, making Angie and Ike forget what Julianne told them—they'd only half-believed her, anyway. Forgetting is easy. Now, listening to the news on the radio, he thought about Bosnia, where another atrocity had just been perpetrated against helpless civilians. Suppose he went to the President and offered to make the Croats and the Serbs forget about the entire thing? Just wipe the slate clean of a thousand years or so of attack and counter-attack. Of course the Yugoslavians would lose a chunk of history if he did that—all the war stories and songs and poems would go, for instance—but at this point, with people being dismembered in the streets, maybe they wouldn't mind. It might be the perfect solution for some of those ethnic or religious conflicts with deep roots—Northern Ireland, for instance. Or Rwanda. Surely such power had come to him for a reason. If he could even partially heal some of these festering sores it would be worthwhile. It was a cheering line of thought, and Rob whistled as he opened Miss Linda's gate.

As usual the kids were delighted to see him. Davey gave Rob's knees a large slobbery kiss, leaving a purple jelly stain on his jeans. Angela said, "Look, Daddo! Look what Annie do!" She turned a leg-thrashing somersault on the rug.

"She just learned that today," Miss Linda reported with pride. "What a big girl, huh?"

"Good gosh, where's the videocamera when you need it! Will you do that again for Mommy when we get home, sugar pie?"

"Sure," Angela said with confidence, and Rob had to laugh.

"Come on, smarty, time to drift." He caught her up in his arms.

"Daddo, can I hold the videocam?" she asked sweetly.

Startled, Rob almost dropped her. Was that unusually articulate for an eighteen-month-old? He glanced at Miss Linda. "She's a clever cookie," Miss Linda said with only mild surprise.

"I wouldn't be surprised if she *could* handle the videocam," Rob said, turning it into a joke. By the time he had both children and all their paraphernalia loaded into the van, he had concluded it was just Angela's latest verbal advance.

Traffic was terrible going back through Fairfax. The rain had cleared, but a big truck had lost part of its load right in the middle of Route 50. Finally Rob was able to edge the van past the light at the intersection. "Lucky we don't have to pick up Mommy today at the station," he told the twins.

"Why? Is she taking the bus tonight?"

Rob's blood froze. Had that been Angela talking? He couldn't stop here in the middle of the highway. Instead he adjusted the rearview mirror to catch a glimpse of the two. Angela was looking out the window, so their eyes didn't meet. Nevertheless there seemed to be an unnaturally intelligent light in the baby face. "Oh my god," he groaned. "What have

I done?" Gritting his teeth he stepped hard on the gas. He had to get them home as soon as possible!

"Sometimes there's a police car hiding here," Davey remarked.

Davey loved police cars—that was why he remembered, Rob realized. He forced himself to slow down. This was not the time to be stopped for speeding. What had he done to them, by his mere presence? Maybe the power, easily driven by emotion, was working through his natural paternal desire to help his kids grow and develop. He rolled through the suburban side streets without seeing them, stopping automatically at the stop signs and making all the correct turns, sick with fear. What will happen to them? Will it get worse? Is this permanent? How can I find out? What pediatrician would know?

He almost whimpered with relief when he pulled into their own driveway. Cutting off the engine, he dashed out of the van and around to the side door. When he slid it aside, both children were staring at him with a kind of mild wonder. Davey was uncharacteristically grave as Rob unlatched his carseat. He held his arms out to be picked up. "Why are you sad?"

Rob flinched. "I can't tell you, son," he whispered. "I can't tell anybody."

"You can tell your family," Angela said reasonably. She sounded so mature, maybe six or eight years old! Rob fumbled at her carseat's latch, fallen Cheerios crunching under his feet.

Davey waited on the sidewalk with a patience totally alien to an eighteen-month-old. "The keys are in the ignition," he reminded Rob. Blindly Rob fetched them out and shut the van up. Ordinarily as he herded them up the walk to the front door they tried to chase butterflies or pick dandelions or eat ants. Now the twins led the way without instruction, and stood clear of the storm door while Rob unlocked the deadbolt.

Inside, on automatic pilot, Rob emptied the diaper bags and rinsed the bottles out. He poured apple juice into sipper cups and carried them into the living room. Dozens of toys lay neglected on the rug. Angela was perched on the footstool, frowning as she pushed the buttons on the TV remote. "You want to see the Lehrer Report, Daddo?"

"No!" Rob said vehemently. "No, please watch cartoons!"

Davey turned over the pages of *TV Guide*. "Power Rangers is too violent for our age group, you know."

"This one time it's okay." Rob set the juice down and bolted from the room. My god, could the kid read already? He ran too fast up the stairs into the bedroom, slamming the door behind him. The blood roared in his ears, and black water seemed to rush over him. He fell half-fainting to his hands and knees. I would love to pass out, he thought foggily. I can't deal with this. Come on, faint! But instead of overwhelming him, the friendly oblivion slowly ebbed. He found himself staring at the carpet, his fingers sunk deep into the green pile.

He crawled up onto the bed and lay face down on the duvet. It was vital to analyze this thing rationally. Miss Linda hadn't noticed any way-out precocity today. Rob remembered how she had been surprised when Angela had talked about the videocam. So this unnatural maturity only appeared when Rob was actually near the kids. With all his heart Rob prayed that this was true. Because then the solution was simple. He would keep away from them, and the children would revert to normal. Maybe even now, downstairs in the living room, it was far enough. Maybe they were babbling and romping and acting like regular toddlers again.

Oh, let it be so! Rob rolled over onto his back and closed his eyes, mentally reaching out. Very gingerly he felt for Angela. In her little treble voice she was saying something about the Israeli-Palestinian negotiations. Rob jerked away. Obviously one storey wasn't nearly far enough.

He rolled to his feet. There was only one course of action open to him now, though he had no guarantee at all that it would work. It was almost six-thirty. Julianne's bus would arrive soon. He kicked his leather loafers off and laced on a pair of athletic shoes. There was no time to pack anything, but he pulled his dark blue toggle coat out of the back of the closet.

He ran downstairs again and into the living room.

"Angela. Davey. I want you to remember this—I love you. Don't ever forget it." They would never forget, he knew it. All of himself, his entire being, was behind the words. He went down on one knee to hug them, first Davey and then Angela. "Mommy will be here in a minute, okay?"

"Where are you going, Daddo?" Angela demanded.

"We're too young to be left," Davey pointed out.

Rob couldn't bear to answer. The truth was impossible, and he wouldn't let his last words to the children be a lie. Without saying anything, he stumbled from the room, down the hall and out the front door. His keys still dangled jingling from the lock. He pulled them out and pocketed them, a last tiny gesture of hope.

The sun was setting. The bus came into sight at the end of the street, and he ran to meet it. With a hiss of air brakes it slowed at the bus stop. He dashed up to the doors just as they sighed open. Julianne stood astonished at the top of the steps. "Goodness, Rob, what's wrong? What are you doing here?"

Rob leaped up the steps into the bus. "Jul, I—I have to go away. On business. A long trip."

Of course she accepted this instantly, because his words had muscle behind them, but still she was surprised when he hugged her tight. "What, you're leaving tonight?"

"On this bus. Right now. The kids are waiting at home for you. Don't worry about me. Kiss me, quick!"

"You know, man, I got a schedule to keep," the bus driver said irritably. "Is she staying on or getting off?"

Rob let her go. "Have a good trip, hon!" Julianne called brightly as she skipped down the steps.

"Good-bye, Jul." Rob stood on the top step as the doors shut.

"Stand behind the yellow line, do you mind?" the bus driver said. "And no bills."

Rob dropped the quarters into the fare box and sank into the nearest seat. The pain in his heart was so dreadful he curled around it, bowing his head to his knees. He didn't realize he was sobbing until the woman in the seat behind him touched his shoulder uncertainly. "Excuse me, are you all right?"

He jerked upright, glaring. "No!" he shouted. "My life has collapsed! I've lost my wife and children! I am not all right!" The bus driver turned, his mouth open. Only a few passengers remained on the bus, and they all cowered. Trapped on a bus with a screaming nut—would he pull out an Uzi and start shooting next? "You don't see me," Rob commanded fiercely. "Forget this happened. Nobody sees me."

And of course nobody did. The tension evaporated instantly. The woman sat back again in her own seat, and the bus driver accelerated to make the light. The bus rumbled through the mild blue evening on its scheduled route, and Rob was alone with his grief.

Two

CHAPTER I

A gaudy dawn came slowly up in the east. Against the purple cloud streaks and pink sky the factory chimneys could have been cut out of black paper. Rob stared out the window at them. He felt gutted, empty. He had wept himself out, but the misery couldn't be eroded by tears. Without thinking about it, he had transferred from bus to subway to the downtown bus depot, paying no fares, cloaked in his invisibility. He hadn't bothered to note where this Greyhound was going. It had been the first departing interstate bus. That was all he cared about.

When the bus stopped and everyone got out, Rob did the same. He followed the other passengers out into a cavernous and grungy bus terminus. From there he wandered aimlessly out into the city: New York City.

I cannot bear this any more, Rob reflected dully. Oh God, if there is a god, take this thing away! It's a curse. It has ravaged my life. I wish I were dead.

Though it was so early, the narrow streets thronged with people. Rob walked like a ghost through them, unseeing and unseen. Millions upon millions of people lived in this city, all steaming with thought, thick with their histories. He couldn't hold their minds at bay any more. It had been madness to come here. New York was the last place for him. He should have gotten on a bus to Michigan, or Tennessee, someplace rural.

He walked at random for hours and hours through a repellent maze of grim commercial streets. At last he came to a park, a tiny wedge of struggling grass and broken bottles. One of the benches had been vandalized, its slats burnt away, but the other was still reasonably whole. Rob slumped down onto it, exhausted. He stretched out on his back and stared up at the slice of sky remaining between the tall gray office towers. The roar of city traffic surged in his ears, and the workings of a million minds scoured through his skull. I am not going to cope with this any more, he thought. I am going to do nothing and think nothing. I give up.

Vaguely he felt the danger of this. When I think it, it happens. If I tell myself to die, I may very well die. But Rob didn't care any more. He willed himself to stillness, to emptiness, to oblivion, and sank gratefully into the dark.

Time passed, an unreckoned period that could have been forever. It was the rain that brought him back. Little annoying drops tapped on his forehead, refusing to go away. Then they rolled down into his eyesockets, forcing him to blink. Of themselves his dry lips parted and the rain trickled in. He realized he was horribly thirsty. He had neither eaten nor drunk since leaving home.

Sullen thunder rumbled in the sky as Rob slowly sat up. His joints creaked, and his arms and legs were full of pins and needles. The rain poured down, digging its cold fingers into his scalp. He was soaked to the skin, right through his coat and jeans and shirt. It was night. The streetlights cast a ghastly pinkish light over the dirty wet avenue. There was only moderate traffic, so it must be very late. His watch said it was quarter to four on Sunday morning. Confused, he could hardly believe it. But he rubbed his chin—at least three days' worth of bristle there. What a horrible city! How come no one had noticed a person lying here, trying to be dead, for three whole days? At the very least somebody should have ripped off his watch.

A man walked briskly by, a bartender on his way to the subway. Rob glanced at himself through the bartender's eyes and saw the problem immediately. He had never stopped doing his tarnhelm trick. He was so strong now, the trick could just run on automatic. His bleak despair might even have subconsciously repelled anyone who wanted to sit on the bench. It occurred to him that all he had to do was quit being invisible, and a mugger would come along and put him out of his misery. He'd be too weak to resist.

Putting it like that made Rob realize he didn't want to die. At least, not by being mugged. Or from starvation and thirst. That single trickle of rain had been enough to revive his will to live. The streetlights wavered and danced as he blinked at them, and he repeated to himself, I am not Superman. If I don't eat or drink I will die. What a laugh if I die now after all, a real triumph of mind over matter. If there is a God, he has a sick sense of humor.

He sat in the pouring rain without the strength to do more than lick the raindrops off his upper lip. More footsteps. He would have to ask this one for help. Rob dropped the tarnhelm trick and whispered, "Help." I'm your friend, he thought at the man, who stopped in his tracks.

"My god! Is that—"

"Rob Lewis," Rob supplied. The tinder-dry creak of the words surprised him. His voice was almost gone.

"Jeez, Rob, what happened? You're hurt!"

"In pretty poor shape, uh—" He fished for the name. "—Jim."

"These gang members, they're everywhere, like roaches! New York's going down the toilet! You must've got knocked on the head—what'd they get, your keys, your credit cards? Come on, I'm taking you home to Marge. Can you walk? Hey! Taxi!"

Jim was a dapper older man, maybe in his sixties, but in great shape. He drew Rob's arm over his Burberryed shoulders and hoisted him to his feet with ease. Probably he went to the gym every day. The first taxi was, naturally, off duty, but Jim bundled him into a second one and gave the driver an Upper East Side address.

Good, Rob thought. Wouldn't want to sponge off a garment worker or a waitress. My buddy Jim can afford to give me a meal. When a uniformed doorman opened the taxi door Rob decided to let all scruples slide. The doorman tenderly helped Rob into the elevator and promised, "I'll buzz Mrs. Deacon and let her know you're coming, sir."

"With Rob Lewis, tell her that," Jim instructed. Boy, will she be confused, Rob thought.

The elevator arrived on the 22nd floor. Halfway down a long carpeted hallway Marge stood in a paisley bathrobe holding the apartment door open. "Jim, who on earth—"

Friend, Rob thought at her hazily. "You remember Rob, don't you, Marge?" Jim called.

"Of course I do! Oh, you poor boy, you're drenched!" Marge was an easy twenty years younger than Jim, but old enough to be motherly. Rob let her take away his sodden clothes and bundle him into a hot shower, Jim interrupting only to press a brandy snifter into his hand. The brandy was excellent, but far too strong for Rob's shrunken stomach. He had to run some of his shower water into it. I think I'm going to survive, he thought.

That first day Rob ate chicken soup and slept, a genuine sleep, not the deathlike trance. In a couple of days he recovered his health and strength completely. By that time he was too uncomfortable to trespass on Jim and Marge any more.

The problem was, saying "friend" didn't make Rob their

friend. He had nothing in common with Jim, a television executive, or Marge, who ran charity banquets. Because he wished it, they adored Rob, plying him with food and liquor, giving him the run of their ritzy apartment. But at the dinner table conversation limped. Rob didn't dare confide his own affairs, and when the Deacons tried to include him in their chat he didn't know or care about any of their concerns. They couldn't remember where they had known Rob before—unsurprisingly—and that tended to throw a monkey wrench into any reminiscence or story.

So as soon as he felt able, Rob took his leave. "You saved my life, Jim," he said. "I'll never forget it."

"It was nothing, nothing!" Jim protested. He squeezed Rob's hand in a painfully muscular grip. "God, it's been so great to see you!"

"Why don't you visit more often?" Marge demanded. "Bring the wife and children next time!"

Rob held onto his smile with an effort. "Thanks for the great meals, Marge." Marge kissed his cheek. Jim hugged him around the shoulders. They walked him down the long corridor and waved as the elevator doors closed on him. As the elevator went down, Rob tried to decide whether he had just committed a crime or not. The Deacons would never prosecute. No court would ever convict. I am not going to worry about it, he told himself. I left all these petty moral agendas in the park. Still it seemed impolite to just walk away from the Deacons' hospitality.

He strolled east towards Madison Avenue. At the corner was a stationery shop. A bread-and-butter note, that's it, he decided. That's the concession I'll make to my middle-class upbringing. He went in and selected the toniest notepaper in the store, in keeping with the Deacons' status. A quick glance into the storekeeper's head showed Rob that nobody ever became a tycoon selling cards in Manhattan. He paid up fair and square.

To camp outdoors in June in New York is no great hardship, at least as far as the weather goes. Central Park had plenty of grassy nooks for Rob to choose from. Rolled up in his toggle coat and tarnhelmed from cops and petty criminals, he slept well. From a street vendor he bought a brown duffel bag to keep the coat in on warmer days. He also scrounged some black plastic garbage bags to use as a groundcloth.

For the first week, money was a worry. Rob wasn't often hungry any more, but eating at coffee shops even once a day soon depleted his cash. And using the credit cards would only shift his expenses to Julianne—No! He wasn't going to think about home, about the family! The effort of holding himself back from that abyss made Rob shake all over. He leaned suddenly against a lamp post, almost unable to stand.

"You're blocking the crosswalk," an Asian woman with a briefcase snapped as she shouldered past. Viciously Rob directed her descending foot onto a storm grating as she stepped off the curb. "Oh shit! My heel!" She balanced on the other foot and pulled off her beige leather pump. But it gave Rob no real pleasure to see her hobbling away, the broken shoe in hand. He slumped down to sit on the curbstone. "What have I done to deserve this?" he demanded of the morning rush hour.

To his astonishment, an older black woman bent to address him. "Look, get yourself a square meal," she said kindly. And she stuffed a ten-dollar bill into his hand.

Did he really appear so seedy? Rob took a look at himself through the eyes of the crowd waiting to cross Lexington Avenue. Since leaving the Deacons he had given up combing and washing and shaving. His light-brown stubble, always thick and vigorous, was fast approaching the status of a beard. His jeans and shirt looked grimy and thoroughly slept in. But it was his eyes and his expression that really marked Rob as strange. He had the desperate look of a man pushed too fast, too far: like a drunk or a mental case.

"Oh great," Rob muttered sourly. First a criminal and now a vagabond. Only two weeks ago I was a completely normal human being. Too bad my former self, that meddling Rob

Lewis who aspired to a cape and tights, won't come along to reform my life!

But he could use this down-and-out appearance to advantage. Panhandling might be time-consuming and unprofitable for other street people, but not for him. Rob plucked a paper cup from an overflowing trash bin and leaned against his lamp post. If everyone on this corner gave him a quarter he'd be set for the week. But the congestion might look odd. So he settled for muscling a quarter from every third or fourth passerby. He skipped anyone who seemed like they couldn't afford it. By lunch time, his pockets were so weighted with coin that he had to transfer some quarters to the duffel bag. This is going to be a snap, Rob told himself. It was much easier being a predator than a benefactor!

On rainy days, and whenever he felt like a home-cooked meal or sleeping in a bed, Rob selected a fat cat and briefly became his best friend. The first time, staying with a hotel magnate in his Fifth Avenue penthouse, Rob didn't even bother to bathe. But the image of a smelly street bum sitting beside a baronial fireplace soon lost its humor. Besides, when the owner of a bathroom the size of a racketball court begged him to try out the hot tub, how could Rob resist?

There were thousands of really rich people in New York City. Rob figured he wouldn't have to leech off anyone twice for years, which was just as well. He didn't want to see any of his hosts again. No application of power would ever make him feel at home among his victims. And without human feeling to season it, luxury cloyed fast. Always after a day or two, Rob returned to Central Park.

Panhandling only took him a couple of hours a week. The rest of his time Rob mostly spent at the library. Particularly in the bad neighborhoods, the branch libraries were dumps compared to Fairfax County. But the main Central Research library at Forty-Second Street was delightful, with a reference collection like a dream. Rob found a dozen out-of-print H. Rider Haggard novels he had never heard of before. Across the street, the Mid-Manhattan branch was more like the circulating suburban libraries he was used to. There he delved systematically through the mystery section. He was through with self-exploration and analysis. It hurt too much. Better to occupy the surface of his mind with fiction.

Whenever the shoot-'em-up stuff began to pall Rob stretched himself by trying poetry. He had never had time to read poems before. Now he began with T.S. Eliot, whose work was tough sledding. Working back in time and reading older poems was easier. He liked Swinburne, and Tennyson and Matthew Arnold were quite understandable.

Instinctively he skipped Dante—the very first lines of the *Inferno* were off-putting—but he spent weeks working through translations of the *Iliad* and the *Aeneid* of Virgil. That, plus the daily papers and the news magazines, kept him busy just about every day shuttling between the two libraries. Except for the occasional thank-you note, he never set pen to paper. Nor did he ever touch a telephone. Let it be a total amputation.

Dimly Rob realized he was systematically severing himself from all meaningful human contact. Adrift, rootless, there were days when he hardly spoke a word to anybody. Certainly he never talked about anything important. The teeming population around him consisted of either patsies or fish too small to exploit. His rich hosts were exactly that, playing contemptible host to his parasite. Like many men, he had few emotional outlets outside of his family. Severed from that natural intimacy he had nothing.

July brought the heat, atmospheric inversions that muffled the entire city like a filthy plastic garbage bag. The air was brown with exhaust and ozone. It was hellish, sullen weather that fostered madness. Tempers shortened, the crime rate soared, and the wail of police sirens and ambulances sliced over and over through the foul air.

As the summer grew nastier, Rob found himself idly considering rather cruel experiments. What would happen, for instance, if that taxi driver lost control of his cab and swerved into the throng of pedestrians at the Columbus Circle cross-walk? If the ticket taker at Radio City Music Hall suddenly refused to let the customers in the door, how long would it take for the management to notice? Would the Rockettes dance to an empty house? It might be kind of interesting to find out . . .

The only time the cold shell cracked a little was one Saturday afternoon. That day Rob didn't get around to walking to the library until well after noon. It was a sweltering hot August day, the sidewalks like a barbecue grill, and he cut south through the Park. Because it was the weekend the park paths were jammed with strollers and roller-bladers. The simmering humid air was laden with the smell of PABA-free, high-SPF sunscreen and spilled sodas. Every rock and patch of grass had sunbathers sprawled on them, playing boom boxes or talking too loud. Rob surveyed all this humanity with a new distaste. There were too many people in New York, all doing too many different and noisy things. Someday he would do something about it—he wasn't sure what yet.

Abruptly a dark-haired man with both a stroller and a boom box jumped up and began to yell, his voice rising in a frightened carrying baritone. Rob stared with only mild interest. Surely he couldn't be shouting "Forceps!" That was pretty unusual even for New York. Then he noticed the kid in the stroller. Her wordless distress surged over him. She was choking.

Rob ran up and, sweeping the shouting man aside, hoisted the baby out of the stroller. She was a small thing, only about a year old. Her face was purple and her eyes bulged. Rob held her upside down over his arm and shook her sharply. A chunk of hot dog shot out of her mouth onto the grass. She drew in a whoop of breath, and began to howl.

In a fury Rob shoved the screaming baby back into the man's arms. "You idiot!" he roared. "Never give a baby a hot dog! At this age they don't chew their food!"

"It never occurred to me," the man said, bewildered. "She's my niece—I don't usually feed her."

"And they *taught* you the Heimlich maneuver, why didn't you *use* it?"

"Oh Jesus! I was so scared, all I could think of was pulling the blockage out with forceps."

Rob snarled with disgust and turned away. Some people shouldn't have charge of children for more than ten minutes, max.

The man grabbed Rob's ragged sleeve. "Wait! Hey, thanks! I'm really grateful—you saved Katie's life! Look, I can see you're, like, fallen on hard times . . ." He set the baby down and fumbled in his shorts pocket. If he offers me money, Rob thought, I'm going to walk him under the wheels of the next crosstown bus.

But the man only pulled out a metal card case. "My name's Edwin Barbarossa. Here's my number. Any time you need help, for any reason, you call me, okay?" Rob made no move to take the card, but Barbarossa pushed it into his hand and with surprising strength closed his unwilling fingers around it. His eyes, green and intelligent, searched Rob's face through the jungle of dirty hair and beard. "How did you know that I can do Heimlich?"

Shit! Rob thought. Must've read his mind! He snatched his hand away. "You don't see me," he said quickly. He continued to stand there though, watching with cold amusement as Barbarossa looked wildly around for him. The little girl was still squalling on the picnic blanket. Rob clocked the time on his watch. It took Barbarossa three entire minutes to finish maundering around and get back to the kid. Incompetent! But the feel of that little ribcage in his hands had been obscurely upsetting. He had better get on to the Periodicals Room and read today's *New York Times*.

✳ CHAPTER 2

W*hen August slid into September, the summer heat mod-*erated. The air no longer thickened with smog to the color of dishwater, and the sky became blue again between the city towers. Rob looked at his coat, threadbare and stiff with dirt, and realized it was not going to be enough come winter.

Where could he go when the cold weather came? Hotels were a possibility. Rob commandeered a suite at the Waldorf-Astoria for a weekend, just to see how he liked it. In theory it would be possible to hop from hotel to hotel, week after week, till spring. But something about hotel beds and canned hotel air repelled him.

Another idea would be to become some rich gull's permanent guest for the season. If he didn't want to deal with his host on a day-to-day basis, he could find someone who was spending the winter months in Palm Beach or Bermuda. In his pocket notebook he listed what this pirated apartment would have to have: view of Central Park, not above Ninety-second

Street, no irritating modern decor, no pets or plants to demand
care. When he stayed with his well-heeled victims these days,
Rob assessed their homes carefully. If a place attracted him sufficiently he might consider muscling the rightful owners out.

Rob was still mulling over the problem in late September
when some entertainment organization threw a fancy awards
celebration. On the sidewalk outside the party Rob seized
upon Denton MacQuie, the has-been hippie rocker. Whether
from age or heavy drug use he was the dimmest bulb Rob had
ever fastened upon, a fifty-year old man with shoulder-length
gray hair and the wattage of a ten-year-old. But it might be
kind of interesting—shouldn't a rock legend have a magnificent home?

When the private elevator carried the two of them up to
Denton's pad though, it was a disappointment. No Wood-
stock memorabilia or sixties souvenirs remained. Some hot interior designer had gone through the place like a steamroller,
scattering Navaho rugs and Southwest furniture, hanging cow
skulls over the fireplace, and painting fake saguaro cactus on
the dining room walls. "Sara had it done," Denton said
proudly. "Hey chick, this is Rob."

"Hey," Sara greeted them from the sofa. She looked like
Janis Joplin would have if she'd lived to see forty-five. Rob instantly slotted her as a cokehead. The buzzing confusion in her
head was entirely characteristic. She stared vaguely at Rob, not
quite focused, and he didn't even bother to say "I'm a friend"
to her. Her brain cells were chutney anyway—she'd never notice.

Denton's glory days were long past, his life style now main-
tained only by licensing old hits for Chrysler advertisements.
"But I'm still writing songs," Denton assured Rob. "Lemme
play you a studio tape."

Rob riffled through Denton's memories of the new music
and winced. "No thanks. Think I'll crash, it's late."

"It is not either late," Sara said indignantly. "It's only like
three A.M. Even Courtenay isn't back yet!"

"Who is Courtenay?" It was important to at least know

of every member in a household, to avoid surprises.

"My daughter," Denton said. "Went to a party. There's the elevator, betcha that's her." A young and painfully thin girl with vivid orange hair came slouching in. "Courtenay, baby doll, this is Rob, an old friend."

"Hi," the girl mumbled ungraciously, and escaped down the hall to the bedrooms.

In spite of himself Rob was shocked. "She's barely in her teens, and you let her run around town till this hour?"

"She turns fourteen in January," Sara said, with a spacey smile.

"Courtenay's got street smarts," Denton said, dismissing the subject. "Hey, I know! My bass player deals. Let's do some hash, like we did in the Haight!"

"Let's not," Rob said, standing up. "Good night." What a contemptible pair! Only the ugly skulls and the blanket-patterned sofas kept him from evicting the MacQuies on the spot.

Luckily he only slept there. In the Reading Room at the main library Rob had worked right back through almost all the major poetry and epics on the shelves. Now he planned to read the very oldest epic of all, the Sumerian myth about Gilgamesh. He had long ago bamboozled the Reading Room librarian into reserving books for him, although that was against the rules. "I've had the Ferry translation of the epic on reserve since July," he complained to her now. "Where the hell is it?"

"Well, it must be misfiled," the librarian said. "We do have over thirty-six million research items, you know."

"Tell me something I don't know," Rob said. "Can't you look for it?"

"You'll just have to be patient, Mr. Lewis," the librarian said soothingly. "Everything that can be done is being done."

The delay put Rob thoroughly out of temper. He stamped out into Bryant Park behind the library and touched off a tremendous shouting match between a cabbie and an old lady by making the cabbie forget that his fare had been paid. The old lady, a game one in spite of her years, put up a surprisingly noisy battle about paying twice. In the end a traffic cop had to intervene. Rob watched until both parties were ticketed, but it wasn't really satisfactory.

He returned early to the MacQuie household. Only Courtenay was home, slumped in front of the TV watching a soap. Today was Monday—why wasn't she in school? For want of anything more entertaining to do, Rob helped himself to a beer and delved into her mind to find out.

She was skipping class, naturally. Rob wasn't surprised. He wasn't even surprised to learn what she was skipping for: to sleep with not one, but two of the boys on the school basketball squad. She was planning to get them all. What an utterly brain-dead ambition! She must've inherited idiocy from her parents.

But the knowledge gave Rob a new idea. He prowled through the apartment, beer in hand, and thought, I could sleep with her myself. The girl's a slut anyway. No one would ever know. And now that he considered it, he hadn't had sex in months, since—well, since. "I can do it," he told a hanging cow skull. "So I will."

He opened doors until he found Courtenay's room. It was the only one so far done in a reasonable style, with flowered wallpaper and a tall white pencil-post twin bed. Stuffed animals were crammed on picture-rail shelves near the ceiling, and beneath hung posters of rap artists that Rob didn't recognize. He began rifling the nightstand drawers and the bureau. This type of girl surely had condoms hidden away somewhere. Right here in the sock drawer . . .

"What the hell?" Courtenay came bursting in and halted in surprise. "What're you doing here?"

Rob stepped between her and the door. Delicacy would be wasted on her. "Let's fuck," he said.

"Asshole!" she spat, dodging past him. "I'm telling Denton and Sara!" How very like the MacQuies, Rob thought, to train a kid to use their first names. He slammed her against the wall, enjoying her sudden terror.

"You want it," he told her, and let her go. With a sigh she flung herself against him. Her kiss tasted disconcertingly of Juicy Fruit gum. He let her probe his mouth with her tongue while he shoved a hand roughly under her sweatshirt. No bra—she didn't need one. "Smaller boobs than I'm used to," he told her, "but these'll do."

He adjusted the dials in her head, forcing her excitement yet higher, and then stepped back and unzipped his jeans. Immediately she was stripping too, flinging her clothes aside and then unbuttoning his shirt for him. "Please!" she begged. "Let's do it, now!" The feel of her skinny naked body against his was wonderfully arousing, almost as exciting as the raw lust he'd sent roaring through her mind.

Rob stroked her, appraising it. She was going to climax at the first thrust. How many times could he get her to orgasm? It might be kind of interesting to find out. He pushed her against the wall again and she clasped him, moaning into the tangle of beard where it hung over his chest. This was going to be a perfectly fair deal after all. He'd give her the best screw of her life, a stellar event that she'd remember fondly forever—far better than the entire basketball team could do.

But standing was awkward. She was too short for him. No problem—Rob picked her up and tossed her lightly onto the white bed. When he climbed on top of her she wrapped wiry arms and legs around him. "Come on, come on!" she begged. He fumbled at her crotch to enter her. Her pubic hair was sparse under his fingers.

Suddenly big soft things were falling on Rob, bouncing on his head and back. Startled, he flung one away. It was a blue teddy bear. The jounce of the tall bedposts had disrupted the balancing act up on the shelf, and the stuffed animals were tumbling off, bears and dinosaurs and walruses and beluga whales raining down onto the bed.

He stared down at Courtenay in a welter of her old toys and thought, I'm having sex with a girl who still sleeps with teddy bears. "Oh, come on!" she wailed. Her fingernails dug into his bare buttocks. "What are you waiting for? I want it!"

"No you don't," he said automatically. "Stop." And she did, like a car slipping into neutral, lying still and blank on her pillow.

He sat on the edge of the bed, his thoughts whirling. What am I doing? This girl is underage, only thirteen years old—a child! All the other stuff I've done is maybe marginal, but this is a crime, a genuine twenty-four-carat crime. I am raping her, the same as if I held a knife to her throat. Is this the kind of person I am?

A sudden and overpowering self-disgust made him nauseous. He stumbled into Courtenay's pink-tiled bathroom and hung over the basin, panting. Cold sweat trickled down his face into his beard, and goosebumps stood out on his naked legs. He stared into the mirror and didn't recognize the person reflected there. A wild man, with hair matted down his back and tangles in his long disheveled beard, glared madly out of the glass. It was a mask of mindless malice, a horror.

"No!" he cried out loud. "That is not me!" His own voice echoing in the tiled room rang oddly in his ears, and he reaffirmed his discovery. "That is not me." From that statement the logical corollary came easily: "I have to find my real self."

He buttoned his shirt. Back in the bedroom he retrieved his ragged jeans. Courtenay still sprawled white and still on her bed. Rob didn't feel even a twitch of desire. He drew the quilt up over her nakedness and told her, "Forget all this. Everything that happened in this room. You're asleep, and you'll wake naturally in time for dinner."

An hour ago that would have been enough, and more than enough. Now Rob thought about the dingbat druggie parents, the basketball team, the condoms in the sock drawer, and knew he had to do more. He sat on the edge of the bed again and looked at Courtenay's sleeping face under the stringy orange-dyed fringe. She needed to straighten out and fly right. But how to achieve it?

He spent a long time flipping through her memories and images. If this was going to work it had to be done carefully, working with the grain of her nature. He didn't want to just pull the plug on her sex drive. She'd need that someday when she got married. What she needed now was some overriding interest, to keep her safe until her emotions matured to match her body. Sports? Not a good prospect in New York City. And in spite of her genes, music might be a bad move—her father hung with too many sleazeball musicians.

Ah, but here was something. Courtenay wasn't a complete ditz. She had liked books until fairly recently: Regency romances, Gothic novels, *Rebecca* and *Gone With The Wind*. He commanded, "You're going to fall deeply in love with the works of—let me see, Jane Austen. Charles Dickens. Anthony Trollope. Read everything they wrote, those nineteenth-century writers. Write papers and book reports. Dive in and enjoy it."

That should do it. Her teachers will be stunned, Rob reflected. As he quietly closed the door on her he envisioned Denton and Sara MacQuie a decade from now, hippies sitting bewildered in a university audience while their daughter graduated summa cum laude with a degree in English Literature. The picture made him laugh, a weak rusty laugh, but a laugh all the same.

Stores in Manhattan do not open early. Rob couldn't get a haircut until after ten. And barbers were apparently an extinct species uptown. There were only hair designers in salons. The Personal Skylines salon on Madison Avenue was far too campily cutting-edge for his taste. Fiberglass Liberty statues stood in the corners holding aprons on their upheld arms. And a large inflatable King Kong clutched a Barbie-doll Fay Wray as he scaled the wall behind the espresso machine. But it was the first open shop Rob found. He muscled the receptionist into overlooking his seedy appearance and giving him the first appointment. He sat down in an opulent white leather styling chair. A classic Billy Joel album popped into the CD player as the boyish young stylist said, "There's *nothing* wrong with long hair on a man these days."

"I want it cut," Rob insisted. "Short."

"But it's so nice, so *long!* Look at mine." He turned so that Rob could see the black ponytail bobbing at his nape. "You know how many weeks it took me to grow it that long? When did you last have a cut?"

Rob had to think. "April."

"You've got roots to die for! Look, let me just trim it up nice for you, okay? Give you an idea how it'll look. And if you're *not* happy, we'll buzz it, I promise."

The stylist pulled the same argument in favor of Rob's jungly tangle of beard. "It'll be far more comfortable for you, believe me, to take it off a step at a time!" Why did people always have to argue? But Rob curbed his impulse to muscle him. If you hired a pro, it was only sensible to heed his advice.

Rob felt like a fool sitting here. The nostalgic Manhattan pop songs pouring out of the speakers, "A New York State of Mind" and "I've Loved These Days," struck him as savagely ironic. The actual haircutting process was curiously unsettling. Rob had not realized until now how stressful it was to be touched, skin to skin. He had gotten into the habit of touching people only to exploit them. Now every time the stylist's fingers brushed his neck he had to fight down an involuntary twitch of power.

Forty-five minutes later Rob still didn't recognize himself, but at least the reflected image was neat—a sharp silhouetted wedge of beard and a George Washington–style tail in back. Summer outdoors had glazed the light brown of his hair and beard with an almost butterscotch gold. "It'll do, I guess." He was too jittery now to demand changes.

"I *knew* you'd love the look!" the stylist exclaimed. Rob tipped him heavily in quarters and made his escape.

His new image flashed in each store window he passed, tattered clothing topped by an absurdly trendy head. But I'm still a wolf, Rob thought. Shearing the wolf to look like a sheep doesn't make it a member of the flock. They touch me, and I want to bite. His isolation terrified him. Where can I go? he wondered. How do I end, and then begin? If I give up life as a wolf, how shall I live? I've built this wall around myself brick by brick, a prison, a bell jar, and now I can't get out.

And all his habits, body and mind, worked against him. Rob looked up after walking and thinking for hours, and found himself at Forty-second and Fifth, in front of the public library. With a grunt of annoyance, he climbed the steps between the big stone lions and went in. Then, it seemed only natural to walk down the cool high-ceilinged hall to the Periodicals Room, and look at today's *Times*. On his way to his usual table, he heard the periodicals librarian calling, "Mr. Lewis? Is that you? There's a note for you from upstairs. Your book has been found, the epic of Gilgamesh."

After waiting two months, it would be a pity to miss the book. Rob gave her the newspaper back again. "Did you get your hair cut?" she asked kindly. "I don't know how I recognized you."

"You don't see me," Rob responded without thinking. Now was that necessary? he thought. She was only making small talk. This tarnhelm trick makes it too easy to be a loner. I've got to get out of the habit. He went upstairs to the main Reading Room, shooed two men away from his favorite place, and sat down. The book arrived in five minutes.

Reading Gilgamesh's story was an eerie experience. For Rob it was like idling through the poetry section, opening a book here and a book there, and then suddenly finding his own biography in blank verse. My god, this guy is me, he realized. Enormous powers that isolate him from his hometown—that means another person had this problem, even if it was five thousand years ago! Of course it was all wrapped up in the usual epic-myth trappings, goddesses and angry demons and magical undersea plants that made you immortal if you ate them, but the skeleton of the story was weirdly familiar. Gilgamesh had even been a rapist.

Rob sat riveted, reading late into the day. Gilgamesh coped with his bell jar by finding an equal, a companion named Enkidu. Rob knew that his instincts had been right. He had to break out of this killer solitude too, or it would twist him out of all recognition until he was a ravening monster. And he would need help to do it. When he was frozen and helpless on that park bench, Jim Deacon had rescued him. But now he had nobody to call on. No quarrelsome Mesopotamian dieties were going to drop an Enkidu into his life. He was stuck, a wolf trapped in the center of a tight tail-chasing circle.

Wait—what about that guy in the park? Rob couldn't recall the name, but he remembered the assurance, the sharp intelligent gaze. What had happened to that card? He felt in his coat pockets without result, then upended the duffel bag onto the table. Quarters rolled everywhere, tinkling to the marble floor. Half a very old soft pretzel fell squashily onto the book. People looked up at the noise, and a librarian came over, her glasses glittering sternly. "No food in the library!" she said.

"You don't see me," Rob said absently. "Go away." Here it was at the very bottom of the bag, a dirty and crumpled card. It read:

Dr. Edwin Amadeus Barbarossa
Microbiological Research Division
National Institute of Infectious Diseases
Building 5, Room 2C 993-A
. The National Institutes of Health
Bethesda, MD 20892

Holy mackerel! After all that worry about being dissected at NIH, would he actually have to go there? And in Maryland! Not only would he have to travel, but Maryland was next to Virginia, too close for comfort to—he broke off that line of thought. Probably the guy had already forgotten his extravagant promises of help. But I wouldn't really be risking anything, Rob argued with himself. What the hell does it matter, where I am? And when this Barbarossa turns out to be a jerk I'll just wipe him and move on.

He stood up and swept all his possessions back into the duffel. The librarian walked by and stared right through him. If this isolation was strangling him, how did it help to be unseen? The tarnhelm trick was just a way to use the weirdness to lie. Rob realized he didn't want to be a liar, that lying was no part of his true self. "I'm visible," he told her, suddenly ashamed. This damned power! That was the entire problem. If he curbed the trawling in heads for information and the casual tarnhelming, surely that would force him to interact more naturally with people.

The librarian took off her glasses, buffed them on her sleeve, and balanced them on her nose again, thrown for a loop. "That won't happen again," Rob told her impulsively. "I promise." Then, already feeling he'd conceded too much, he pushed past her and hurried down the aisle towards the door.

Three

CHAPTER I

*T*he huge *National Institutes of Health complex baffled* Rob. If you number buildings, then they ought to be in numerical order, right? But no, the numbers seemed to be entirely random. Armed with a map and the exact address of where he was going, it still took Rob an hour to find Dr. Barbarossa's office. When he found the right building, he wandered through the corridors trying to decipher the room numbering system.

The entire building was chockablock crowded right out into the hallways, which were lined all down one side with padlocked refrigerators and freezers. These bore handwritten notices like Sterile Samples or The Storage of Radioactive Materials Is *Prohibited* In This Unit! Every refrigerator also had names and phone numbers taped on, in case of machine failure. The constant hum of the machinery made the hallways hot and claustrophobic.

With a determination that surprised him, Rob tried stubbornly to stick to his rash resolution not to use the power lightly any more. Unfortunately he was driven to make endless exceptions. For instance, how could he possibly explain his errand to the NIH security guard? And without a proper building pass he couldn't ask passersby for directions. Easier to walk unseen.

At last he came to the correct room. The window in the door was blocked with a roller shade, and beside the door were four black plastic nameplates, one above the other. Edwin Barbarossa Ph.D. was the third one down. Rob stood for a long time staring at that door. I'm not nervous, far from it, he told himself. It's just that my stomach is in a knot. The longer he stood there the worse he felt. With a sudden convulsive effort he dropped the invisibility and opened the door.

Inside, surrounded by a welter of pipette trays and slide holders, a tiny swarthy woman in a white lab coat perched on a tall stool and peered through a microscope larger than she was. "Dr. Barbarossa?" Rob asked, and she silently pointed on towards the connecting room without looking up.

The next room was full too, more bulging shelves and mysterious instruments and crammed-full filing cabinets. Nobody sat at any of the desks. But the room farther beyond had a light on. Rob peeked around the corner. This office was yet smaller, not much bigger than a decent bathroom. A large desk with a computer-stand ell took up half the space. Above it rose shelves piled with three-ring binders, glass laboratory jars, sheaves of electron micrographs, and microscope slides in boxes. Pinned to the wall were some family pictures, two postcards, and a large blowup of an unrecognizable oval object, possibly a plate of moldy spaghetti. On the floor a bitten doughnut perched on a napkin in an open soft-sided briefcase.

Rob recognized immediately from Central Park the CD boom box perched precariously on top of a stack of scientific journals. Classical piano music tinkled from it very softly. Dr. Barbarossa himself was almost invisible, slumped in his office chair with his feet on the desk. Only the top of his head, with a slightly thin spot in the dark curls at the crown, could be seen. When he turned a little, Rob saw that he was typing at great speed on a small computer propped on his lap. Rob waited to see if he was going to stop or slow down. But Barbarossa could apparently keep it up for hours. So Rob knocked on the open door.

"Come!" The voice was confident and cheery. Barbarossa sat up and turned as Rob stepped in.

At least he had given his first words some thought. "How's Katie?" Rob said.

"Katie? My niece? She's fine . . . Are you—holy mike, it's the Heimlich guy from Central Park!" He bounced up and shook Rob's hand. "How are you? You look to be in better shape than before! What's your name, by the way? Mine's Edwin."

Somehow it hadn't occurred to Rob that he'd have to tell his name. And Barbarossa made an intimidating figure, in a white lab coat with pens and an X-acto knife stuck in the pocket. Under his tan the skin had an olive cast. He was a little shorter than Rob, but more strongly built, with a deep chest and powerful shoulders. In another decade or so, his round cheeks and clean-shaven chin would be imposing. But now his face was too open and youthful to merit the word—cute rather than handsome. He looked entirely capable of dissecting Rob at the drop of a hat. But there was no time to chicken out now. "I'm . . . Robertson Michael Lewis," Rob said haltingly. ". . . call me Rob."

He stuck there, completely out of practice at normal conversation. Luckily Edwin had no difficulty holding up both ends of the talk. "I remember last time, you called me 'Idiot!' It was great, exactly true. I looked up the statistics on infant choking when I got back. Enough to make your blood run cold! Let's go down to the cafeteria and grab a cup of coffee. You want to leave your bag? It's safe enough while Dr. Lal is here."

He turned the CD player off, and swept Rob along the maze of stuffy corridors and down the stairs, chatting easily about nothing. But when they sat down in the cafeteria with their coffee, Edwin suddenly said, "I owe you, you know. You came here for a reason, didn't you? What is it?"

Rob forced the reluctant words out, one by one. "I guess . . . just to talk. It's scary. I don't . . . know anybody anymore. So I picked you. Because I had your card."

It didn't make much sense, but Edwin said, "Okay." Rob stuck here again a little, so Edwin continued, "Were you homeless in New York? How long have you been on the street?"

"Not too long. Just the summer. I—I think that's what I need to tell. How I hit bottom. I want to come back. And I can't. Unless I tell."

Edwin nodded. "Confession is good for you."

Nettled, Rob retorted, "No, it isn't. It's going to be horrible. Because *I've* been horrible."

Edwin grinned at him over the brim of his plastic coffee cup. "You won't shock me, Rob. How old are you?"

"Thirty-one," Rob said, surprised.

"I'm thirty-four. I've had three whole extra years on you, to pile up sins. Nothing you say can surprise me."

Now it was Rob's turn to smile. "Want to bet?"

After all his worries, Rob was astonished at how easy it was. With practice, the logjam on his tongue went away and his whole story poured out, painlessly and without stress, as if it had all happened to someone else. Edwin was a world-class listener, instinctively knowing when to be silent and when to ask a prompting question. Even the gravest difficulty Rob had foreseen—the complete impossibility of his entire situation— didn't weigh on Edwin at all. "But isn't the whole thing unbelievable?" Rob demanded.

"I've believed as many as six impossible things before breakfast," Edwin replied. Oh great, Rob thought. I get it. He thinks I'm a nut.

They bought sandwiches and walked across the campus to a picnic table near the Clinic building. It was a perfect autumn day, with the trees turning saffron and red against a diamond-clear sky. "When you come right down to it," Rob said, "I know so little about what's happened to me, it's pathetic. I do stuff without knowing how. Sometimes stuff happens when I don't intend it, and I never can break on through understand how or why. I spend all my time thrashing around in the dark."

"So is that your goal? To understand your condition, the how and the why?" Edwin unwrapped a submarine sandwich as long as his forearm, and squirted mayonnaise from a deli packet onto the cold cuts with a generous hand.

Rob had chosen the smallest sandwich on offer, a Monterey Jack-and-pita which he probably wouldn't be able to finish. As he poked the alfalfa sprouts around into a more even and biteable layer, he noticed his dirty broken fingernails, revolting crescents of black. He stuck his hands into his coat pockets, and said, "You won't believe this. It's embarrassing to admit it. But once, at the very beginning . . . You ever read comic books when you were a kid? Superman, the Fantastic Four? That's what I thought I could do. Fight crime. Save the world."

Edwin stopped in midbite to look at him. "You wanted to do good things. That's so great!"

Rob's smile felt as wry and twisted as a lemon peeling. "And look what I actually accomplish. I bully weaker people, and rape teenage girls."

"But you didn't actually go through with that." Edwin spoke gently, without even a tang of condemnation.

A little comforted, Rob took his hands out of his pockets again and bit into his pita. The taste of food reawakened his appetite, and he ate rapidly. "Another thing I thought about," he said between bites. "I'm so isolated, it drives me crazy. If I just had someone to share this with, an equal! It's the terrible imbalance of power that makes it so lonely. I wonder," he added, struck by the idea, "if I could just split it with somebody? With you, say. It might be interesting to try."

Edwin was so calm that Rob was sure now he was just humoring him. "Is it the sort of thing—like this sandwich, for example—where if I give you half I only have half left? Because then giving bits away might be helpful to you. Or is it more like the flu—you give the virus to me and then we both get equally sick?"

"I don't know," Rob admitted. "I told you I know squat about this thing. You think it's even possible?"

"I was putting that question aside, because I don't think it is. This is part of you, not me. You couldn't share your hair color with me, for instance. And I don't believe that equality and friendship work like that."

"With me it's different," Rob said.

"So you've got strong gifts. So? Other people will have other gifts."

"You don't understand," Rob said with despair. Damn it. Should he just muscle the belief into Edwin's head? But that had really bombed, the last time he tried it. Rob realized how desperately he yearned to be believed and understood in his own right, without weird mental meddling—to be treated like an ordinary human being.

Edwin put down his sandwich and set his right elbow on the picnic table between them. "Look. Arm wrestle?" His hands were solid and square, with the clever strong fingers of a musician or surgeon. Black hairs sprouted from the backs of his palms and furred the wrists up to the cuffs of his white coat.

"What for?" But Rob put his arm up.

The other man's grip was surprisingly warm, and implacable as a table clamp. Edwin pushed his arm over without even straining. "Come on, two out of three."

"Forget it!" Rob said, laughing. "I've lost too much weight this summer!"

"But you see what I mean. In one way you've got it on me, but in others I've got it on you. It's a waste of time running around making comparisons." Edwin took a large bite of his sandwich and chewed. "That's the unselfish reason why I'd decline the honor," he said. "The selfish reason is, I don't want anything to keep me from passing my physical."

"You need a physical to work here?"

"No, but I'm on the NASA long list for the manned Mars mission."

"Wow! That's super! But what do they need a microbiologist for on Mars?"

"Rob! Don't you read your science fiction? If there's life on Mars at all it's at the cellular level. Good grief, if they don't bring a microbiologist they might as well not go at all!" Rob had to laugh at this lopsided view, and Edwin laughed too. "Actually my chances aren't so great. But it's nice to dream about it."

"I envy you," Rob admitted. "Not Mars, but having a dream, a future. I guess—to answer your question—I don't know what I want any more. This summer I've been lost, drifting without an anchor."

"Well, we haven't even begun to work on you yet. Have you finished your lunch? Let's go back up to my lab and begin."

When they went through the outer office Dr. Lal was still motionless at her microscope. Rob wondered if she ever budged at all. Edwin cleared a chair in his nook by moving a clutter of slide trays to another stack. "There's some seltzer water behind those books there," he said, turning the music on again. "Help yourself. I just want to look something up. Do you remember your old phone number in Fairfax?"

"Sure, it was 246-2741." Rob found the water bottle and poured while Edwin dug into a cupboard. Then he saw that Edwin was consulting a Northern Virginia White Pages. "You're not going to phone Julianne, are you?"

"Oh no—I'm just seeing if she's still listed."

"Checking up on my story?"

Edwin tossed the book back into the cupboard. "I want to help you, Rob, truly I do. But I don't know if I'm the right person."

Rob smiled without humor. "Maybe you know a reputable psychiatrist."

"Well, that's certainly an idea. Rob, just now you said you didn't know what you wanted. But I think I hear what you want, loud and clear, all through everything you told me. Understanding your problem, doing things with it, giving chunks of it away—those are just side issues. Your central desire is: you want to return home, to your wife and family. Am I right? And if a little Thorazine would get you there—"

Rob didn't hear any more. "That's true," he whispered. "My family. Oh god, it's true." Suddenly he was choking with tears, the iron fingers digging mercilessly into his throat and chest. Julianne. Angela. Davey. Memory and loss ambushed him, piercing him through and through.

The twins would be coming up on their second birthday, and he wouldn't be there. Did they still demand nightly readings of "The Three Billy Goats Gruff"? Would they still yell in stereo? How had Jul made ends meet on just her salary? He had told her not to worry, but how long could that command hold? The leaves would need raking, the gutters clearing. Every emotion that he had suppressed since spring, that he had been so safe from when he was just telling it all to Edwin, seared him now. He was so close to them, so damn close! Not even a toll call away, and yet the distance was unbridgeable. He leaned his face on his hands and wept.

And through his pain it came to him. I was looking for my real self. This is me: the father and husband. As long as I'm separated from my family, this anguish will be an essential part of my being. When I denied that, I became a stranger.

From far away Edwin was shouting in his ear. "Rob! Rob, drink this!"

He pushed the seltzer cup into Rob's hand. The liquid looked like water but went down like a hand grenade. "What the hell?" Rob sputtered and coughed.

"Topped it off with ethyl alcohol from the lab," Edwin said. His face was ghastly pale under the olive skin tone. "Oh, holy Jesus. Rob—this is not all just in your head, is it. It's not a delusion. It's real."

"You idiot," Rob said without heat. He wiped his wet face on his coat sleeve. "What convinced you?"

"Listen." Edwin went to the window and hauled the sash up. From somewhere not very far away came the howls of the damned—shrieks and ululating bellows and the pounding of metal on metal.

"Is that your lab animals?" Rob asked, coughing. "Wait till the animal rights people nail you."

"It isn't us, Rob. It's you. The chimps went absolutely nuts just a minute ago. You're transmitting something that they can feel."

"Not just the chimps, Ed," Rob said. "Look at you."

Beneath the thick dark hair Edwin's face had gone the color of cold chicken gravy. "I can't deny it," he said with a weak smile. "It was like—I don't know, being hit by an invisible truck. I'm sorry I didn't believe you. Oh Lord, and your poor children! You did the right thing leaving them. Forgive me, for poking at the scars."

"It's okay." Rob was shivering with reaction. "I guess I thought if I muffled the wounds up, time would heal them. But time doesn't do much for an amputation. You know, I still have my house keys there, in my bag."

Edwin shut the window and turned on the heat. "I know some folks at the Mental Institute who'd kill to meet you," he remarked.

Suddenly Rob was swept with paranoia. As long as Edwin thought he was crazy it was safe. But now Edwin knew—what would he do? Who would he tell? Had that cup contained only seltzer and ethyl alcohol? Rob jumped to his feet. "You don't see me," he gasped. He could make Edwin forget, wipe all the knowledge out—

"No!" Edwin shouted. He barreled past Rob and stood in the open office doorway, his broad-shouldered frame blocking it almost completely. "It's all right! I would never sell you out. Rob, you swore you were going to give this up! You can't cop out now, or you'll always do it!" He couldn't see Rob, of course, but he glared stubbornly around the tiny room.

Exasperated, Rob let the tarnhelm effect drop. "You seriously think you can block that door against me?"

"Can't I?" Edwin grinned faintly and raised an eyebrow. "Show me."

With a short sigh, Rob pushed aside Edwin's control of his own limbs and pre-empted them himself. He walked Edwin like a marionette to his office chair and dropped him into it before releasing him.

For a long moment Edwin stared down at his own arms and legs. "So I didn't really beat you arm wrestling, huh? Wow, that was weird. I didn't like it."

"Shall I make you forget it?"

"No . . . ! Can you really do that?"

"I can. I don't have to trust you, Edwin. Everything we did or said today is written on sand. I don't have to take any risks. I could wipe today right out of your brain, like erasing a video-tape. And more—I could dig deeper, pull your neurons a hand-ful at a time, drive you to idiocy or perversion or screaming madness. You see what I mean, about an imbalance of power."

"God help you, it must be unbearable. Rob, you poor fel-low!" He jumped up and clapped Rob on the shoulders with both hands.

This close, face to face, eye to eye—touching—it was al-most impossible not to read his mind. But Rob held back. I have to trust a little, he told himself. Besides, his face is as open as a book. Only sympathy there, not a trace of fear for his own safety. He trusts me, even though I could destroy him with a gesture. Of themselves the words came out: "Ed, help me. What shall I do?"

"Oh boy. That's a tough one. I'm going to have to think hard about it. But we'll come up with something, don't you worry."

"Nothing invasive, okay?"

Edwin laughed. "You don't fit under an electron micro-scope, so you're safe from me! But seriously, I won't say or do anything without your full consent. Cross my heart."

"Good, I'm glad." Suddenly Rob was exhausted. Too much emotional turmoil, too much contact. A step at a time is easier, the hairstylist had said, and that applied to more than haircuts. "Ed, I have to go. I'll come back, okay?"

"Make it soon. Phone me. Hey, but where are you going? Are you staying anywhere?"

"I'm homeless, remember? But I'll be fine." Rob turned and went quickly out through the connecting rooms, shutting the office door behind him.

Acres of green space surround the NIH buildings. Rob curled up in his coat in a thicket behind a parking garage, and slept for twenty-four hours straight. When he woke it was raining, a cold steady drip from thick, flat gray clouds like carpet padding stretched from east to west. A gloomy day for a gloomy situation. Tramping down Wisconsin Avenue, Rob thought about his own foolhardiness yesterday. He knew zero about Ed Barbarossa. The fellow could be calling a press conference right now, or notifying the CIA. The picture made his empty stomach jump. Something had to be done.

It was about three in the afternoon. He turned in at the Pizza Hut on Wisconsin and ate a very early dinner, or a very late lunch. But a fast-food joint with its Muzak and bustle was too noisy for what Rob had in mind. He looked in the phone book, but the Bethesda library was already closed for the day. Annoyed, he continued on down the street. A cold trickle of wet went down his collar and onto his shoulder blade, and his sopping jeans flapped annoyingly around each ankle. I need quiet, he thought. And to get out of the rain, of course.

Now there was a possibility, across the street: a fur salon. Rob jaywalked across the avenue, adjusting his tarnhelm trick, and pushed through the heavy glass revolving doors under the green awning. Inside, squelching across the deep plush carpet past racks of fur coats, he found a long sofa in a large mirrored dressing lounge at the back—the sort of area laid out for husbands and sugar daddies to relax in while their women shopped. An elegant sales clerk strolled by without looking at him. Rob sat down, dripping onto the upholstery.

For months now he had deliberately kept his weirdness on the surface—no thought, no analyses, just using it. It had grown to be almost mechanical, pushing buttons and turning dials in people's heads. But Rob remembered clearly now that it had been different at the beginning. The power had been far more deeply real then, with an entirely more organic flavor, images of gardens and growth. He particularly recalled an episode with crystals. Suppose now he searched out Edwin's crystal? It would be a way of checking him out at one remove, metaphorically, without actually rooting through his head. He leaned back on the luxurious sofa cushions.

It was different, of course. So far he had never come to the same inner landscape twice. What's the rule that governs what it looks like? Rob wondered. Is it sunspot activity, or the Dow Jones Industrial Index, or just my own emotional weather? This time it was very different indeed: a broad featureless plain at twilight, shrouded in blowing mist. A fitful wind blew without ever blowing the fog away. Rob could scarcely see three yards ahead through the skeins of gray and yellow. This is no better than Bethesda in the rain, Rob thought as he walked along. And it would help if I knew where I was going or what I was looking for.

Nevertheless he kept walking, stumbling every now and then on rocks or unevennesses of ground hidden by the fog. There didn't seem to be any road, and the weather hid any stars or moon. Boring, Rob decided. Not fun. Didn't it used to be scary, but a little fun too?

Suddenly through a clearing in the mist he saw something. It looked like a fence post. For lack of a better destination he walked towards it. As he got closer it looked more like a milestone, or an oddly proportioned grave marker. Finally he stood right in front of it. It was a midget Washington Monument, an obelisk about eight feet high.

Was it made of stone? He touched it, just a casual brush of the fingertips, and instantly letters appeared on one side. They were carved deeply into the stone, as both eyes and fingers told him, but he was certain they hadn't been there a second ago. "This is really bizarre," Rob said aloud. It came to him that this was a foreign object, quite alien to his inner landscape. Someone had put it here. To tell him something? "Well, it's a bust if I can't read the writing." The letters weren't alphabet, but half a dozen wedgy and angular shapes like cuneiform.

Maybe he could look up the word at the library. Anyway it was an occasion, the very first communication of any sort he'd received here in the realm of his power. Impulsively Rob felt in his pocket for the notebook and, with mild astonishment, pulled it out. Well, if his clothes and shoes came along on these journeys, why not the notebook too? He sat down cross-legged on the gritty bare ground and set about copying the inscription.

When he was done he had another thought. With his palms he brushed away the sand beneath his knees. Underneath was stone, big blocks laid without mortar. This was no natural plain, it was a pavement. But there was nothing else, no inscription or painting or anything. He stood up and dusted off the ragged seat of his jeans, stuffing the notebook back into his shirt pocket. It was very quiet and cold here in the half-dark, and Rob felt a twinge of doubt. Could he find his way back? It had never been a problem before, but then it had never been so gloomy and joyless here before either. Had he gotten to the right place? When he came here with an end in view, a way would turn up to achieve it. The inner travels were always indirect and dreamily odd, but never random.

He pushed tentatively at his environment, and it gave way like paper. This is nothing but a stage set, Rob thought. A detour into a dead end. As the reality came roaring in, he knew this was where he had been going.

Rob found himself on a rocky sea shore. White-tipped breakers pounded against wet brown rocks, as picturesque as a travelogue. He picked his way down the slope to the water. The wind smelled of salt and the sea, reminding him of very early in the morning in Pacific Grove when he was a boy. The sun was still behind the hill, but farther out the ocean danced with light, sapphire with purple shadows in the hollows of the waves.

He squatted down at a tidal pool and rinsed gritty dust off his hands. This was the right place. It was always interesting and complex and alive here, more so with every visit. He scrambled along the shingle just beyond the reach of the waves. It could have been any northern California beach.

But here was something different. Between a pair of huge boulders was a large tidal pool. Its water teemed with little fish, billions of shiny silver creatures the size of a thumbnail. There were so many of them the water quivered and boiled as they swam. Rob wondered how they could survive in such a chowder of their fellows, but the little fish seemed perfectly happy.

He lay down on the rock on his stomach and dipped a hand in. There was almost more fish than water, their tiny cold bodies pouring between his fingers like BB shot. Touching, skin to skin, he recognized them instantly. These were the flowers and the crystals from before. These were people. Every person in the hemisphere must be represented here. Rob found he couldn't remember the current population of the New World, but it must be a good few billions. There were surely that many fish here.

With both hands he tried to isolate just one specimen. It was difficult to catch one, and then even harder to keep the fish under water and yet separate for more than a few seconds. There were so many! Finally he imprisoned one in his cupped hands for a minute and peered at it. They weren't really fish, more like tadpoles, so delicate that he could see the internal organs through the thin silvery skin. This particular little thing was a schoolteacher near São Paulo in Brazil. He relaxed his fingers and let it go, trailing his hands through the water again. A fisherman in the Barbados. An old lady in Montreal. A Chicago street sweeper. He had the entire population of the hemisphere flowing through his hands.

His original game plan now seemed foolish and petty. Edwin was here, of course, but it would take hours of paddling to find him. On such a pretty day it was more energy than it was worth. Rob got up and wiped his hands dry on his pants.

By climbing and jumping from rock to rock, Rob gradually worked his way out to sea, farther from the main shoreline. Had he somehow traveled to a real place, or was this amazingly detailed landscape still a construct, like the jewel or the garden? He didn't recognize the coast, though it had such a familiar air. He might not even be on Earth at all. Those had definitely not been regular fish. Wouldn't Edwin be envious if he knew!

The coast shelved steeply into the water and very soon Rob could go no farther. Was there any way to tell where he was? When he looked back at the coastal mountains the sun still hadn't risen above them. Backlit, any houses or roads were invisible. He turned and scanned the ocean horizon. No boats, no contrails in the sky.

Then, a couple of hundred yards away, a long gray back rose wetly above the waves. A whale! Delighted, Rob watched as the magnificent animal undulated in and out. He tried to remember what he had learned on the whale-watching field trip in high school. Did a humpback have such a very long tail?

The creature vanished, then suddenly reappeared much closer. It had seen him. Scenes from *Jaws* came fleetingly to mind, but Rob dismissed them. This is my place, my image, he told himself. Nothing can hurt me here—I think.

About ten yards away the whale turned and cruised past. For a breathless moment Rob stared into a mild black eye the size of a soccer ball. "Hey, pal," he called. It almost looked like a human eye—definitely not a whale! With a ponderous flick of the overlong tail, the glorious thing turned away. When it rose again, spouting, it was far down the shore.

An unreasoning joy filled him. Rob clambered back to the beach, bounding along over the rocks like a goat. At the foot of an enormous boulder he announced, "I bet I can jump right up to the top!" A standing high jump! He leaped it easily, though it was at least ten or twelve feet. Was this not his realm? But then he bungled the landing and fell on his nose onto something smooth: a sofa.

He lay breathing deep and staring into the dimness. The fur store seemed to be closed now. That was wonderful! he thought. If all these images and places are ways for me to handle the power, I may be getting somewhere. Then he thought, if everybody on earth was imaged as the tadpoles, then what was the whale?

Rob sat up. His clothes and shoes had dried nicely on him. Consulting his watch he saw with surprise that it was past six in the evening, on Saturday. Another day gone—amazing.

He pottered around the empty and locked store, using the bathroom, exploring the little refrigerator, rescuing yesterday's paper from a trash can. He felt almost sociable. Well, Edwin had urged him to phone. He dug the card out of the duffel bag. There was a phone conveniently right by the sofa.

Hard to believe that anyone would still be at work at this hour. Sure enough, Rob got the voice-mail system. "Hi, you've reached Edwin Barbarossa's extension. If you want to leave a message, wait for the tone. If you're calling because of freezer failure, *or* if this is Rob Lewis, press one. Thanks!"

Considerably surprised, Rob pressed one. A new message kicked in: "I can be reached at home, at 432-1059. Rob, this means you!"

"Good gosh!" Rob exclaimed mildly. To alter a voice-mail message was no big deal, but still he was impressed that Edwin had gone to the trouble. He dialed the new number.

"Hello?"

"Hi, Edwin, this is Rob."

"Rob! Good grief, where are you? It's been pouring rain all weekend!"

"Has it really?" Rob leaned over to look out into the main showroom. Sure enough, rain was scouring down outside the big front windows.

"You shouldn't have just vanished like that the other day. We could've found you someplace! Look, I'm going out tonight anyway, to a pot-luck. I'll swing by and pick you up. Where are you?"

Rob hesitated. "Don't bother, Ed. I'm in good shape."

"Don't be ridiculous! Rob, they're predicting a freeze tonight!"

"I'm not wet. I'm not in the rain at all. I'm stretched out on a very comfortable sofa. It's upholstered in green velveteen."

"The dickens with the velveteen! Where is it?"

"Well . . ." Rob was pretty sure Edwin wouldn't approve. "It's in a back lounge at Gartenhouse Furs on Wisconsin Avenue."

"What?" A clatter as the receiver on the other end fell down, and very distantly Rob heard Edwin roaring with laughter. It was impossible not to smile when Edwin laughed. "I'm wasting my worry on you, buddy!" he said when he came back.

"I'm not your usual homeless person," Rob agreed. "Besides, the store is closed. They have security gates locked down over all the windows and doors. I don't think anyone can get in or out until they open up tomorrow. I'm not even going to try to step into the main showroom. I bet they have cameras and motion alarms."

"Couldn't your, uh, vanishing trick fool them?"

"I don't really vanish, Ed. I only make people not see me. I probably show up on videotape just fine."

"Hmm, and mirrors too, I'd think. Listen, can you come to the lab tomorrow? I have some ideas."

"Sure. After noon—they open the store then."

"Right, see you then."

Rob hung up and lay back on the sofa. Maybe he really had a chance to get out from under this. If there was any other case like it, a treatment, even just a name for what he had become, someone at NIH would know. With Edwin as an ally, there was hope. Suddenly he felt ravenously hungry. When had he eaten yesterday? A fur saleswoman had left some lunch in the little fridge—half a ham sandwich and a banana yogurt. He went to investigate.

T he research buildings were relatively empty on Sundays.
Only an occasional light showed through the windows in the
lab doors. In the outer room, the monster microscope rested
under a plastic dustcover the size of a bedspread. From Edwin's
nook came the sounds of Cole Porter and conversation.

Rob peered in warily, but Edwin was only talking into a
machine. He pointed at a chair and mouthed, "Hello." Then
he said, "Carina, you know any sweater's fine with me. I have
no objection to llamas. But no hat. I'm convinced that wearing a hat causes premature hair loss, and I'm already getting
too thin on top . . ." While he spoke he unzipped his briefcase
and took out a box of Girl Scout cookies. He handed them to
Rob and made silent opening gestures.

Rob opened the box and ripped open one of the cellophane
inner packets. Edwin took a cookie, still talking. He was using
a ham radio rig, Rob decided. He ate a cookie himself. When
had he last tasted a Do-Si-Do? It must have been in Pacific

Grove when his sister was a Girl Scout. He could vividly remember Angie's splendid Girl Scout uniform. How many
memories he had cut himself off from this summer!

"All right!" Edwin was snapping switches off and un-
plugging things. "Sorry, Rob, but Carina doesn't surface often,
so I have to catch her when I can."

"Who is Carina?"

"My fiancée." Edwin pointed at a blurry Polaroid on the
wall, of a dark girl in a cowboy hat. "An archaeologist. She's
in Peru, so we use the radio—no reliable phone service at the
dig in Cuzco."

"From Peru to Mars? You're going for a Guinness record
for long-distance relationships, right? I'm sorry, Ed, I just noticed I've wolfed half the box."

Edwin laughed. "I brought them for you—finish them! Or
leave them till after lunch. I was thinking we should go out.
The cafeteria's too pricey."

An active man, Edwin apparently never used the elevator.
Halfway down the staircase Rob said, "You know, Ed, I'm not
dressed for restaurant dining."

"Neither am I. You don't think we're going to Lion d'Or?
Bob's Big Boy is more my speed."

As they walked Rob noticed that Edwin wore not the lab
coat but gray jeans with paint stains and a three-cornered hole
at one knee. And he'd chosen the budget restaurant with its
all-you-can-eat Sunday buffet to make sure Rob got enough
to eat. The subtlety of Edwin's courtesy made Rob think. He
would never catch Edwin performing wholesale mental reno-
vations at Lorton Reformatory.

At the restaurant, Edwin zoomed down the buffet heaping
his plate with bacon, eggs, biscuit, and pancakes, while Rob
followed more slowly. He had got out of the habit of big
meals. They sat at a corner booth furnished with a large jug
of coffee and some dessert cards, and ate in companionable
silence.

After Edwin refilled his plate with three kinds of salad, he
sat down and said, "I've been thinking your problem over,

Rob. In a theoretical mode, you understand—trying to lay out a game plan. We know your goal now: to go home. We established that last week, right? And what is preventing you? Not the weirdness per se, but the possibility of inadvertently endangering people around you."

Rob said, "You know, I never thought about it that way." How long had he been wandering, lost and alone, in the heart-freezing jungle of his own fear and bewilderment? Now he might find a way out of the tangled midnight forest by the glimmer of a lamp in Edwin's hand: the light of reason.

Edwin frowned thoughtfully at his lettuce-laden fork. "Suppose you had some dangerous disease, AIDS or Lassa fever. How would we achieve your goal then? Putting aside the question of whether you'd die of the bug yourself, there'd be two logical ways to go on it. One would be that we cure you. Drive the virus out of your body and make you a healthy human being again."

"That's what I've been hoping for! How would you do it with the weirdness?"

Edwin shook his head as he sliced a tomato into pieces. "I told you this was theoretical. I'll have no idea at all how to implement without data. The other possibility is, you learn to contain and control your problem. Here the analogy to AIDS would be using condoms and being careful about sharing your body fluids. You got into trouble at home when the power leaked out without your knowing it, am I right? And began doing stuff you hadn't intended?"

Thinking about the twins made Rob lose his appetite. He pushed his plate away. "You hit it on the head. So, we either cure or contain."

"No reason we couldn't do both. AIDS research is double-pronged too. Some people concentrate on finding a cure, while other researchers specialize in figuring out how HIV spreads and finding ways to prevent that. In your case, we'd think about ways to permanently remove the weirdness, and in the meantime work on containing your 'leak.'"

"Okay, I'm in. Let's do both. You have no idea, Ed, how

good it is to talk to someone who has a systematic outlook."

"Don't start throwing bouquets yet. Like I said, I have no idea how to actually accomplish either. I'm just applying the common sense of a microbiologist! What would really help, on both fronts, is to know how you do this stuff. Data! That's what I need. Where does this thing come from? Is it contagious? Is it genetic, hormonal, neurological, or what?"

Rob set his cup down slowly. "Would there be any other cases in the NIH files? I'm tired of making up my own terminology."

Edwin's eyes gleamed. "Rob, if there'd been anyone like you, ever, in the past hundred years, I would've heard of it. We all would. Heck, they'd have his or her body pickled in a jar on display down at the Smithsonian."

Rob grinned at him. "Tell you what. When I make my will, I'll leave my body to science."

"Don't laugh, Rob," Edwin said, laughing. "It might be the most important thing you could ever do. Finding out what makes you tick is a Nobel Prize–caliber project! In fact, in the interests of future research, I'm going to start keeping notes."

"Well, in the meantime get that wistful look off your face— I'm not nearly done with my remains yet!"

Edwin topped off his coffee cup and took a gulp. "I can't believe you've had this thing for so long without trying any experiments."

"I have," Rob said. "But not like you mean. In New York."

"You could say a lot about your actions in New York, but nobody would call them systematic. Like that remote control trick you pulled on me Thursday. You've always used the remote on unsuspecting people, am I right? What happens when you try it on someone who's ready for you—like right now? Give me some data!" Without the slightest warning or transition Edwin startled Rob by bursting into one of the Cole Porter songs he had been playing in his office:

Experiment!
Make it your motto day and night

> *Experiment,*
> *And it will lead you to the light!*

As the tuneful voice rang through the room, the other diners turned and stared, smiling. Rob eyed Edwin's unselfconscious grin with some envy. He had never met a man who was so together, in whom mind and heart moved in such concord. "The idea doesn't frighten you?"

"Well sure, it gets on my nerves a little. But don't you see, Rob? That's precisely the attraction. That's why I want you to try it again."

Rob shook his head at this folly. To repeat a nerve-wracking experience until it became old hat? Rob himself would never confront a fear in that way. But it might be a useful trait in an astronaut candidate. He couldn't help smiling at Edwin's expression. A terrier watching the progress of a dog biscuit out of the box could not have been more eager. "Okay, Ed," he said. "You're on. You take your coffee black, right?"

"Yeah, but—oh come on, Rob! Not sugar! At least make it Sweet 'N Low!"

They both watched as Edwin's hands tore the white paper packet of sugar open over his half-full cup. "Saccharin causes cancer," Rob remarked.

Unfaltering, Edwin's clever fingers picked up another sugar packet. "Only if you eat saccharin by the carload," Edwin objected. "No more—I absolutely refuse to do it . . . Darn, it's not working. That's number three. I'm kind of disconnected from my hands, is that it? This is like when I was eight, and got the chicken pox. Four. My fever hit a hundred and three degrees, and I could watch my hands shake, and listen to my voice mumbling about the World Series, out of my control. Five."

The sugar in Edwin's cup now rose in a soggy brown atoll above the surface of the coffee. "Had enough?" Rob suggested.

"Could be . . . So you're manipulating my hands and fingers, and in addition to that you're short-circuiting my willpower. That's six. My volition is totally out of the loop. Am I right?"

"Oh, yeah. Shall I prove it?"

Edwin's hand picked up a spoon. The coffee was so sludgy now, stirring it was slow work. Rob made Edwin lift the spoon. Undissolved sugar coated the bowl like wet sand. Edwin yelped, "Hey, no! This is disgusting!"

"I can be very precise, Ed," Rob said softly. "Open your lips, insert the spoon, force your tongue and throat to swallow something that revolts you. It's not absolutely necessary, but it helps to be close to you, even more to touch you. Helps me focus."

With clinical interest Rob watched Edwin struggle in his grip. Possibly because he was a scientist, Edwin had a very different mode of thinking, precise and analytical. His mind was like a brand-new surgical instrument, supple but shiny-sharp, a scissors or a scalpel perhaps. Even as the repulsive spoon rose inexorably to his mouth, Edwin was coping, the scissors snipping the problem into smaller and hopefully more solvable bits that floated on a larger restless surface. It took Rob a second to recognize this increasing turmoil as fear. Instantly he let Edwin go. "I—I'm sorry," he said. "That's one of the things I was going to quit doing."

Edwin dropped the sugary spoon into the cup again, slumping in his seat. "Wow. So that's what a fruit fly on the dissecting tray feels like. The way you were staring at me . . ." He rubbed his eyes with both hands, knuckling them like a boy.

"I'll keep out of your head from now on, Ed," Rob said, alarmed.

"No, it's all right. Don't look so worried! We learned something, didn't we? And I asked you to try it. I wish I knew more about the latest brain-body research. I better read up on it. If I could just design some nice tight simple experiments . . ." He snagged a clean coffee cup from the table behind.

Rob poured fresh coffee into it, marveling at this resilience, and Edwin took a long thirsty swallow. When he was sure

Edwin was okay, Rob said, "Listen, Ed. You know I spent the summer reading books. I did read about one guy like me."

"You did? Holy mike!" Edwin banged his new cup down on the table.

"Don't get excited," Rob begged. "It was a guy five thousand years ago. A king, name of Gilgamesh."

Edwin looked blank. "Never heard of him. Is he a Biblical character?"

"I don't think so. I read a long poem about him."

"I guess I better get a copy of it." He pulled out a notepad and a pen.

Rob nodded in approval. Then the sight of Edwin's notepad brought something else to mind, and he took out his own. He almost expected the page to be blank. If you copy an inscription in a dream it shouldn't be there when you wake. But he knew it hadn't been a dream, and his careful copy of the funny writing was there where he drew it. He tore the leaf out and passed it over. "Can you read that?"

"Nope." Edwin shot a humorous green glance across the table. "I am actually not all-knowing, Rob. I may act like I know it all, but don't be deceived."

Rob laughed. "I didn't really expect you could. You think we could find someone to translate it?"

"I guess, if it's really writing. But why? Where did you get this?"

"I was lost," Rob said slowly. "And I was looking for directions. And I found a signpost, with this message on it. I never found writing before, it's not that sort of place, so this must be important."

Edwin leaned back and stared at him. "I've fallen off the sled here."

"I—I'm sorry, Ed. I don't think I can explain better." All his inner journeyings were incommunicable, Rob realized. Describing his own actions and crimes was straightforward. But his inner adventures were too vivid, too intimate, for mere words. He might never be able to convey their reality. It was the guy thing, in spades. For a moment he felt utterly desolate.

"Don't worry about it," Edwin said quickly. "There's plenty on the plate to deal with. Let me see what I can do. Would it be okay if I digitized it and uploaded the writing onto the Internet? That'd be the fastest way to find out what it is."

"Sure, why not."

"So let's leave it there for the moment. And now, moving on to the next item on our agenda—would it be all right, Rob, if we discussed your personal situation?"

Rob frowned. "What for?"

"I can't believe that it's comfortable sleeping outdoors in October." Edwin pushed his empty cup aside and leaned forward on his elbows. "And in no time the snow'll be flying. You can't crash at a fur salon forever, Rob. Suppose you came and camped out on my sofa-bed?"

"I appreciate the offer, Ed, but no thanks. It would be an imposition."

"All right. How about a homeless shelter? My church helps run one in Silver Spring. They offer job counseling and sleep space."

"An Open Door Center."

Edwin raised an eyebrow. "You know it?"

"There's one in Fairfax too. I sent a bum there once."

"But you've never stayed at one yourself, am I right? So it would be a new experience for you. Why not give it a try?"

Edwin was so persuasive that it was easier to give in. "All right," Rob said. Somehow the former ease of their talk had slipped away. He sat silent, staring down at his hands folded on the red Formica tabletop.

Edwin rubbed the back of his neck. "Look, Rob, I have to ask you this. I know you said you were giving it up. But, except for just now—have you been messing with my head?"

Rob looked up, shocked and yet unsurprised. "No! I mean—I don't know, Ed. I haven't deliberately done a thing, I swear it. But—I told you, about Angela and Davey. I do stuff without knowing it. I'm so damned strong. That's why it would be crazy to stay on your sofa. I can't get too close to anybody. I don't dare. It's not safe. I'm not safe. Maybe even this homeless shelter is a dangerous idea, maybe even the street. Sometimes I think I should get right away from everybody, live in the Arctic tundra—"

Edwin reached a sympathetic hand across the table to touch his clenched fingers. Rob jerked away from the contact, the words trembling on the tip of his tongue, You don't see me! But Edwin spoke first, cutting them off: "It's okay, Rob, it's okay! You don't have to escape. Everything's fine!"

"There, you see?" Rob said bitterly. "How did you know that I was going to tarnhelm, unless I transmitted it to you?"

"Sherlock by name, Holmes by nature," Edwin said. "I didn't need the weirdness. Anyone could see what you were going to do, written in your face. I didn't mean to upset you, bud. It's just that—the things you told me Thursday would unsettle anybody. And when it began raining cats and dogs I woke up in the middle of the night on Friday and thought, Is Rob out in this? And then I lay in the dark and thought, Is he making me care, making me get involved? So it sort of got on my nerves."

"Oh god, I wish I were dead."

"Don't say that! It's okay, Rob, truly it is. If you're drawing me in, that's fine. I—I consent, all right? People need to care more, not less. I'm a younger brother. I can deal with strong-minded people. You must meet Carina sometime. No one could stand up against your deliberate manipulation, you've proved that, but your unconscious influence can't be malevolent."

"Not malevolent?" Rob demanded incredulously. "And you're supposed to be smart. I told you about New York!"

"That wasn't really you, Rob. You recognized that yourself. This whole thing had dropped on you like a grand piano, and you were miserable. You aren't really a bad person."

"It wasn't really me," Rob repeated. The kindly words were an overwhelming relief. He himself wasn't the liar or rapist; it was some separate unsavory entity that he could expel or defeat. But Rob felt impelled to add, "But I'm still dangerous."

"Dangerous, what's to worry? We'll deal with it somehow. In the meantime, what I want to deal with now is dessert. Our family motto is, Dessert Always."

With a flourish he held a dessert card out. Rob took it, saying, "I appreciate your trust, Ed. But you're crazy, you know that."

"I may not get to do many crazy things in future," Edwin said absently, studying the menu. "No scope for it in the space program. Hot fudge for me—how about you?"

*R*ob *had never set foot in a homeless shelter before. The* Open Door Center was in Silver Spring, a suburb a couple of miles around the Washington Beltway from NIH. A big crumbling gray bungalow on a transitional street had been converted into offices and dorm space. Rob gave the man at registration a minimum of information, pocketed the house rules without reading them, and went straight to bed in the men's dorm room at the back of the ground floor.

He woke the next morning to raindrops on his face. For a second Rob was back on the park bench in New York City again, despair filling his chest like quick-set concrete, but then he came fully awake. A large grayish stain was spreading on the plaster ceiling above the folding cots, and water dripped down. A few beds over, another man burst into tears, and someone else bellowed, "Hey! The fucking *roof* is fucking *leaking* fucking *again!*"

Rob rolled out of bed, muttering, and put his shoes on.

Wasn't anyone going to pick up the ball? Going up the stairs he met a very pink young man coming down. "The roof is leaking down here," Rob barked. "What's being done?"

"Um, I don't know. Let me go check the volunteer's manual."

The carrot-headed young man skittered on downstairs. Growling, Rob ascended to the smaller upper floor and went from room to interconnecting room inspecting the ceilings, ignoring the sleepy complaints of the mothers and kids. He was looking for an attic access hatch. He found it in the bathroom ceiling. By standing on the old-fashioned bathtub's rim he was able to pop it open. The pink youth came in just as Rob was preparing to climb higher. "You got a flashlight?"

He blushed even pinker. "You're not supposed to be here. This is the women's john!"

"The roof is leaking," Rob explained patiently. "You never ignore a roof leak. Especially when it's not even raining. Now—I need a flashlight."

After some delay a flashlight was found. Rob hoisted himself into the attic. The slanting ceiling was so low he had to squat. The space was cobwebby and littered with mouse droppings, but quite innocent of insulation. This at least made it easy to find the large pool of water on the floor near the dormer. "You should insulate," Rob said.

The young man stood on the bathtub below, staring through the hatch as if Rob were proposing to hang upside down from the rafters like a bat. "That would cost a fortune!"

"You probably blow a fortune in oil every winter—this place has oil heat, right?" Rob could feel the old Harry Homeowner instincts kick in. Leak first, then insulation! He shone the flashlight at the pool of water on the floor. Where was the water coming from? Not from overhead—it was a frosty clear morning outside. He peered between the louvers of the gable vent. "I get it, here's your problem. Look at that!"

"What is it? What is it?"

"The gutters. Come on." Rob climbed down again, swinging by his hands from the edge of the hatch until he could balance on the tub. "You got a ladder?"

"No, of course not."

Rob swept past him and down the stairs, where one of the boards was missing, to the front door. The front porch spanned the width of the house and had once boasted gingerbread and fretwork railings, all broken and faced with plywood now. Rob climbed up and stood on the rickety rail, and then shinned his way up the corner porch post. Leprous chips of paint and chunks of spongy rotten wood shredded away under his hands and legs. "Don't do that," the young man begged from the unkempt lawn below. "We should ask the committee! We should call Pastor Phillipson!"

Rob sat on the edge of the porch roof and glared down at the little twit. If there was anything he despised it was deliberate incompetence. But after all, the kid was a volunteer. "How old are you?"

"Uh, nineteen. I'm Jonathan, by the way."

"I'm Rob. Shouldn't you be in school?"

"I am! At Montgomery Junior College. But I don't have Monday morning classes, so the college fellowship tapped me for the Center here."

"Well, Jonathan, maybe they haven't taught you yet that dealing with gutters is one of an American male's duties and prerogatives."

"You're kidding!"

"Says so right in the U.S. Constitution—go look it up. It's just after the right to bear arms." Jonathan actually seemed to be seriously considering this. "Besides, the ladies admire this kind of work," Rob couldn't resist adding. "Girlfriends. Mothers. That's the sort who particularly abhor roof leaks. You should take this opportunity to learn about them. It will have a significant impact on your relationship with the opposite sex."

"Golly! Maybe I better take you up on it."

Rob gave him a hand up onto the porch roof, thinking, If

I teach him, then the next time this happens *he* can fix it. And I won't be climbing on a rickety roof at eight A.M. "See, here's the attic. This flat bit must be the roof over the men's dorm. And here's the water. It must be coming in under the dormer, and then on down into the bedrooms."

"Wow! No wonder it's leaking! Why doesn't it run down to the ground?"

Rob splashed through the standing pool which had formed near the base of the attic dormer. "Here's the downspout, all blocked up. Hand me that stick, will you?"

With the stick Rob fished wet clots of leaves out of the downspout. The water began to seep away immediately with a satisfying trickling noise. Jonathan helped by tossing more leaves over the edge of the roof. Like an old war-horse at the sound of the trumpets, Rob leaped into battle. He circled the entire roof and cleared the gutters all around. "It's autumn," he pointed out. "The leaves are still falling. Come early winter, say on a nice dry day in November or December, you climb up here and do this again. Then you'll be all set for the winter. No more roof leak."

"I can't believe it," Jonathan said. "It's like a miracle."

Rob rolled his eyes and climbed down to ground level again. It was ten o'clock and he was starving. Hanging out with a food fiend like Edwin had gotten him into eating far more than he used to in New York. He left Jonathan to explain the miracle of gutters to another Center counsellor, and went inside to wash up. Because of zoning regulations there was no kitchen at the Open Door Center. For meals the residents were supposed to hit a nearby soup kitchen. Rob foresaw having to do that someday soon, but at the moment he still had quarters. He'd walk a couple blocks over into downtown Silver Spring and have a decent breakfast.

They were still yattering on the porch when he came out. "Rob!" Jonathan said. "This is Mrs. Ruppert, the jobs counsellor and daytime manager."

"Hi," Rob said reluctantly.

"You are handy," Mrs. Ruppert pronounced.

He looked down at his feet in their tattered athletic shoes. "Thank you."

"We should have *no* problem placing you."

Rob tensed. He knew, without any mental stuff, that he shouldn't say he didn't want a job. Not to a jobs counsellor. "Maybe after breakfast," he muttered.

"But before we begin the placement search, we were wondering, do you know anything about—plumbing?"

"You see," Jonathan broke in, "the downstairs toilet has never worked right. Every now and then it just runs over. It's gross."

Rob couldn't help smiling into his blond beard. "I'm not a real plumber, but I can do fixes on toilets. I have—I mean I used to have an old house we were fixing up."

"If you would look at it, at your entire convenience of course, we would be so grateful!" Mrs. Ruppert, a very short middle-aged lady, beamed adoringly up at him. Obviously working toilets loomed large in her concept of happiness. Rob hoped that Jonathan was absorbing the lesson.

"Let me make a pass at it after breakfast," he said. "While I'm gone, maybe Jonathan can scout around for a pipe wrench."

That morning Rob replaced the innards of all three of the Center's toilets. In the afternoon he cleared a slow drain, caulked all the shower stalls, and began on the windows. It took all day Tuesday to finish caulking the outsides of the windows and doors, with only one short break to patch a hole in the drywall near the office. By Wednesday Mrs. Ruppert had twisted Pastor Phillipson's arm and gotten authorization to replace some long-missing floor boards and linoleum squares. Rob began installing them immediately. He also made the radiators quit knocking by bleeding the sediment out of them.

It was an almost poignant pleasure to work with his hands again around a house. No wonder he had been so desperately unhappy in New York. Looking back, Rob wondered how he could have been so stupid. After working all his adult life and years of being an energetic homeowner, and then entering the marathon called raising twins, he had switched to idleness, just panhandling and reading newspapers all day long. A recipe for misery! It was much better, much more fun, to do things. And this building needed work. From something the hardware store man had said when Rob was buying spackle, he gathered that the Center was not considered an asset to the neighborhood.

On Wednesday evening Rob sat cross-legged in the hall measuring the last board for the floor and pondering lawn care economics. On the one hand grass was merely cosmetic. Spreading fall fertilizer on it wouldn't increase the comfort of the residents one bit. On the other hand it could be argued that any improvement in the way the place looked might placate the neighbors. Rob was realistic about the Not-In-My-Backyard phenomenon. Having a homeless shelter on your street did nothing for your real estate values. Heaven knew that if the county had proposed one on the Lewis block in Fairfax, Julianne would have hit the ceiling.

Julianne. She never fertilized or mowed the grass—that had been Rob's task. Had she just let the lawn go to hay this summer? More likely she'd hired a lawn service. Rob looked up at the pay phone, which hung in the hall near the front door, and temptation seized him.

His hand was on the receiver, the other fishing for quarters in his pocket, before Rob got a grip on himself. What exactly would he say to her? "Hi honey, I'm in Tanzania . . . No, I don't know when I'll be back . . . No, no paycheck . . ." The lies he'd have to tell wouldn't deceive a baby, yet he'd have to muscle her into swallowing them. And what good would it do? At least he'd had the sense to command her not to worry about him. There was nothing more he could add to that. He swallowed hard and leaned his forehead against the graffiti on the wall. It had been so much less painful to just not remember.

The doorbell chimed right above his head, making Rob jump. He looked through the glass, and flung the door open. "Ed! Thank goodness you're here!"

Plump as a robin in a red down parka, Edwin said, "Hey, Rob, what's wrong?"

Rob shook his head. "Nothing. Just—just a little homesick, that's all. Come on in, you're letting in the cold."

"Is that okay?" Edwin looked uncertainly towards the common room, where some residents were watching a sitcom.

"Well technically, no—no visitors allowed. But we're not supposed to go in and out at night, either. So either you come in, or we yell through the door at each other."

Rob ushered him across the hall to the dingy little office, and unlocked it. "You have a key," Edwin noticed.

"Have to, to put away the tools. Some of these guys you wouldn't trust with a lollipop stick."

"But they trust you, eh?"

"A guy who can repair a toilet commands respect around here, let me tell you . . . And another rule is, no food in the facility." Rob laughed out loud at the politeness struggling with dismay in Edwin's face. "But I still have that half-box of cookies—let me get them."

"I was telling Pastor Phillipson about you," Edwin said. He took out a small Swiss Army knife and slit open the cellophane wrapping.

"Yeah?" Rob took a cookie. "I hear he doesn't understand the value of attic insulation."

Edwin pushed a cookie whole into his mouth, and laughed. "Mrs. Ruppert told the pastor you were an angel specifically sent from above."

Rob almost choked on a mouthful. "You must be kidding. I hope you corrected them!"

"Come on, Rob, how could I? I made a promise I wouldn't breathe a word about your shenanigans. So instead I told about how you saved Katie."

Rob glared at Edwin, who leaned back grinning and

propped his feet on Mrs. Ruppert's blotter. "I don't want a halo. I'd rather have a cape."

"If you had a halo, we would get your remains."

"I think I had better will my body to a dog food factory!"

Edwin laughed so hard he almost lost balance. When he recovered he sat up and said, "Last night I had an idea, a really good one."

"Not another experiment!"

"This is perfectly safe and innocuous, Rob. Look, I'll show you some of the elaborate and technical equipment I've prepared." Edwin pulled a shiny new penny out of his jeans pocket and held it up between two fingers. "Okay. You want to hear it?"

Rob relaxed. There was not a lot of trouble anybody could get into with a penny. "All right."

"So let's consider this penny. I flip it." He did so, catching it neatly and clapping it onto his hand. "Call it."

"Tails."

Edwin looked. "Sorry, it's heads." He flipped it again. "Now—neither of us have looked at this penny, right? You don't know if it's heads or tails, and neither do I."

"Right."

"Is there any way, by the exertion of power, that you could influence the flip: make it come out heads or tails? Or find out which it is before I lift my hand?"

"No. This is all in the brain. No super-strength, no x-ray vision. The only way to do it would be to seize control of your hand—" Rob did so for a moment. "And lift it. Looks like it's heads again."

Edwin shook his right hand in the air. "Ack, that's creepy. Okay, now what if I flip the coin and then go down the hall and show the guys watching TV. You could find out then."

"No problem—I fish the information out of their heads."

"Suppose then we change the game. Flipping coins is a matter of pure chance. What if we play blackjack, a game of both chance and skill?" He took two poker decks out of his parka pocket and laid them on the desk.

Rob shook his head. "I don't think I know how to play, but you don't want to play cards with me anyway, Ed."

"You would win—but how exactly would you be winning? The chance component you have no influence over, we've established that."

"Ed, I can look through your eyes and see your cards."

"Suppose you don't read my mind to see my cards. Would you still have an influence on my judgment and skill?"

"I think so. Wanting things, feeling strongly about something, I notice that a lot of the time that's what does it. The whole point of playing blackjack is to win. That alone would ensure that I couldn't help it."

"And if you made a concerted effort to play dead fair?"

"I guess I could try," Rob said. "But it'd be tough to find players. How would people know I was trying?"

Edwin's eyes gleamed as he leaned forward. "There *is* a way to know, Rob. At least, over time, and if you stick to one consistent system of play. The odds in blackjack have been analyzed to a fare-thee-well by statisticians. I used to play around with the theory myself, in grad school. They've determined that when you play dealer's rules the house has an edge of about six percent. Suppose you don't deliberately pick up on anybody's cards. Over a very large statistical sample it should be possible to calculate exactly how much your powers are *inadvertently* affecting the play."

"And where does that get me?"

"Rob, don't you understand? You could tell if your abilities were leaking. Your entire problem with this weird thing is that right now you can't see it working. It's inside your head, out of view. If you could discern it somehow, you'd have a chance to control it. You know that you can teach people to produce alpha brain waves, by letting them watch their own EEGs? Blackjack would give us a window to observe the workings of your ability. Over time you could learn to contain your powers, and we could chart your progress by analyzing your blackjack wins. We'd have hard numbers, data we could crunch and lay out in graphs or pie charts. And we would know when your control was perfect—when your loss rate gets to six percent."

Rob stared across the desk at him. "Oh my god. I guess I better learn to play blackjack."

Edwin opened the decks and began to shuffle the cards together. "I'm sure you've learned this. It's a really easy game. Number cards count as their number, and picture cards are worth ten. Aces can be either one or eleven. The idea is to add up to twenty-one, without going over."

They played a few hands. Rob won them all. "I'm not doing anything, either," he said gloomily.

"Three hands isn't enough data points. In theory any game that combines chance and skill would work—bridge, poker, gin. But blackjack is a particularly good choice."

"Yeah? Why?"

"Because first we have to accumulate statistics, get a base line. Then, perfecting your control might take months of practice. I can't play blackjack with you all that time. I have a research project, and a textbook deadline, all these things I have to do. Already there aren't enough hours in the day. But we could go to the casinos in Atlantic City and scoop a lot of data fast."

"That's a good idea," Rob had to admit.

"Have you ever been there? I haven't."

"Me neither."

Edwin dealt again, two cards apiece. "Maybe we should go. You free this weekend?"

"I'm nothing but free," Rob said with amusement. "Another card, how about."

Edwin dealt him another. "Good! Let's leave on Friday. I'll take off a couple hours early. I figure eight hundred hands will give us a nice base line. Take maybe twenty hours."

"Twenty hours—that's ten hours a day! Can anyone play that much blackjack?"

"Sure, lots of folks do. You'll see. Hmm, that's bust me. Lucky we're not actually betting. Remind me—while we drive there I'll coach you on how to bet. And the jargon. Unfortunately there's no way to play blackjack in casinos without betting. That's always the drawback to blackjack statistical research."

Rob glanced at him. "You're very knowledgeable, for a nice church-going fellow."

"I'm a Nevada boy—put myself through MIT working at Caesar's Palace. My father played clarinet in the band for the floor shows. Oh, and another thing, it would help if you— well, blended in. Has Mrs. Ruppert offered to revamp your wardrobe yet?"

"She made noises about it yesterday but I didn't pay attention. I guess I should, if I'm going to be a high roller."

"I'm hoping that won't be a problem. We'll stick to the two-dollar tables. We're after numbers, not money." He shot a merry glance at Rob. "This homeless thing is just a façade for you, Rob. A secret identity, if you like. Mrs. Ruppert is going to suit you up, reveal your true colors."

Rob laughed at this. "Next time you see that pastor, tell him I lured you into gambling."

CHAPTER 4

It felt very strange to wear new clothes after all this time.
Mrs. Ruppert, with job interviews in mind, took Rob to the
Salvation Army store and bought him a blue jacket, a red tie,
and a pair of khaki pants. He was surprised to find that his
waist size had gone down more than two inches. No wonder
he had needed string to hold up his ragged old jeans. In the
mirror he saw a figure that didn't look unduly odd at all—
weathered, tall, blond, a little too thin. Meeting the gaze of
his reflection gave him a peculiar feeling, however—as if there
was someone else, a stranger, behind those ice-chip eyes.

"I don't know," Edwin said when he arrived on Friday and
saw the result. "Maybe it's because I've only known you in
your old clothes."

"I kind of miss them," Rob admitted. He stared, awed, at
the sleek vehicle at the curb. Edwin's car cast a startling new
light on his character. It was a sexy red Mazda RX-7 with a
spoiler, a moon roof, and leather upholstery—curvaceous as

a centerfold model. Somehow Rob had imagined that as a nice nerdy type Edwin would drive a very different sort of car.

Rob wedged himself into the low-slung seat and shut the door. The car had such tight suspension, and was so close to the ground, it was like sitting in a roller skate. It made a powerful contrast to Rob's own minivan. From the state-of-the-art CD sound system came the supple voice of Barbra Streisand singing Broadway show tunes. Rob said, "And I thought of something else."

Edwin let in the clutch. "Oh? What?"

"I'm going to learn how not to win at blackjack, right?"

"Strange but true," Edwin said, nodding. "Ideally, months of training and careful coaching will finally enable you to lose your shirt."

"But until I do learn, I'm going to win. Won't this be cheating the casino, sort of?"

Edwin's grin lit up his face. "Funny you should mention that. I thought of it too." The light turned green and the car swung with smooth power out into Colesville Road. "During the first few sessions, I expect you'll take the poor fellows to the cleaners. That would be a severe blow to an honest business."

"It would be terrible. We can't do that!"

Edwin didn't slow down. "But suppose the casino was a dishonest one."

It was a new idea. Rob thought about it. "Are there any?"

"My very question to Gary."

"And Gary is?"

"Katie's dad, my brother-in-law. He's also the number three guy at the FBI office in Albany, New York."

"You know somebody everywhere, Ed. It's amazing."

"Well, my older sister deserves most of the credit for my acquaintance with Gary. He especially urged me to keep out of the Lady Luck Casino Royale, the least savory establishment on the boardwalk. It's a money-laundering operation for a Colombian drug cartel, and under investigation by New Jersey's Casino Control Commission. I think the Lady Luck has earned a visit from you. You want to fight crime? We fight crime."

With the flick of a button Edwin cut off Barbra in mid-croon. He revved the Mazda's engine and tapped a rhythm on the steering wheel, humming and singing an old TV theme song: "Batman, Batman, Batman!" Rob leaned back in the bucket seat and laughed.

It was more than a three-hour drive to the Jersey shore, and Edwin insisted on taking time out for a proper dinner outside Wilmington. The autumn evening had closed in by the time they reached Atlantic City. The neon casino signs stained half the sky with their glow. As they drove through the tawdry tourist area looking for the motel Rob said, "And people come here for fun?"

"They say the beach can be nice. Not my cup of tea, though—too developed."

"It's not a place for kids." For Rob that was the ultimate condemnation.

Edwin had selected a motel from the AAA guidebook. It was too far from the casinos to be first class, a fact Rob entirely approved. The room had cable TV, two double beds, and an instant coffee machine in the john. "I'm beat," Edwin yawned. He slung his overnight bag onto a bed. "Early start tomorrow, okay?"

Perhaps because of the unaccustomed quiet—there were always noisy residents in the dorm at the Open Door Center—Rob slept deeply. He found himself in a perfectly familiar place: the basement of the house in Fairfax. He realized he was asleep and dreaming, but doing the weird stuff too. Somehow the inner domains were connected—not continuous, but hooked up in some ways. You learn more every day, Rob thought. Maybe this is the only way I can access my subconscious self. And that's why this is the basement. When I'm upstairs, I'm awake.

The silly symbolism delighted him, and he set out to enjoy it. To deliberately guide a dream along was a new experience, and this was a particularly friendly setting for it. He moseyed over to the furnace and had a look at the air filter. Maybe a new one next month. He admired the cross-brackets he had installed between the ceiling joists, to correct a sag in the dining room floor above. The sump pump seemed to be doing fine too.

The basement had never been livable because it was so low. Over by the sump pump Rob had to duck his head under the ceiling beams. Since he was six feet tall, that meant the floor would have to be lowered more than a foot to bring the basement up to code. Such a major renovation would have been a gross overimprovement to the Fairfax house. But this house is me, Rob realized. Here, I could do it. I could do anything.

He sat on a cobwebby old crate and considered this. All major home improvements are rooted in the basement, as Rob well knew. And there were things he didn't like about himself. Anyone who could think or do some of the things Rob had, only this year, could use some renovation. I could make myself into a happier person, a better person, he thought. The equivalent of installing ceramic tile flooring and a whirlpool tub.

Ah, but there was the problem. He would be a different person. It would be like letting Julianne railroad him into becoming President. Just as with real houses, any changes had to be carefully worked into the existing building.

He was sitting, chin on hand, staring at the floor and thinking all this, when he noticed the crack in the concrete foundation slab. Rob jumped up and fell to his knees to examine the place closely. It was a very straight deep crack. Here under the low place it was rather dark, but Rob traced the crack with his fingers. It turned a right angle, and then another. It was a trap door.

The flashlight, in Fairfax, hung on its own recharging unit near the dryer. Rob fetched it and shone the beam on the door. There was no bolt—very dangerous in a house with kids! But there was a crude handle, just a loop of leather protruding from the crack. Rob grabbed it and pulled. If there's a subbasement, then the sump pump shouldn't be on this level at all, he thought. The jerks who sold and installed that pump are going to hear about this!

The door rose easily on well-oiled hinges. The space beneath was utterly black, swallowing up the feeble flashlight beam. But how deep could it be? Rob put the flashlight in his pocket, sat on the edge, and then hung by his hands. "Gosh, it goes down a ways," he said aloud, and dropped.

It was a very long ways, at least twenty feet. Rob landed awkwardly, twisting his ankle a little, on a coarse dirt floor. At least the space was dry. There was only the smell of damp, no standing water. When he pulled out the flashlight and pushed the button nothing happened. He must have broken the bulb when he came down.

"It wouldn'ta worked here anyway."

The hoarse whisper was electrifying. Rob's heart seemed to turn right over in his chest. He couldn't see anybody. Only a faint yellow light trickled down from the single light bulb in the basement above. He stood up with difficulty and gasped, "Who's there?"

"Behind you."

Rob whirled and half-fell backwards until his back hit a dirt wall. The space down here must be very small, only a deep slot or chute cut into the clay soil: an oubliette. When the speaker stepped forward into the light he was only an arm's length away. Rob recognized him instantly. He last saw that face glaring out of Courtenay MacQuie's bathroom mirror. This is only a dream, he said to himself. A nightmare. I'll wake up any minute. Still he had to bite his lip to keep from screaming.

"You think you're so smart," the tramp with the face of a madman said. "I'll show you. I know something you don't."

"What?" Rob whispered.

The old Rob grinned at him, a grimace full of glee and hate behind the jungle of hair and beard. "I'm not gonna say. You'll have to go ask *him.*"

Somehow this spiteful answer increased the horror fivefold. Rob's breath sobbed in his throat. Then he thought, the vicious bastard, he's *doing* this to me. Sure this is a dream, but it's also a vision. He is me—but I am him. It's my power he's using to terrify me. Nothing can hurt me here. Here, I don't need a flashlight. "Light!" he commanded, and the light came, a cone of sunshine as if a skylight had been let into the basement ceiling.

Rob's eyes watered in the glare but he could see now a rusty cast-iron pipe running down one corner of the space here. Of course—the sump pump! He could have shouted with relief and joy. He scrambled, panting, to escape. The pipe was six or eight inches in diameter, easy to climb. Rob was almost at the top when he suddenly woke. Edwin was drawing the curtains, and the dawn light poured in across Rob's face.

"If that didn't wake you I was going to turn on the TV," Edwin said. "No way I was going to touch you. Tell me that was just a nightmare, okay?"

Rob sat up, panting. "Oh my god, yes. How did you know?"

"I'm glad we're moving on this containment thing." Edwin spoke naturally, but Rob could see it was an effort. "You were right. It's getting dangerous. It looked like heat lightning, I guess, around your head and pillow. Saw it when I came out of the john, and it almost scared me spitless . . . Tell you what. I always run before breakfast. You come too. We can go down the beach."

"All right." Rob flung the sweaty covers aside and stood up. The pain in his ankle was a surprise. He sat down heavily on the edge of the bed to look at it. The joint was only a little swollen. "Maybe I'll just walk, okay?"

"Sure—but how'd you do that? Was it last night?"

"I fell, just now. It was good you didn't touch me." He got up more carefully and tottered to the bathroom.

The tide was all the way out, uncovering a very wide beach of clammy gray sand. It was so early, nobody was around except for one girl with a Labrador retriever. The wintry wind whipped the waves into cat's paws, and the seagulls had to flap hard to make any headway. Rob turned north to walk into the wind, with the ocean on their right. He sucked in a deep cleansing breath. "If this doesn't blow the cobwebs away, nothing will."

"Cold, isn't it?" Edwin agreed. He wore a faded green warm-up suit. "Like it's blowing straight from the North Pole. Look, let's walk to those rocks there. Then I'll run. You can either wait, or walk on, or go back."

"Fine. How far do you go?"

"Oh, three or four miles. Just enough to keep the cardiovascular system rolling around nicely."

Rob smiled at his airy tone. "NASA will appreciate it."

Edwin laughed. "I sure hope you were getting weird just then. I don't want to be obvious."

They came to the rocks, and Edwin jogged on. Rob sat down to rest his ankle and watch Edwin recede up the beach. Rob's coat—the same old dark blue toggle coat, threadbare but thoroughly dry-cleaned now—hardly seemed to strain the wind. He shivered under its blast.

This has got to work, this blackjack stunt, he told himself. Otherwise I'll move to—to Saskatchewan, or Tierra del Fuego, someplace unpopulated. I will not put people in danger. He thought about total solitude. So many of his problems would fall away into unimportance, if only he didn't have to deal with other people. But becoming a hermit necessarily meant never seeing Julianne and the kids again. So Rob knew he had no choice. He had to try. He got up and began to walk back to the motel.

They were finished with breakfast and ready to start by ten. Rob felt the first doubt when he saw Edwin's laptop computer. "Do you think they'll let you bring that into a casino, Ed?"

"Sure, why not? I'll just explain that I'm a postdoc gathering statistics for research."

It sounded reasonable to Rob, who had never done this before. It was still early enough that there was little traffic when they drove to the casino. Atlantic City endured far more than its fair share of snack joints, T-shirt shops, and souvenir stands. Beyond the main streets the town seemed stunted and poor.

All the juice of civic life was sucked up by the casinos. They dominated the boardwalk, huge gaudy establishments, the Trump Plaza and the Sands and Bally's Park Place, frosted with more neon than Rob thought possible. The Trump Taj had neon in the shape of a dome, the Trump Castle had neon outlining its turrets and parapets, while the Grand confined itself to awnings and arches picked out in lights.

Among these grander casinos, the Lady Luck Casino Royale made a poor show, having fallen well behind in neon one-upmanship. The outdated façade displayed a vaguely Moroccan style, with pointy windows and curlicues of gilt ceramic tile. "But the original Casino Royale was in France," Edwin complained. "By the Riviera. It said so, in the James Bond novel." He hopped out of the car, the laptop under his arm, and locked the doors with care.

"Maybe these guys only saw the movie." As they walked towards the big canopied doors Rob said nervously, "Now, today I just let it rip, right? No deliberate muscle, but no effort to stop leaks."

"Right. You'll try to play four hundred hands. That'll take all day. I'll keep track of your cards on the computer. Tomorrow, you make an effort to keep your weirdness strictly to yourself, and we'll compare the results."

Two big doormen in fakey yellow satin Arabian Nights costume stood at the big brass doors. They had evidently been chosen not only to look alike, but for size and strength. Between the sequinned fronts of his vest the nearer doorman's chest rippled with muscle. The laptop made him scowl. "No card-counters," he told Edwin.

"Oh, I wouldn't do that," Edwin said reproachfully. "I don't want to count the cards to cheat. I just want to collect the statistics and enter them on."

The second doorman came up, as tall and hulky as the first. "And what'll you do with these statistics, huh?"

"Um, write a paper, that's it. 'A Statistical Analysis of Doubling Tactics in Atlantic City Casino Play,' that sounds good." Edwin smiled, so visibly lying that it was painful to see. "I wonder if *Microbiology Review* would consider publication?"

Suddenly everything began to happen very fast. One doorman jerked the laptop from under Edwin's arm. At the same moment the other one gave him a sharp shove. As Edwin tumbled backwards, the first doorman's satin-slippered foot was there to trip him up. It was all as choreographed and neat as a circus routine, except that Rob jumped forward to grab Edwin's arm and break his fall. Still Edwin rolled sprawling onto the red-carpeted boardwalk.

"Spazz," Rob snapped, and both doormen collapsed onto the ground. Rob scooped up the computer and hauled Edwin to his feet. "Come on!"

He shouldered through the heavy brass doors and into a huge noisy space packed with rows of whizzing slot machines. Their electronic boops and whoops precluded all possibility of talk. But to one side was a dimly lit bar. Rob hustled Edwin into a booth there and said, "We're invisible, both of us."

"What's happening?" Edwin said bewildered. "Rob, did you just *do* something?"

"You damn well bet I did." The belated adrenaline rush made every nerve in Rob's body taut. "Do you even realize what they were doing there?"

"That big guy in the fez pushed me, didn't he? And—hey, where's my laptop?"

"Here." Rob slid it across the table. "They were going to stomp it flat as a pancake, after splitting your head open."

"But I *said* I wasn't using it for card-counting!"

"And surprise, surprise, they didn't believe you. Ed, when you worked at Caesar's Palace over the summer, was it in the casino?"

"Of course not," Edwin said. "I was just a college kid. It would've been illegal. I was a lifeguard at the hotel pool. I got into blackjack while I was taking a statistics course for my doctorate."

For a second Rob wanted to burst out laughing. "Look, Ed, we better rethink this."

Edwin dusted off his jacket, still looking confused. "You want to explain?"

It came to Rob that Edwin might be a little older, and considerably smarter, than he. But Rob had him, hands down, on horse sense. He said, "What we are proposing to do is to take a large sum of money away from professional criminals."

"You're going to win it," Edwin corrected him.

"Look at it from their perspective," Rob said. "They have the money. We take it. Naturally they get mad." Edwin muttered something about the New Jersey Casino Control Commission. "Ed, these people are criminals. They've just proven it. Wolves do not fight fair. Believe me, I was one—I know!"

"But we're not intending to rip the casino off," Edwin argued. "It's just a temporary side effect. You'll get it together and start losing like a good boy."

"You really expect them to trust you on that? Your problem, Ed, is that you are too nice a guy!"

"Yeah, yeah. And I warned you, didn't I, that I do not know it all. Well, what do you propose then? Do we bag it and go home?"

Rob hesitated. "I don't think I can afford to pass up even the smallest chance of getting a handle on this thing," he said at last. "Besides—what's the point of being powerful, if some two-bit heavies in fezzes can scare me off?"

"Attaboy," Edwin applauded. "So it's a go. Break out the cape."

"But we have to be very careful, Ed. I mean it. We cover our backs, we take precautions, we don't do anything stupid."

"You better take the lead on that," Edwin said. "The computer here is really only a recording device. I can easily note down your games on paper, and enter them later."

"That'd be twice the work for you." Rob was beginning to feel stubborn about it. If the wolves wanted unfair, he'd show them unfair. "I think the most sensible way to cover all the bases today is for you to not appear at all. I'll keep you tarnhelmed, but be visible myself. Then you can load data onto your program all day, and nobody will bother you."

"This will be fun!" Edwin said, bouncing to his feet.

The gaming rooms were past the slots. A repellent haze of cigarette smoke hovered near the ceiling. Though it was early, there were plenty of people sitting on the attached stools pumping coins into the slot machines and pulling the levers, over and over again. Their fingers were grimy gray from touching so many coins. The noise of crashing silver and the clangor of the electronic sound effects was deafening. "That doesn't look amusing," Rob said, pitching his voice to carry over the racket. "It actually looks a lot like factory labor."

"Slot jockeys are the lowest on the feeding chain. So am I really invisible now? Nobody can see me?"

"You're invisible." Rob glanced at him. "You can go anywhere, do anything. Nobody would know. Listen to private conversations. Help yourself to chips off the gaming tables. Look up women's skirts. Take credit cards out of handbags. Everything's open to you."

"Oh, but I'm too nice to do that," Edwin said smiling. Then he said, "Rob. Did you?"

Rob remembered the dark narrow oubliette, the burial smell of clay and solitude, and shivered. "I've got a monster locked inside, Ed. Power hasn't been good for him."

Edwin said, "We're every one of us flawed."

The blackjack area was cavernous too, with big chandeliers and carpet that would have been Oriental if it hadn't spread from wall to wall. Edwin pointed out the two-dollar tables. Rob sat down at one and bought a hundred dollars' worth of chips from the dealer. Edwin had loaned him the money. The smooth green baize table looked huge. It occurred to him that if somehow he lost heavily, if Edwin's theories were bunk, they might both be in trouble.

He put a chip down, and the dealer dealt from the shoe. Edwin had coached him to play an extremely simple and overly-conservative strategy—take a card up to 17 and then stand. Over time an ordinary player could expect to lose with it. Rob sighed as the dealer bust and he won. Edwin had predicted it, of course, and it was actually a good sign, since it showed he was on the right track. Still it was depressing, after an hour's play, to be sitting behind the biggest stack of chips at the table.

"At least you're not winning every hand," Edwin pointed out. He sat on a chair near Rob's, clicking quietly away every now and then on the laptop.

After lunch they chose a different table. Edwin said, "I figure that so far you're winning more than half the hands. That's way out of line, just like I thought. Look at the numbers here. The ratio shouldn't be more than eight out of seventeen."

Rob squinted at the laptop's screen. "We've got to whip the data into better shape. Maybe bar graphs, what do you think? That thing should have enough capacity to do graphics."

"That's right, you're a software wizard . . . What's wrong?"

Rob stared tensely at the back of the room, where the service doors were. "Damn it, I'm a fool," he said quietly. "I forgot about the video cameras. They must have them in the ceiling to keep an eye on the gambling. Ed, you're still invisible. Go over and stand near that cigarette girl, will you?"

Edwin began to say something, but Rob jerked a thumb for him to hurry. A half-dozen men in casino uniform were fanning out around Rob's table. Safely unseen, Edwin slipped past. Rob ignored them, even when one of them came up and examined Edwin's chair. They might have seen Ed on the video, Rob reflected with cautious satisfaction. But to actually get him they need human hands and eyes and brains.

After about ten minutes of subdued confusion and discreet searching the men went away. Rob nodded at Edwin, who came back. "So what were your cards?" he demanded.

"Aren't you even interested that those goons were looking for you?"

"Well sure, but let's keep our eye on the ball here. More data, more!"

"I lost, on a queen and an eight. The dealer hit twenty-one. Now if I jog your elbow again, you nip over and wait by the ladies' room there."

It happened three times more in the next two hours, and became rather comic. Different groups of burly and unhappy men came out to look for someone who haunted their video pictures but could not be found in real life. To further confuse them, Rob had Edwin circulate around the room and pretend to observe other players. "You just remember the hands I miss," Edwin said.

Rob had been stowing extra chips in his pockets for some time now, but he knew the pit bosses had him marked as a heavy winner. They had already given him complimentary food and entertainment passes, all the incentive goodies other winners received. His huge luck plus Edwin's uncanny presence were sure to provoke some more reaction, and Rob waited for it with watchful interest.

Finally one more group came out. These men were much better dressed, in neat dark suits instead of the yellow sports jackets. In the middle of the group was a tall thick man in a very expensive suit indeed: a wolf dressed like a sheep, the front man. He came straight up to Rob and said, "How do you do, sir? I'm Conrad Baskin, manager of the Lady Luck Casino Royale." He held out a hand.

Rob took it without hesitating. "Hi, my name is Jones."

Baskin smiled. His handshake was smooth and dry. "An alias, surely, Mr. Jones."

"Oh yes—my wife doesn't know I'm here, you see."

"And how long have you been playing casino blackjack?"

"This is my first visit to a casino, ever."

Rob, carefully observing Baskin's thought processes, saw that Baskin didn't believe him. With amusement he watched Baskin ape surprise and genial pleasure. "My goodness, your beginner's luck is phenomenal, then! Fred, Marie, do the honors!"

A smiling waiter appeared with champagne and an ice bucket. The camera girl snapped Rob's picture as Baskin put his arm around his shoulders. The cork popped loudly. People turned to look as Baskin announced, "His very first visit to the Lady Luck, ladies and gentlemen, and he's won, what?

Ten thousand dollars or so, in one day's play! And he's not done yet, right, Mr. Jones?"

"Oh no," Rob said. "It's too early yet."

"That's the spirit! Here, let me present you with this—" More goodies appeared, a yellow Lady Luck T-shirt, vouchers for rooms and more meals, tickets to see Regis and Kathie Lee. "And did I understand that you're traveling with a friend? We'd be happy to offer him a room voucher too—where is he?"

Rob smiled. What a lot of rigmarole, to work up to that question! "He slipped on the boardwalk and sprained a wrist, so he went back to our room to watch cable TV."

"We have cable too, the adult channels, everything. Please, both of you, be the Lady's guests!"

"I'm sorry, we've already made other arrangements for this evening." Rob watched to see what lurid interpretation Baskin would put on this: call girls, of course. Baskin's men would probably waste hours trying to find and suborn these phantom call girls.

"Perhaps some other time very soon then," Baskin said cordially, shaking Rob's hand again in farewell. "You're always welcome here!"

As soon as the fuss died down Edwin came back. "I thought they'd want to sock you on the jaw or something," he said. "What's with the cornucopia?"

"They can't possibly assault me here," Rob said. "It'd be horribly bad advertising. Would you like some of this champagne? They want me to stay—first, because I might lose all this money back again, and second, because they haven't figured out our scam yet."

"This is terrible," Edwin said, sipping from a plastic champagne flute.

"The cheapest money can buy, I'm afraid. How much longer do I have to do this?"

Edwin checked his numbers. "Another fifty hands will do it. Say another hour."

"It's getting tiresome," Rob grumbled. He persevered,

however. Thanks to Mr. Baskin, his pleasant anonymity was gone. Other gamblers made side bets on him, and tourists goggled at his pile of chips. An admiring crowd followed him to the cashier when he went to cash in. The camera girl popped the flash at him.

"Wonder if I should buy one," Edwin said. "I'll turn out in her pictures, won't I?"

"Neither of us will. She took her lens cap off, and then I had her put it back on."

Edwin laughed. "But they still have your image and mine on videotape."

"That I don't care about. What I don't want is for Julianne to open the paper tomorrow and see my picture with a caption: 'First Time Blackjack Player Wins Big.' "

Rob was supposed to fill out IRS tax forms too. He handed them back blank to the cashier and had her return them to her drawer. No way these people were going to get his name and address. Then she began to count out money, an enormous wad of limp old bills, greasy with the sweat of losers. "—and twenty makes thirteen. Thirteen thousand, one hundred and five dollars! Thank you for playing at the Lady Luck Casino Royale!"

The cashier beamed. With difficulty Rob wedged the rolls of fifties and twenties into every pocket he had. Cameras flashed. Mr. Baskin appeared, flanked by confetti-tossing showgirls, and cried, "Congratulations, Mr. Jones! We're sending you home in the casino stretch limo!"

"I'm sorry, but I've already arranged for my friend to pick me up." Rob nodded slightly at Edwin, who took the hint and went to fetch the Mazda. A huge white stretch limo pulled up at the awning anyway. Rob recognized the doorman who opened the door, and the fellow stared stonily at Rob from under his ridiculous yellow fez.

But nothing was going to happen here, in a crowd of admiring tourists and onlookers. Rob smiled easily at the cameras and promised Mr. Baskin he'd come back tomorrow. When Edwin pulled up Rob noticed the ripple of astonishment instantly—a car rolling along with no driver! Hastily he dropped the tarnhelm effect. With luck nobody would believe their eyes. "You're visible," he told Edwin as he climbed into the front seat. "Wave at the nice doorman!"

Edwin waved and grinned. "This is a gas," he laughed.

"Don't laugh too soon. This is where we start being paranoid."

"You didn't stay in their hotel, you didn't get into the limo. How else can they get their claws in you?"

"Well, they could follow this car and catch us at the motel."

"I never thought of that!" Edwin slowed down to look in the rearview mirror. "Do you want to drive then?"

"No, you do it. I might need to do other stuff. Let's tour the town a bit."

It was fully dark now, but the garish neon signs pushed back the night. The side streets and minor avenues were sleazier than ever. Rob stared through the window without seeing them. He was sure someone was following their car. It would be what he would do in the same situation. The only problem was pinpointing it. A slight effort, though, and in a few minutes he said, "Got them. That blue sedan."

Edwin looked. "What do they have in mind?"

"Oh, they just want to know where we're staying."

"And what are you going to do about it?"

"Hmm. Driving is so complex, there are lots of possibilities. Usually I have the driver confuse the brake pedal with the gas for a while." The blue sedan suddenly stopped with a screech in the middle of an intersection.

Edwin kept on driving. "Can we go to the motel now?"

"Fine. But park across the street, in that little shopping center. Driving a car like this is better than wearing your own neon sign. Oh, and if you feel nervous about sharing a room again, I'm sorry—but we really should stay together."

"I do not either feel nervous," Edwin said indignantly.

The following morning, Rob commandeered the motel bill and paid it from his winnings. "You would never have had to come here, but for me," he pointed out.

"But you'll need that money," Edwin argued as he tossed his bag into the back seat. "You're homeless and jobless."

"That's not a problem if you have money, and now I do. Oh, and your stake." He passed Edwin two fifties. "You remember at NIH that first day, Ed—when I told you I might just give you a parcel of the power?"

Edwin stared at him across the glossy low-slung roof of the sports car. He looked utterly horrified. "You wouldn't really, would you? You haven't already begun, with that invisibility?"

"No, no—that was just a tiny loan, very temporary! I wanted to say that you were right that day, with the arm wrestling. People don't have to be equal. Diversity is a strength. I could never have done this alone. I needed your insight. It took the two of us, together, to get this going."

Edwin blushed visibly under his tan and ducked into the car. "Don't let's get excited till we see how it works out, okay? We're still only assuming that you can control the 'leak' at all. Have you thought about how you'll do it?"

"No," Rob admitted. "I'm going to have to experiment with it. That's why I think we should simplify things today. No more James Bond stuff. If I cash in every time I'm ahead a couple grand, I'll never be holding a flashy mountain of chips. And I'll modify the tarnhelm trick a little, and just tell everyone in the entire building they don't recognize either of us. That should cover us completely. No more veiled confrontations with the management. You won't have to slink around like a ghost."

"Aw, that was kind of fun." Edwin shook his head in mock disappointment. "And the laptop?"

"They won't recognize that either. If anyone asks you, say it's jewelry."

"Did you learn to be such a great liar?" Edwin asked laughing. "You sure have me beat! Or is it a gift?"

"I, I learned it," Rob said, flushing with shame. "In New York."

With the pressure from the casino management removed,

and the novelty of blackjack worn off, it was a calm day. Rob spent a lot of his time at the tables in a brown study, fumbling for control. Images, he thought. For me the weirdness is image and metaphor—as if it's too big, or too strange, for a regular person to fully understand. I have to choose the right picture and impose it on the power.

At last he settled on the idea of a laser. This thing has been like a light bulb, shooting out energy all over, Rob thought. I've tried lampshades and wimpy stuff like that as it's gotten stronger and brighter. Now I want to contain and focus the light, shoot it out in one direction only. It was the first time he'd ever tried to apply his own template to the situation. He realized the only lasers he'd ever seen were on TV and in movies. He'd have to read up on them at the library to get a detailed idea of how they worked.

At the end of the day, however, Rob felt he had made a little progress. "Only twelve thousand–some dollars," he reported with pride as they walked to the car.

"That might just be within statistical variation," Edwin said. "We have to crunch the numbers some."

"I want to tinker with your software in there. It's just the standard spreadsheet, right?"

Edwin handed him the laptop. "Mess with it while I drive home. It'll be good to get back to the lab."

"Next time I'll come by myself, Ed—now that you've got me started."

"You think this'll really do it?"

"I don't know, but . . ." Rob found he was grinning like an idiot through his beard as he got into the car. "I think I have a chance!"

"That's great!"

"And I think I'll have to move out of the Open Door Center. It'd be dumb to live in a homeless shelter with more than twenty grand stuffed in my duffel bag. I'll rent a room someplace."

"I knew you'd turn around," Edwin said happily. "We'll stop for dinner in Delaware to celebrate!" He pushed the buttons on the CD player, and Gwen Verdon began to sing songs from "Sweet Charity."

It was a nippy evening for October, frosty-clear and smelling of snow. Traffic east on Route 40 was moderate. Thinking about the future, Rob felt the approaching malice only at the very last instant. "Ed!" he shouted.

Edwin jumped. "What?"

There was no time to explain, no time to even grab the wheel of the Mazda. Rob resorted to his Kmart remote trick. He shoved Edwin out of the saddle of his brain and seized control of his hands and feet. The sports car rocketed forward as Edwin's foot pushed the gas pedal, and Rob made his hands spin the wheel. The Mazda screamed across all four lanes of the highway, right into oncoming traffic. The headlights were blinding. Horns blared and tires screeched before the Mazda went roaring back again. A crash came as a side rear window shattered. The winter wind suddenly shrieked through the interior.

"Don't lose control, Ed," Rob snapped, twisting around in his seat. "I'm letting you have yourself back."

The Mazda jerked and slowed as Edwin took charge of it again. "What the heck are you *doing*, Rob? What's happened to the window?"

"Someone's shooting at us," Rob said furiously, looking back. Their assailants' car had dropped well behind, hiding in traffic. "Give me a second to get onto them . . . Oh damn it, am I stupid! I forgot they'd recognize your car! They noticed it in the casino lot and followed us."

"But they can't know we did anything!"

"They knew we were doing *something*, and why bother to analyze it? Just pump a few rounds of automatic rifle fire into the car and the problem goes away." Rob was so angry he could hardly see. But he had a hold of them now, the driver and the gunman in the attacking car. "I'll fix them," he said between his teeth.

"Oh my God!" Edwin gasped. The car came zooming up from behind with headlights glaring. It swept past at eighty miles an hour, the engine howling in protest. "Rob, what are you doing?"

"An accident." Rob smiled a small savage smile as he turned around again and sat back. "Excessive speed and spin out, right through the rail of that overpass up there."

"You're going to *kill* them?" The Mazda lurched as Edwin pulled over onto the shoulder and stopped. "Rob, no!"

"They were going to do us." Coldly Rob watched the tail-lights wink out of sight ahead.

Edwin gripped his arm, the strong fingers digging in hard. "No, Rob! Are you insane? You can't murder them!"

Rob wrenched free. In an icy whisper he said, "You *dare*?"

Edwin hesitated for only a fraction of a second. Then he glared back, bristling. "Of course I dare! Who else is going to tell you this is wrong?"

"You idiot!" Rob's vision suddenly seemed to clear as he said the words. With a sharp exhalation of breath he relaxed. "Okay . . . they're off the hook."

"Oh, Jesus." Edwin leaned on the steering wheel, gulping. "You wouldn't have really done it?"

"Oh sure. I—I got mad, I guess . . . Thanks for stopping me. I'm sorry." Rob leaned back, shaken and sick.

"You can be one terrifying dude, Rob, you know that?" With unsteady hands Edwin put the car in gear again.

"I'm sorry," Rob repeated unhappily.

Edwin drove on, well below the speed limit. Incongruous Broadway show music filled the silence. A mile up the road the headlights picked out the other car slewed sideways in the median. The driver and passenger were barely visible in the bushes beside the car. "They're begging the Virgin Mary for mercy," Rob reported as they drove past.

"They have the right idea. Look, Rob, you try as hard as any man I know to be a decent human being. But you can't save yourself. You need help."

"I know it."

"There are answers. You want me to tell you about them?"

"Not right now, Ed. I don't think I can take it in." Rob

hardly heard him, staring wearily out the window. He was bitterly ashamed of himself. With great power comes great responsibility. He was as bad as Julianne with her White House ambitions, as contemptible as Denton MacQuie smoking hash in his Santa Fe–style New York penthouse. Every time he made progress on one front things seemed to collapse somewhere else. And what about Edwin? With typical courage Edwin had ignored his own peril, but Rob knew what he had been capable of. He would have swatted his only friend like an annoying bug. The self-contempt was crushing. Even moving to Antarctica wouldn't solve this one. The monster in the sub-basement would go with him everywhere, lying and murdering. No matter where I run, I meet myself there.

The wind blustering through the broken window rapidly made the car unbearably cold. Edwin turned into a restaurant parking lot and swept the broken crumbs of safety glass out of the back seat with his gloved hands. Rob worked to plug the window with duct tape and a plastic garbage bag. "Here's a little souvenir for you," Edwin said. He held it out on the palm of his hand—a misshapen bullet. "You can see where it punched right through the side there. Don't look so miserable, okay? You really saved our bacon."

Rob picked the bullet up between thumb and forefinger. "You never would be in such a situation, except for me. I don't think I'm good for you to know, Ed."

"Too late now—I already know you. I think we've gone as far as we can with duct tape. Let's go have some dinner."

". . . so I should be moving out in a couple days, as soon as
I find a furnished room."

"Oh Rob, I am so very glad!" Mrs. Ruppert's eyes were
moist with gentle emotion. "You know you *never* were one of
our more usual residents, quite a different caliber. It's the Open
Door Center's mission to be a turning point for the homeless,
and to fulfill it just moves me more than I can tell."

"You've taught me things I want to hang on to," Rob said
honestly. "And that brings me to a favor I'd like to ask. I noticed that the front porch is really shot."

"Oh, isn't it terrible? Pastor Phillipson is worried that it'll
blow right off this winter."

"I'd like to rebuild it," Rob said. "Even if I'm not living
here I could come over a couple days a week, maybe keep the
tools here."

"Why—that would be marvelous, but—won't it be very
difficult? And expensive?"

"It would be the biggest carpentry job I've ever tried," Rob admitted. "But I'd supply all the materials, so if it's a bust the Center won't lose much. The porch'll fall off any day now, the pastor's right about that. And if the front of the building gets spruced up, your neighbors won't mind."

"They'd certainly be less catty! Oh, I don't see *how* we can say no, Rob! Let me just run the idea by the church. Thank you, thank you so much!"

"Please don't thank me, Mrs. Ruppert." Rob smiled down at her. "It's my pleasure, believe me."

So that was one lifeline secured. With Edwin and Mrs. Ruppert as references, Rob had no problem renting a partly-furnished room in the back basement of a house a mile away. It was dark and prison-like, the one window barred with an iron security grille, but Rob didn't care. For him any place that was not home was a sorry substitute, and where he slept didn't matter. "I'll say this for you, Rob," Edwin said at the end of November, when he saw the Spartan room with its single bed. "You have simple needs. You're going to embarrass me when we get to my place."

"Let me guess." Rob pulled the ill-fitting apartment door shut with a firm tug. He'd have to plane it down one of these days and install weatherstripping. "Your place looks just like your NIH office, piled with stuff. An explosion in a scientific supply warehouse." He led the way up the steep flight of concrete steps to the street.

"It's my co-authors' fault," Edwin said. "If they hadn't sent me all their chapters to collate and organize I'd be tidier."

"What's the name of your book?"

"It's a college textbook: *Eukaryotes and Prokaryotes.*"

"Oh!"

"That's the usual reaction," Edwin said grinning. "I can't imagine why. They're unicellular organisms. You've seen one—the poster in my office. That was *Euglena.*"

"Was that what it was? I thought it was a close-up of food gone bad."

Edwin laughed so hard at this that he almost missed the

turn into the computer superstore. After borrowing Edwin's laptop for a couple of solo blackjack trips Rob had decided it was silly not to buy one of his own. The salesman tried to steer him to a fancier machine than he needed but Rob knew exactly what he wanted. "Gee, you're fast," Edwin said. "It took me weeks to make up my mind, and I exchanged the thing twice."

"Read up on it in *Byte* at the library," Rob explained. He counted out twenty-three hundred dollars in worn fifties and handed it to the cashier.

Edwin stared. "Tell me you're not carrying it all in cash."

"I don't worry about muggers, you know! But actually the money got really bulky to haul around in the duffel. I've made maybe sixty thousand since October. So I started a few savings accounts. As long as I spread my deposits around, the banks won't get suspicious."

They drove to Edwin's apartment in Takoma. It was on the second floor of a garden block near the park. Edwin flung open the door and said, "Behold my nemesis! If I don't whip the manuscript into shape by the new year the publisher will strangle me."

There did seem to be a lot of paper in the room, and also a lot of furniture and high-tech toys. A fancy motion sensor turned on the stereo automatically, so that a Wynton Marsalis septet filled the room as they came in. The apartment was spacious, with a balcony and a dining ell, but it held two sofas and half a dozen tables, big and small. Edwin also had another computer, an electronic music keyboard, two CD players, and innumerable stereo speakers trailing wires everywhere. Bookcases held fat textbooks on the lower shelves and paperback science fiction on the upper ones. Near the sliding doors, a Lifecycle stood draped with damp T-shirts and jogging shorts. Out on the balcony a mountain bike hung from a rack. Packing boxes stood in towers in the corners. Everything was topped with piles of typescript and folders bulging with photographs of cells.

"Boy, I knew I didn't want to crash with you," Rob remarked. "How did you come by two sofas?" He tripped over a pair of rollerblades and sat down on the only clear space on a sofa.

"Oh, half this stuff is Carina's. It didn't make sense for her to keep an apartment when she was going to Peru for a year. And, speaking of archaeologists, I have something for you." Edwin turned the litter on one of the tables over like hay. "Here."

He handed over a sheet of paper. Clipped to it was Rob's own torn-out notebook sheet with the inscription copy on it. The paper had the same wedgy characters on it, printed out big on a laser printer. Beneath them were syllables in English. "A - Kwe - Ben - Ni (Silent)," Rob read aloud. "Aqebin. Who is Aqebin when he's at home?"

"It's an archaeological site in the old USSR. Uzbekistan, one of those newly independent republics. During the heyday of the Empire, a team of British archaeologists began digging there in the late nineteen-hundreds. Then the Communists came in and the Brits got tossed. Since then nobody much has worked there. So says the assistant professor of ancient Near Eastern studies who saw this on-line. He's mailing me a xerox of the team's preliminary survey. That was all they ever published." Edwin looked expectantly at Rob and rubbed his hands in anticipation. "Now it's your turn. How does a defunct dig in Asia figure in? Does a rabbit pop out of a hat, or what?"

Rob shook his head. "I'm sorry, Ed. It doesn't ring a bell for me at all. Never heard of the place. I guess it was a waste of time, a dead end."

"Oh well—win some, lose some. Let's boot up your new toy and load the software. Does it take three-and-a-half inch diskettes?"

Rob dropped the paper into an overflowing wastepaper basket. "Of course—bring 'em on. I've made a few changes in your graph program, by the way . . ."

It took several hours to set up the new laptop and transfer all the numbers Rob had been accumulating. On the bus back and forth from Atlantic City, Rob had written a graph-ics program to display the numbers in bar graph form. It printed out in a continuous sheet a couple of feet long. When the dot matrix's buzz stopped Edwin tore the paper off and spread it out over the litter on the table. "What do you think?"

"It's too easy to fool yourself with numbers," Rob said. "Massage your data right and you can get any result you want. But it sure looks good, doesn't it?" He noticed his voice was unsteady.

Edwin scanned the printout, pencil in hand. "Not *any* re-sult," he said. "You can't get any old answer. You're definitely progressing here. If this is normal down here, and we draw a line here where you'll intersect it . . ."

"It'll take me years," Rob said sadly. "At the rate I've been going."

"Maybe it's like working out at the gym," Edwin said. "As you get stronger it gets easier. What you mustn't do is give up."

Rob leaned a shoulder against the wall and stared down at the graph. "It's just . . . it's the end of November already. The kids' second birthday is December twenty-fourth. And then it's Christmas. It's going to be hard to hang on to my courage."

"They arrived on Christmas Eve, how cool! But you poor guy, December's going to be a double whammy for you this year." Edwin began to fold the long sheet up. "Was it a bum-mer, going to Atlantic City for Thanksgiving?"

"If there's a rehearsal for hell, they have it there then. Commuting in from this area was the smartest decision I've made. Two or three day trips a week is plenty. If I had to live in Atlantic City, I'd lose my mind."

"I'm going to Tucson to see Carina over Christmas. She'll be there on vacation, with her folks—one of those huge ex-tended Latino families. You come too."

Rob shook his head. "A reunion with your girl, and you want to drag me along? Don't be silly. Besides, do they have casino gambling in Arizona? I have to keep this up."

"Let me work on the problem," Edwin said thoughtfully.

. . .

Dismantling the Open Door Center's front porch took almost no time. Once Rob pried off the peeling roof shingles the rotten wood framing practically fell apart of its own weight. He had to rent a small dumpster to take the debris. When he was done only the stone steps and support piers were left. The house looked odder than ever, and the shelter residents had to use the back door.

But then the fun could start. Rob had Hechinger's deliver a truckload of pressure-treated lumber, and began the framing. The Center had on hand only the simplest and cheapest tools, so Rob bought himself a square, a four-foot level, a D-handle drill, a worm-drive circular saw, and—an irresistibly enchanting toy—an electric hammer.

After the unusually chilly fall, December was mild. Rob was able to get by in just his old clothes and the blue toggle coat, saving his more decent outfit for casinos. It was enormously satisfying to be outdoors measuring and cutting two-by-sixes, hammering them into a sturdy framework to support the decking. He dragooned Jonathan into helping to hold beams while he nailed. If the weather held up, he hoped to get the roof framed and shingled before the new year. Then when winter really closed in, he could sit under cover and work on the floor and rails.

He was leveling and squaring a floor joist one morning, squinting in the sunshine at the bubble in the level, when a female voice said, "Excuse me—Mr. Lewis?" It wasn't Mrs. Ruppert, who still tapped Rob for the occasional sink stoppage or radiator adjustment, but an entirely different woman, fortyish and conservatively dressed. "I'm Pastor Amy Phillipson."

Rob straightened up and stared in surprise. But at least no impolite comment slipped out—women became clergy all the time these days. "Hi, I've heard about you." He wiped his hand on his faded and tattered jeans and took hers as she held it out.

"And I've heard a lot about you! Show me what you're doing here. This must be the new porch!"

Awkwardly Rob pointed out the new framing bolted to the old stone piers. Was she checking up on him? It had been so much easier when he could just scope out people's minds. "Once I get some joists up, I can set up a temporary walkway with plywood. Then folks won't have to go around back."

She was like a brown sparrow, her eyes bright and bird-like as she assessed him. "Mrs. Ruppert says you've been a godsend. I'm sure you've had a very interesting life, Mr. Lewis. How did you ever come to be homeless?"

"There were things," Rob said evasively. "People have been nice to me, though. You know Edwin Barbarossa."

"Isn't he a sweetie? He mentioned to me that you'll be at loose ends over the holiday. So I came by to invite you to Christmas dinner."

"Umm . . ." Acute embarrassment made him tongue-tied.

"Nobody much will be there—my family of course, Jeff and the children."

Rob felt his stomach tense. "How old are your kids?"

"Eleven and eight. Oh, and my husband's daughter and her family will be there too. Their baby was born in September."

Big kids and infants he could handle. If there had been tod-dlers Rob knew he'd decline. As it was, he ought to accept. "I appreciate it," he said slowly.

"The house is nearby, over on the other side of Colesville Road—here's the address and phone number. If it's raining, call and someone will give you a lift. Around three, all right?"

When she was gone Rob shook his head in amazement and picked up his hammer. He was a reformed criminal, currently supporting himself on blackjack winnings. What was a nice lady minister doing inviting him to dinner? Edwin should have warned her.

Above him the front door opened a cautious crack. Rob had barricaded it with some boards to prevent accidents. Mrs. Ruppert looked out over the block, her small plump face puckered in dismay. "Oh Rob," she wailed. "All the lights have gone out upstairs in the women's dorm!"

"I'll look at it. It must be the circuit breaker." Rob put his hammer down again.

Christmas week was fully as bad as Rob had foreseen. He had learned to sleep anywhere, in a pile of leaves in the rain, or by a crowded freeway. But now he couldn't sleep in his stuffy little basement room. He lay awake night after night, staring up into the dark. It was so stupid! He had total power, if he cared to exert it, over other people's heads and hearts. But his own were unmanageable. One morning he went into a Toys "R" Us and began toy shopping, torturing himself with speculations about what Angela and Davey might like. It wasn't too late—Federal Express could handle the delivery. But the thought of the note or card defeated him. He abandoned a heaping shopping cart in the middle of the aisle, and went to the homeless shelter to hammer plywood.

I could phone her and not talk, he thought as he worked. Just hear her say, "Hello." I could ride the Metro and the bus, and just look at the house as it goes by. The weather's so warm, the kids might be out in the yard.

Even changing diapers would be a pure delight. The palms of his hands recalled emphatically the heft of solid toddler bodies. Then, with an equal and frightful vividness, he remembered the last time he had touched them: the TV blaring out the Lehrer Report, the smell of apple juice, the treble voices speaking with preternatural clarity. No, he couldn't go back yet! It wasn't safe—and the hammer came down, wham! on his thumb. Rob dropped the hammer and gripped the throbbing finger with his other hand gratefully. Here at least was a perfectly allowable reason for the tears rising to his eyes.

Early on Christmas Eve morning, he took the subway downtown and visited museums. The National Gallery and the Sackler would counterbalance the tackiness of Atlantic City, he thought. He looked at Renaissance paintings and toured a visiting exhibit of Mesopotamian sculptures, eerie colossal statues of big-eyed curly-haired kings. It was hard to picture these stiff smug figures as the Gilgamesh of the epic.

But the exhibits were full of families and kids in town for the holiday. Their simple happiness oppressed him. At midday he gave up on culture and set out to walk. If I could just wear myself out I'd sleep, he told himself. Walk until I drop.

He went north up Connecticut Avenue towards Dupont Circle. The leafless trees were hung with glittery white lights, and red bows adorned the lamp posts. All the store windows were decorated for the holiday. Was Julianne going to have a birthday party for the kids? Had she set up a Christmas tree? He stopped to look at a menu hanging in a bar window. I could get drunk, he thought. Six or eight whiskies and out like a light. Or if I'm thinking lowlife chemical solutions, some dirtbag would sell me cocaine or heroin even on Christmas Eve.

But it was the runup to oblivion that scared him. Three drinks, maybe, and the trap door to the sub-basement would pop open. He'd just spent months working towards control—what was the point if he tossed all that progress away? Reflected in the dark glass he noticed his own face, a little haggard from lack of sleep but much more human than this summer. I am getting there, he told himself. No more self-destructive craziness. And a haircut wouldn't hurt either, if I'm going out to dinner tomorrow.

He walked on and found a barber shop in the lobby of an upscale hotel. "Off with the ponytail," he told the girl. He felt he endured the touch of her fingers wielding the scissors and the clippers very calmly. When she held up the mirror he inspected the close-cropped fair hair and beard with mild surprise. I don't look like a derelict any more, he realized.

He still had the evening to get through. Up near the circle was a big bookstore. He went in and chose an armload of action-adventure paperbacks with titles like *MIA Hunter* or *The Destroyer*. On his way to the register he saw a new paperback edition of the Gilgamesh epic, and added it to the stack. There was a Metro station at Dupont Circle. He would ride back to the room and read, all night if necessary.

Still he couldn't sleep. After reading the night through, Rob's head was thick with cliff-hangers and blazing M-16 rifles when he arrived at the Phillipsons on Christmas Day. Their house was a suburban archetype, a split-level set in the center of a green lawn. Rob leaned on the picket fence and swallowed his envy. His life had looked like this once.

"Come on in!" Amy Phillipson waved from the front door. "Isn't it warm? It could be spring! This is my husband Jeff, my son Theo, and my daughter Janey. My father-in-law Buck is watching TV with Mark, and my stepdaughter Anne is upstairs nursing the baby."

The new names swirled around in Rob's head without hooking up to their proper faces. He stood dumb, acutely uncomfortable. Then the older kid, a brash carrot-topped girl in a blue soccer team shirt, said, "I love it when Mom brings home a hunk."

"Janey!" Both Phillipsons pounced on her. Rob laughed so hard at this picture of himself that he felt better right away.

"Girls," young Theo said in disgust. He had red hair like his father too. "I got a new baseball mitt for Christmas. You wanna go out back and catch a few?"

"Sure, I'm in," Rob said.

The air was so mild the birds sang just as if it were April, and snowdrops showed bravely in the flowerbeds. Only the bare branches of the trees betrayed the season. Theo had ambitions to be a pitcher, so Rob undertook the batting. "You watch yourself," Jeff warned when he came out with some eggnog. "Theo's idea of a strike zone is loose at best."

"We could use a catcher and a fielder," Rob invited.

"I'm basting the turkey," Jeff said. "But I'll turf out the couch potatoes. It's too nice a day to watch TV."

In the end almost the entire family joined the game. Amy Phillipson was astoundingly fleet chasing ground balls, and the old father-in-law could hit anything Theo pitched. The atmosphere was so comfortable and normal that Rob felt himself fitting right in, as if he were a cousin or a distant nephew in town for the holiday. I've rejoined the human race, he thought. It's a miracle.

At dinner, Rob could have been eating turkey with these people all his life. Jeff had stuffed the bird with fresh oysters and breadcrumbs, a recipe of his own invention which he refined every year. "This year I put in brandy and mushrooms," Jeff said, chewing thoughtfully. "I don't know. Maybe if it was Madeira instead . . ."

Rob was fascinated. It was something he was sure he could do. After all, from carpentry to cooking was not so far a step—they were the same sort of creativity. He remembered his scant repertoire of two recipes at home. "When this is all over," he confided, "I want to learn to cook."

"When what is all over?" Janey asked.

"Umm, stuff."

"Janey," her mother said warningly, and the girl pouted.

"It's okay," Rob said. "I have kids of my own . . ." Suddenly it was alien again, the dining room, the laden table, the faces young and old around it. The fellow feeling switched off with an almost audible click. What am I doing here? he thought. Only common decency kept him from jumping up and running out of the house.

In the uproar of dessert, which was a Christmas cake decorated with sprigs of holly, he hoped his sudden silence would pass unnoticed. When they all pitched in to clear the table, though, Amy Phillipson drew him aside into the window bay. "I'm sorry," she said. "Janey touched on something hurtful, didn't she?"

"Not her fault," Rob muttered.

"Can we do anything to help?"

He shook his head, forcing himself to break out of the ice, to make a reply. "I—I got into a deep dark hole, and I have to work my way out. And it takes so long . . ."

She gazed thoughtfully out the window at the leafless trees ringing the lawn, and quoted, " 'It is easy, the descent to Avernus. Morning and night the gates stand open. But to retrace the footsteps, to light again return, there indeed lies toil.' "

"Virgil," he said, surprising himself. "The *Aeneid.* I read it this summer."

"You are a very unusual person," she said, surprised in her turn.

"Is it ever really possible?" Rob asked her impulsively. "To return to the light?"

"Oh, never doubt it!" Her voice and eyes were full of certainty. "You can't do it alone, of course. But there are those who can build bridges, and unlock doors, and even plunder Avernus."

Out of his depth now, Rob said, "Edwin's good that way."

She looked up at him, surprised but smiling. "I hadn't thought of him in that context, but you're right. He's an excellent representative. We always sing carols after Christmas dinner—you will too, won't you?"

Rob wanted to say no, but knew it would be a mistake. No half measures, he told himself. If I'm in the human race, I'm in all the way. "I can't carry a tune in a paper bag," he said. "But if you can live with that, then let's go for it." So the evening passed off fairly well after all. And whether it was the carols, or merely eating a large dinner with oyster stuffing, that night Rob slept.

O*n his return in the middle of January from another* Atlantic City day trip Rob found three separate phone messages from Edwin waiting for him at the shelter. He called back right away. "Is something wrong?" he demanded.

"Of course not. I wanted to tell you I got a new toy."

"You and your toys! What is it, another CD accessory?"

"No, this one is really cool, Rob—an EEG machine. To record your brain waves, you know? I borrowed it from a friend at the Mental Institute, just for you."

"Ed, no needles, please!"

"There aren't any needles," Edwin said indignantly. "Just electrodes to paste to your scalp. This is as simple and as low-tech as you can go in brain studies, short of running mazes or doing pencil-and-paper tests. Oh come on, Rob, in the interests of research, aren't you wildly curious to see if your brain wave patterns differ from everybody else's?"

"I've never considered it," Rob said. "Haven't you had enough of the experiments?"

"Never! It won't hurt, Rob, cross my heart and hope to die. And if you want we can set it up right here in my office. You can recline in my desk chair."

Rob laughed. "I'm just having you on. Of course I'll come give it a try."

The following afternoon Rob rode the Metro to NIH and walked to Edwin's lab. Winter had set in at last. A powdered-sugar sprinkling of snow overlaid the grounds and made them a setting for a fairy tale. The heat thrown off by all the refrigerators and freezers in the hallways felt good. "I'm going to have to bite the bullet and buy myself a heavier coat," Rob said as he came into the lab.

"I don't understand your attitude," Edwin complained. "You have the money—why not spend it?"

"I want to travel light, I guess. Until I get home. Is this the toy?" The machine sat on its own cart, taking up almost all the space in the small room.

"Yep. Come and take her for a spin."

Edwin's eagerness made Rob laugh. He obligingly sat in the chair while Edwin fussed with wires and connections, crawling under the desk to attach the cables to his computer. "Does microbiology involve work with EEGs?"

"Nope. But Maureen—she lent me the machine—coached me good."

"Oh great. You inspire confidence, Ed."

"It's not a complicated technology, I tell you, Rob. Now, quiet in the peanut gallery. I'm going to stick these electrodes on."

"You're going to put paste in my hair."

"At least I'm not shaving it off, right?"

It was not actually uncomfortable to be wired up with electrodes, but Edwin's inexpert fingers felt shivery on his scalp. Every now and then, being touched still brought the power snapping into unwelcome focus. But he didn't mention his difficulties to Edwin.

"See? Isn't that cool?" Edwin adjusted the colors on his computer monitor. "That's you!"

To Rob they looked like eight ordinary sine waves snaking slowly across the screen. "What do other people's look like?"

"Here's some charts that came with. Let me adjust it down here . . ."

Edwin fiddled with the equipment out of sight below, while Rob flipped through old charts. He had no idea what the various lines signified at all. So far as he could tell his brain patterns on the screen were very similar.

"Okay," Edwin said, re-emerging. "Now! Do some stuff."

"Like what?"

"Oh—how about the invisibility thing?"

"Fine. You don't see me."

Edwin rubbed his chin, his eyes narrowed to a green glint. "Now I know empirically that you're there in my chair," he said. "I can see the electrodes, even. And it's not that you're actually transparent. But it's hard to actually discern you somehow . . . Let me get a mirror. I've always wanted to test that." He fetched a square mirror from the lab next door. "Now, how about that. I can't see you here either."

"Vision's mainly in your head, you know. The photons hit the retina, the optic nerve carries the signal, but your brain does the signal processing. It's not that I'm invisible—I keep on telling you that. It's that you, the viewer, don't see me."

"True. It might be fun to reverse it someday—try me on the EEG, while you vanish." Edwin scribbled notes on a pad of paper. "Do something else. Uh, no, not the remote control bit, that gives me the creeps. Something else."

Rob watched the colored lines wiggle and change on the computer screen as he dropped the tarnhelm. So many of his tricks involved influencing another person—there weren't that many that he did to himself. Ah, but how about a little voyage to inner space? "Watch," he told Edwin. "This should be different." And he let himself drop.

To his astonishment he found himself on the barren plain again. He had never come to the same place twice, but even though it was night he recognized his surroundings. It was very cold, the black wind cutting like a razor blade and kicking up irritating powdery grit. He looked up and recognized the stars, Orion and the Big Dipper. So this was an Earthly place! But a dull one. "What is this," Rob grumbled, "a trailer before the main feature?" He reached, to tear the fake landscape away.

Right overhead out of the clear night sky came a crack of lightning. For one strobe-like second, the sizzle of light drove the darkness back. The thunderclap sent Rob diving flat into the dust, his hands over his ears. Still his ears rang with it, and in the ringing were words: You had a hint, and you didn't take it. Now you get an order. Come to Aqebin!

Rob felt the command pierce into him like a blade. This is what it's like when I do it, he realized. Someone's doing it to *me*. Instinctively he fought back. Pulling an unwitting puppet's string is one thing, he thought grimly. But I have teeth. This is my place, my head. Nobody's bossing me here. Dust was thick on his tongue as he struggled against the intrusion.

Then he was out, free, on his feet again. The enforcing order was gone. This is some automatic system, he thought. Somebody left me an e-mail message here. Somebody had the power to do that, to invade my sphere and hang up a paper landscape with a note on it. The realization stunned him. He had to get back, back to ordinary life, to think about it. He blinked and he was there.

Not, disconcertingly, in Edwin's desk chair, but on the floor. His feet were painfully cramped under the instrument cart, and his head was jammed up against a bookcase. A small dark face hung over his, frowning. "Dr. Lal?" Rob asked, surprised.

"Good, you recognize me." Her English was clipped, with a heavy Hindu accent. She folded up her stethoscope and sat back on her heels.

Behind her Edwin hovered holding a glass of water. "Here, bud, drink this. Is that okay?" he asked the doctor.

She nodded, and they both watched like hawks as Rob sat up and sipped. His hands were trembling, and he wiped something thick off his mouth. He had thought it was dust, but red showed on his sleeve—blood. He had bitten through his tongue.

"A seizure of some kind, not a typical grand mal," Dr. Lal said. "I am M.D., but not a neurologist. Your friend must see a good one, very soon. Show him or her that." She nodded at the computer screen, where the colored lines now stood motionless. The electrodes had been jerked off his scalp and hung forlornly from their cables over the arm of the desk chair. "From the brain scan they can diagnose, you understand? Brain tumor, epilepsy—" She held her tiny hands wide, to show she didn't know.

"You got it," Edwin said fervently. "I'll set up an appointment ASAP."

"No!" Rob protested, alarmed.

Dr. Lal rolled her dark eyes eloquently and got up. "I'll deal with him," Edwin promised. "Thank the Lord you were here!" He went out with her. Rob hauled himself to his feet and dropped into the desk chair again. He hurt all over. It had never hit him like this before. A gray gritty haze seemed to overlay the world.

Edwin came hurrying back. "I thought I was electrocuting you! But Dr. Lal said it wasn't the apparatus. You have to see a doctor, Rob. Epilepsy is no joke. They've got the best in the world here—"

"I am not sick, Ed," Rob said tiredly.

"I don't want to debate this with you, Rob. I saw what I saw. There's something definitely wrong, completely aside from the weirdness. You know we were all set to call 911 just now?"

Rob closed his eyes, sorely tempted to just command him to lay off. It would be so much easier than explaining, arguing, persuading. But the sharpened blade that had almost impaled him just now made him think. It was very unpleasant to be muscled like that, to be the bug on the dissection tray.

Maybe he should just pull down the invisibility, walk out of Edwin's life forever? But friends didn't do that to each other . . . He opened his eyes. Edwin was picking his telephone receiver up. "Hey, don't do that! I was just thinking!"

Edwin put the phone down. "You looked like you were zoning out on me again! Tell me the truth, Rob, please—how do you feel?"

"A little logy, but all right, okay? There's nothing wrong with me physically, I'm sure of it. It was . . . a message."

"You're receiving messages. From UFOs, maybe."

Irrational anger seized him. "Damn it, Ed, you do not have to participate in this. I only need one thing from you and then you can bail out."

"And that is?"

"That antique archaeological report, about the dig at Aqebin."

Edwin slowly leaned forward and banged his forehead, gently, against the file cabinet. "Now that is so bizarre, it's just like you. So it must make sense somehow. All right. You're not ill. Explain it all to me."

Rob rubbed a hand down his face, feeling the sticky blood in his short beard. "Let me wash first. And could we go have coffee or something? I need ballast."

"Food! You're right, that's exactly what you need, nutrition!" Edwin leaped out of his chair. "Come on!"

It was close enough to dinner time that Edwin insisted they eat a proper meal at the cafeteria. "You can pull the wool over everyone else, but you can't lie to me," Edwin said. "You looked like hell warmed over before, but would you admit it? Noooo."

Cleaned and fed, Rob had to agree. "It's never been like that before."

"What hasn't?"

"The . . . the places I go. I can't explain the basic experience to you, Ed. It's like it's not meant to be put into words. All I can tell you is how this time it was real different. In fact," he added, struck by the thought, "what did the EEG show?"

"I didn't look," Edwin confessed. "You began to convulse, and I forgot all about it. But it's captured on disk."

Rob sighed. "I went—in, to where I go when I do this, and there was a message waiting for me. It was like—like logging on to a computer net, and finding an e-mail in your box."

Edwin nodded vehemently. "Stick with the net and the e-mail, and you got me. Let's keep away from in, and the places you go, and the basic experience. You got an e-mail. What did it say?"

"It was in the same place that I got that inscription."

"I remember you said back then that it was a message, too."

"It was a hint," Rob said grimly. "Today I got the message. It was, 'Come to Aqebin.' And it had muscle behind it."

"Muscle? You mean—wait a minute . . ."

Rob sat back and waited to see what Edwin would conclude. He imagined the gears and precision wheels spinning in Edwin's head, the trained intelligence, so different from his own thought processes, swinging around to bear on the problem.

"If someone can enforce a command like you can—and if they can use your bulletin board system—holy mike, Rob! There's *another specimen!*"

Rob burst out laughing, rocking back in his chair and slapping his knee. "And maybe this one won't be so pernickety about dissection, huh?"

Edwin grinned. "You better make that will before you go. Are you going? Do you have to?"

"Whoever it was isn't making me do it, if that's what you mean. But I think I have to go find out. If there's somebody else, someone who's been through this before, I could learn so much, Ed. They'd be my equal in power, and with a lot more experience. Maybe they've figured out the control question. Maybe they know where it comes from. Even if I could learn the name of the weirdness, that would be progress."

"You wouldn't be alone any more," Edwin said.

Rob looked at him. "I haven't been, Ed. Not really. Not since I moved down here."

"You know what I mean," Edwin said, embarrassed. "I wonder why this other guy is in Asia. Or girl—can't be sexist about it. With such a wide separation you can't be sharing a microbe or a virus. You don't have any Russian ancestors, am I right? Have you ever traveled to Europe or the Middle East?"

"Went to the Virgin Islands on our honeymoon, that's it. My folks have been Californians for three generations. Before that they came from Massachusetts, and before that, Ireland."

"Then a genetic link isn't very likely. Maybe a random mutation? You were right—we have to find that site report. Let's not go off half-cocked on this. Let me ask around about the dig and the area, do the background research."

"Wait a minute, Ed. What you mean, 'we'? You don't want to come, do you? Not to Kurdistan or wherever it was, in January."

"Of course I want to come! I've been wanting to get to the bottom of this for months!"

Rob thought about it. If he traveled alone he could go faster, without tickets or passport in fact, like a ghost. What about Edwin's job and family? Carina surely would not approve of his jauntering off like this. On the other hand Rob now knew the perils of becoming a ghost. Edwin was a smart and resourceful fellow, excellent in the planning phase, though he tended to collapse in a crunch. It would be fun, Rob realized, to travel with a friend.

Edwin rested his elbow on the table and leaned his chin on his hand. "I hate it when you do that piercing ice-blue stare," he remarked. "I know you're not rooting through my thought processes, but it *looks* like you are."

"Sorry," Rob said, glancing away. "No, I was just wondering if it was really a good idea for you to come. What about your book? Your research?"

"The manuscript's gone to one of my co-authors for revision. And I can take some vacation. How long is this likely to take, anyway? A week?"

"Longer, I bet. It sounds pretty well off the beaten track."

"A travel agent." Edwin wrote it in his notebook. "Equipment. Boots. Clothes. I know, let's go shopping for you!"

"No toys," Rob begged. "Let's travel light!"

Of course they did not. Rob had to get a copy of his birth certificate by mail from California to apply for a passport, and then they both needed visas. All this took more than a month, and during that time Edwin contrived to gather an astounding amount of luggage. "All these things are essential," he insisted. "You've never been to a primitive dig, Rob. Believe me, sometimes Ziploc bags and paper towels are a life saver. I went with Carina to Chile once—thought I would die."

"We're not going to dig," Rob argued. "We're just going to visit. We're tourists! We are not going to need case lots of paper goods."

Then Edwin hauled Rob to his favorite outdoor equipment store. "Everything for him," he told the clerk. "From the skin out, for outdoor winter work. Boots, Polarfleece, thermals, parka, Thinsulate, everything."

"Is this really necessary, Ed?" Rob pleaded.

"Do you want to turn into a popsicle? We're going camping in Central Asia in March. Get real, Rob!"

"We're not going to the North Pole," Rob began, but then he subsided. It came to him that Edwin had been itching for weeks to get him into thoroughly weatherproof clothing—as if Rob might suddenly start sleeping on street corners again. How could he thwart such a paternal motive? So he meekly let them put him into a plaid flannel shirt, a green waterproof down parka like Edwin's, Vibram-lugged hiking boots lined with both Gore-Tex and Thinsulate, and flannel-lined jeans. Dressed, he felt twenty pounds heavier. In the mirror he looked rugged and competent, a blond bearded lumberjack, ready for anything. "I'll never be cold again," he remarked.

"Polarfleece mittens," Edwin muttered. "They're warmer than gloves. Gore-tex overmittens. Wool hat, wool hiking socks. Long underwear." He piled these garments on the counter.

It was certainly different from shopping at the Salvation Army store. When Rob saw the grand total he blinked and looked again. Luckily he had thought to close out one of his savings accounts. "I can tell you where my next stop will be," he remarked.

Edwin looked up from his own stack of minor purchases: a folding shovel, three cheap disposable button lights, some nylon webbing luggage straps, and a quartz-krypton 360-degree camping lantern that could be recharged from a car battery. "Yeah? Where are you going?"

"Atlantic City," Rob said, and Edwin laughed.

✳ CHAPTER 7

During that month Rob hustled as hard as he could on the Open Door Center's front porch. Shingling a roof in January was so crazy that passersby stopped on the sidewalk to watch him. But once the crucial weather-flashing was installed he could relax. No water or ice could creep in between the house and the porch roof to loosen joists or rot wood. The electric hammer made installing the flooring fun and easy. He laid all the floor boards and ran the circular saw around the perimeter of the porch to trim them even.

"What's the rush, dear?" Mrs. Ruppert asked, astonished at this efficiency. She was always bringing him hot chocolate or coffee, to keep off the chill. "You'll catch your death working outside in this cold."

"I'm going to be away a few weeks the beginning of March," Rob explained. "If you have a floor, the porch is basically useable. I'll do the railings and banisters when I come back."

It was beyond his skill to duplicate the old gingerbread trim, and anyway he had no table jigsaw. So he opted for a more Southern effect, with big square porch columns and stepped pediments and moldings. To keep kids from falling off until he could build a railing, he strung two-by-fours between the pillars.

Even on the day of their departure Rob was working at it, balanced on a stepladder shooting nails into the final dentil trim. "This is gorgeous, Rob," Edwin exclaimed when he pulled up in the Mazda. "It's the same old porch, only brand-new. Are you going to paint it white?"

"Not till spring—you can't paint in freezing weather." Rob pulled off his work gloves and dropped them into the tool box. "And I'll tell you, a fresh-painted porch will stand out like a sore thumb against this siding. Ideally, I'd paint the whole house to match."

"This is neverending—I thought you were almost done!"

"The slogan of the home improver: It's never done," Rob said. "Let me put these tools in the office. I've got my bag here."

When he saw the old brown duffel bag, Edwin said, "Oh, you're joking. That's all you're bringing?"

"This is everything I own, except a few books and the lap-top. One of us has to travel light." Rob popped the passenger seat forward and tossed the duffel into the back on top of the five fat bags already inside—Edwin's absolute minimum. "They're not going to let you on the plane with all this junk."

"Books—I forgot to bring something to read!" Edwin exclaimed.

"I'll lend you one of mine."

"You have reading material in there too," Edwin muttered as he started the car. "I don't believe it."

Their plane left from Baltimore-Washington International Airport, and connected in New York to the overnight Moscow flight. There was hardly time to settle down on the first short leg, but once the jet left JFK Rob said, "Well, I'm going to sleep. I've been up since five, putting the final licks on that porch."

"You can sleep? I can never sleep on planes. I get too excited about traveling."

"I can sleep anywhere. I'm glad I let you have the aisle seat."

"Let me have a book too, or I'll go buggy. The magazine rack only has *Golf World* and *Working Woman*."

"You do have your Diskman and the laptop," Rob pointed out. But he unzipped his duffel and handed over an MIA Hunter paperback. "So I'm a lowbrow—sue me."

"Surely not. Pastor Phillipson told me you quote Virgil."

"She's a liar. She quoted, I recognized it. Wait, here's something else." He handed Edwin the Gilgamesh book.

"And you say this guy is you." Edwin pointed at the cover, which showed a bas-relief of a rather sticklike ancient warrior holding a lion up by a hind leg in either hand.

"No, not exactly. But read it, and tell me what you think." Rob leaned his seat all the way back and closed his eyes. He felt more nervous than he wanted Edwin to see. I'm getting nearer, he thought. Getting to the bottom of this. My life has been upside down since last May. Now I might find out how and why. He had been looking backwards so long, back to an old life as perfect and complete as the jewel in the bezel of a ring. Now he looked forward, and the future was unknowable, blank. He could not imagine what they would find in Aqebin, but surely it was unlikely to lead him back to his old happy life in Fairfax County. He would never be able to return completely even if he found a cure there. He himself had changed too much. Even his shirt size had gotten bigger. He'd noticed that at Edwin's outdoor store—probably from doing so much physical labor. He fell asleep thinking about the fun Julianne would have choosing new clothes for him.

It was a long flight, more than thirteen hours. Edwin had managed the bookings, because he had the credit cards to clinch reservations. "But even American Express isn't all-powerful," he said. "I predict glitches."

"I thought we had tickets, paid for in hard currency."

"I talked to folks who had to bribe the pilot to take off in Novosibirsk."

"At least we won't have that problem," Rob said smiling.

"Weren't you going to give up muscling people?"

"Ordering innocent folks around is one thing. But if I buy and pay for something, at an agreed price, and the guy welches so as to screw more money out of me—then I think a little push might be in order."

Moscow was deep in snow and bitterly cold. At the Aeroflot desk they learned that their flight to Samarqand had been cancelled. "You've got to be kidding," Edwin said. "There's only four a week, and you cancel one?"

The pretty airline clerk shrugged one shoulder, uninterested. "Fuel shortage."

"I bet that's what you tell all the guys." He turned to Rob. "You want to spend a few days seeing Moscow, till the next flight?"

"No." Rob leaned an arm on the counter. "Could we speak to someone in higher authority?"

The clerk's big eyes got bigger. "How well you speak Russian!"

"I do?" Rob recovered fast. This was a perfectly reasonable extension of the weirdness. "I'm anxious to get to either western Kazakhstan or Uzbekistan. Can you help?"

"Your accent is perfect! That's rare in an American." She gave him a flirtatious half-smile. "I will call my superior. He will know."

Edwin nudged him as she vanished into a side room. "You understand her?"

"It sounds like English to me. And she just said my Russian accent is perfect."

"What about written Russian? That sign over there—what does it say?"

Rob shook his head. "Sorry, Ed. Maybe the meaning has to jump from a living brain to mine."

Edwin stared into the distance, a look of dreamy abstraction on his face. "After all this is over I'm going to write a paper about it."

"How about 'Superhero Sidekick Tells All'?"

Edwin laughed. "I never thought of that! No, it'll be more on the order of 'Glossolalial Behavior as an Aspect of the Lewis Phenomenon.' "

The supervisor was an entirely bald man in an ill-fitting blue suit. "No flight to Samarqand today," he announced.

"But I have tickets." Rob passed them over.

The supervisor flipped through them, clicking his tongue in annoyance. "Very sorry for your inconvenience, but if there is no plane, what can be done?"

"Are there other flights to the area? We can be flexible."

"Probably no."

"Anywhere in Uzbekistan, how about that?"

"Let me see."

He disappeared into the back. Edwin said, "So what's happening?"

"We may well see the sights of Moscow after all. This guy says there's no plane, and he believes it's true—no question about greasing him. I wanted to get close to him to be sure."

"Oh, come on!" Edwin slumped exhausted against the counter. "Can you, you know, do anything?"

Rob sat on one of Edwin's bigger bags. "Sure. I could twist his arm, push him into overdrive, get him to pull some other plane or something. But should I do it? The problem is, Ed, the stronger I get, the less casual I can be about using this thing. In fact, if you carry the logical progression to the very end, you could imagine a time when I'm totally all-powerful—and can do absolutely nothing."

"Sounds real Zen. And boring. You really think you'll come to that?"

Rob stared out through the foggy window at the dull gray tarmac and wintry sky. If he couldn't get a grip on the weirdness, if the monster inside became impossible to keep down . . . "If I have to," he said. "But maybe it'll be like traveling near the speed of light—I'll approach it, but I'll never get there."

"Good. Navel-gazing is not your style."

"You got the map? They might be able to route us through some of these smaller towns. There's nothing set in stone about Samarqand, right?"

Edwin pulled a map out of the side pocket of his briefcase and unfolded it. He had marked their destination on it in pen. The northern swathe of the old USSR, now labeled the Russian Federation, swept across the large-scale map from the Baltic to the Sea of Japan. Cuddled beneath this enormous mass was Kazakhstan, itself the size of a third of the US. South below that dangled the smaller breakaway republics, Turkmenistan, Uzbekistan, Kyrgyzstan, and Tajikstan. The Aqebin site was on the border between Kazakhstan and Uzbekistan.

"The big hassle is, there's no there there," Edwin said. "The Brits were digging in the middle of the Kyzylkum Desert, a couple hundred miles from any settlement. The Intourist people were going to have some sort of car for us at Samarqand. If we go anywhere else we'll have to dredge up wheels ourselves. So don't commit us to too long a drive." He compared the distances by measuring with the edge of the paperback novel.

They waited for almost an hour before the pretty clerk returned. "Zarafshan, all right? It's not on the Intourist lists at all, so we usually don't send Westerners there. But you won't have any problems!"

Edwin stared expectantly at Rob, who consulted the map. "Close enough," he said, pointing the town out to Edwin. "All right."

Distances here were so tremendous that Rob's expectations were confounded. The flight would take ten hours, but that seemed far longer than their crossing from America to Europe. The old Tupolev-154 plane did not inspire confidence as it labored through the air. The wintry tan and white landscape below was endless, a continent broader than many an

ocean. "And it's so old," he said, looking out. "People have
been crossing these plains since—since when, Ed?"
    Edwin was valiantly clicking away on the laptop. "Oh,
probably ever since we started walking upright. Couple million years or so." After twenty-four solid hours awake, he was
running on empty, nodding as he sat. When he dozed off at
last Rob reached over and powered the computer down, to
save the battery. Then he leaned back in the uncomfortable
seat—designed for a shorter passenger—and took out his
pocket notebook.
    He headed the list Questions, and began marking off sec-
tions, leaving space for further additions: Origin. Control.
Dealing with Regular People. After some thought he added,
Other Place.
    When he wrote this down it struck him. Had his private
kingdom been invaded, spoiled forever by the mysterious visitor? Suddenly it really worried him. The inside place had
always been there, part and parcel of the power. He had forgotten it for weeks together, taken it entirely for granted as it
had developed and changed inside his head. Now the prospect
of its loss hit him with something like panic. He closed his eyes
and dove within.
    The important thing was not to get drawn into the dead-
end paper landscape. He was obeying, going to Aqebin, so the
unknown arrogant commander had no beef. Besides, if he
went into another seizure Edwin would get upset. Whether because of his deliberate effort or not, all went well. He found
himself in a deep window alcove lined with books. "A library!" Rob exclaimed aloud.
    It was no library he'd ever visited in real life. American li-
braries didn't usually have carved ceilings and polished marble floors, or window seats cushioned in balding sun-faded
corduroy. Perhaps it was a very large research library at a
major British or European university.
    He ran his fingers over the spines of the books, pulling out
a volume here and there. A large collection of old books has
its own aroma, a smell of paper and leather and glue all mel-

lowing together. Rob sniffed it joyfully. None of the titles was familiar and many weren't in English. As in Moscow, his language skills apparently only extended to spoken words.

Beyond the first alcove was another, and then another. "This is great!" Rob said. He pottered happily for a long uncounted time through the maze of rooms, which connected and interlocked in a way that brought to mind the library in *The Name of the Rose*. If the books were organized, he could not fathom the system.

There were other patrons in the library too, quietly pulling books off the shelves or sitting at tables and taking notes. Rob hardly noticed these first human residents of his domain. They fit in so well they seemed like part of the building: typical library patrons, shabby-intellectual men in tweed jackets, and women with glasses and bulging leather portfolio briefcases.

Then, browsing down a long aisle, he saw something new—a small bright yellow object on the marble floor. It was a toy dump truck, a Matchbox. Rob picked it up. Around the corner sat the owner of the toy, a little boy.

Rob flinched. Davey? But this was an older kid, maybe four or five years old, in some kind of school uniform—knee pants and a blazer and cap to match. In Rob's opinion though he was too young to be alone. "Where are your parents?" he asked.

The child accepted the toy that Rob held out but said nothing. Did he not speak English? Or had he merely been thoroughly drilled about talking to strangers? From the tears in the big brown eyes Rob judged it was the latter. The kid was lost, and unwilling to admit it. "Come on then—we'll look for them," Rob said, and held out a hand. The boy thought it over, and took it.

There is a protocol about lost children, at least in America, that Rob instinctively adhered to. Never take the kid into a car, or into your house, or even to the potty. Go straight to the people in charge of the place and hand the kid over. The distraught parents would go there too. A reunion could then be achieved through the mediation of the building management, without lawsuits or accusations of molestation or kidnapping.

But this library was different. Search as he would Rob never came to the circulation desk, or the checkout counter, or the reference librarian, or even an exit. The bays opened out into galleries which led to interlocking rooms that petered out in dozens of alcoves. It was endless. He had not known there were so many books in existence. The scholars and researchers at the tables and carrels didn't look up as they passed.

Rob was beginning to worry. Surely there must be a librarian in the place, if only to create and maintain order in the collection. He wasn't in the right place. The boy's mother or father must be getting frantic. The boy clung trustingly to Rob's hand, a new sensation—his own two had been too small to walk hand in hand with a tall man. If he'd had any sense he would have circulated right in the immediate vicinity where he found the kid. Probably the parent had been right there, one row over or something. Now he wasn't even sure if he could find the original aisle again. His good intentions were only making things worse.

The only thing to do, though it was not protocol at all, was to ask the other library patrons. He stopped at a long table where two scholars sat at opposite ends, each surrounded by stacks of musty fat books. "Excuse me," Rob said. "I have a lost child here. Could you direct me to the librarian?"

The older reader, an elderly man with a goatee, put his finger on the yellowed page to mark his place and looked with surprise up at Rob. Then he looked down through his glasses at the little boy and said, "We've landed, Rob. Time to boogie."

"What?" Rob blinked. Edwin was standing in the aisle of the plane, leaning on a seat back and staring humorously down at him. For a second Rob panicked—he'd left a child in trouble, unattended! Then he relaxed. The other library patrons could pick up the ball.

"You weren't kidding," Edwin said, "when you said you could sleep anywhere. You missed a landing I never want to go through again. Everyone's gotten off the plane but us." He held out Rob's brown duffel bag.

Rob took it. "Did you see anything unusual? Or touch me?"

Edwin frowned at him. "Oh, I get it. No, you were smiling in your sleep, perfectly normal. I did give you a good poke when the seatbelt light came on, but you didn't stir so I hitched you up myself."

"Good. Thanks." Elated, Rob followed him up the narrow aisle. Much better than in the motel, he thought. I'm really getting there.

The Zarafshan airport was small and painfully ugly, a cinderblock building erected by Stalinists. The new independent government had removed the Communist emblems and the statues of Lenin without making any other improvements. As Edwin stepped through the door onto the sidewalk he was instantly engulfed by drivers, touts, and pimps, all shouting offers of cars, hotels or other services. Staggering with a bag under each arm, Rob burst out to rescue him. "Cut it out," he snapped.

"You speak Uzbek!" an astonished hotel tout said. "But aren't you foreigners? Americans?"

"That's right," Rob said recklessly. "And you are driving us to your hotel for an honest fare. Take this bag, please."

In no time their gear was loaded into a rust-pocked Lada. Rob wasn't using muscle, but still the driver gave him startled and curious glances in the rear-view mirror as he drove them into town. "How'd you pick this guy?" Edwin asked.

"At random. Sometimes any firm decision's better than dithering."

Zarafshan was a tiny dust-colored town with no industry and no obvious tourist attractions. Cold winds swept powdery sand across its washboard roads under a brilliant blue sky. If Alexander the Great or Tamerlane had come through here on their conquests, they had left no signs of their passage. An older mud-brick central square was surrounded by a few tatty concrete blocks in poor repair.

The hotelier also seemed to find a tall fair man, visibly American but speaking perfect Uzbek, disconcerting. Rob had no trouble negotiating a reasonable rate for an open-ended stay. The hotel was tiny and primitive, a private house incompletely and badly converted for commercial use. It boasted only three guest rooms, but it was a block off the central square and therefore quiet.

In such a small town, organizing the next leg of the trip was going to be excruciatingly difficult. They spent a day resting up and adjusting to the time change before making plans. Edwin said, "Our problem breaks down into two sections. First, we need a vehicle that can handle the desert. And second, we need as detailed a map as we can get. The site map shows only ten miles or so of terrain, and the big national map doesn't give the road detail we'll need."

"Intourist was going to set us up with a car in Samarqand," Rob reminded him.

"Probably it would've been one of those Ladas. Didn't the one from the airport sound like a lawnmower? I want four-wheel drive and a decent engine under the hood, if there is such a thing here. A vehicle we can rely on for desert travel."

"You dreamer, Ed—in central Uzbekistan? Well, take a stab at it. I'll find us a map first, and then work on the car problem with you."

They were sitting in the only restaurant in Zarafshan, a liquor and wine shop that also served drinks and the local shish kebabs. Edwin held his glass of harsh red Uzbek wine up to the light. "I remember," he said meditatively, "when you first turned up at the lab in October. You were in rags, practically inarticulate, scared spitless—am I right? Running on raw courage. And here you are six months later, full of confidence, total master of the situation."

Rob squirmed uncomfortably in his green parka. "Don't

let me push you around, okay? I'm trying to quit bullying people. I just thought that having credit cards would make it easier for you to do the car rental."

Surprised, Edwin looked at him over the glass. "I was
speaking with admiration, bud. You've come a long way, and
I don't just mean to Uzbekistan."

The unexpected praise made Rob so embarrassed he had
to look around the room. Most of the store customers wore
local dress, loose woolen robes and baggy pants and sheep-
skin hats. But at the bar sat somebody different, a gray-haired
man in a long tailored gray-green coat. Rob recognized the garment but it took him a moment to recall where he had seen
one like it—in photographs of the old Communist regime, of
course, worn by grimfaced old codgers on reviewing stands
watching armored divisions and soldiers parade by. This must
be somebody who used to be with the old government. And
government people would have maps. Impulsively he stood up,
carrying his glass with him. "Come on, Ed."

"Where are we going?"

"A friend of mine just came in, and we have to say hello."
Edwin stared around, startled. "Here? Who?"

"I don't know his name yet, but hang on." Rob went to
the bar and stood beside the old Soviet. There were medals
pinned to the front of his coat—better and better, a military
type. Rob said, "Hi, I'm Rob Lewis. I'm a friend."

The old soldier goggled at Rob, astonished. "Why—why
so you are! How do you come to this godforsaken place, Rob?
It's been a long long time!" He seized Rob's hand and pumped
it enthusiastically. On his other side Edwin shook his head in
amazement, not needing to understand the talk.

"I wanted to see some ruins in the Kyzylkum Desert, and
I need a good map of the district."

"Yuri! Bring vodka! We have to celebrate, my friend!" He
beamed at Rob. "You have hard currency, yes? Your best
vodka, Yuri!"

The best that Zarafshan had to offer was not very good.

An hour later Rob had sipped enough bad vodka to thoroughly upset his stomach. "You see, it's a security issue," Anatoly confided. "You say you are not CIA, and I believe you. But will the authorities believe me, when I tell them? An American speaking perfect Russian would make a baby suspicious, you know. You have been carefully taught."

"But there's nothing there," Rob said. He topped off their vodka glasses. "It's just a desert, right, Ed?"

Edwin pulled out and unfolded their map. Anatoly examined it with suspicion. "They used spy satellites to make this map!"

"I bought it from the National Geographic, for three dollars. It was in their magazine."

"You're joking, really? Holy mother, I'm ashamed for us. Gorbachev drove the country to the dogs."

Rob tried to stick to the point. "Why should anybody care, if we want to tour the Kyzylkum Desert? There's no security issue at all. They quit excavating the site at Aqebin in 1918."

Anatoly drained his glass in a gulp. "If your interests are solely archaeological, I can say you waste your time here. Whatever the ruins, however important or beautiful they were in 1918, they're gone—pssssshhh!" He waved his hand parallel to the bar top, to indicate flatness.

"Good gosh, how?"

Anatoly stared down at his glass so hard that Edwin took the hint and refilled it. "Don't tell us if it makes you uncomfortable, Anatoly," Rob said. He felt terribly guilty now about manipulating the poor old man. How had he been able to blithely do this so often in New York last summer? "I wouldn't want to get you into trouble on any account."

"Oh, my friend, you are so kind!" Anatoly flung an arm around Rob's shoulders. "And it's ridiculous, just security paranoia. There's no reason you shouldn't know. It's old hat! But I've been a soldier too long to change my ways easily. When I was young Stalin was in power, you understand? So we learned to be circumspect. Look, come to my house—I will give the map to you. Tell who you like, print it in the magazine, sell it to the Western press for hard currency. It's no longer important."

"That's so very kind of you, Anatoly." Rob felt worse than ever. It was unfair doing this, like arm-wrestling a child.

Anatoly nodded, his gray eyes bleary. "The fact is, that area was used for an H-bomb test in the fifties. Mostly they did that sort of thing near Semenovka, northeast of here. An ugly place there, whew! But they also dropped one not far from your site. I suppose it was an experiment. I don't know why they didn't keep it up. Since nobody lives there, and it's a desert, it was a very suitable target."

"Oh my gosh!" Rob repeated the information for Edwin's benefit. "Does that mean it's still dangerous to go there?"

"I wouldn't think so, after forty-some years," Edwin said thoughtfully.

Anatoly confirmed this. "But play it safe, my friend. Don't eat anything that grows there, not that there is any farming, only a few nomads. And don't drink the water. That's an American joke, ha ha!"

The vodka bottle was nearly empty, and Rob paid the barman. He thought that Anatoly had probably had enough for one day. They walked with the old soldier back to his dismal concrete apartment building in the more modern street of the town. The hallway was filthy and smelled of cabbage and urine. There were no bulbs in the light sockets, and many of the doors were secured with padlocks. An old woman in the dingy apartment, a wife or a sister dressed in black, glared bitterly at Rob and said, "Drunk, again!"

"I'm very sorry," Rob said sheepishly. "I didn't mean him to."

Anatoly stumbled to a desk and pulled a drawer open. "Your map, my friend!" He pushed the folded map into Rob's hand and leaned on his shoulder, sniffling. "We will do this again, yes? Tomorrow? I will meet you at the bar!"

The old woman positively bared her teeth at Rob, snarling a silent warning. Rob said, "You remember I'm going to the desert, Anatoly. Some other time, all right? Good-bye, thank you again!" He broke away gently, and ducked back out to the dark splintered stairway where Edwin was waiting. "I feel terrible. Let's go back."

Edwin said, "It's a very different way to make an acquaintance, that's for sure." They groped their way out into the street and began walking back to the hotel. The short winter day was over, and it was cold.

Rob pulled on the double mittens and his hat. "Ed. What I did just now. Was that right?"

There were no streetlights in Zarafshan, nor any billboards or neon advertisements. And local motorists dangerously pinched pennies by driving only with their parking lights, turning on the headlights only in the most dire of emergencies. So the moon reigned unrivalled in a broad dome of sky. Edwin stared up at it. "I don't know, Rob. It's not like they refer to the instant friendship stunt in the Ten Commandments. But I think the fact that you feel bad about it is significant . . . Does the issue of mental privacy ever bother you?"

"Huh?"

"You wouldn't make yourself invisible and then peek down women's blouses, am I right? We established that in Atlantic City. Suppose then that people have a right to mental privacy, as well as physical privacy."

Rob had never thought of it that way. "It does sound reasonable," he said slowly. "But if I'm rigid about that, I'll never do anything at all. This entire weird thing is in the head. I'd wind up all Zen, like you said. At some point my own agenda overrides these issues."

"Mmm, that's a tough one all right—to know when that action point has arrived. Your problem, bud, is that you have no societal channels to guide your abilities. Suppose you had tremendous physical strength instead. There are acceptable things to do with that gift: you could be a lineman for the Washington Redskins, for instance. But you, you don't have any models except maybe in the comics. That's one of the reasons why it's so important for you to find these people at Aqebin. With them to help, maybe you won't always have to invent yourself from scratch."

"Ed, you've been really cogitating on this." Rob was touched and impressed.

Edwin grinned at him, his teeth white in the moonlight. "Well, it was just a thought. And it is very nice to have a good map, and Anatoly had a blast of an afternoon. It's a reasonably fair exchange."

"If he'd had any more fun I would've been sick right there in the bar," Rob said with feeling.

"We'll go home and dose you with Pepto-Bismol," Edwin said soothingly.

*F*inding *a car was far more difficult. People with four-*
wheel drive vehicles needed them for farming or other work, and were not about to rent them out casually. Rob systematically interviewed the various touts and brokers around town, and rejected several possibilities as too unreliable or under-powered. "We're trusting our lives to this vehicle," he pointed out. "If it breaks down out there, we're toast."

"I'm not questioning your judgment at all," Edwin assured him. "I wish the local drivers believed in automotive maintenance, but I suppose out here there's a parts problem."

A week had gone by, and Rob was beginning to feel desperate. At some point, as he had told Edwin, he had to override other people's agendas. Perhaps that action point was approaching. He lay on the bed and considered the problem. If he had to, if no other possibilities opened up, Rob could muscle somebody into renting them a good car. When would it be okay to do that?

The beds in their hotel were very foreign, lumpy kapok mattresses on squeaky iron-sprung frames. Edwin had made them more comfortable by spreading the Therm-a-Rest pads and the down sleeping bags on top. The door opened and Edwin put his curly dark head in. "Is this a good moment, or are you doing something weird?"

"I'm here. I was just thinking."

He came in. "What would you say, Rob, to a Land Rover? The only problem with it is that it's from England—the steering wheel's on the right side."

"You're kidding, Ed! Where'd you find one? You don't even speak the language!"

"There are folks who are fluent in English in Zarafshan. I just met all two of them, at the monthly church service."

"I didn't even know it was Sunday. How'd you get onto it?"

"Asked at the bar, of course. Would you be willing to have dinner with Reverend Pallet and his wife? They're Wesleyan missionaries from England. They have to go to Kabul for a month—he needs new dentures—and if you act reasonably respectable and trustworthy tonight they'll rent us their precious Land Rover while they're gone."

"This is astounding, Ed. Is there a place on this planet where you couldn't find a friend?"

Edwin laughed at him. "I might say the same thing about you, bud!"

What struck Rob that evening at dinner was the genuine friendship Edwin could kindle. It was nothing at all like his own false vodka-fueled intimacy with poor Anatoly. The Pallets were like something out of Rudyard Kipling, an elderly British couple in the wildest outposts of the empire. Rev. Pallet had a thick white mustache and a bald head fringed all around with white. He greeted Rob with a deep startling bark: "Can you manage a standard transmission, young man?"

"Sure," Rob said, considerably rattled.

"Good!" To his relief, Edwin rescued him by asking a question about the Wesleyan mission organization.

But this left Mrs. Pallet to Rob. She looked far too fragile to be living in Central Asia, a silver-haired old lady with loose thin transparent skin. It was hard to think of things to say to her. He sat dumb, ill at ease. How pathetic, to be able to read thoughts, and control minds like a god, and yet not be able to converse! The self-imposed limitations he had put on his own power bound him now hand and foot. He couldn't trawl in her mind for topics of mutual interest. Maybe in Aqebin he would find somebody he wouldn't have to control himself with.

Mrs. Pallet seemed to take pity on him, because she said, "You have a great look of my grandson, Mr. Lewis. He went up to Oxford last year. Would you like to see his picture?"

"Very much," Rob said with sincerity. The dullest family photographs would be better than sitting here silent. She took out a huge old-fashioned scrap book. Rob didn't see any resemblance to the grandson, a too-handsome young towhead in a scholar's gown. "But who are these?" he asked, pointing to a snapshot of a pair of babies.

"Oh, those are the darling twins, my niece's girls. She named them Hermione and Henrietta. I can't imagine why, the poor mites!"

Then everything was all right. Rob agreed with Mrs. Pallet that the naming of twins, particularly identical twins, was a high and arcane art. They discussed teething, and Mrs. Pallet told him all about the work they were doing to promote child health care and vaccinations in Uzbekistan. They sat down to a stubbornly Western meal, lamb chops with potatoes and turnips. Afterwards the entire party adjourned to the garage, where Rev. Pallet showed them the air filter and the radiator cap on the old but well-loved Land Rover, and lectured them about hoses.

"What a wonderful pair," Rob said as they walked back to the hotel. "I admire a man who's obsessive about regular oil changes."

Glowing with food and good fellowship, Edwin laughed. "It sure gives a guy confidence when he borrows his car. I'm glad you enjoyed the evening. We'll drive them to the airport next week, and then we can start. That will give us plenty of time to scare up supplies."

Only a few more bureaucratic obstacles remained for that last week. Even renting a privately owned car involved filling out forms and getting minor officials to sign off on them. For a while it looked like the entire expedition would collapse for want of the signature of a deputy assistant undersecretary. Rob had been ready to get tough, but the more experienced Edwin came to the rescue with cigarettes and chocolate bars.

A week later Rob drove cautiously north out of Zarafshan. Until he actually took the wheel, he hadn't realized how disconcerting a right-hand drive could be. If traffic in the former USSR had run on the left, then he could have just made a complete switch. But driving on the right, in a car with the steering wheel on the right, was endlessly confusing. The Land Rover persisted in drifting into the center of the road. Luckily traffic was sparse, mostly pedestrians, with donkeys and camels and one bicycle.

Beside him Edwin wrestled with Anatoly's map. It was very large, paper backed with cloth, and lettered in Cyrillic. Correlating it with the National Geographic map and the photocopy of the 1918 hand-drawn site map was no easy task. "As long as we keep heading north it should be all right," he decided at last. "I told you the compass would be useful."

The old gray Land Rover was fully loaded. By Edwin's advice, jerricans of gasoline and plastic canisters of water made up most of the load. That and the food had made a big hole in Rob's hoard of casino dollars. Since he didn't know how many days the trip would take, he had gone long on staples: potatoes, strange Central Asian noodles, and bags of the flat local bread. "You won't mind eating lean for a week or so," he joked to Edwin.

Zarafshan was too small to have suburbs. The country began when the asphalt quit and the dirt road carried on.

Goats and sheep grazed on the tamarisk as they passed, and the shepherds stared at them. By afternoon the land had become true desert. Rob saw now why "Kyzylkum" meant "Red Sands." The road meandered across stark red rocky ridges and down into sand-choked valleys where only tough camel thorn and saxaul grew. A stiff wintry wind stirred the pinkish dust into the air and carried it along for miles. The horizon was hazy and brown with it. Even when he looked straight up, the sky didn't seem perfectly blue.

Before the short winter day began to end they stopped for the night in a steep little valley. The wind whistled down at what felt like a hundred miles an hour. "Wow, it's cold," Rob remarked as he stepped down. "I'm glad we're sleeping in the Rover. A tent would blow right away."

"Let's light a fire so we can have a hot meal. Oh, for my LP camp stove! Open wood fires are the dickens in windy weather."

"Just build it downwind of the car."

"Trust me, Rob. Do I look like a greenhorn?" Edwin gathered pale brittle twigs from under the saxaul bushes and expertly lit a cooking fire. They toasted lamb kebabs over the fire and ate them on flat bread. "How long will the meat hold out?" Edwin asked.

"I got half a lamb's worth at the market. Even in this cold it'll probably go bad before we can eat it all."

"Good, then let's barbecue a few more!"

Rob felt very strange, sitting cross-legged on a rug in the desert eating slightly gritty grilled lamb and drinking Uzbek wine. Edwin reclined on one elbow like an ancient Roman, nibbling on a sword-shaped skewer, perfectly at ease. Rob couldn't help saying, "I can't believe we're doing this. What if it doesn't pan out?"

"You worry too much, Rob," Edwin said lazily. "Take it as it comes. If Aqebin turns out to be a bust, we'll have had an extended camping trip. A vacation."

"In the Kyzylkum Desert in Uzbekistan."

"You've spent too much time in Atlantic City. Exotic and

unusual vacations are the best. That casino jaunt with you was the tamest trip I've made since I was a kid, when we went to see the Hoover Dam."

Rob paused to chew. The local lamb was sinewy-tough, even after marinating all day in oil and spices in one of Edwin's Ziploc bags. "What do you think our destination will be like?"

Edwin waved his skewer around. "Probably it'll look like this—a rocky desert. But maybe . . ." He sat up straight and pointed with his free hand at Rob. "Maybe there'll be, I know, a large starship lying crash-landed on the sands. The surviving space-travelers need the human race's help to get back to Beta Centauri. So they call on you for help, and give you the muscle to persuade the United Nations for them. Am I right?"

Rob applauded, laughing. "Or how about a more H. Rider Haggard scenario—a lost city of adepts in the desert, all of them tarnhelming like mad to keep out of view."

"They'd have a problem with surveillance satellites. Maybe an *underground* city, that would be very cool. Ruled by a babelicious native queen."

"I'm a married man, so she'll have to fall madly in love with you."

"Carina will mount an expedition to rescue me. She'd like that—she approves of breaking down gender barriers."

The only camping equipment available in the local market was cheap woolen rugs. Rob had picked up half a dozen of these for sitting and sleeping on. The idea was to transfer all the fragile baggage, like Edwin's laptop and the bread, into the Rover's front seat. Then they could spread some rugs and the mattress pads over the load in back and sleep on them under cover, the bed of the old-fashioned Rover being just long enough for this.

It was completely dark now, so cold that touching the metal of the car with bare fingers hurt. In the sky hung endless stars, more than Rob had ever seen. Repacking the car was difficult even in the 40-watt glow of Edwin's fancy camping lantern. The jerricans, water jugs and suitcases made an ex-

traordinarily lumpy surface. Also the load was so high in back
that there was hardly room to squeeze in under the roof, especially for Edwin's broad shoulders. With a lot of grunting
and thrashing in the narrow space they rolled themselves in
the down sleeping bags. "You wouldn't let me bring my tent,"
Edwin complained from close beside him. "It's from L.L. Bean,
a geodesic that sleeps four."

"You're horribly spoiled, Ed. Believe me, this is miles better than Central Park."

"And you're going to do your sleeping like a baby bit, too,
I can tell."

"You want me to *make* you sleep?"

"Oh, no thanks!"

Rob had to laugh at his tone. Contrary to expectation,
Edwin began to snore almost immediately, a small comfortable noise like a young pig. Rob lay with his shoulders wedged
against the roof of the Rover, his back in the sleeping bag
pressed against the bulge of Edwin's shoulder in its sleeping
bag. There was a simple comfort in lying so close to another
human being. It had nothing to do with sex. Some primitive,
almost childlike hunger, unfed since he last slept beside Julianne, was assuaged now by just the contact, the warmth of
another person. How could I ever be a hermit, he reflected
drowsily. Stupid idea. I need people too much. And he fell
asleep.

As they drove the country continued rough, but very gradually dropped, a slope that eventually would terminate hundreds of miles to the north and west at the Aral Sea. After a
day or two, the road became a mere track, and sometimes vanished altogether under windblown sand. Only once in the distance did they see nomad shepherds with their flocks. There
were no signs or postings to mark the border between Uzbekistan and Kazakhstan, but they were somewhere in that area
when the country flattened out into a wild and dry plateau.

Wind-hewn hills crowded it on the eastern side. "And look at that!" Rob exclaimed.

"Let me just get her out of this sandy bit . . . okay. So what is that?"

"Looks like the desert beyond this plateau's been hit by a hammer." Even from miles away the deep dimple in the land was visible. It looked like a gigantic cereal bowl set in the ground, half full of sand.

Edwin cut the engine. "Let's look at Anatoly's map. He didn't mark the site of the nuke test—I'm sure the exact spot is still way classified—but I think we've found it."

They got out and spread the various maps out on the hood of the car. "It would help if our maps were drawn to the same scale," Rob grumbled.

"And used the same artistic conventions, eh? It's taken me weeks to figure out the chicken scratches the archaeologists used . . . As near as I can figure it, we're very close to the old site. It should be right around here someplace, at the edge of these hills." He scratched at his unshaven chin, where a sprinkle of dark stubble showed too uneven to ever make a decent beard.

Leaving Edwin to mutter and calculate mileage and direction, Rob walked a little way off. If you bring two magnets together, he thought, they don't have to touch. As soon as they're near enough they affect each other, to attract or repel. I had the entire population of the western hemisphere pouring through my hands. If there's another power of that caliber around here, it should have spotted me long ago. I should have spotted it. He reached out, searching, and the desert all around felt as desolate as it looked.

"I have no desire to see Ground Zero," Edwin announced. "Do you? Okay then, I think the old dig is around that way. If we can't find any ruins after a few passes, we may have to assume that Anatoly was right, and they got nuked to rubble."

The plateau was seamed with ravines and gullies. There was no road at all now. For another hour Edwin eased the

Rover along in low gear, heading east to skirt the plateau. "The terrain's getting too rough," he finally said. "I hate to think what Rev. Pallet would say if we broke his baby's axle. And the land's changed so much, this old British map isn't much use. But we've got to be real near." He cut the engine and looked sideways at Rob. "Can't you get weird, and find it?"

"I ought to be able to. I can't understand it. There doesn't seem to be anyone here. Maybe that atom bomb killed them."

Edwin sighed and unclipped his compass from the dashboard. "Okay, where weirdness fails, orienteering may save the day. Let's take a little hike."

The wind was a little less strong now, and the sky overhead burned clear and blue. In the brilliant midday desert sunshine, the rocks and rosy-pink sand looked entirely ordinary. Decades of wind and weather had eroded any scars from the bomb test away. With his gift for living in the moment, Edwin seemed to be enjoying the exercise after driving so long. But Rob was too worried to relax. It occurred to him that he might be too late. Time ran at a different rate in inner space. How long had those messages been waiting there for somebody powerful enough to receive them? As long, perhaps, as it took for Aqebin to crumble into ruins? He hunched up in his green down parka and bent his head into the wind as they clambered up a long slope of reddish scree.

At the top Edwin consulted his compass again. "Do you think this could be the place? We've come far enough around the plateau." The pebbly ridge sloped downhill again to a flat place about the size of a football field. The wind whipped sand up into little dust-devils over it. Beyond, the ground dropped sharply down again in a cliff, so that the space was like a terrace in the side of the hill. Lying in the middle of the flat was a long finger of rock, half buried in sand-drift.

Rob's breath hissed between his teeth as he sucked it in. "I've been here before," he whispered.

Edwin stared. "You have? Then this is it?"

But Rob was already moving, sliding down the shallow slope to the bottom. He walked up to the fallen rock. It was worn almost shapeless, but surely once it had been an obelisk. Edwin caught up, his papers flapping in the wind as he pulled them from an inner pocket. "The Brits said there was a stele," he said, turning the pages with gloved fingers. "They translated the inscription. You want to see?"

"Sure." Rob leaned to look.

The picture was a precise hand-drawn copy of rows of wedgy characters. The English was noted underneath:

The [city] of eagles, fed by [a large number, a thousand?] rivers and beloved of Ishtar, builded this temple and [consecrated] it to myself, the great [one], who knows all his subjects may do, powerful to sway the [hearts of] men, king who is mighty [like? as?] a god.

Rob didn't think the old inscription was especially informative. "When I saw it," he said, "the stone was new, standing up."

"You know, weird is a good word for this whole thing." Edwin knelt and dusted the surface off. "No writing here now. Maybe the inscription's on the underside."

"No." Rob pulled off his mitten. Touch was the trigger, his own skin to the stone. He squatted and put his bare hand gingerly on the cold gritty surface. The shock made him jerk back.

"Wow! Did you see that? Are you okay?"

"Yeah." Rob sat down, deliberately relaxing himself. If he didn't calm down he'd be sick, just like on the first day of kindergarten. "I know where to go. This thing told me. Another little e-mail. Let's get back to the car."

Edwin pulled off his glove and touched the stone himself. "Hmm. Either it doesn't work for anyone but you, or you've already emptied the box and there's no more mail left inside. Darn it, I wish I'd tried it first! All right, let's go."

When they got back to the dusty Rover Edwin said, "Shall I drive?"

"Better let me." Rob took the offered keys. He felt certain

of the route now, but it was not the sort of certainty that he could direct someone else to follow. He steered the Land Rover slowly north and east, deeper into the hills.

Edwin shaded his eyes to peer ahead. "Is it my imagination, or is it beginning to be a road again?"

If it was a road, it was not much more than a footpath, winding uphill around the shoulder of a steep barren slope. There was no doubt an hour later when it ended, though, on a natural balcony of dust-colored rock. There was just room to carefully turn the Rover around, ready to descend again. From this height they could see for miles north and west. All the way to the horizon the country was lifeless, a desolation of pink rock and wind-driven sand. The indifferent emptiness was crushing, awesome.

"And look! It *is* going to be an underground city!" Edwin pointed at a dark cleft in the rock and bounded joyfully out of his seat.

Rob went around to dig the big camping lantern out of the back. "Wait up, Ed."

Edwin stopped and looked back. "Rob. Do you know what's inside?"

Once more Rob extended himself, feeling all around, bringing the full power of his unnamed weirdness to bear. "No." Perhaps they were all dead years ago. You could set up quite elaborate automatic answering systems—look at Edwin's voice-mail at NIH.

"But you're nervous about it. Very natural."

Rob forced himself to smile. "Not nervous, exactly."

"Fine, don't admit it. Do the raw courage thing instead." He came and took the flashlight out of Rob's grasp. "The two of us together can cope with anything. Let's go in, shall we?"

O*ut of the wind the cave seemed almost warm. They* paused to pull off hats and gloves, and let their eyes adjust to the dark. The sound of the wind had been a constant presence for so long that the quiet now rang in their ears. The narrow gap in the hill was obviously a natural formation, like the rock platform outside. "But look," Edwin said. He bent and tilted the lantern so that it shone at a low angle across the gritty floor. In the glow the imprint in the sand could be clearly seen: an ordinary human footprint. "Not aliens," Edwin sighed in disappointment. "Let's see where it went."

The passageway went deep into the hill, twisting and turning. The roof was so low Rob could easily touch it. Around a final corner, and it ended abruptly in a small cavern scarcely bigger than Edwin's NIH office. Edwin flicked the beam around the dark little space. "Empty," he said. "Is this all? What a bummer."

"No," Rob gasped. The tarnhelm trick, how stupid of him

not to think of it! "There's someone—sitting right there!"

And there was. Rob couldn't tell how he was seeing it in the dark, but a towering figure sat enthroned on a ledge of the unhewn rock only ten feet away, a living man in the dress of men five thousand years gone. A robe fringed with gold wrapped his legs. His splendid brown chest was bare except for a massive pectoral necklace set with rubies. He had a black and elaborately curled beard, but no mustache. Long black hair hung in gleaming corkscrew curls down his back, and his eyes were huge in his face, black and brilliant. He was a statue from the ancient Mesopotamia museum exhibit come to life.

Rob thrust Edwin behind him so roughly the lantern fell with a clatter. This was a sophisticated illusion, he could tell: not much different from appearing as somebody's best friend. And who could say what lay behind? Instinctively he responded in kind, flinging up a false seeming of his own. The homeless man, of course—rags, and a piece of string for a belt, and his familiar threadbare blue toggle coat over all. It was a standoff, façade faced with façade.

"I can't see anything," Edwin grumbled at his back.

"You don't see him?"

"See who? You better not have bust my flashlight, Rob. Wait a minute, here we go." The light flickered and steadied as Edwin turned the lantern all the way up. "Holy Mike!" The light dipped wildly as Edwin fumbled it again.

Rob didn't look around. "Keep behind me, and set that light down before you break it."

A new voice spoke, low and hoarse: "Perhaps we should drop the masks, eh?" Its sound was jolting, like a hidden door suddenly flung open.

"I will if you will," Rob said warily.

"Agreed."

Edwin jammed the lantern into a crevice, and drew in a long breath of wonder. The magnificent god-king had shrunk. A skeletally thin figure, very short by modern standards, sat slumped on the ledge. The long hair hung lank and thin in black streaks over his shoulders, and the beard straggled. His ribs showed, and the yellow-brown skin stretched tight over his knobbly elbows and knee joints. He wore sandals and a ragged brown robe. Only the huge eyes were the same, eerily big and sharp. "You are not doing it right," he croaked pettishly. "Illusion is supposed to make you look grander and more impressive, not less. That is not the way it should be done."

"I see," Rob said, very taut.

The skeletal man frowned sourly up at him. Their faces were scarcely ten feet apart. "So you have youth. And beauty, though not of the Asian style. It does not impress me. Tell me your name."

"Tell me yours first," Rob said.

The man smiled. "I am that I am."

"No way!" Edwin exclaimed, his eyes kindling.

"You understand him, Ed?"

"Yes, and he's lying!"

Rob didn't understand how Edwin could know this, but he said, "You want to try again?"

"Speak with respect," the skeletal man said, still smiling so that all his yellowish teeth showed. "For I am your father."

Rob could feel Edwin's uneasy gaze prickling on the back of his neck. "My father passed away in 1989. He was a retired civil engineer."

"I seduced your mother," the man suggested.

Rob folded his arms. He couldn't fathom the motive behind this rigmarole. "I'm the living image of Dad. Everyone says so. We even wore the same shoe size."

"I think then you must guess my name," the man said grumpily. "You are not doing this right. And who is that?" He glanced at Edwin.

"A friend." Danger signals shivered down Rob's spine. He didn't want to tell Edwin's name. Though he couldn't avoid giving his own. "My name is Robertson Michael Lewis. And I bet I can name you. You are Gilgamesh son of Lugalbanda, once king of Uruk in Mesopotamia."

Edwin's mouth opened in astonishment. The skeletal man's

eyes got even wider. "My name is still spoken," he said, pleased. "And my epic is still sung!"

"I have the book out in the car."

"Later on you must show it. How did you know me?"

"Yeah," Edwin interjected. "That was some stunt, even for you!"

"I recognized you right away when I read the book," Rob said slowly. "I knew that Gilgamesh was someone with the power—like me. I told you that," he added to Edwin.

"I thought you were being metaphorical! And the plant," Edwin said, struck by another thought. "The magical undersea plant that gives immortality. I read about it on the plane. The story said you lost it to a snake."

"A story is only a story," Gilgamesh said, baring his teeth in a skeletal smile again.

"Holy Mike! That means you're maybe five thousand years old! You wouldn't by any chance consider visiting NIH, would you?"

Rob had to set his teeth to keep from laughing out loud. Gilgamesh stared at Edwin with annoyance. "Silence," he rasped. Rob could feel the subtle crackle of power, and when Edwin opened his mouth no words came out.

"I don't feel that's necessary," Rob said mildly. He had never seen that trick before. But merely seeing it done was disproportionately informative. With a mental gesture he easily undid Edwin's dumbness. "Although you might consider taking the hint," he suggested.

"Right," Edwin gulped.

"Oh, you are a bold one," Gilgamesh said to Rob. "I will give you your true title then. Not slave, nor son—but brother."

The whispery creaking voice held for Rob the note of truth. Here was someone with exactly his abilities, an equal, just as he had once wished for. "I've been looking for you," Rob said in a low tone.

"Now that sounds right." Gilgamesh nodded in approval, the black strings of hair shifting on his shoulders and chest. "You alone fully understand, then. I am a king and the son of a king, monarch of humanity's first city, the mightiest hero of my age. Tell me: How do I come to the desert, my subjects only a few nomad shepherds?"

Rob looked into his own heart, and knew the answer. "You couldn't stand it. The pressure, dealing with all the people, all around. You had to get away, to where it was empty."

"Very good! One insect, a hundred even, I can smash, but it becomes a weariness." Rob began to speak—that hadn't been quite what he'd meant—but Gilgamesh was already going on. "Even the shepherds here were too near. I made the overlords of this land drive them farther off."

"You had them drop an H-bomb?" Rob said, horrified.

"Is that what it is named? The noise was impressive. But recently I decided it was time to turn again. I felt a need for a companion, an equal, an Enkidu as of old. And . . ."

The rasping voice trailed away. Gilgamesh stared at Rob out of his huge glittering eyes, and raised a bony hand in an inviting gesture. Rob could feel the blood draining away from his face. "Oh my god." It burst out of him in a sob. "Oh my god. You did this to me. This power is from you."

Gilgamesh clapped his bony hands together. "Oh, well done. Very good. Yes, I divided my godhead with you. Half— a fair sharing, remember that. We are equal, and exactly alike. Except for the immortality, of course—that is mine alone. It should be very diverting."

"You mean—you did this to me, you trashed my life, broke up my family, drove me almost insane, for a *diversion?* Just to amuse yourself?" A pure and towering fury filled Rob, making his voice crack. Through his down sleeve and all the thermal layers he felt Edwin's restraining clutch on his arm.

"You talk as if this were a whim," Gilgamesh said. "Since we are brothers I will admit to you what I would tell no other. It is a solitary business, being divine."

Again Rob felt the prickle of recognition. The same horrible isolation had oppressed him. The weirdness could sever a man from his fellows like a sword. You became too strong, too different, no longer on the same level as other people. Rob himself had only broken out by luck—with Edwin's help. And the epic had told of the death of Enkidu, how in spite of all his power Gilgamesh had been helpless to save his best friend. Over the thousands of years, and through the dozens of translations from language to language to language, the poem still ached with grief. Perhaps Gilgamesh had been struggling against the glass walls all the centuries since then, moving further and further away from humanity, undying and yet eternally alone. And his strange slanted approaches to Rob were his last gasp for help, the final attempt to break free from this cave and all that it meant. Only the utmost desperation could have driven a proud ancient king to give away half his power to a stranger.

Edwin seemed to be acting on the same thought. He stepped around the warning arm Rob flung out and said, "You poor old fellow! You didn't have to do it this way. That's not how making friends works at all. We'll cook you some dinner. Maybe you don't need to eat, but you ought to. And this cave is way too cold for a bathrobe. Here, take this . . ." He went down on one knee to talk to Gilgamesh on the level, unzipping his red parka.

For a second Rob thought it was really going to happen— his faith in Edwin's genius for friendship was that strong. Surely no one was beyond Edwin's warm rescuing grasp: the bridge builder, the opener of doors, standing at the edge of the dark wood with a rechargeable camping lantern in one hand. But a look at the old king told the story. Rage suffused the brown skeletal face. "You *dare* to pity me," he creaked. "You dare, you insect. You worm, you—"

"Microbe," Edwin suggested, smiling.

Rob could have punched him, the idiot! "Look, he only wants to help," he began. "We both do—"

With a shimmer like heat lightning Gilgamesh lashed out. Edwin tumbled backwards with a choked cry. Rob shouted, "No!" and jumped forward.

He towered above the frail old man, his fists clenched. A physical fight would have been no contest at all. But to his horror, this contest was a stalemate. Rob put his full strength into pushing Gilgamesh out of Edwin's head, and he couldn't do it. He could hold his own position, but that was all. Between them at their feet Edwin moaned, a shrill and terrible sound. "We shall kill him between us," Gilgamesh said. "Such slaves have not fiber enough to endure our battle."

The truth of this was shatteringly obvious. Rob was forced to retreat. "If you are Gilgamesh," he panted, "so am I. This one has stood as Enkidu to me."

"Yes indeed," Gilgamesh said almost fondly. "Very good! You have it right. You are Gilgamesh too. You are I. If I made you to serve my need, you made this one. He is not your friend, he is your pawn, your tool. And now we have met, you have no more need of him." He poked Edwin with a sandaled toe. "Up, you. Stand."

Edwin reeled upright. His face was slack, as blank as a dummy's, but his eyes were still his own. Repetition had not yet worked its dulling magic. His gaze was luminous with terror. Rob stuck his hands deep into his pockets, fighting down another impulse to try and grab the strings out of Gilgamesh's control. The old man's words were like a knife-blade, stabbing him with truth. *The difference between what he's doing to Ed and what I did is only a matter of degree. We're equal and exactly alike, indeed.*

"Go back to Aqebin," the old king commanded. "Behind the temple was a cliff. Throw yourself off it."

Rob held back a gasp of protest. Let Gilgamesh think he concurred. Edwin pivoted like a puppet. Rob felt his pleading gaze, but kept his face impassive and looked at his watch. It was two o'clock. He listened to Edwin's slow footsteps receding down the passage and clenched the fist in his pocket tight: around the keys of the Land Rover.

Edwin would have to walk back. It had taken them an hour to drive here from the site. It would take Edwin longer than that to return on foot. If Rob could fudge up some excuse to step outside soon, he could drive back, catch up with Edwin, and release him from the enforced command. It could be done!

"I agree that we must begin with a battle," Gilgamesh was saying. "It is an old, old tradition—the way all heroes become friends. But a single human mind is too small a battlefield, and too frail. The planet itself shall be our arena. Return you to your western lands, and conquer them. Meanwhile I shall subdue Europe and Asia to my will, and be a king of men again. We can then battle: with pawns. Let us agree to begin the war one year from today. That should be plenty of time."

Rob was unable to keep silent any more. "You have it all planned, don't you?"

"I have spent centuries in thought," Gilgamesh said with smiling pride. "After the war we can be reconciled. You shall call me Gil, and I shall call you Rob. Is that not the parlance of these times?"

"Why bother to ask? You have it all taped out." Rob's voice slipped from his control again, shaking with emotion. "You are insane. I will have no part of this!"

"But we are brothers!" The old man sounded genuinely surprised.

"You don't want a friend or a brother," Rob said savagely. "You want a pawn or a tool, you murdering psychopath. And you can go to hell!"

"I *made* you," Gilgamesh rasped. "Long and long did I search, sifting through tiny vermin minds around the world, until I found one that might grow to match mine. I raised you up from the slime to sit beside me. You are as I now: a god. You should be on your knees with gratitude!"

"I never wanted this thing," Rob shouted. "You pushed it on me in a lump without asking, and left me to struggle with it. And now I'm going to leave you to it. Play your little games alone!"

Rob turned on his heel. There was plenty of time—Edwin had scarcely fifteen minutes' start on him. Nevertheless he moved fast down the shadowy cramped passage, so fast that he tripped on the rough floor and fell.

In the instant of falling, Rob knew he had made a huge and

possibly fatal mistake. He had turned his back on Gilgamesh. His body was probably still in the cavern, sprawled on the gritty stone floor. Severed from it, his mental self fell and fell, an endless tumbling drop through the dark.

He landed hard, on his back. Harsh summer sunshine filled the cloudless desert sky above him. Its heat was like a furnace. Rob rolled quickly to his feet. Big square stones polished to a glossy sheen paved a wide plaza. Around the sides cyclopean stone buildings stood empty, their windows blank and dark. In the center the gleaming obelisk stood tall, graven deep with the boasts of a god-king. This was the Aqebin site as it had been thousands of years ago. And this was the original of that paper landscape, the reality that Gilgamesh had photocopied to mail to him. Definitely the wrong playground, Rob realized. This is going to be ugly.

Now there were no more decisions to make, Rob felt icy-calm. He only had to fight and get out, fast, before too much time passed. "Hurry up, damn you," he called.

"Listen to the little rooster crow," a deep voice bellowed. From the black yawning doorway of the biggest building, a tall figure came striding out into the sun, a Sumerian warrior in full battle dress. A glittering round bronze helmet protected his head. Bright overlapping metal strips armored his chest, which was once more superbly muscled. He carried a long flashing battle-axe with a curved edge. The black beard was braided and tied with gold, and above it, full red lips curved in a wide terrifying smile. In spite of himself Rob was impressed. Gilgamesh in the center of his power made an awesome sight.

"You think mighty well of yourself, Gil, old pal," Rob said. "And you sure don't worry about fighting fair." Gilgamesh here was head and shoulders the taller. Without armor or weapons, Rob could not hope to stand against him. In fact, his down parka and flannel linings handicapped him with their heat and bulk.

"I have no wish to fight you, brother," Gilgamesh rumbled.

"We are too nearly matched. It could be unpleasant. I only want you to do as I say. After all, I am considerably your elder. You should heed me."

"I deny the relationship," Rob said between his teeth.

"Then I must convince you to alter your mind."

Rob tensed, getting ready to dodge that long deadly axe. But suddenly Gilgamesh was gone, between one eye-blink and the next, like a special effect in a movie. Rob was alone. Something more complicated than just a whack from an axe was coming.

"Oh god," Rob said aloud. "I *am* alone." In this huge and illimitable inner landscape there was not one living thing. Gilgamesh had paved it over, smashing everything flat, nuking everything except himself. Rob had never known either agoraphobia or claustrophobia, but both seized him now at once. He was both isolated in space and yet closed in. Sheer terror bore him to his knees. Sweat poured down his face. "The bastard, he's doing this to me," he whispered, as he had in the subbasement. But this time it didn't help. In this place Rob was defenseless, and Gilgamesh's power was supreme.

In New York City the isolation had been a bell jar. Here it descended on Rob in glass bricks, weighting him down, crushing him flat against the hot pavement. Gilgamesh was squeezing him like a bug under a glass paperweight. Rob was being deliberately driven insane. Strange voices chanted in his ears, and a dizzying vertigo made the world spin even through his clenched eyelids. No, he thought, clawing at his wits. Been there, done that. I am not going to go crazy again. He writhed, pushing out and away with desperate strength, back to the cool reality of the cave.

"You astound me!" Gilgamesh said, in his rusty-iron voice. "Have you indeed the boldness and artifice to escape?"

Rob gasped on his hands and knees at the old man's feet. "How can you stand it there?" he panted. "How can you do that to yourself? There's nothing alive there. It's all dead!"

"Have no worry about me, pretty boy," the old king chuckled. "Taste this instead. You may not know it."

Suddenly every muscle in Rob's body locked rigid in cramp. His back arched and his limbs twisted. A shout of pain tore out of his throat before his windpipe closed. The agony was unspeakable. Under the breastbone his heart turned traitor, galloping wildly faster and faster. A hot red haze filled his eyes, and the long bones in his legs and arms creaked under the strain. In another second they would snap, or his overdriven heart would collapse. I'm dying, he realized. He's using my own brain to murder me. But I can't die yet. I have to, to . . .

For a moment he couldn't remember. Rescuing Edwin, returning to Julianne, raising his children, everything slipped away into the scalding mist of pain, and death nearly had him. Then an image came to him: fifty feet of porch railing and a pair of stair banisters in Silver Spring, Maryland. And the commitment to finish them was so mundane, so specific and ordinary and down-to-earth, that it was obvious he wasn't going to die. Carpenters and handymen do not get themselves racked to death by Mesopotamian monarchs.

He didn't die. Gilgamesh let him go just in time. The smiling skull-face swam into Rob's view as the haze of pain cleared. "That was interesting," he said happily.

Rob's breath rasped unevenly through his raw throat. His nose was bleeding. In his chest his heart jumped and slowed, trying to return to its normal rhythm. He lay on his side, shuddering and throbbing as if he'd been worked over with a baseball bat. The sadistic swine, he thought foggily. Another one like that will kill me.

And yet this was familiar too. The monster in his subbasement would get on with Gil just fine. That's why he chose me, Rob realized. Gil was looking for a brother, someone whose personality matched his, equal and exactly alike. And in the basement I have a psychopath too, every bit as bad, a rapist, a bully, a murderer. All I have to do is let him out, and Gil will be my best friend.

The sandaled foot by his head took a few practice swings and then kicked him in the face. The old man was too starved and slight to do more than gash Rob's eyebrow. All Rob could

do was blink the hot sting of blood out of his eye. He was too
drained to stir.

"That," Gilgamesh said, "was for being defeated. For you
are defeated. I wasn't quite truthful when I said we were completely equal. I do have the advantage of experience, little
brother." He set his foot on Rob's mouth and chin. "In time
to come," he said, "I want you to remember this moment. Remember who had the mastery. Admit it!"

The taste of chilly leather and sand ground into his mouth.
If I could just turn his own trick on him, Rob thought. I saw
him do it, so I know how. Pull him in. Touch him, skin to skin.

With a tremendous effort Rob turned his head a little. The
crushing foot slipped a bit in the blood, and for a second the
papery cold ankle touched his nose and cheek. Instantly Rob
grabbed through that contact at Gilgamesh. He pulled, falling
backwards to drag the old king into himself. He had no idea
what the inner landscape was doing today, but he trusted it
would answer his need as it had always done.

Rob stood up. His pains dropped away. Times Square
swirled around him, neon signs and skyscrapers and traffic signals and crowds of people, a glorious heart-lifting sight. Power
and joy surged through him. "My playground, Gil," he
shouted laughing. "New York, New York!"

The traffic lights changed and the pedestrians hurried
across, every one of them layered with their different histories.
As properly cool New Yorkers should, they stepped around
the Sumerian monarch crouched on the sidewalk without
looking at him. Gilgamesh stared wildly around, his mouth
open. Jet contrails threaded the sky. The towering buildings
were festooned with advertising banners. Cars honked. Bicycle messengers whizzed past. Everything, however small, revealed an infinite complexity the moment it was examined.
Millions of people, billions of artifacts and toys, zillions of
magazines and books and newspapers—there was a galaxy of
information here, enough and to spare to totally overwhelm
any reclusive ancient king.

"How do you stand it?" Gilgamesh moaned, covering his eyes.

"Stand it? I *made* it!" Rob said, with a shock of delighted discovery. This wasn't the real New York City—he could see differences in the skyline, and the sidewalks were impossibly clean. It was only a reflection: the reflection in himself of the real city. It all hooked up, all of it, right back to that very first day when he had admired the chocolate artists and the Star Trek fans at the office luncheon. Diversity, that was the theme. Nothing the same, not one person, not one flower in the endless garden he had surveyed, not even one grain of sand, and yet a unity. E pluribus unum, just like on the dollar bills.

"Gil, I'm pleased to say we are fundamentally different after all," Rob announced. "You pruned everything inside away and made a desert. I opened up and let things grow. You ground things down to be the same, and I love things that are different. We really have no common ground to stand on. And now—I don't suppose you read comic books? Well, watch this!"

Here Rob knew he could do anything. He had always wanted to fly, and now he did. He jumped up into the air and it held him up nicely. He paddled higher, up among the pigeons fluttering between the concrete towers. His horrible experience inside Gilgamesh's universe had been educational. The trick was to call the reflection's basic character into play. He knew exactly what to do now.

About sixty stories up Rob halted, treading air. From here he could see most of downtown. The city throbbed with life, a community yet chockful of diversity, more complex and beautiful and unique than anything he could imagine. It's only a reflection, he told himself. But a really good one. I'm proud of it.

Rob called on that quality now. Gilgamesh had socked him with undiluted isolation. Rob was going to return the favor, with pure community. It rose up behind him in an invisible tidal wave, a whole city's worth of everything that people did or made or said to hook themselves up with other people, and followed him as he zoomed down, in an irresistible curving breaker right onto Gilgamesh's dazed head.

Rob swooped clear in the best superhero style, leading with one fist like Superman in flight. Then he looped back to inspect the result. The old king lay prone, unmoving, his long lank hair and beard spilled onto the sidewalk. Rob landed with a grace he could not hope to duplicate in real life, and hauled Gilgamesh by the arms into a nearby bus shelter. He had to find a permanent fix for Gil. The guy was far too dangerous to let go. And he had to do it now, before the old king recovered.

Rob propped the limp old man in the corner against a Mostly Mozart poster, and sat on the bench to consider the problem. Could Gilgamesh be killed? If a magic sea flower had endowed him with eternal life that was a real question. He'd already hung around for millennia. If it was possible at all then some accident should have done him in long ago. Perhaps Rob could strip him of his powers. He had been given half of them already. Would it be possible to remove the other half by force?

We are equal and exactly alike, Rob reminded himself. He did it to me, without my participation or knowledge. So I should be able to turn the tables on him. And here I can do anything. It's a reflection: I can bend it to my desire if I find the right image to do it in. He put his will behind it, leaning his forehead against his clenched hands.

Then, looking down, he noticed a small rectangular tag at the base of Gilgamesh's skinny neck, between the protruding points of the collar bones. It looked exactly like a zipper tab. When he looked closer he even saw the brand name "Talon" imprinted on the plastic. "It's not any more unusual than swimming in the air, I guess," he said out loud. He took the tab between finger and thumb, and pulled it down.

Gilgamesh unzipped very tidily down the middle past his navel. He looked like an untenanted wetsuit, his skin as thick as neoprene rubber and showing the seams on the inside. There were no organs inside the hollow shell. In the middle only two little objects rolled around. Rob reached in and scooped them up before zipping the old man back together again. He examined the things carefully. They were beads, one a pearl and the other a gleaming red-orange crystal like a fat drop of juice from a blood orange. In the epic, Rob remembered, Gilgamesh won eternal life by plucking a magic flower from the bottom of the sea. That would make the pearl the symbol of his immortality.

The old man stirred suddenly. Intelligence returned to the huge black eyes, and he sat up. "What have you done to me?" he whispered hoarsely.

Rob held out the two gems, the red and the white, so that Gilgamesh could see them. Here in this realm of joy he was no longer driven by wayward impulses. He could say with calm and perfect truth, "In the cause of justice, Gilgamesh, I'm returning to you what you truly need: your humanity. You wanted a brother. Welcome back to the brotherhood of man." Rob dropped the two gems into his shirt pocket, safe inside the green parka.

The old king's eyes bulged in horror. "No! Not after all this time, not mortality! I need to live forever—"

With a finger's gesture Rob cut him off. In this place he didn't have to agonize or debate himself. At this moment he was briefly the unity he was so rarely in real life, and his confidence was total. Of course Gilgamesh didn't want it this way. And the cons in Lorton hadn't really wanted to go straight, and if consulted, Courtenay MacQuie would have scorned to read Dickens. Nevertheless it was right, and Courtenay and the jailbirds would agree someday.

Would Gilgamesh agree too, maybe years from now? Somehow Rob rather doubted it. The old king sat glowering in the corner, full of hate but unable now to do anything about it. He might not even be able to speak anything other than

Sumerian, or whatever it was they spoke in Mesopotamia five thousand years ago, now that he had no power to bridge the language gap. Rob looked up at the glorious neon signs, and leaped to his feet in shock. The clock under the Sony sign said 5:30 P.M. Surely it couldn't be so late! Time ran at a different rate here. How much had passed, in reality?

"Come on, Gil—we've got to get back!" Without ceremony Rob stepped back into the desert cave, dragging the helpless old man with him. It was a nasty drop back into his battered physical body. His mouth tasted of blood and vomit, and sand gritted between his back teeth. His bruised limbs were almost crippled, stiff from lying on the clammy stone floor. Awkwardly he hauled himself to his knees and fumbled at his wrist. To his dismay the watch was broken. The digital face must have smashed against the rock during his spasms.

Rob staggered to his feet. "I'll be in touch," he flung at Gilgamesh, and ran. His joints groaned and his muscles protested as he forced them to move. His cold wooden fingers could hardly tug the car keys out of his pocket. Outside he leaned against the dusty Rover for a second. Physically he might be shot, but his mind was sharp and icy-clear.

He concentrated, searching the nearby desert all around. Maybe pulling the plug on Gilgamesh had released Edwin from the death sentence. But Rob found nothing and nobody. For miles around the wasteland seemed empty of life. Was Edwin already dead at the bottom of a cliff? Maybe Rob had just missed him. It was hard to know how accurate his searches really were. Why hadn't he listened to Edwin, and tested his skill systematically? Or, most likely, that tricky swine Gilgamesh had rigged some kind of cloak again. Mustn't give up hope. The sun was still above the hills. The afternoon wasn't over yet. He climbed painfully into the Rover.

How fast could Edwin have walked? Rob drove down the steep nonexistent track like a maniac, jouncing over the rocks as fast as he dared. The Rover bounced and skidded, rattling every bone in his aching body. Around every curve he looked for Edwin's red parka, but the stony desert hillside remained stubbornly empty.

Once on the flat he could push the Rover along in second gear. Mustn't lose the way, Rob told himself grimly. Mustn't break an axle. Oh God, if there is a god, let me be in time!

As he approached the site he could see the long pebbly ridge, empty. Rob brought the Rover to a skidding halt at its foot and hauled on the hand brake. He ran up the slope, his Vibram boot soles sliding in the red gravel, his heart pounding in his throat.

He came over the crest and halted, sagging with relief. There was Edwin on the far side of the pavement, his red parka still hanging open from when he had unzipped it to give it away. No tarnhelm trick could cloak him from Rob at this close range. "Ed!" he shouted.

Edwin turned, and instantly Rob knew something was wrong. Edwin stood unmoving a few yards from the verge, saying nothing, not even waving in greeting. Rob sharply focused his power and felt it right away—the command of Gilgamesh, still in force. And the ancient king had learned too, from how easily Rob had undone the silence command. Rob couldn't override this one fast enough: It was laden with safeguards and locks. He began to run.

Rob slithered down the gravelly slope in a cloud of red dust. The central plaza of Aqebin seemed enormous, Edwin's figure tiny on the far side. "Ed!" he called as he ran. "Hang on for one more second!" If he could just touch Edwin, grab his hand!

Rob was close enough to see his expression now. A look of hurt and horror distorted Edwin's face. He stepped backwards, one step, and then another. "No!" Rob screamed hoarsely, as Edwin stepped over the edge.

Rob skidded to his knees at the stony lip. The actual drop was more than twenty feet and sloped away into a steep rubble-choked valley. Edwin tumbled down like a discarded doll, loosening a small avalanche of pebbles and rock. He slid to a halt halfway down, partly buried in the scree. Dust settled in his hair. "Ed!" Rob yelled. But Edwin didn't move.

An icy clarity filled Rob. He couldn't climb down from here—more rocks would slide down. He ran well to one side, where the cliff was lower, to climb down and then over. As he clambered down the slope, he realized it would be impossible for him to haul Edwin back up alone. The hill was too steep and unstable. He had to have help, fast. What had Gilgamesh said about nomad shepherds?

He scrambled across to Edwin and touched him gently. In its torn sleeve Edwin's left arm was bent back at an impossible angle. Rob straightened it gently, and the sound of the broken bone ends grating against each other made him shudder. Blood pouring from a gaping scalp wound masked Edwin's face. When Rob tried to clear away the boulders pinning his lower body, more rocks threatened to roll down, and he had to stop. Rob pulled out a Polarfleece mitten liner, the only piece of cloth to hand, and pressed it to the head wound. The skull bone gave sickeningly under his fingers. He didn't dare to apply firm pressure. A familiar terror filled Rob, the odd panic that had possessed him in the hospital ER after the Chasbro fire. Edwin was dying.

But now Rob was almost a year older, and far more experienced. He didn't have to thrash around in frantic and selfish dismay. He could really act this time. The plight was desperate, long past what Edwin had called the action point. Rob reached out, questing, feeling for the nearest help. He sensed Gilgamesh, immured in his cave, and moved outwards. About ten miles west at an oasis, some shepherds living in yurts. Come, he silently commanded them. Farther out now, in a widening circle. Aqebin was between Uzbekistan and Kazakhstan. Zarafshan to the south had been a small town, but farther north and east was Qyzylorda, a provincial Kazakh capital. No airplane could land at the site here, so he needed a helicopter . . .

Edwin sighed, stirring a little. He was sinking. Rob could feel it. Deep in the central stronghold of himself Edwin was perhaps even now pulling on a white lab coat for his final stand, marshaling an electron microscope and a laptop computer for weapons. None of the summoned help could arrive in time. The distances were just too great. Shivering, Rob stared down into the blood-smeared face and thought, this is how Gilgamesh felt when Enkidu died. Gilgamesh has sat gazing into the face of a dying friend, and suffered this same pain. Equal and exactly alike.

Suddenly Rob threw down the dripping gory mitten. He had brought his copy of the Aqebin inscription back to everyday life once. And once he had twisted his ankle in a visionary sub-basement and woke up limping. What now was in his shirt pocket? He wiped his sticky hands on his jeans and groped in the flannel pocket with trembling fingers.

He drew the beads out and cupped them carefully in his palm. In the last sunset light they glowed strangely, the pearl with a cool luster and the gem like a tiny live coal. They were metaphors made real, constructs, symbols for processes or magics he could not comprehend. What exactly did eternal life entail? Escape from the aging process, obviously, and liberty from trivial details like eating and drinking, but what else? Healing of mortal wounds, perhaps? Rob barely hesitated. The gamble had to be taken. Whatever happened, Edwin could hardly come to worse harm now. Gently, he forced the pearl past Edwin's pallid lips and onto his tongue.

Nothing happened, no flash of light or alarm bell or anything. Rob felt Edwin's pulse but wasn't able to say whether it was getting weaker or stronger. The head wound had stopped bleeding, but applying pressure could be responsible for that. He could only watch and wait.

The light was going fast. The sand-laden wind scoured like emery paper across the darkening hill, teasing fluffs of goose down out of the rents in Edwin's parka. All this time Rob had been clutching the red gem in his left hand. But suddenly, with a horrible start, he realized the hand was clutching emptiness. If he had dropped the jewel on this rocky hillside no one would ever find it again! Rob opened the hand, cursing his own carelessness, and was jolted to see a vivid red-orange dampness on his palm. Even as he watched, the color sank into his skin and vanished. The gem had melted like an ice cube and apparently been absorbed. It was so dark now he could almost believe he'd imagined it. It wasn't as if his hands weren't already smeared with red wetness. Yet the jewel was gone. If only he had worn mittens, or kept the thing in his pocket! I am in big trouble now, Rob thought wearily. And, damn it, I left the lantern with Gilgamesh.

It was fully night before half a dozen shepherds arrived riding two-humped Bactrian camels. A strangely compliant crew, they wasted no time on questions, but lit torches and dug Edwin carefully out of the hill. Chilled and pain-wracked, Rob could only help a little as they rolled Edwin in woolen rugs and carried him to safety. He still clung to life, but Rob wasn't quite able to hope yet.

"Do you have medicine for him, great lord?" the chief shepherd asked.

"No. But a helicopter will arrive in a couple hours," Rob replied. He sat bone-weary by the campfire that someone had lit near the Rover. Very tentatively someone else offered him a metal cup of the local green tea. Rob took it and drank thirstily, nodding his thanks.

"Are you—" The shepherd hesitated. He was a starved-looking man in worn woolen robes and a shaggy fur cap, his bronze face weathered into a hundred wrinkles. "Are you the new god? Is the old one gone at last?"

Rob almost crushed the thin metal cup in his hands. "Don't call me that! Don't you dare, not me or him either, or I'll, I'll—" He couldn't think of anything frightening enough to use as a threat.

But the shepherd didn't need threats. He groveled in the dust at Rob's feet, whimpering, "Mercy, great lord! Forgive me!"

"It's all right. Get up, please! You know him, then. The old one, in the cave." Of course—these unfortunate nomads were Gilgamesh's nearest neighbors in the desert. He had probably been muscling the tribe to cater to his whims for centuries. No wonder they were scared rigid.

"When you called to us, we thought it was him." That accounted then for their speed and docility.

"You keep it in mind, then, all of you—I am a man, and he is a man. Never believe anything different." The shepherds squatting around the fire nodded obediently. Rob rubbed his dirty beard, thinking hard. "Would your people be willing to take him in?"

"Who, the old one?" The chief looked anything but enthusiastic.

"He is without power now. He may not even be able to speak to you. I doubt if he knows Kazakh. He is old and helpless, and weary of being alone in his cave." Rob was careful not to use any muscle. These men deserved to make their own choice.

"Well . . ." The chief looked around at his men. "It would be an act of hospitality. Allah smiles upon such."

So there was one burden gone. "Good. Now, does anyone in your tribe know how to drive a motor vehicle?"

Another round of glances, and a tribesman volunteered, "My son can drive."

"Would he be willing to drive this Land Rover back to Zarafshan for me? I'll write down where it should go. In return I'll give your tribe all the baggage."

That got a big positive reaction. The shepherds jumped up, chattering excitedly, to look over their bonanza. Rob claimed only his duffel and Edwin's black nylon briefcase with the laptop, with a few extra clothes stuffed in the top. Edwin's toys would be a gold mine for these impoverished people, and there was no way to fit all this junk into a rescue helicopter. From the bottom of the duffel he dug out the box of classy letter paper he had bought on Madison Avenue. By firelight he scribbled a brief note to Rev. Pallet, explaining that an accident had forced them to evacuate by air. He gave the note and the keys to the shepherd with the driver son.

Then Rob could let himself relax. Everything else he'd

worry about tomorrow. It was almost midnight. He was so exhausted the campfire seemed to split into two fires, then three,
before slipping into focus again. Warmly wrapped, Edwin
slept beside it. Rob lay down on the bare ground beside him
and fell asleep instantly.

*Y*ou *remember, Rob, when I called you a terrifying dude?"*
Edwin asked in cheerful tones. "That's what you call reasoning ahead of your data. I take it back. Beside old Gil you come
off like Woody Allen."

It was barely after sunrise, but they were already over the
Aral Sea flying west. The cargo plane was only half full, so
Edwin's body-board stretcher was strapped across four of the
folding canvas seats that ran down one flank of the interior.
Rob sat on the seat at his feet. Edwin grinned happily at him
from under the heavy white bandage around his head. He was
almost unrecognizable. His hair was matted into points with
dried blood, and the slurry of blood mixed with dust had
dried into his skin. Dr. Mitchells, the Red Cross doctor, said,
"His pelvis is fractured. He should be screaming in pain. I
don't understand it." He stuck the last piece of white adhesive
tape down on the leg splint and cut off the end with a scissors.

"I didn't think I could bear it," Rob explained tautly.

"*You* couldn't bear it?" Dr. Mitchells shot him an odd glance.

"I get by with a little help from my friends, doc." Edwin looked down at his splints and bandages. "Guess I'm not going to pass my NASA physical, huh?"

"Don't give up hope, Ed—please!" So far there had been no chance to bring Edwin up to date. The prospect made Rob almost too tense to sit still.

"You're sure now?" Dr. Mitchells demanded once again. "This is important. It will affect his future treatment, you understand? They didn't administer morphia in the helicopter, nor at the airfield? And you didn't medicate him? No experiments with hashish, no opium cigarettes, no nothing?"

Rob shook his head. Edwin said, "He wouldn't know how to medicate a house plant, doc."

"This is so weird," the doctor muttered. "And I have a quarterly report to write in Qyzylorda. I have no idea why I'm zipping off to Istanbul on a cargo flight with a pair of tourists." He pulled the blanket up to Edwin's chest.

"It's a mystery," Edwin agreed. "Am I done for the moment? Good! I wonder, could you look him over now?"

"There's nothing wrong with me," Rob objected. The old reluctance to be touched possessed him.

"You should see yourself." Edwin met Rob's eye and winked a permission. Rob took a quick glance at himself through Edwin's eyes, and was startled. He had forgotten how many knocks he had taken yesterday. His fair hair and beard were crusted with dark dried blood, and his face was bruised all along one side from falling onto rock. And he was filthy— not as spectacularly grimy as Edwin, but pretty bad.

Grumbling, the doctor swabbed his cuts clean. "You should have a stitch in that eyebrow. Let me give it some xylocaine."

"Don't bother—just sew it." If Rob could short-circuit Edwin's pain response it was no trouble to briefly disconnect his own too.

"It's a macho contest, right? You two are trying to see

who's tougher." The doctor rooted in his medical bag, swearing under his breath.

When the doctor was finished with Rob he retreated to the cockpit to swap grievances with the pilot. Rob took a deep breath of nervous anticipation. "Does it bug you that I'm messing with your head? Anytime you want, I'll quit."

"Don't be ridiculous. To scream like the doc thinks I should would embarrass me. I can tell I'm hurting, but it doesn't bother me at all—like it's happening somewhere far away."

"Are you tired? You want to sleep?"

"Maybe a little later. Right now I want to think and talk. The usual Barbarossa agenda. You got some pretty major bruising there, bud. Is that what's bothering you?"

"Golly, no!" Rob hastily buttoned his flannel shirt back up, cursing the doctor for insisting on listening to his chest. Opening the shirt had revealed that he was black and blue all over.

"Well, what's on your mind?" Edwin's eyes narrowed in suspicion. "This pain thing you're doing on me, you're not actually toting the load or anything?"

"Forget it, it's a snap." Rob unbuckled his seat belt and moved to sit cross-legged on the floor beside the stretcher. "Ed, I have something extremely important to say, okay? And I want to apologize in advance. Anything I can do to help you with it in future, you got it. That's a promise."

Edwin shook his head. "Come on, Rob. I'm sure this isn't going to be a permanent disability. People break their pelvic bones all the time. It's no big deal."

"No, Ed, that's not it at all. Let me tell this my way." Rob couldn't think where to begin. "The doctor told you about your injuries, right? The leg, the pelvis, the arm, the ribs."

"Funny thing," Edwin said. "I remember everything up to the actual fall. Just as well, I guess."

"Shall I tell you why that is? Because the worst injury was your head."

"What, this?" Edwin touched the head bandage with his uninjured right hand. "It's just a scalp wound. The doc said so. Fourteen stitches, though—a personal best for me."

"When I got to you, Ed, it was a dent in your skull. About this big." Rob made a circle with his fingers and thumbs. "And–and squishy. You must have hit a rock."

"Oh, you must be mistaken, Rob," Edwin said with maddening assurance. "Cranial trauma like that? I would've been herniating, bleeding into the brain with a burst aneurysm or an epidural hematoma. People don't survive injury like that without immediate surgery to relieve the pressure inside the skull. And a brain injury usually entails obvious neurological consequences. I mean, here I am talking quite connectedly to you, sound as a dollar, at least on the cognitive front. Scalp wounds are way messy—that must have confused you."

"I'm not telling this the right way," Rob said, frustrated. "Look. When I nailed Gil I stripped him of everything. The power, and the eternal life too. I had to do it. He was too dangerous to let run around with it."

Edwin blinked up at him. "Did you kill him?"

"Not outright." When he thought back on it Rob was appalled at his own serene cruelty. "I should have. To suddenly be an ordinary average person, after all these centuries—he'll go nuts. It's worse than how he did it to me. At least I had a week or so to gear up to speed. Gil lost it all in one instant."

"And out there in the desert alone—the poor old guy, Rob, he'll freeze! And starve!"

"No he won't. The shepherds will take him in. Ed, don't distract me. I climbed down and found you dying from a massive head injury. I swear it—it's absolutely and objectively true. I had to save your life the only way I could. And I had it on me: the magic sea flower that confers eternal life. So I gave it to you."

Edwin lay and stared consideringly at him for a long moment. When it became obvious he wasn't going to speak Rob said impatiently, "Oh, spit it out, Ed. We've been through so much, you can be up front with me."

"I think," Edwin said gently, "that you've taken some pretty heavy hit points, Rob. Obviously you've defeated Gilgamesh, but it's cost you. It must have been brutal. Look at those bruises. And you haven't come to an accomodation with the tiger side of yourself, am I right? If you had to kill him, it's perfectly normal to suffer emotional stress, and feel a need for a coping mechanism . . . You don't agree with me."

Rob covered his sore face with his hands, partly in frustration but also to hide his unwilling smile. "Be fair, Ed. Have I ever told you anything that wasn't the plain and simple truth? But there's an easy way to prove this one. Back in Kazakhstan Dr. Mitchells said your pelvis was broken. That's why you're strapped to this body board. Let's get him to look at it again." He got up.

In the cramped airplane cockpit Dr. Mitchells refused point-blank to leave the copilot's chair. "There's no necessity whatever to check the injury. The less stress we put on the break the better. I never saw a plainer fracture. He'll probably need surgery, and be bedridden for months."

Rob was nettled by his self-satisfied tone. "I don't agree with your diagnosis," he said deliberately.

The doctor glared at him. "And who awarded you an M.D.? You want him to scream, is that it? I tell you, Meg, there are some sick people in the world."

The pilot glanced over her shoulder at Rob. "Oh, be a sport, Bill. Go check him out—maybe there's something really wrong."

"No such luck," the doctor growled, grabbing his medical bag.

Back in the cargo bay Edwin was restless. "Maybe we should wait for an X ray," he said nervously. "Or an MRI. You know, Rob, it's not that I don't trust you. It's just that you see things in a more creative way sometimes."

"Creative," Rob repeated, with a straight face. "Very tactful, pal. I appreciate it."

Ignoring all this, the doctor knelt and threw the blanket back. Underneath, what remained of Edwin's blood-boltered clothing hung in tatters from where the doctor had cut things away. The bulky splints on his right leg immobilized it from hip to ankle. Black padded nylon straps snugly criss-crossed his body from armpits to knees, binding him immoveably to the body board. "This ought to hurt," Mitchells said. "If it doesn't, it's another goddam mystery." He worked his fingers into examination gloves and delicately probed the hipbones. "You're going to tickle me," Edwin fretted.

Mitchells sat back on his heels for a moment. "That's not right," he muttered. He put a palm on the point of either hip and leaned, rocking the dish of bone with his full weight. "Could it be that . . . Damn it! Wait a minute though. You felt something, didn't you?"

The layer of grime stood out starkly on Edwin's stubbled face as he went suddenly pale. "Not a thing," he said in a stunned tone. "It's just—I'm thinking, that's all."

With brusque angry motions the doctor began unbuckling the nylon straps. "It's got to be broken. It was broken when we strapped you down! Here, sit up, will you?"

Rob helped the doctor hoist Edwin up, maneuvering the clumsy splinted arm and leg into position. Edwin sat on the edge of the board looking merely bewildered. It was obvious the action gave him no trouble at all. Hopelessly, the doctor flexed his good leg in several directions. Then he stood up and announced, "Okay. There's no pelvic fracture. I give up. I do not understand. The sooner you two get out of my life, the happier I'll be." He turned and marched back to the cockpit.

Rob sat down in his own canvas seat. "Ed, I'm truly sorry. I know the last thing you wanted was to get sucked in like this."

Edwin rubbed the back of his neck with his good hand. Loosened dust pattered down all around him. "What I wouldn't give for a cup of coffee. And a shower. I still can't believe this is happening. Tell me more, Rob. Tell me everything. How did you get the thing away from Gilgamesh? Is it connected to your own weirdness? How did you give it to me?"

Rob stuck for a moment, trying to surmount his usual difficulty in putting the experience into words. Finally he said, "You swallowed it, Ed. Like a piece of candy."

Edwin leaned his bandaged forehead on his hand. "No, Rob. You can't do the inexplicable explanation bit any more. This time I really have to understand. Let's rewind a bit, and go through it in order. When I left the cave, go back to that. Who said or did what, next?"

"He . . . I—" For a moment Rob wanted to beg off, just repeat that it was too hard to explain. But hadn't he just promised Edwin he'd help him cope? No one had been there to tell Rob the score last year, but at least he could help Edwin find a balance now. "Well, we—we discussed conquering the world."

Edwin watched him narrowly from under the head bandage. "The two of you were going to take over the world. Like Pinky and the Brain."

"Um, not quite. He was going to take over his bit, Europe and Asia, while I managed the Americas. And then we were going to have a war, just for kicks."

Edwin raised his eyebrows so high, the dried blood and dirt fell off his brow in flakes. "I can't dismiss old Gil as a wacko with delusions of grandeur. I've seen too much now. Rob, truly—did he have that caliber of power?" Rob nodded, and Edwin slowly added, "Do you?"

"Gil told me he was a god. And—and that I'm one too."

Rob could hear the edge of anxiety, the shameful plea for reassurance, in his own voice. But Edwin didn't fail him. "I have some slight acquaintance with God," he said gravely, "and I can assure you there's not much resemblance. Besides, didn't the epic poem say that Gilgamesh was only partly divine?"

"Two-thirds god and one-third man," Rob recalled.

"Well, there you are," Edwin said with satisfaction. "That's flat-out impossible, the way DNA replication works. He'd have to be one-half, or maybe three-quarters. The ancient Sumerians wouldn't have a clue about the Mendelian laws of inheritance. So Gil planned to rule the world. Obviously you didn't go along with this ambitious agenda."

"No. In fact we, uh . . ."

"Disagreed. Vehemently. You fought him." Edwin pointed at Rob's plaid shirt, which hid the bruises completely. "How?"

"In our . . . There's a place you can get to, Ed. If you get sufficiently weird. It's your own place, individual as a fingerprint, sort of . . . like your own personality, expressed as an environment." Edwin's blank expression drove Rob to greater clarity. "Like the way a Web page is you, expressed on the Internet. I told you about mine. How Gil left me an e-mail there."

"Right, I remember that."

"So when we fought, he dragged me into his own head."

"Holy Mike!" Edwin pulled the laptop out of his briefcase and powered it up. "I wish I could've seen it—what was it like in there?"

"It was a desert, exactly like the country we drove through. Just looking at it, you'd know Gil was really bad news. And he tried to nail me. But I wiggled out, back to the cave, and that's when I got so dinged up."

Without looking up from the keyboard Edwin shook his head. "You're abridging, Rob. I can tell. But how'd you get the drop on him?"

Edwin was hunt-and-pecking notes on with one hand, his right. Rob noticed that the left hand in its shoulder-to-knuckle splint kept trying to help too, particularly with the space bar. Without mentioning it he withdrew the pain blocker from Edwin's head. Edwin didn't seem to feel a change. Rob said, "I saw how he did it. Pulled me into his own head. So I did the same. Pulled him into me."

"What's it like there?" Edwin asked, as he had before.

But this was utterly impossible for Rob. The strange joy and power, the sense that he had truly come together in that place—he knew it was a ridiculously inadequate description of that glory and beauty to say, "It was like New York City . . . I'm sorry, Ed. If I were a poet, or a songwriter, if I had the words . . ."

"It's okay." Edwin's glance was speculative but full of sympathy. "Maybe we'll work on that later, bud. Right now let's stick to the straight narrative. What did you do to him? How did you take away his power?"

Recounting the vivid unreality of the battle was like trying to grasp a dream. "I got him down," Rob said slowly, "and then I, I unzipped him. The two things, they were like beads inside his tummy: a pearl and a ruby. And I took them out. But I knew from the epic that eternal life was the pearl."

"And this is the pearl you had me swallow like candy."

Edwin sat staring at his computer screen, his splinted leg sticking awkwardly out to one side. "Darn it, I have to cook up a way to get a better grip on this. An inarticulate fellow like you is the worst possible observer. Rob, does this mean you have Gil's power? Is it a sandwich, or a virus? I mean, do you now have twice as much as before?"

"I guess so. I haven't tried anything much with it."

"But won't it be twice as hard to ride herd on?"

"Probably. I should've given the red jewel to you too, but you wouldn't have liked it."

"I'm very glad you didn't," Edwin agreed. "This pearl bit is going to be plenty weird enough, as it were."

"Let me see your arm." Rob began picking at the adhesive tape on the splint. "There's only one more vital thing for you to know, Ed. You're not in my situation. You're not stuck with this. I gave it to you, and I know how to take it away again. If having eternal life gets on your nerves, I can unzip you and take the pearl out—though I'd like you to put up with it until your bones all knit together, first. Any time you want out, you just say." He ripped the fastening tape free and began unwinding the cloth bandage.

"I see a problem with that, Rob. I may well outlive you, and if I do I'm in dutch." Edwin's grin was still a little crooked. "I do not at all want to live forever. I'd rather do my threescore and ten and then die in peace. But it does occur to me that an astronaut who can't get killed might be really useful on a space mission. So don't predecease me until after I come back from Mars, and then you can have the immortality back again with my blessing."

"Right. When the photon torpedoes need new dilithium crystals you could just step out into warp space and install them."

"You're no Trekkie—photon torpedoes don't take dilithium crystals!" Edwin's laugh had something of its old exuberance now.

"Okay, how does it feel?" Rob let the splints drop in a tangle of padding and bandage strips.

Edwin flexed the arm without difficulty. "I can see the fracture sites," he said, pointing. A livid bruise near the crook of his elbow and another near the wrist were all that remained of the injuries. Already the marks looked yellow and old, fading at the edges. "I wonder if the bone would sustain pushups yet?"

"Give it another couple hours," Rob suggested. "Shall I start on your leg now? That splint doesn't look comfortable."

"Dr. Mitchells is going to be so pissed," Edwin said, shaking his head ruefully. "Sure, get it going. I'll start rolling up some of these bandages. Maybe if we put them neatly back into his bag you can convince him it was all a bad dream."

Four

O_n the first afternoon in May, Rob arrived at Edwin's apartment. He had walked all the way from the bus terminal. Now he ran up the stairs two at a time, the old duffel bag on his shoulder and the laptop carrier in hand. He rang the bell and then turned the doorknob. Edwin didn't bother to lock the door when he was at home.

Stepping into the hallway, Rob almost ran into a young woman. With an effort he kept his mouth from dropping open. She was not tall, but stunningly beautiful, with a mass of dark curly hair and fiery brown eyes under delicate eyebrows. The moment she saw him, the butterfly eyebrows slanted together. "You," she said. "I recognize you. You must be that world-class louse, Rob Lewis!"

Rob clutched his laptop to his chest. "Holy mackerel. And you must be Carina. Ed's told me so much about you."

"Edwin," Carina declared, "hasn't the common sense God gave a hen. And you take him on a rock-climbing vacation in the Ural mountains! He could have gotten really hurt—of all the stupid, ill-considered expeditions, and in March, no less! Nobody with two brain cells to rub together visits Central Asia in winter. You could have frozen to death!"

Rob recognized the rock-climbing story they'd agreed on. In the face of her righteous fury he could only shrink. "I'm very sorry," he mumbled. "I'll never do it again, I promise."

"Oh dear!" A stricken look spread over her tanned face. "And I promised Edwin faithfully I wouldn't yell at you! I'm sorry. You have to excuse me—I have to make a phone call."

She darted into the bedroom and banged the door. Rob went more slowly into the messy living room. Dressed in jean shorts and a baseball T-shirt, Edwin was working out on his Lifecycle to the pounding beat of Van Morrison. The latest issue of *Journal of Microbiology* was clipped open on the book stand, and he was eating a large slice of apple pie from the pan. He picked up the remote and powered the stereo's volume down. "Hi, Rob, want some?"

"You don't have to pack in the calories any more, you know! Ed, have I caused trouble between you and your girl?" Rob moved a pair of rollerblades from a chair to the floor before sitting down.

"Impossible. What, did Carina lay into you? Ignore it. She has a lot on her mind. I think we're going to tie the knot at last."

"Congratulations! She's a gem—that Polaroid you have of her at the lab doesn't nearly do her justice."

Edwin raised his dark eyebrows in mock alarm. "You didn't tell her that, did you?"

"I wouldn't have the nerve!"

"She hates it when people judge her by her looks." Edwin grinned, remembering. "In fact, at the ceremony, be sure and tell her that her wedding gown makes her look intellectual."

Rob laughed. "I'll do that, and I'll tell her you told me to! When is it going to be?"

"In August sometime. She's calling her folks now to coordinate calendars. You see, we have to do it after July twentieth."

Edwin's voice suddenly quivered with suppressed excitement. Rob asked, "And what's so important about that day?"

"This came yesterday over the net." He put the pie pan down and scooped a piece of paper from a table to pass over. It was a printout of an e-mail message:

> Eddie!!! The list's FINALLY been handed down from
> on high! I spent all morning chasing it down, they
> DON'T want it all over the place yet, but YOU'RE
> ON IT!!!!! <virtual confetti and champagne> The
> official wheels will start turning next week. You can
> tell your family of course, but don't steal the
> President's thunder, okay? There'll be a White House
> announcement, on July 20, natch.
> CONGRATULATIONS!!!!! Jeremy
> P.S. Bring me back a souvenir—how about a T-shirt?
> "My college roommate went to Nix Olympica, and
> all I got was this lousy T-shirt!" :):):):):):):)

"July twentieth," Rob said, thunderstruck. "I remember, that's Apollo Day. Does that mean—"

"A good day to make the Mars announcement, don't you think?"

"So you're in!" Rob shook Edwin's free hand with both his own. "Congratulations again! You've been having a very busy week!"

"I'll be busier yet. I have to move to Houston to do astronaut training. You want to take over my apartment lease here?"

"No, I . . . Gosh, I didn't realize you'd have to move. And you'll be in space for years." Rob's heart sank a little.

"They're only just building the space station. I figure it'll be five years easy, before they're ready for lift-off."

"That's practically forever," Rob said with relief.

"Just what Carina said. Hence the wedding." The timer dinged. Edwin leaped off the machine and wiped his sweaty forehead and neck with an old towel. "I couldn't sleep last night, I was so jazzed up. And if we don't talk about something else I won't sleep tonight either. What are you doing with your laptop there? Do we need to print you another graph?"

Rob nodded. "I spent all this week in Atlantic City."

"And?"

From pure excitement Rob could hardly get the words out. "I lost my shirt, Ed. Every dime."

"You did? Let me have that disk! But I thought it was going to be at least twice as tough?"

"Let me do it. I can't really describe it, but I figure it's like this. It's sandwiches, not viruses. Gilgamesh gave me half his power, and it was like one wheel—a unicycle. It's tough to learn to ride a unicycle, but after a while I was doing okay with it. Then I got his other half, and I'm riding on two wheels now—a bicycle. And bicycles are easier, not harder. I'm a whiz now, with total control—look at this."

Rob took one hand off the keyboard and held it up. The heat lightning effect, the only visible sign of his power, leaped obediently from fingertip to fingertip and back again.

"Holy Mike! Then that means you did it! Thank God!"

Edwin gave him a high five. The open joy on his face was wonderful to see. Rob grinned happily back at him and said, "So I was wondering, do you have a razor I could borrow?"

"I've fallen off the sled here," Edwin confessed. "Are you taking off the face fuzz? What for?"

"I can tell you're not a parent, Ed. Angela and Davey have never seen me in a beard. The transition will be easier for the kids if I look pretty much the same as a year ago."

Edwin clapped a hand to his forehead. "Of course! I wasn't thinking. You're going home!"

"Tonight." His happiness was so great Rob felt almost sick with it. If he should ever get swell-headed his nervous stomach would keep him humble.

Carina passed through briskly from bedroom to kitchen, remarking, "Edwin says you have tummy trouble, Rob. So it's tea and toast for you. No apple pie—it'll be too rich."

"Besides, I ate it all," Edwin said. As the printer began its chatter he moved over to sit at one of the two dining tables.

Carina set a Corningware casserole dish of leftover vegetarian lasagne down. "Oh Edwin, how could you, before lunch?"

"It's not slowing me down, now is it?" He cut himself a generous portion, laughing up at her.

Rob sat down. It seemed easier not to argue with Carina, and it was too early to leave yet. Rush-hour bus service in Fairfax didn't start until four. He ate chewy whole-grain toast and drank organic herbal digestive tea, another Carina import— Edwin only ever served coffee and designer water.

Rob felt old and wise as he watched the electricity between the two, and more than a little amused. To see two such confident and self-possessed people so deeply enamored was a riot. It was obvious to his experienced eye that they were not yet sleeping together. In her worn khaki shirt and shorts, Carina looked like Miss America doing an Indiana Jones impression for the talent competition. It was particularly comic to watch Edwin assessing the fit of those shorts, and the mutual blush when Carina noticed him doing it. Just as well the wedding would be this summer.

After lunch Rob piled the dishes into the sink, and would have washed them if Carina hadn't turfed him out. "I have to put the chicken mole on," she said. "You two go and analyze your graphs." She dropped a kiss on the top of Edwin's head and went into the kitchen.

"I thought we should look over the entire file," Edwin said when they moved into the living room. "Here, hold this end."

Spread out, the bar graph showed a truly notable progress. Rob could see how he had slowly and steadily decreased the leak since autumn. "And you know, this wasn't a waste of time," he said. He slid the long sheet of paper through his work-calloused hands. "If I hadn't gotten a handle on the power, Gilgamesh would have trashed me. He nearly did anyway."

"I think you had better stick to Gil," Edwin said. "The name Gilgamesh will excite Carina unduly. There isn't an archaeologist on earth who wouldn't kill to meet him. Even without the weirdness and the live-forever thing, he's a treasure trove. To talk to someone who's actually lived in Uruk and Dilmun . . ."

"Go back to Kazakhstan then and look him up."

"Oh, don't tempt me, Rob! Maybe when I get back from Mars. You'll have to come too, you know, to translate. Sumerian's a dead language."

"I just promised Carina I'd do no such thing!"

Edwin shouted with laughter until the room rang. "You know, there never used to be enough hours in the day for everything I wanted to accomplish: the books and papers to read and write, the research to do, the people to know. Now I realize, I literally have all the time in the world."

Rob looked at him carefully, not quite sure what he was trying to perceive. Edwin looked exactly as always, tanned and fit and blithe—if anything, more clean-cut than usual, since his hair had been trimmed for Carina's visit. But Rob remembered, that first day at NIH, foreseeing that his friend's dark comeliness would mature. That would never happen now. Edwin had always looked young for his age, and now he always would. Without the sound of time's winged chariot hurrying behind him, would Edwin be able to change and grow? He had gained eternal life, but what had he lost? "Immortality is going to suit you, is it?" Rob said cautiously.

"Well, it did occur to me that a lot of really useful research could be done, and now I don't have to rely on the unwilling cooperation of a nervy subject. It would be fascinating to find out exactly how eternal life is done. Just for starters I'm having a friend over in the Blood Institute do me a full blood workup. Me, I'm not afraid of needles, no sirree."

Rob laughed. "You can still count me out. For a minute

you had me worried, but you're still yourself, Ed."

"Yes," Edwin said more soberly. "And I'm going to do my level best to stay that way. Call it denial if you want, but I'm hanging onto my self and my goals. I'm going to eat meals, and get married, and start a family, all the ordinary stuff. Your experiences have been kind of . . . frightening."

Rob nodded. "Yeah, by all means avoid my mistakes. No point in two of us making damn fools of ourselves."

Edwin swirled the tea around in the bottom of his mug. "I don't know how you survived this past year, bud. Now I've come a little way into weird with you I can appreciate it."

Rob sat up, alarmed. "Are you in bad shape, Ed?"

"Nah, do I look it?" Edwin gave his barrel chest with its orange Orioles T-shirt a resounding slap. "But even though being immortal doesn't have a day-to-day impact, it—sometimes it haunts me, Rob. The implications. Like, do I tell Carina? She's going to be my wife—how can I not trust her with such an important fact about me? So I've decided I have to, maybe after the wedding. And what about NASA? My oxygen consumption rate tests really worry me."

"Your what? What does oxygen have to do with it?"

"Rob, think about it. I don't need to eat or drink. I don't need to breathe either. The other day I held my breath for fifty-five minutes just to see if I could do it. If this shows up on the metabolic rate tests, how long will it be before the whole story runs on the front page of the *Washington Post?*"

"You don't need to eat, but that isn't keeping you from scarfing down lasagne and apple pie," Rob pointed out.

Edwin leaned back, considering. "That's a thought. Perhaps I'm burning oxygen anyway, as long as there's plenty around. There are ways to find out . . . And you, your weirdness is way scarier. It trashed your life. You're still not finished pulling the pieces together. You could have been hell on wheels squared and cubed, Rob. Bad as old Gil in his cave—"

Edwin stopped, watching him, and Rob realized he had frozen in mid-sip, the mug halfway to his mouth. He set it down carefully on the arm of his chair. "That's—that's more true than you know, Ed," he said quietly. "I never thought I'd find out why this thing happened to me. But Gil told me."

"He was lonesome," Edwin recalled. "Wanted some peers."

"He wanted to have some fun," Rob corrected him. "And he chose someone who could share his interests. Rape and murder, for instance."

Edwin jumped to his feet. "No, Rob! What is this, a self-esteem issue? That's simply not true! You are nothing like the old guy. I can attest to it."

"Self-esteem be damned!" Suddenly Rob was frightened, with the violent unreasoning despair of a child in the dark. Gilgamesh had named the prisoner in the sub-basement: His name was Gilgamesh too. "And so is mine," Rob said aloud, his voice barely above a whisper. "I defeated Gilgamesh. But he is I. I'll never be rid of him." It had all been for nothing, the worry and striving. He had conscious control over the power now, but what about his control over himself? How could he return home, knowing that the next time Jul cut off another driver, he might lose it and kill her? The enemy within was unbeatable.

"Rob," Edwin was repeating. "Rob! Will you listen to some plain reasoning?"

"Sure." The habitual reply escaped without thought.

"Firstly, I want to point out that old Gil was a liar. Practically the first thing he told you was an untruth. He wasn't God, nor your father, or any of that stuff. Am I right?"

Rob had forgotten that. "But we thought so much alike, Ed. It gave me chills. Some of the things he said—"

"I'm not saying he was mendacious from beginning to end. But don't forget to consider the motives behind old Gil's words, Rob. Can you say that he wasn't just pulling your chain?"

Rob couldn't. "It would be just like him," he realized. "And for Gil it would be easy. So easy."

"Like it would be easy for you," Edwin agreed. "He

claimed to be in control of the situation, to have selected you. What if he didn't?"

"But if he lied, then there's no rhyme or reason to it at all."

"It's natural to look for patterns and logic, Rob. But maybe there isn't any. Maybe old Gil has just gone through the rinse cycle too often. So take him with a grain of salt, okay? Secondly . . ." Edwin paced the limited space between the Lifecycle and the second sofa. "You're only a human being, Rob. You have the power to act like a god or a devil. But you're only a man."

The unexpected statement made Rob's mouth drop open in wonder. He had needed to hear that. More than anything in the world, those were words he had needed to hear. But how had Edwin known?

Pursuing his train of thought rapidly around the room, Edwin didn't notice. "Your capacity to turn tiger bothers you. Okay. But that capacity is an essential component of the human personality. You need it to survive—not every day or every year, but when push comes to shove, at the action point we talked about. It's Darwinian, you understand? A survival trait bred in our bones, yours, mine, everybody. Keep the tiger on a leash, use him to the right degree and not too often, and you'll be fine."

Rob stared doubtfully up at him. Edwin's insight was always so keen—surely he was right about this too? But on the other hand, Edwin was too nice a guy. In some things he was as innocent as a boy. He had no real knowledge of evil, had difficulty recognizing it even when it pushed him off a cliff. Just now he'd even talked about returning to Kazakhstan and interviewing Gilgamesh again! "How can I be sure, Ed?" he said at last. "You don't know, it's impossible for you to know, what my monster is like."

"Impossible?" Edwin grinned down at him. "A funny word from you of all people, bud. You're so weird, you can do anything. So why don't you get a second opinion on him? Introduce me."

Taken completely aback, Rob sputtered, "But—Ed, you're out of your mind! Take you on a tour of my inner sewers—do you think I want to destroy our friendship?"

"You can't do that, Rob. You confessed all your crimes to me already, remember? And I'm very well-read—you can't shock me."

Offering books as proof of worldliness was so typical of Edwin that Rob laughed in spite of his turmoil. The kitchen door opened and Carina came in, frowning with concentration and drying a skinless chicken drumstick on a paper towel. "Edwin, do you have any chicken stock? Or bouillon cubes?"

Edwin put his hands into the pockets of his denim shorts and turned them out. "Nope, sorry. Do you need some? Shall I pop out and pick up a few cans? I live to serve you, my darling! Rob can come with—you want to, Rob? We can walk across the park to the store and get some exercise."

Before Rob could formulate any objections he was out the door and heading down the steps with a grocery list in hand. Edwin loitered, ostensibly looking for the canvas shopping bag. But from the blissful satisfaction of his grin when he caught up at the bottom of the stair, he had more likely been stealing a kiss. "It's going to be so much fun being a married man," he told Rob happily. "We're talking three kids to start with, maybe up it to four if the NASA scheduling works out. Don't you think I'll do great as the patriarch of a large brood?"

If anything Rob found the idea comic. It was impossible to imagine Edwin as a parent. Rob carefully kept a grave countenance. "Do you have a lot of hands-on practice with babies, Ed?"

"You mean, human ones? I've raised a lot of bacteria and fruit-fly larvae. How much of a difference can there be?"

"Umm . . ." Rob decided it would only be kind not to disillusion him now. Let that first baby do it!

Edwin grinned at him. "Do I sense an aura of skepticism, Rob?"

They had crossed the parking lot and the intervening street into the park. Suddenly Edwin put on a spurt of speed and ran at a park bench. He grasped the top slat of the seat back and without apparent effort flipped up into a briefly perfect handstand. Then he overbalanced and toppled, flailing his legs and nearly catching an ankle on the seat. "Ed, you idiot!" Rob exclaimed, laughing.

"Don't you understand, Rob?" Edwin said as he bounced to his feet. "There's nothing beyond me today. Carina is going to marry me, and I'm an astronaut! The world and everything in it is wonderful! I'm invincible—if we went to Atlantic City, I'd break the bank! I'll manage a family, tidy up your loose ends, anything and everything! Come on, let's run!"

He loped down the path past the soccer field on through a strip of trees, singing as he went:

> *And everything is so complete*
> *When you're walkin' out on the street*
> *And the wind catches your feet*
> *And sends you flyin', cryin'*
> *Wooo, ooooh, ooooo-wheee!*
> *Wild nights are callin'!*

Beyond the trees was another suburban avenue with a convenience store at the corner. Edwin whirled down the aisles like a joyous tornado. The cans of chicken broth paid for, he said, "There's a pond with ducks beyond the game field there. And it's Monday, so nobody will be around. So that'd be a good place."

"A good place? For what?"

"To tour your inner landscape, Rob. Are you familiar with the terminology of personality theory? Shadow, ego, and self? It's time the pieces of your psyche got on better terms. And today, I'm just the one to facilitate it."

"No, Ed." Rob shook his head stubbornly as they walked. "I appreciate your good will, but it would be very dangerous."

"This is where it's going to work out so great, Rob. Only I can do this for you. For me it won't be dangerous at all. I can't die. I'm immortal."

"But what about mental damage? Emotional injuries?" Rob argued. "You're not proof against those."

"How do you know?"

Rob fell back, stumped. How did he know? He realized he knew even less about Edwin's condition than he did about the weirdness. Trotting to catch up, he said, "Is this how you're going to manage on Mars? Just plunge headfirst into the unknown and count on the immortality to save the day?"

"This is not unknown territory, Rob, I keep telling you. I know you. Besides," he added after a pause, "the moment you told me Gilgamesh got a tour, I wanted to go too." He laughed uproariously at Rob's incredulous expression.

The pond was a small municipal one, the shallow sunny water surrounded by flagstones. Fat puffs of white cloud were reflected in the still surface. Ghostly green in the shadowy depths, the young leaves of a water lily unfurled towards the light. The sidewalk widened out to accomodate some pink-flowering azaleas and another slatted wooden park bench. As Edwin sat down, three brown mallard ducks carved vees in the water towards him, hoping for a handout. Edwin set the canvas grocery bag clanking beside him, and pointed at the remaining space. Reluctantly Rob sat. "I've heard of scientific curiosity, but this is crazy," he said.

"Come on, Rob—you can't *tell* me about it, we've already seen that. So why not *show* me?"

Rob realized that, ever articulate and far the faster thinker, Edwin had an answer to objections that Rob hadn't even dreamed up yet. And it would be undeniably interesting to see what happened. Today was his lucky day too. Impulsively he said, "Okay. You really mean it? Then let's go. Hold out your hand."

"My hand?" Edwin laid his left hand on top of the grocery bag.

Rob watched him sharply, but saw no signs of nervousness or second thoughts. Very lightly he brushed his fingers across the back of Edwin's wrist, drawing him gently in.

CHAPTER
2

*R*ob *found himself lying on the grass looking up at a fath-*omless sunny blue sky. It was framed by drifts of fairylike pink blossom. Beside him was an old stone Japanese lantern. He sat up, and a chubby man in polyester plaid pants said, "Say, mate, take a kip again, wouldjer? You're coming into the shot."

The man was focusing an enormous camera balanced on an inadequate-looking tripod, otherwise Rob wouldn't have known what he was talking about. "Sorry," he said. "Let me move out of your range." He looked around and saw Edwin sitting nearby, against a gnarled gray tree trunk. "How do you like it, Ed?" he asked.

"This is the Tidal Basin, in Washington, D.C.," Edwin said, enthralled. "See the Jefferson Memorial? And the Lincoln's over that way. What happened? Did you teleport us? I thought you said it was like New York City."

Rob shook his head. "It's different every time, did I mention that? This isn't the real Washington, Ed. This is me, my playground, and today it happens to reflect downtown. Your body is untenanted, left to sit on a park bench in Takoma Park. I just hope passers-by will assume we're stoned or drunk."

"But this is so real! Are you sure?"

"Think back, Ed. Did you watch the local evening news last night? When did they say the cherry blossoms peaked?"

"Ten days ago," Edwin said, stunned. "During the cherry blossom festival. Wow! And who are they?" He pointed at the plump tourist, who had posed with his family around the lantern and was now using a remote to take the picture.

Rob shrugged. "I don't know. A lot of things here I don't understand. Shall we go on?"

Edwin stared out at the sunny sparkling Tidal Basin. Someone in a paddle boat was halfway across to the Jefferson Memorial, glowing snowy white against the blue sky. "What a beautiful day! Even if it isn't real. This is so great! Where are we going?"

Rob smiled at this enthusiasm. "If we go that way we'll come to the Potomac, and the Lincoln Memorial. Head east, and we'll be at the museums on the Mall."

"The museums! Let's go to Air and Space, and look at the Mars colony model!"

"There may not be one there," Rob warned him. "Keep it in mind every minute, Ed. This is a construct, a metaphor. You're pretty safe with me—this place is the core of my power, and I can literally do anything here. But we have to stay together. If you get lost in here, I don't know what would happen to you."

"Are you kidding? I'm going to stick like glue—you have to answer my questions!" Edwin took the small notebook and a ball-point pen out of the back pocket of his shorts. "Did you make this place, Rob? Did you know beforehand it would be D.C.? What exactly are we looking for?"

"I suppose, no, and I don't know," Rob said laughing. "I'll know when we find it."

It was impossible to be wary on such a glorious day. The

cherry trees were so excessively gorgeous, and there were so many of them, that it was difficult to believe they were real. The beauty was superfluous, a generous gift pressed down and running over, unasked, undeserved. Cars full of gawking tourists armed with videocams and pocket cameras thronged every road around the Tidal Basin. The traffic chugged slowly past Rob and Edwin as they strolled down the sidewalk. Everything was glorious yet mundane, sunny and safe. It occurred to Rob that in defeating Gilgamesh he had routed the monster in the sub-basement too. Perhaps this was all there was now, a bright and sane interior universe.

Edwin's glance was full of what Rob was startled to recognize as respect. "And you say I'm too nice? If this is you, your true self, Rob, you keep some impressive inner beauties hidden under a bushel."

Rob shook his head. "I've changed a lot, Ed. Do you remember when we met, in Central Park? I bet it wasn't so pleasant in here then."

"I recall. You looked like a crazy person—if you hadn't helped Katie I would never have spoken to you. You've recovered amazingly since then, bud. It's a miracle."

Rob stared at him. "But Ed—you're the one who did it. How can you not have noticed? If it's a miracle, you worked it. You made the darkness bright, and built the bridge. If I hadn't met you first, before meeting Gil, he would have had me by the short hairs, you know that? I'd still be in Aqebin, being groomed to be the next Hitler."

Edwin laughed with genuine astonishment. "Holy Mike, it's true. Superhero sidekick saves the world from disaster, film at eleven. No, don't you dare thank me, I can't stand it. Tell me instead, why Washington? Why not Paris, or Singapore? I've never been to Singapore."

Rob stared up at the limpid sky. "I never know what it's doing in here, or why. Maybe it's Washington because I've never been to Singapore either. Maybe the weather is good only because I'm happy."

Edwin stopped for a moment, and then excitedly began to

walk again. "That is a really significant statement, Rob, do you realize? You hardly ever confess, even to me, how you're feeling."

"That's true." Rob knew that out in reality even that simple admission would have made him stammer with embarrassment. "I wonder why that is."

"I can guess," Edwin said, thinking hard. "It's because here we're really inside you. Somewhere out there—" He waved an arm at the cloudless blue sky—"either about four inches away, or a hundred billion light years, depending on how you think about it, is your face, Rob. Your mask. Your reserved tough-guy interface with the rest of the world."

Rob laughed. In a strange way it all made perfect sense. He had given up expecting this place to be logical in any mundane way. "How does a guy who holds by all the articles of Christianity know so much psychobabble?"

"Nonsense, Rob, I'm the epitome of consistency. Taking apart the toy to see how it works just increases your respect for the toymaker."

The path dwindled drastically as the road crossed over an inlet of the Tidal Basin. Rob led the way along the foot-wide sidewalk, separated by an ordinary steel highway barrier from the clogged tourist traffic idling along beside his right hip. Under his left hand the ugly W.P.A.-era bridge rail was made of concrete uprights and clunky rectangular ironwork painted green. Edwin followed at his heels, still simmering with questions. "And suppose we walked over to the White House? Would there be a President there? Who would he be? George Bush, or that other guy who ran against him, I forget his name, Clinton?"

Suddenly the water beside Rob burbled and boiled. A deep and gluey voice roared, "Who's that tripping over my bridge?"

Rob halted, completely unalarmed. He recognized that voice. It was his own, the ominous troll-voice he had perfected for Angela and Davey. In his opinion this overpass barely merited the honor. "Ed," he said. "Does this even rate as a real bridge?"

"There's water on both sides," Edwin pointed out, gulping. "Rob, who was that?"

Rob smiled. "It's the troll, Ed—did you ever read the fairy tale? He lives under the bridge."

Big oily bubbles rose to the surface, bringing up a smell of swamp and decay. "Who's that tripping over my bridge?" the troll yelled again in earthquake tones.

"This is uncanny," Edwin said.

"That's what this place is like," Rob agreed. "Scary, but fun too." Serene, he leaned over the iron rail. In the shadow of the low bridge the water was gloomy gray. There was no gap between the bottom of the overpass and the sullen surface of the water. "I'm Rob Lewis," he called down.

"Then I'll eat you up!"

"You don't want to eat me," Rob said. He had nearly said "meeee," in billy-goat bleats! "There's another guy coming just behind me, with a lot more meat on him."

He grinned back at Edwin, who waved his hands in negative denying motions and pulled a comic horrified face. "Leave me out of it, why don't you?" Edwin whispered. "Why doesn't the troll yell at all these cars?"

"He doesn't know there are people inside? He doesn't want to become a traffic fatality? Don't sweat it, Ed—just refer the troll to someone even bigger and tastier following us. That's how it worked in the story."

The water blurped and bubbled disgustingly again. "No," the troll bellowed. "I want—you!"

Something shot with a tremendous spurt of icy water straight up at Rob, a greenish slimy paw at the end of an impossibly long boneless arm. With horrible sticky strength, it clutched Rob's chest and throat. He gasped, thrashing in terror as the thing dragged him down. He tore at the cold strangling grip with desperate hands.

"Holy Mike! This is impossible!" Edwin stared around wildly, searching perhaps for a policeman.

"Ed—help me!" Rob choked. "It's pulling me over—"

Just in time Edwin locked his powerful hairy arms around

Rob's waist. "Don't worry, bud," Edwin panted. "I've got my legs hooked around a concrete baluster. We're rooted like Gibraltar. Holy Jesus, why isn't anybody getting out of their car?"

But the vehicles crept by without pause. It was as if underwater monsters plucked pedestrians off this bridge every day. Fire swam in his eyes as Rob forced first two fingers, and then three, between his throat and the stinking green death-clutch. He was stronger than this monster. He had defeated Gilgamesh and stripped him of everything. This troll wasn't going to get him. He dragged the paw relentlessly off his neck.

As if it sensed defeat, the watcher in the water abruptly switched tactics. The oozy grip turned itself inside out with rubbery ease and fastened with numbing strength on Rob's wrist. "No!" he gasped. But the swift outward jerk on his arm nearly dislocated his shoulder, and plucked him neatly right out of Edwin's grasp.

"Rob!" Edwin yelled, lunging.

With a splash, Rob was reeled under. The water bit icicle cold through his khakis and sports shirt. Here at the edge, the Tidal Basin couldn't possibly be more than a couple of feet deep. Yet the implacable arm sucked him down and down with fearful speed into the gelid sunless water. He could see nothing, and a roaring noise filled his ears. I'm going to drown, he thought in terror. I didn't breathe properly before I went under. I'll black out and then drown. He struggled feebly, hopelessly, and felt something dragging on his right foot. Something warm, clinging to the ankle—Edwin!

The knowledge calmed Rob's panic a little. This is my place, my country, he told himself. I can't drown here. Nothing can hurt me. Still he didn't quite dare to open his mouth and inhale the water just yet. He could hold out another few seconds—

With a rush and a buffet Rob's head broke the surface. He had arrived. The grip on his wrist was gone, and the darkness was absolute. Gasping, he groped forward and touched a slick rough surface. It was a narrow place, a ledge perhaps. Wheezing for breath, he levered himself onto it. He was deep under the foundations of the bridge, in a tiny underwater nook that had trapped a bubble of air.

Edwin fumbled at his leg, and Rob reached in the dark to help him up. The sound of their rasping breath echoed close around their ears. The place must be very small.

When he recovered a little, Rob wiped away the water streaming from his beard and hair. "Told you so," he panted. "Dangerous."

"Right. Rub it in." Water splashed and dripped in the dark as Edwin shifted to sit on the narrow slope beside Rob. "What do we do now?"

"I don't know." In this country he could speak the truth without self-consciousness. Rob leaned back against what felt like a stone wall. He knew what was coming, very soon. "Ed, I—I'm terrified."

"Very sensible," Edwin panted. "I'm scared spitless myself. Lost my notebook, too. But if I still have my Swiss Army knife . . ."

It was so dark Rob could distinguish no difference if he opened his eyes or shut them. He glared out into the void anyway, stubbornly hoping to glimpse his enemy. How could he have ever dreamed the monster had fled? Fear jerked and plucked at his nerves, grinding in his stomach like gravel. "We're not really trapped here, Ed," he said, steadying his voice with an effort. "Takoma Park, the bench by the pond— we can get back in a second. Then he can't get us. I'm in control. I can push the 'abort' button any time."

"Let's think about that," Edwin said. "Is this troll here the monster you were talking about?"

Rob nodded, but then remembered Edwin couldn't see him. "Yeah," he said huskily. "Up there on the bridge. He knew my name."

"Then he's the gent we've come to see. There's no point in running away from him—you did that before, am I right? Let's try to see it through this time."

Rob hitched himself up onto the slippery ledge again. It

was true that nothing horrible was happening right this moment. At any time he could pull out. Nothing could hurt him
here. He swallowed the lump of irrational fear in his throat
and said, "You want to just sit here in the dark for a while,
before we go?"

Close beside him, Edwin gave a grunt of satisfaction. "It's
a shame I'll never be able to tell anyone how clever I am." And
a tiny spark of light came to life in Edwin's hand, pushing back
the dark.

Rob goggled at it. "Ed—how?"

"Halogen button light," Edwin said, grinning with justifi-
able pride. "I buy them at the camping store, mainly for the
Mazda—so I can unlock the door at night without scratching
the finish. I keep it on the ring with my knife. It's only powered by a couple watch batteries, though. So it won't last us
long. Here—since the troll is after you, you take this."

He passed over the Swiss Army knife. It was the little one,
not the massive four-inch Gerber multi-purpose tool Edwin
kept for camping trips. Rob snapped open the biggest blade.
He had seen Edwin use this to slit open cookie packets and
cut the tape on parcels. It was less than two inches long, totally comic as a defense. Rob gave a laugh so weak it sounded
like he was choking. "Ed, this thing wouldn't stop a mouse."

"It's wonderful what a little light will do," Edwin said, re-
plying to the tone rather than the words. "Let's boogie, huh?
Come out, troll," he called softly, lifting the light. "Come
where we can see you."

The tiny glow just barely illuminated a rough concrete
ceiling. It was very low, too low to stand under, and came
down to the black water all around. Their slimy ledge, the only
footing, was about three yards long. Rob held his breath and
listened. The only sound was the drip from their sodden
clothes.

After a long moment Edwin said, "You want to give it a
try?"

"No," Rob admitted. "But I will." He raised his voice.
"Where are you? Come out!"

The space was too small for a creature of any size to hide. Rob stared at the ominous black surface of the water, wondering if trolls were amphibious. Edwin shifted to a crouch, his tennis shoes squelching. As the light moved with his motion Rob caught a glimpse of something out of the corner of his eye. In the dark, beside him in the shadow—"No!" he yelled, throwing himself back.

Edwin grabbed Rob by the shoulder before he plummeted into the water again. "It's okay, Rob!" he said. "I—I know you."

Edwin was staring past him at the troll. Rob looked too, and gulped. It was not really a movie monster with slimy tentacles. Or the green spiny troll from the twins' favorite book, or even a Mesopotamian monarch. The third person in this tiny space looked like a drowned man. His face was greeny-white, and weeds clogged his long pale hair and beard. Water streamed from his colorless rags, and he glared at them out of deep-set icy gray-blue eyes—the eyes of a wolf.

"I know you," Edwin repeated, kneeling up. He ducked his head under the low ceiling, watching the drowned man intently across Rob's sprawled body. "You did a Heimlich on Katie. You stood up to the casino doormen. You fought to save my life. You are not a bad person. You are Rob Lewis too."

The truth of this struck Rob with the force of revelation. Of course! This wasn't a monstrous aspect. It was an emergency weapon. It had always been here, down in his unconscious. Newly armed this past year with the weirdness, this inner tiger was as dangerous as a nuclear missile. But like a nuke, this terrifying lurker had on occasion been a genuine asset. Galvanized, Rob began to sit up.

Suddenly the drowned man spoke, with difficulty, a thick oleaginous voice. "Who asked you, smart guy?"

"Rob asked me," Edwin said, disconcerted.

The words were like matches to gunpowder. With a wordless bellow the drowned man dove across Rob and seized Edwin's throat in both hands. The impact carried Edwin backwards halfway off the ledge. In the scuffle, the little knife squirted out of Rob's hand into the water and was lost. The button light also went flying, bouncing off the wall behind Rob's head. Gibbering with rage, the drowned man straddled Edwin's chest and held his head under.

Fifty-five minutes, Rob recalled, fighting down panic. Ed's okay. He held his breath the other day for fifty-five minutes. Rob knew he had to use smarts, as he had against Gilgamesh, not force. Now was the time to start exerting that control he claimed. He scrabbled to find the light—thank goodness it hadn't bounced off into the water, too—and held it up to the manic dead-white face.

"You don't have to do this," Rob stammered. "Edwin's a friend, remember?"

Edwin's legs thrashed. His strong hands clawed at the drowned man's tattered sleeves, and with a final writhe he kicked free. He slid with a splash into the dark water. Sleek as a seal, his head immediately broke the surface, and he sucked in a huge furious breath. He trod water and croaked, "Try me fair, you trog!"

"Ed, cut it out." Rob kept his attention fixed on the cunning crazy face not six inches from his own, gleaming with wet in the tiny light between them. What could he say to calm the creature? Some glib and plausible fiction, anything! "You are me," Rob said insistently. "And I am you. I can exploit people for my own gratification. Lie without blushing. Threaten my friends, steal and cheat and kill. I am you."

Then Rob's heart almost stopped in his chest. Here in the depths he could not lie. What he had said was indeed true. His very intention, paradoxically, showed it—to placate the monster with tarradiddle. In desperate situations, under sufficient stress, there was no crime beyond him, no trough he could not plumb. "You are me," he repeated, in a trembling whisper. "Brother. Self."

The drowned man sat back on his ragged haunches, a sardonic glint in his eye. "Thought I was old Gil."

At least the logical corollary to that came easily. "No, no," Rob said. "He was lying about that. I see it now, the old lunatic. You are the worst of me, and still you're miles better than him. Gil is the sort of real bad-ass we save the rough stuff for. You did a fine job on him in Kazakhstan, by the way."

The drowned man grinned wolfishly. "That was fun, wasn't it? When do we get to do that again?"

Edwin hoisted himself up onto the ledge again on Rob's other side. "How about right now," he wheezed. Rob glanced back in surprise at him. He had never known Edwin to be so aggressively hot-headed.

Suddenly, without the slightest warning, the button light died in his hand. In the illimitable darkness Rob could only see blurry afterimages of Edwin sprawled on his left and the drowned man squatting on his right. Quickly, before he lost track of positions, Rob put both hands out to touch his companions. Edwin's furry arm was humidly warm, trembling with some strong emotion, but the drowned man's hand was boneless and cold, slick with wet.

"Oh Jesus," Edwin gasped, coughing. "Oh Jesus, where's the light?"

"You shouldn't've brought him," the drowned man grumbled. "This place is bad for his like. How come you take him around to all these dangerous places, anyway? He's a drag."

"No, he isn't," Rob said. "In fact, he mostly drags me!"

"Well, take him away, or he'll go buggy. I'll be in touch."

The drowned man pulled his icy hand away, and was gone. Rob could neither feel nor hear any trace of him. On his other side Edwin was panting unevenly, obviously in distress. Rob tugged gently on his hand and Edwin tackled him, a clumsy fumbling hug in the dark. Here no foolish shyness impeded Rob's tenderness. He held Edwin the way he would Davey or Angela, feeling the strong heart thudding desperately with fright under the deep ribs. The drowned man was right. Down here was no place for a child of the light. "Hang on, pal," Rob said. "We're out of here."

And they were rolling over and over together in the shallow warm water of the duck pond. The sun blazed down so high and bright in the sky that it must still be early afternoon.

With an irritated quack, a mallard duck fluttered away from their flailing limbs. Rob stood up shakily in the knee-deep water. "Ed, are you okay?"

"Better now." Edwin wallowed over and clung gasping to the flagstone verge.

To his horror Rob saw ferocious crimson finger-marks sunk deep in Edwin's throat. "My god, Ed! Let me see—we've got to get you to a doctor. You're bleeding!"

"Rob, this is *me*, remember? Give me ten minutes in the sun here, and I'll be fine." He rolled over onto his back in the water and leaned his head on the verge. Rob climbed out and lay prone on the sun-warmed stone. For a long time they rested, panting. Then in a stronger voice Edwin said, "Besides—if we went to the emergency room—I bet these marks would match your fingers, bud. I wonder what a passerby would have seen."

The thought made Rob gulp in dismay. "Oh yeah. I'm glad this is a quiet park." A brief silent struggle, and then Rob went on, "It *was* me, Ed. I can't shove the responsibility off onto anybody but myself. I just tried to rip your head off. I'm really sorry."

"Nonsense, Rob. Perfectly okay. I can take it, thanks to you. Maybe I shouldn't have pushed you so hard to let me in. I didn't realize how—how deep we were going to go. I was intruding, so I deserved some hassle."

"No—it was okay. You did good." Rob had to smile at the shy, inadequate words. Out here he could say little more, entrenched once again behind his reserve. It was just the way he was—he could never change.

After some consideration Edwin added, "I will say though, that I never want to do that again. The next time you need help with your psyche, I'll give you advice from the outside."

Rob sighed. "I don't know quite what I've achieved just now, Ed. Except that—I know I'll always have to stay in control. Keep a tight hold on my temper, my impulses. With great power comes great responsibility, you know."

Edwin raised his head. "I've heard that someplace before. Who said it, Virgil?"

"Believe it or not, the Amazing Spider-Man."

Edwin snorted with laughter. After another long reflective pause he said, "I don't know why I began to lose it in there. That's unusual for me. And here's a good question: what happened to my stuff? The notebook, the light, the Swiss Army knife—they're not in my pocket now. I dropped them in your head. So where are—yeowtch!"

Rob started, bumping his chin on the flags. "Ed, what is it?"

Edwin rolled over and heaved himself splashing out onto the flagstones. "A duck bit my toe, right through the sneaker!"

Rob laughed. Suddenly his heart was absurdly light. Somehow, from the dark below the bridge, he had brought back some smatch of that inner joy and serenity. "Let's take the hint, and get moving."

The canvas grocery sack was still on the bench. "I wonder if we just sat there on the bench awhile," Edwin mused, "and then fell forward into the water?"

Rob noticed that the savage red marks on Edwin's neck were nearly gone. Amazing! He said, "Maybe you should tell Carina we were just horsing around, and fell in."

"What, lie to her?"

"It's the truth—you'd just be leaving out some details. On second thought, let me do the talking. When you lie you always look like a guilty baby. You can take our clothes downstairs to the laundry room instead." Whether from the duck pond or the Tidal Basin, their clothes exuded a growing swampy reek in the hot sun.

With relish Edwin declared, "If you're going to walk from the laundry room up to my apartment, and pitch a story to Carina, all without a stitch on, I want to see it."

Rob laughed at the picture. "No, I guess that wouldn't work!"

In the end they both went upstairs, sneaking into the apartment like naughty schoolboys. A heavenly smell of chicken mole made Rob's mouth water. Carina was sitting out on the balcony, chattering rapid-fire Spanish into a cordless phone.

"Suppose you take first whack at the shower," Edwin said. "Towels are under the sink, the shaving stuff in the cabinet." He snatched a blue terrycloth bathrobe off the hook behind the bathroom door. Rob dove into the bathroom and stripped off his wet casino clothes for Edwin to wash. After a thorough shower he spent a long time painfully and clumsily shaving. Rob had last handled a razor a year ago almost to the day. The face that emerged from the final toweling was not the same as the one in the bathroom mirror in Fairfax. He looked older and thinner. Pain and madness had etched their lines around his eyes and mouth. Threads of gray contributed to the new butterscotch brightness of his hair. The icicle-blue glint in his eyes was new too, and his chin was pasty pink against the rest of his weathered face. But overall he thought the family would recognize him, and that was all he cared about.

He put on a fresh set of clothes, the heavy jeans and a plain white Salvation Army T-shirt, and snatched up his bags. He ran downstairs, intercepting Edwin near the mailboxes.

Edwin stared at him. "Holy Mike, is that you, Rob? I've never seen you without the beard. You look so, so ordinary!"

With a self-conscious grin Rob said, "I shouldn't have let it slide for so long. I better leave you to it, Ed. It'll take me a couple hours to get home by Metro and bus."

"That's right, leave me holding the bag. Could it be that my bride makes you nervous?" Edwin set the box of laundry detergent down on the stair and rubbed the back of his neck thoughtfully. "I suppose you can pick up your clean clothes any time. Rob, will it be all right? You think you should maybe phone ahead?"

"Of course not," Rob said confidently. "Everything'll be great." He held out his hand, and Edwin took it in a firm grip. "Look, Ed . . . I was thinking. You're right—what you said by the cherry trees. It is a miracle. I've been really lucky. So lucky it's crazy. There were hundreds of times I could've gone under this past year, but I didn't. I'm—thankful, I guess."

"Now I warned you, Rob, not to make a habit of thanking me. It'll get on my nerves, and then I won't invite you to the wedding."

"I wasn't thanking you," Rob said indignantly.

"You're not, huh?" Edwin looked at him, his gaze very sharp. "Then who? We'll talk later about it. Right now you have a long-awaited date. God bless you, bud."

Rob turned away, and then remembered. "Ed, I forgot! I'm flat broke. I lost every cent I had at the casino. Could you lend me ten bucks for the bus and subway?"

Edwin began to laugh. Reaching into the pocket of his terrycloth bathrobe, he drew out his sodden wallet.

**✳ CHAPTER
  3**

*R*ob *rode the Metro Red Line downtown in such a turmoil* of happiness he could hardly think straight. He almost missed the transfer entirely at Metro Center to the Virginia train. He tried to get a grip on himself. He had worked for this day, dreamed about it for so long, it would be a pity to be incoherent about it.

The twins wouldn't be the same, of course. At that age children grow and change daily, almost hourly. They'd be taller, smarter, maybe even approaching the potty stage. Angela would sing new songs for him, and Davey had probably mastered the playground monkey bars long ago. Perhaps they'd learned to use forks—that would be a major improvement in the household ambiance.

And Julianne. Rob was overwhelmed with yearning: the memory of her kiss, her touch, the smell of her skin. She would have new clothes, of course, and probably a new haircut, but she herself would be exactly the same . . . wouldn't she?

The train stopped at the end of the line. Rob rode the escalator up to the bus stops. Suddenly he was uneasy. It was illegal, he was sure of it, to just up and abandon your wife and children. He had vanished from his Fairfax life like smoke. He hadn't called, or sent word, or written. Suppose Julianne had given up on him? Didn't love him any more? Divorce would be an entirely reasonable reaction, given her situation. Desertion was sufficient grounds, wasn't it?

And if she'd gone through with a divorce, she might even have remarried by now, a full year later. People did that every day. In her style, Julianne was as lovely as Carina. There'd be hundreds of guys waiting in line for her. Rob realized that, as always, Edwin had been right. He ought to phone ahead. But just at that moment the commuter bus pulled up at the stop in a cloud of blue diesel exhaust. If he didn't take it, he'd have to wait forty minutes for the next one. The doors sighed open, and he got on. He'd have to go through with it.

The bus wasn't full. He set the ancient brown duffel bag on the seat beside him and searched inside. Down at the bottom corner he felt a clump of metal bits: his keys. He drew them out and held them. If I were marrying a young divorcée with kids, he thought—or, my god! if I bought the house from her when she moved away! If I did that, I would rekey all the locks and bolts. It would be the sensible, Harry Homeowner thing to do. Even if Julianne has just axed me, the first thing she'd do would be to change the locks. So I don't have to phone. I don't even have to ring the bell and see her new man open the door. Or the new owner of the house. All I have to do is try my key in the lock.

Rob sat and stared tensely out the window as the subdivisions rolled by. He was afraid now, afraid as he hadn't been at Aqebin. Power sang through his bloodstream and bent to his will, power enough to totally dominate the entire earth and everyone on it. And he couldn't use it, not now, not for this. If Julianne had moved on, emotionally or physically, he couldn't muscle her into coming back. She was free to make her own choice, and he would have to accept her decision. He

could do absolutely nothing about it. For all his strength, he
was helpless as a child when it came down to what really mat-
tered.

The thought should have been fearful, but was in fact glo-
riously freeing. Here, arguably at the pinnacle of human
power, Rob was only a small step above everyone else after
all. He wasn't a god, had never even been close. In the family
of humanity he wasn't the dad, but only a younger son. The
realization was a tremendous relief, like a titanic rock rolling
off his back. Somebody else had the job of being God. He had
never for one second wanted that burden, and now he knew
he would never have to shoulder it. Dimly he saw, not the details, but the broad contours of belief, a wide new country to
explore some day.

When the bus halted at his stop Rob felt dizzy. It roared
away into the sweet spring evening, vanishing around the corner before Rob mustered the nerve to cross. I am not going to
chicken out, he insisted to himself. I have to know. I've faced
so much, I can face this.

His own street now. The house at the corner had a new
roof, and someone was barbecuing—Rob could smell the
burning charcoal. The azaleas were just coming into flower in
masses of clashing reds and pinks. He marched slow but steady
down the sidewalk, putting one foot ahead and then the other,
watching for the first glimpse of the house.

And there it was. The maroon Plymouth van was parked
in the driveway—they hadn't moved away. The lights were on
in every room, so that the Cape Cod house glowed a welcome
in the twilight. The yard looked in reasonable shape too. Jul
had probably hired a lawn service after all.

Rob went slowly up the front walk and set the duffel and
the laptop on the stoop. The keys jangled in his shaking hand,
and in the shadows he had problems sorting out the right one.
She never remembered to put the porch light on.

He pulled open the storm door, the familiar door he had
bought and hung himself, and it was too much. He leaned his
forehead on the door jamb, silently pleading for mercy, from

whom he didn't quite yet know. Then he straightened and pushed the key into the lock.

It fitted. It turned. The deadbolt snicked back, and the door opened. From inside came the aroma of microwave pizza, and the thunder of galloping small feet. Davey's ululating Tarzan cry echoed down the hall. Rob took one more deep breath, right down to the bottom of his stomach. "Thank you," he said aloud. Then he stepped in and shut the door behind him.

✳ AUTHOR'S NOTE

*T*he central alteration I have made in the ancient story of Gilgamesh—that the king actually retained the gift of eternal life instead of mislaying it—is my own. Everything else about the hero I have borrowed from many sources. Of the epic, translator Maureen Gallery Kovacs says, "As was traditional in Mesopotamian literature, 'authorship' consists largely in the creative adaptation of existing themes and plots from other literature to new purposes." I have happily aligned myself with this tradition.

In the New York Public Library, Rob reads David Ferry's *Gilgamesh* (1992), the most vivid verse rendering available today. The paperback epic he buys on Christmas Eve is the Penguin Classics edition, translated into prose by N.K. Sandars. Randall Garrett coined the term "tarnhelm effect" for his Lord Darcy stories. *The Individuated Hobbit,* by Timothy R. O'Neill (1979), explicated for me the use of Jungian archetype in fiction. And the marvelous and obvious truth about immortality—that it is a pearl, not an undersea plant—is pointed out by Geoffrey Bibby in *Looking for Dilmun* (1969).

Many on-line geniuses supplied answers to my inordinate array of questions, ranging from trucks to casino blackjack to EEG machines to the adventures of Mandy Patinkin. David Singer told me about travel in the former USSR and the inmate population of Lorton Reformatory. Dr. Louise Abbott sneaked me into the bowels of buildings at NIH for a private tour. Greg Feeley wrestled mightily with title problems, and Carol Kuniholm and Larry read the manuscript. To all these generous people, my thanks.